Stories from
ONTARIO

Stories from
ONTARIO

a selection by
GERMAINE WARKENTIN

Macmillan of Canada

ISBN 0-7705-1068-X cloth

ISBN 0-7705-1069-8 paper

Library of Congress Catalogue
Card No. 73-92693

Printed in Canada for
The Macmillan Company of Canada

Acknowledgements

*For permission to reprint copyright material grateful
acknowledgement is made to the following:*

John G. Aylen, Ottawa for "Expiation" from *The Witching of
Elspie* (1923) by Duncan Campbell Scott.

The Canadian Forum for "The McCrimmons" by Alice Boissonneau which first appeared in *The Canadian Forum*, December
1952.

Shirley Faessler for "A Basket of Apples" which first appeared in
Atlantic Monthly, 1969.

Hugh Garner for "One-Two-Three Little Indians," copyright Hugh
Garner, 1952, 1966, 1973 from *Men and Women*.

Harper & Row, Publishers, Inc., for "Sir Watson Tyler" in *From
the Life* by Harvey O'Higgins, Copyright, 1919 by Harper &
Row, Publishers, Inc. By permission of the publishers.

House of Anansi Press Limited, Toronto, for "They Heard a
Ringing of Bells" from *When He Was Free And Young And
He Used To Wear Silks* by Austin Clarke.

The Macmillan Company of Canada Limited for "Adrift" from
The Yellow Briar by Patrick Slater, "Last Spring They Came
Over" and "Ancient Lineage" from *Morley Callaghan's Stories*
by Morley Callaghan, and "The Way Back" from *The Kissing
Man* by George Elliott; all reprinted by permission of The
Macmillan Company of Canada Limited.

McClelland and Stewart Limited, Toronto, for "The Marine Ex-
cursion of the Knights of Pythias" from *Sunshine Sketches of a
Little Town* by Stephen Leacock. Reprinted by permission of
The Canadian Publishers, McClelland and Stewart Limited,
Toronto.

McGraw-Hill Ryerson Limited, Toronto, for "Walker Brothers
Cowboy" and "The Peace of Utrecht" from *Dance of the Happy
Shades* by Alice Munro and "Where the Myth Touches Us" from
Flying A Red Kite by Hugh Hood, all by permission of McGraw-
Hill Ryerson Limited.

The Montreal Standard Publishing Company Limited. "May Your
First Love Be Your Last," by Gregory Clark, is reproduced by
permission of The Montreal Standard Publishing Company
Limited. It first appeared in *Weekend Magazine* on January
26, 1968, and is the title story of the best-selling book published
in 1969, copyright The Montreal Standard Publishing Company
Limited.

Oberon Press, Ottawa, for "In Exile" by David Helwig, reprinted
from *The Streets of Summer* by permission of Oberon Press.

Press Porcépic for "Out in Chinguacousy" by Dave Godfrey, an
excerpt from *Death Goes Better With Coca-Cola*, reprinted by
permission of Press Porcépic.

James Reaney for "The Box-Social" from *The Undergrad Magazine*, 1947. Reprinted by permission of the author.

University of Ottawa Press for "The Loading" from *Selected
Stories of Raymond Knister* and "Great Godfrey's Lament"
from *Selected Stories of E. W. Thomson*.

Contents

WHERE THE MYTH TOUCHES US

EPILOGUE

Introduction

Highway 400 stretches out across the Ontario countryside through the township of Medonte, reaching up to Georgian Bay from the distant city south of the slowly rising uplands of Simcoe County. To either side, there are concession roads, silent byways that repudiate this recent slash across their antique grid. Threading a way through the confluence of roads at the end of the journey, the traveller experiences a shock, for he crosses almost in a moment from the serenity of this quiet landscape to the suddenly presented obstacle of the north. Beyond Port Severn, the highway enters another world, and one moves, as everywhere in Ontario, across an unexpected boundary. Everywhere I look, the Ontario experience seems to me to be defined by the presence of boundaries in the midst of places intensely known, yet haunted at the same time by a continuity of experience never quite described.

When I was an Ontario child, I found it difficult to imagine that the place I lived in, downtown Toronto, was not the whole world. Yet wherever I went, experience contradicted me. Downtown was not uptown, city was not country. The first world I possessed totally is fixed in my memory by the image of an autumnal Toronto street. It looks like one of Thoreau MacDonald's drawings; the trees are bare, and there is rain, but since the picture has the sound of quiet music, no unhappiness. But even then, there were other worlds to be explored. At the northern end of the Yonge car line, we could leave the red-brick houses, street after street, and embark on a journey among the paradisal willows and along the rutted lanes of York Mills and Lansing. On one occasion, we moved from city to country, and later came back again. This wartime disruption made me the confused possessor of two unrelated bodies of experience, which were soon to be even more severely demarcated by the boundaries drawn by time. Both of the worlds I possessed pleased me; what puzzled me was the relationship between them. I would ask myself what these different places were, and why they seemed to be connected only in me, as I explored yet a third milieu (new to me, though venerable with apparent age), the Edwardian streets of Toronto's Annex.

All this I left behind when as an Eastern bride I travelled by train to Winnipeg, where I had never been, and met my new Western family. We parted from all my known worlds four hours out of Toronto. But we did not leave Ontario behind until the next night. From the lighted midnight platform at Sudbury to the twilit circle of the lake next day at Kenora, it came with me on my journey, and as before, all that I watched from the window of the day-coach was new and unknown.

The stories collected in this volume are a testimony to these paradoxes. All of them are by Ontario authors, and of all of them Ontario forms the setting, either stated or implied. They are, I suppose, "regional" stories, or would be if those ubiquitous boundaries did not prevent us from attaining some notion of what "region" means for Ontario. A sense of place, or a question as to its nature, is one of the things a writer can usefully begin with in Canada, knowing that his audience will share his desire to name and comprehend it. Consequently, perhaps the strongest thread of fiction-writing in the country lies in the regional novel; our prose is built layer by layer out of such evocations of place. And when that locality already has its own cohesion—the prairie of Grove and Laurence and Wiebe, the Maritimes of Haliburton, Roberts, and Nowlan—the diversity of local and individual experience can be channelled powerfully at an early stage. It is this strain in our literary history that leads to *The Stone Angel*, which has its origin somewhere in the regional idyll, but instead of being parochial, has become a central work to which we can all pay homage, no matter where we come from.

But considered solely as a locality, Ontario is not a region of Canada. No image of place informs it, for as a geographical entity it is as various as any of the larger nations of Europe. No historical experience confirms its unity, for the shots fired at Queenston Heights do not, for the Northern Ontarian, signify a symbolic moment in his past in the way that Duck Lake and Batoche do for Westerners. No obvious way of life defines it, for what Cobalt shares with Kingston is often more fundamental to their shared existence as communities of men than as communities specifically Ontarian. Anyone who has been here long has acquired a tumbled assortment of images of life within its boundaries: the main street of Cochrane full of afternoon shoppers in windbreakers, the calm activity of the Elmira farmers' market on a cold autumn morning, Nathan Phillips Square in the bustle of Caravan week, a cottager sitting silently on the end of a dock at Go Home Bay, two young bureaucrats in conference in the National Gallery cafeteria, an aged derelict slipping slowly to the pavement at the corner of Jarvis and Shuter. The continuous thread that binds this diversity into one is something we just work out as we go along.

It is part of the perversity with which Ontario refuses to be defined that *outside* its borders, everyone knows what Ontario means. If you are a Maritimer, Ontario is "Upper Canada," someplace dangerously more new and brash than your own familiar shores. If you are Québécois, Ontario is a synonym for the puritanical and philistine. If you are a Westerner, Ontario represents all that is conservative and self-gratulatory. And behind those beliefs (diverse and regional themselves) lurks the common notion that Ontario husbands a dangerous power, that decisions made on Bay Street can make rivers disappear in Newfoundland, that Ontario lures Western poets to the wine cellars of Jarvis Street, and never gives them back.

Worse still, these things are all true. Even in Canadian terms, Ontario is new. A hundred years after the Hudson's Bay Company had cast its frail but powerful network of posts across the West and North, Southern Ontario was relatively unorganized wilderness. Within very recent memory, Northern Ontario presented a considerable obstacle to travel by any method except train. Ontario has been—and still is, perhaps—intensely philistine; it took years for a regional theatre like those in Winnipeg and Halifax to be established in Toronto, where the patronage of a touring Broadway show is still thought in some quarters to be synonymous with culture. And Ontario is conservative in all three senses of

that term: best, worst, and political. Our most significant date
is probably August 17, 1943, when the present Tory government began the reign which has made it the most persistent
feature of community life here since the passing of the Orange
Lodge.

A sense of unknown and frightening power attaches itself
to the meaning of Ontario in the minds of people who do
not live here, and for good reason, for Ontario is power incar-
nate in place. To get to each other, Canadians have to go
through, or over, or past it, and as at every portage, the
travellers meet and talk, and share what they have in common
without devoting much attention to where they are standing.
To an extraordinary extent, in Ontario, they tend to settle
down and stay, always exiles from their own region, yet drawn
by the powerful sense of "centre" that they feel when they
get here. Though it isn't particularly praiseworthy, it is thus
not surprising that to an Ontarian, his place is not a region
but the centre of the world. Many of the decisions taken here
which antagonize people elsewhere arise from the easy
assumption that all the rest of Canada is like Ontario: diver-
sified, lacking in social cohesion, relying on power and entre-
preneurship to sustain itself, and eaten by the self-doubt that
arises from all these things.

Yet beneath this surface disunity, there can be seen a
stubbornly evolving set of characteristics. In the 1940s, a
western journalist called it "the Ontario Mind . . . closed,
filled with prejudice, and intolerant." This spiritual conserva-
tism, which used to express itself in a narrow range of human
values and a morose resistance to creative change, is still
found in Ontario, and novelists such as Robertson Davies,
Graeme Gibson, Marian Engel, and Richard Wright have
all tackled its problems. But here and there we can see it
being transformed into something more attractive. Old ways
of doing things are more important for all North Americans
than they used to be, now that we are turning back from the
pursuit of progress to settle for goals less glittering and less
destructive. It may have been Ontario's good fortune not to
have moved fast, for its people to have lived in small houses
on quiet streets, and actually enjoyed the infamous Toronto
Sunday. Some such habit of life is perhaps what really unites

the tranquil Victorian avenues of the long-settled south, and the bungalow-lined suburban streets of Geraldton and Longlac, which stretch out into wilderness.

Confronted with these possibilities, the Ontario writer's primary task is not, as elsewhere, to secure and confirm himself by naming and identifying his place, but to ask the much more puzzling question: "What is going on here?" And the problem of the relationship between different, bounded worlds tends not to be solved by finding a sense of locality, but in a confrontation with time. Walking in the cathedral stillness of White's Wood, near St. Thomas, one is among the last titanic relics of the great pine forest that once covered Southern Ontario. Curiously, this small acreage, which has never been cleared, does not seem particularly dense, and standing there I know it ends a hundred yards beyond me at the busy highway. But to the first Europeans who came here, the forest stretched everywhere. Today, as I sardonically reflect, the pine is not in the woods, but in the antique shops. Nevertheless, cupboards, chairs, and chests made out of these great trees seem to provide some of the first symbols of our idea of Ontario as a place. They are human artifacts, to be understood only through the human dimensions of time and art.

The layers of literary experience in Ontario are many. Nineteenth-century vignettes and sketches are succeeded by early twentieth-century wilderness romance. The cosmopolitan realism of the twenties and thirties gives way to "Western Ontario Gothic" and semi-autobiographical urban pastoral in the fifties and sixties. In few of these stories, except perhaps the very recent, does the sense of Ontario as a place define the story itself.

Instead, the stories draw their character much more than anything else from what people thought a "story" *was* when they were written. In selecting the ones included here, I've tried to cast my net very wide, and to include stories that are fine examples of their mode, even if that mode is now out of fashion. Some of that variety can be grasped in every section of the book, which as well as including brilliant modern short stories such as Alice Munro's "Walker Brothers Cowboy" also includes Greg Clark's fine sentimental vignette "May Your First Love Be Your Last" and James Reaney's historic shocker "The Box-Social." Some of the stories like those by Harvey O'Higgins and Alice Boissonneau are little-known. Others are famous, much-anthologized pieces, like Hugh Garner's "One-Two-Three Little Indians" and Morley Callaghan's "Last Spring They Came Over," which insofar as Ontario has ever been "caught" in the short story are surely definitive. It goes without saying that in limiting my choice to stories that make Ontario their starting point I have had to overlook many others.

Those that I *have* selected I've arranged in a curious and probably too personal order. The paradoxical nature of the Ontario experience is caught beautifully in one of the finest pieces of Ontario writing, Stephen Leacock's sketch "The Marine Excursion of the Knights of Pythias," which I have used to introduce the collection. Between Leacock's comic tale of the sinking Mariposa Belle, which ends in the rescue of its rescuers, and Dave Godfrey's elegiac "Out in Chinguacousy," which seems to ask whether rescue is possible, are four groups of stories, all containing pieces from different historical periods. The first section, "In the Clearings," contains stories about existence in a wilderness of some sort, all of which suggest why being an immigrant is not something that people in Ontario very rapidly outgrow. The next section, "Is This the Way to Sunshine?," contains four stories and one novel excerpt that all concern the problems of building human institutions: mercantile, political, familial, and spiritual. "Men and Women" contains five stories about different kinds of love; for reasons I don't understand, in almost all of them a sense of place is nearly as important as the relationships of the people involved. The final section is called "Where the Myth Touches Us," from Hugh Hood's story of that name. Gathered here are stories which take their character from the Ontarian confrontation with time. Except for one instance, the people in these stories are not preoccupied with history for its own sake. Nevertheless, they all turn back in a reflective gesture to look across boundaries between worlds of experience, by examining the way in which the past has turned out to be alive in the present.

Oddly, this sense of past-in-present is one of the things we can see in the Ontario landscape too. Despite its diversity, Ontario is slowly being unified as a place by the quantity of human experience that has left its mark here. One is always being surprised in the present by the signs of some past way of doing things that cannot be rejected or passed by. The modern highway that slashes through the century-old grid of concession roads seems at first an offence to the natural pattern of life. But after a while one settles down to adjudicate the debate between them; a tough task, but a necessary one, if we are not merely to live in our environment, but to *know* that we are living there. The collecting of these stories involved just such a debate for me, and I hope the reading of them does for you.

Germaine Warkentin
Victoria College
University of Toronto
1974

Prologue

Stephen Leacock

THE MARINE EXCURSION OF THE KNIGHTS OF PYTHIAS

Half-past six on a July morning! The Mariposa Belle is at the wharf, decked in flags, with steam up ready to start.

Excursion day!

Half-past six on a July morning, and Lake Wissanotti lying in the sun as calm as glass. The opal colours of the morning light are shot from the surface of the water.

Out on the lake the last thin threads of the mist are clearing away like flecks of cotton wool.

The long call of the loon echoes over the lake. The air is cool and fresh. There is in it all the new life of the land of the silent pine and the moving waters. Lake Wissanotti in the morning sunlight! Don't talk to me of the Italian lakes, or the Tyrol or the Swiss Alps. Take them away. Move them somewhere else. I don't want them.

Excursion Day, at half-past six of a summer morning! With the boat all decked in flags and all the people in Mariposa on the wharf, and the band in peaked caps with big cornets tied to their bodies ready to play at any minute! I say! Don't tell me about the Carnival of Venice and the Delhi Durbar. Don't! I wouldn't look at them. I'd shut my eyes! For light and colour give me every time an excursion out of Mariposa down the lake to the Indian's Island out of sight in the morning mist. Talk of your

Papal Zouaves and your Buckingham Palace Guard! I want to see the Mariposa band in uniform and the Mariposa Knights of Pythias with their aprons and their insignia and their picnic baskets and their five-cent cigars!

Half-past six in the morning, and all the crowd on the wharf and the boat due to leave in half an hour. Notice it! —in half an hour. Already she's whistled twice (at six, and at six fifteen), and at any minute now, Christie Johnson will step into the pilot house and pull the string for the warning whistle that the boat will leave in half an hour. So keep ready. Don't think of running back to Smith's Hotel for the sandwiches. Don't be fool enough to try to go up to the Greek Store, next to Netley's, and buy fruit. You'll be left behind for sure if you do. Never mind the sandwiches and the fruit! Anyway, here comes Mr. Smith himself with a huge basket of provender that would feed a factory. There must be sandwiches in that. I think I can hear them clinking. And behind Mr. Smith is the German waiter from the caff with another basket— indubitably lager beer; and behind him, the bartender of the hotel, carrying nothing, as far as one can see. But of course if you know Mariposa you will understand that why he looks so nonchalant and empty-handed is because he has two bottles of rye whiskey under his linen duster. You know, I think, the peculiar walk of a man with two bottles of whiskey in the inside pockets of a linen coat. In Mariposa, you see, to bring beer to an excursion is quite in keeping with public opinion. But whiskey—well, one has to be a little careful.

Do I say that Mr. Smith is here? Why, everybody's here. There's Hussell, the editor of the Newspacket, wearing a blue ribbon on his coat, for the Mariposa Knights of Pythias are, by their constitution, dedicated to temperance and there's Henry Mullins, the manager of the Exchange Bank, also a Knight of Pythias, with a small flask of Pogram's Special in his hip pocket as a sort of amendment to the constitution. And there's Dean Drone, the Chaplain of the Order, with a fishing-rod (you never saw such green bass as lie among the rocks at Indian's Island), and with a trolling line in case of maskinonge, and a landing net in case of pickerel, and with his eldest daughter, Lilian Drone, in case of young men. There never was such a fisherman as the Rev. Rupert Drone.

Perhaps I ought to explain that when I speak of the excursion as being of the Knights of Pythias, the thing must not be understood in any narrow sense. In Mariposa practically everybody belongs to the Knights of Pythias just as they do to everything else. That's the great thing about the town and that's what makes it so different from the city. Everybody is in everything.

You should see them on the seventeenth of March, for example, when everybody wears a green ribbon and they're all laughing and glad—you know what the Celtic nature is—and talking about Home Rule.

On St. Andrew's Day every man in town wears a thistle and shakes hands with everybody else, and you see the fine old Scotch honesty beaming out of their eyes.

And on St. George's Day!—well, there's no heartiness like the good old English spirit, after all; why shouldn't a man feel glad that he's an Englishman?

Then on the Fourth of July there are stars and stripes flying over half the stores in town, and suddenly all the men are seen to smoke cigars, and to know all about Roosevelt and Bryan and the Philippine Islands. Then you learn for the first time that Jeff Thorpe's people came from Massachusetts and that his uncle fought at Bunker Hill (anyway Jefferson will swear it was in Dakota all right enough); and you find that George Duff has a married sister in Rochester and that her husband is all right; in fact, George was down there as recently as eight years ago. Oh, it's the most American town imaginable is Mariposa—on the fourth of July.

But wait, just wait, if you feel anxious about the solidity of the British connection, till the twelfth of the month, when everybody is wearing an orange streamer in his coat and the Orangemen (every man in town) walk in the big procession. Allegiance! Well, perhaps you remember the address they gave to the Prince of Wales on the platform of the Mariposa station as he went through on his tour to the west. I think that pretty well settled that question.

So you will easily understand that of course everybody belongs to the Knights of Pythias and the Masons and Oddfellows, just as they all belong to the Snow Shoe Club and the Girls' Friendly Society.

And meanwhile the whistle of the steamer has blown again for a quarter to seven—loud and long this time, for anyone not here now is late for certain, unless he should happen to come down in the last fifteen minutes.

What a crowd upon the wharf and how they pile on to the steamer! It's a wonder that the boat can hold them all. But that's just the marvellous thing about the Mariposa Belle.

I don't know—I have never known—where the steamers like the Mariposa Belle come from. Whether they are built by Harland and Wolff of Belfast, or whether, on the other hand, they are not built by Harland and Wolff of Belfast, is more than one would like to say offhand.

The Mariposa Belle always seems to me to have some of those strange properties that distinguish Mariposa itself. I mean, her size seems to vary so. If you see her there in the winter, frozen in the ice beside the wharf with a snowdrift against the windows of the pilot house, she looks a pathetic little thing the size of a butternut. But in the summer time, especially after you've *been* in Mariposa for a month or two, and have paddled alongside of her in a canoe, she gets larger and taller, and with a great sweep of black sides, till you see no difference between the Mariposa Belle and the Lusitania. Each one is a big steamer and that's all you can say.

Nor do her measurements help you much. She draws about eighteen inches forward, and more than that—at least half an inch more, astern, and when she's loaded down with an excursion crowd she draws a good two inches more. And above the water—why, look at all the decks on her! There's the deck you walk on to, from the wharf, all shut in, with windows along it, and the after cabin with the long table, and above that the deck with all the chairs piled upon it, and the deck in front where the band stand round in a circle, and the pilot house is higher than that, and above the pilot house is the board with the gold name and the flag pole and the steel ropes and the flags; and fixed in somewhere on the different levels is the lunch counter where they sell the sandwiches, and the engine room, and down below the deck level, beneath the water line, is the place where the crew sleep. What with steps and stairs and passages and piles of cordwood for the engine—oh, no, I guess Harland and Wolff didn't build her. They couldn't have.

Yet even with a huge boat like the Mariposa Belle, it would be impossible for her to carry all of the crowd that you see in the boat and on the wharf. In reality, the crowd is made up of two classes—all of the people in Mariposa who are going on the excursion and all those who are not. Some come for the one reason and some for the other.

The two tellers of the Exchange Bank are both there standing side by side. But one of them—the one with the cameo pin and the long face like a horse—is going, and the other—with the other cameo pin and the face like another horse—is not. In the same way, Hussell of the Newspacket is going, but his brother, beside him, isn't. Lilian Drone is going, but her sister can't; and so on all through the crowd.

* * *

And to think that things should look like that on the morning of a steamboat accident.

How strange life is!

To think of all these people so eager and anxious to catch the steamer, and some of them running to catch it, and so fearful that they might miss it—the morning of a steamboat accident. And the captain blowing his whistle, and warning them so severely that he would leave them behind—leave them out of the accident! And everybody crowding so eagerly to be in the accident.

Perhaps life is like that all through.

Strangest of all to think, in a case like this, of the people who were left behind, or in some way or other prevented from going, and always afterwards told of how they had escaped being on board the Mariposa Belle that day!

Some of the instances were certainly extraordinary.

Nivens, the lawyer, escaped from being there merely by the fact that he was away in the city.

Towers, the tailor, only escaped owing to the fact that, not intending to go on the excursion, he had stayed in bed till eight o'clock and so had not gone. He narrated afterwards that waking up that morning at half-past five, he had thought of the excursion and for some unaccountable reason had felt glad that he was not going.

*   *   *

The case of Yodel, the auctioneer, was even more inscrutable. He had been to the Oddfellows' excursion on the train the week before and to the Conservative picnic the week before that, and had decided not to go on this trip. In fact, he had not the least intention of going. He narrated afterwards how the night before someone had stopped him on the corner of Nippewa and Tecumseh Streets (he indicated the very spot) and asked: "Are you going to take in the excursion tomorrow?" and he had said, just as simply as he was talking when narrating it: "No." And ten minutes after that, at the corner of Dalhousie and Brock Streets (he offered to lead a party of verification to the precise place) somebody else had stopped him and asked: "Well, are you going on the steamer trip tomorrow?" Again he had answered: "No," apparently almost in the same tone as before.

He said afterwards that when he heard the rumour of the accident it seemed like the finger of Providence, and he fell on his knees in thankfulness.

There was the similar case of Morison (I mean the one in Glover's hardware store that married one of the Thompsons). He said afterwards that he had read so much in the papers about accidents lately—mining accidents, and aeroplanes and gasoline—that he had grown nervous. The night before his wife had asked him at supper: "Are you going on the excursion?" He had answered: "No, I don't think I feel like it," and had added: "Perhaps your mother might like to go." And the next evening just at dusk, when the news ran through the town, he said the first thought that flashed through his head was: "Mrs. Thompson's on that boat."

He told this right as I say it—without the least doubt or confusion. He never for a moment imagined she was on the Lusitania or the Olympic or any other boat. He knew she was on this one. He said you could have knocked him down where he stood. But no one had. Not even when he got halfway down—on his knees, and it would have been easier still to knock him down or kick him. People do miss a lot of chances.

Still, as I say, neither Yodel nor Morison nor anyone thought about there being an accident until just after sundown when they—

Well, have you ever heard the long booming whistle of a steamboat two miles out on the lake in the dusk, and while you listen and count and wonder, seen the crimson rockets going up against the sky and then heard the fire bell ringing right there beside you in the town, and seen the people running to the town wharf?

That's what the people of Mariposa saw and felt that summer evening as they watched the Mackinaw lifeboat go plunging out into the lake with seven sweeps to a side and the foam clear to the gunwale with the lifting stroke of fourteen men!

But, dear me, I am afraid that this is no way to tell a story. I suppose the true art would have been to have said nothing about the accident till it happened. But when you write about Mariposa, or hear of it, if you know the place, it's all so vivid and real, that a thing like the contrast between the excursion crowd in the morning and the scene at night leaps into your mind and you must think of it.

*   *   *

But never mind about the accident—let us turn back to the morning.

The boat was due to leave at seven. There was no doubt about the hour—not only seven, but seven sharp. The notice in the Newspacket said: "The boat will leave sharp at seven"; and the advertising posters on the telegraph poles on Missinaba Street that began, "Ho, for Indian's Island!" ended up with the words: "Boat leaves at seven sharp." There was a big notice on the wharf that said: "Boat leaves sharp on time."

So at seven, right on the hour, the whistle blew loud and long, and then at seven fifteen three short peremptory blasts and at seven thirty one quick angry call—just one—and very soon after that they cast off the last of the ropes and the Mariposa Belle sailed off in her cloud of flags, and the band of the Knights of Pythias, timing it to a nicety, broke into the "Maple Leaf for Ever!"

I suppose that all excursions when they start are much the same. Anyway, on the Mariposa Belle everybody went running up and down all over the boat with deck chairs and camp stools and baskets, and found places, splendid places to sit, and then got scared that there might be better ones and chased off again. People hunted for places out of the sun and when they got them swore that they weren't going to freeze to please anybody; and the people in the sun said that they hadn't paid fifty cents to be roasted. Others said that they hadn't paid fifty cents to get covered with cinders, and there were still others who hadn't paid fifty cents to get shaken to death with the propeller.

Still, it was all right presently. The people seemed to get sorted out into the places on the boat where they belonged. The women, the older ones, all gravitated into the cabin on the lower deck and by getting round the table with needlework, and with all the windows shut, they soon had it, as they said themselves, just like being at home.

All the young boys and the toughs and the men in the band got down on the lower deck forward, where the boat was dirtiest and where the anchor was and the coils of rope.

And upstairs on the after deck there were Lilian Drone and Miss Lawson, the high-school teacher, with a book of German poetry—Gothey I think it was—and the bank teller and the young men.

In the centre, standing beside the rail, were Dean Drone and Dr. Gallagher, looking through binocular glasses at the shore.

Up in front on the little deck forward of the pilot house was a group of the older men, Mullins and Duff and Mr. Smith in a deck chair, and beside him Mr. Golgotha Gingham, the undertaker of Mariposa, on a stool. It was part of Mr. Gingham's principles to take in an outing of this sort, a business matter, more or less—for you never know what may happen at these water parties. At any rate, he was there in a neat suit of black, not, of course, his heavier or professional suit, but a soft clinging effect as of burnt paper that combined gaiety and decorum to a nicety.

* * *

"Yes", said Mr. Gingham, waving his black glove in a general way towards the shore, "I know the lake well, very well. I've been pretty much all over it in my time."

"Canoeing?" asked somebody.

"No," said Mr. Gingham, "not in a canoe." There seemed a peculiar and quiet meaning in his tone.

"Sailing, I suppose," said somebody else.

"No," said Mr. Gingham. "I don't understand it."

"I never knowed that you went on to the water at all, Gol," said Mr. Smith, breaking in.

"Ah, not now," explained Mr. Gingham; "it was years ago, the first summer I came to Mariposa. I was on the water practically all day. Nothing like it to give a man an appetite and keep him in shape."

"Was you camping?" asked Mr. Smith.

"We camped at night," assented the undertaker, "but we put in practically the whole day on the water. You see, we were after a party that had come up here from the city on his vacation and gone out in a sailing canoe. We were dragging. We were up every morning at sunrise, lit a fire on the beach and cooked breakfast, and then we'd light our pipes and be off with the net for a whole day. It's a great life," concluded Mr. Gingham wistfully.

"Did you get him?" asked two or three together.

There was a pause before Mr. Gingham answered.

"We did," he said "—down in the reeds past Horseshoe Point. But it was no use. He turned blue on me right away."

After which Mr. Gingham fell into such a deep reverie that the boat had steamed another half-mile down the lake before anybody broke the silence again. Talk of this sort—and after all what more suitable for a day on the water?—beguiled the way.

* * *

Down the lake, mile by mile over the calm water, steamed the Mariposa Belle. They passed Poplar Point where the high sand-banks are with all the swallows' nests in them, and Dean Drone and Dr. Gallagher looked at them alternately through the binocular glasses, and it was wonderful how plainly one could see the swallows and the banks and the shrubs—just as plainly as with the naked eye.

And a little further down they passed the Shingle Beach, and Dr. Gallagher, who knew Canadian history, said to Dean Drone that it was strange to think that Champlain had landed there with his French explorers three hundred years ago; and Dean Drone, who didn't know Canadian history, said it was stranger still to think that the hand of the Almighty had piled up the hills and rocks long before that; and Dr. Gallagher said it was wonderful how the French had found their way through such a pathless wilderness; and Dean Drone said that is was wonderful also to think that the Almighty had placed even the smallest shrub in its appointed place. Dr. Gallagher said it filled him with admiration. Dean Drone said it filled him with awe. Dr. Gallagher said he'd been full of it since he was a boy and Dean Drone said so had he.

Then a little further, as the Mariposa Belle steamed on down the lake, they passed the Old Indian Portage where the great grey rocks are; and Dr. Gallagher drew Dean Drone's attention to the place where the narrow canoe track wound up from the shore to the woods, and Dean Drone said he could see it perfectly well without the glasses.

Dr. Gallagher said that it was just here that a party of five hundred French had made their way with all their baggage and accoutrements across the rocks of the divide and down to the Great Bay. And Dean Drone said that it reminded him of Xenophon leading his ten thousand Greeks over the hill passes of Armenia down to the sea. Dr. Gallagher said that he had often wished he could have seen and spoken to Champlain, and Dean Drone said how much he regretted to have never known Xenophon.

And then after that they fell to talking of relics and traces of the past, and Dr. Gallagher said that if Dean Drone would come round to his house some night he would show him some Indian arrow heads that he had dug up in his garden. And Dean Drone said that if Dr. Gallagher would come round to the rectory any afternoon he would show him a map of Xerxes' invasion of Greece. Only he must come some time between the Infant Class and the Mothers' Auxiliary.

So presently they both knew that they were blocked out of one another's houses for some time to come, and Dr. Gallagher walked forward and told Mr. Smith, who had never studied Greek, about Champlain crossing the rock divide.

Mr. Smith turned his head and looked at the divide for half a second and then said he had crossed a worse one up north back of the Wahnipitae and that the flies were Hades —and then went on playing freezeout poker with the two juniors in Duff's bank.

So Dr. Gallagher realized that that's always the way when you try to tell people things, and that as far as gratitude and appreciation goes one might as well never read books or travel anywhere or do anything.

In fact, it was at this very moment that he made up his mind to give the arrows to the Mariposa Mechanics' Institute—they afterwards became, as you know, the Gallagher Collection. But, for the time being, the doctor was sick of them and wandered off round the boat and watched Henry Mullins showing George Duff how to make a John Collins without lemons, and finally went and sat down among the Mariposa band and wished that he hadn't come.

So the boat steamed on and the sun rose higher and higher, and the freshness of the morning changed into the full glare of noon, and they went on to where the lake began to narrow in at its foot, just where the Indian's Island is—all grass and trees and with a low wharf running into the water. Below it the Lower Ossawippi runs out of the lake, and quite near are the rapids, and you can see down among the trees the red brick of the power house and hear the roar of the leaping water.

The Indian's Island itself is all covered with trees and tangled vines, and the water about it is so still that it's all reflected double and looks the same either way up. Then when the steamer's whistle blows as it comes into the wharf, you hear it echo among the trees of the island, and reverberate back from the shores of the lake.

The scene is all so quiet and still and unbroken, that Miss Cleghorn—the sallow girl in the telephone exchange that I spoke of—said she'd like to be buried there. But all the people were so busy getting their baskets and gathering up their things that no one had time to attend to it.

I mustn't even try to describe the landing and the boat crunching against the wooden wharf and all the people running to the same side of the deck and Christie Johnson calling out to the crowd to keep to the starboard and nobody being able to find it. Everyone who has been on a Mariposa excursion knows all about that.

Nor can I describe the day itself and the picnic under the trees. There were speeches afterwards, and Judge Pepperleigh gave such offence by bringing in Conservative politics that a man called Patriotus Canadiensis wrote and asked for some of the invaluable space of the Mariposa Times-Herald and exposed it.

I should say that there were races too, on the grass on the open side of the island, graded mostly according to ages—races for boys under thirteen and girls over nineteen and all that sort of thing. Sports are generally conducted on that plan in Mariposa. It is realized that a woman of sixty has an unfair advantage over a mere child.

Dean Drone managed the races and decided the ages and gave out the prizes; the Wesleyan minister helped, and he and the young student, who was relieving in the Presbyterian Church, held the string at the winning point.

They had to get mostly clergymen for the races because all the men had wandered off, somehow, to where they were drinking lager beer out of two kegs stuck on pine logs among the trees.

But if you've ever been on a Mariposa excursion you know all about these details anyway.

So the day wore on and presently the sun came through the trees on a slant and the steamer whistle blew with a great puff of white steam and all the people came straggling down to the wharf and pretty soon the Mariposa Belle had floated out on to the lake again and headed for the town, twenty miles away.

* * *

I suppose you have often noticed the contrast there is between an excursion on its way out in the morning and what it looks like on the way home.

In the morning everybody is so restless and animated and moves to and from all over the boat and asks questions. But coming home, as the afternoon gets later and later and the sun sinks beyond the hills, all the people seem to get so still and quiet and drowsy.

So it was with the people on the Mariposa Belle. They sat there on the benches and the deck chairs in little clusters, and listened to the regular beat of the propeller and almost dozed off asleep as they sat. Then when the sun set and the dusk drew on, it grew almost dark on the deck and so still that you could hardly tell there was anyone on board.

And if you had looked at the steamer from the shore or from one of the islands, you'd have seen the row of lights from the cabin windows shining on the water and the red glare of the burning hemlock from the funnel, and you'd have heard the soft thud of the propeller miles away over the lake.

Now and then, too, you could have heard them singing on the steamer—the voices of the girls and the men blended into unison by the distance, rising and falling in long-drawn melody: *"O—Can-a-da—O—Can-a-da."*

You may talk as you will about the intoning choirs of your European cathedrals, but the sound of "O Can-a-da", borne across the waters of a silent lake at evening is good enough for those of us who know Mariposa.

I think that it was just as they were singing like this: *"O—Can-a-da"*, that word went round that the boat was sinking.

If you have ever been in any sudden emergency on the water, you will understand the strange psychology of it— the way in which what is happening seems to become known all in a moment without a word being said. The news is transmitted from one to the other by some mysterious process.

At any rate, on the Mariposa Belle first one and then the other heard that the steamer was sinking. As far as I could ever learn the first of it was that George Duff, the bank manager, came very quietly to Dr. Gallagher and asked him if he thought that the boat was sinking. The doctor said no, that he had thought so earlier in the day but that he didn't now think that she was.

After that Duff, according to his own account, had said to Macartney, the lawyer, that the boat was sinking, and Macartney said that he doubted it very much.

Then somebody came to Judge Pepperleigh and woke him up and said that there was six inches of water in the steamer and that she was sinking. And Pepperleigh said it was perfect scandal and passed the news on to his wife and she said that they had no business to allow it and that if the steamer sank that was the last excursion she'd go on.

So the news went all around the boat and everywhere the people gathered in groups and talked about it in the angry and excited way that people have when a steamer is sinking on one of the lakes like Lake Wissanotti.

Dean Drone, of course, and some others were quieter about it, and said that one must make allowances and that naturally there were two sides to everything. But most of them wouldn't listen to reason at all. I think, perhaps, that some of them were frightened. You see, the last time but one that the steamer had sunk, there had been a man drowned and it made them nervous.

What? Hadn't I explained about the depth of Lake Wissanotti? I had taken it for granted that you knew; and in any case parts of it are deep enough, though I don't suppose in this stretch of it from the big reed beds up to within a mile of the town wharf, you could find six feet of water in it if you tried. Oh, pshaw! I was not talking about a steamer sinking in the ocean and carrying down its screaming crowds of people into the hideous depths of green water. Oh, dear me, no! That kind of thing never happens on Lake Wissanotti.

But what does happen is that the Mariposa Belle sinks every now and then, and sticks there on the bottom till they get things straightened up.

On the lakes around Mariposa, if a person arrives late anywhere and explains that the steamer sank, everybody understands the situation.

You see, when Harland and Wolff built the Mariposa Belle, they left some cracks in between the timbers that you fill up with cotton waste every Sunday. If this is not attended to, the boat sinks. In fact, it is part of the law of the province that all the steamers like the Mariposa Belle must be properly corked—I think that is the word—every season. There are inspectors who visit all the hotels in the province to see that it is done.

So you can imagine now that I've explained it a little straighter, the indignation of the people when they knew that the boat had come uncorked and that they might be stuck out there on a shoal or a mud-bank half the night.

I don't say either that there wasn't any danger; anyway, it doesn't feel very safe when you realize that the boat is settling down with every hundred yards that she goes, and you look over the side and see only the black water in the gathering night.

Safe! I'm not sure now that I come to think of it that it isn't worse than sinking in the Atlantic. After all, in the Atlantic there is wireless telegraphy, and a lot of trained sailors and stewards. But out on Lake Wissanotti—far out, so that you can only just see the lights of the town away off to the south—when the propeller comes to a stop—and you can hear the hiss of steam as they start to rake out the engine fires to prevent an explosion—and when you turn from the red glare that comes from the furnace doors as they open them, to the black dark that is gathering over the lake—and there's a night wind beginning to run among the rushes—and you see the men going forward to the roof of the pilot house to send up the rockets to rouse the town—safe? Safe yourself, if you like; as for me, let me once get back into Mariposa again, under the night shadow of the maple trees, and this shall be the last, last time I'll go on Lake Wissanotti.

Safe! Oh, yes! Isn't it strange how safe other people's adventures seem after they happen? But you'd have been scared, too, if you'd been there just before the steamer sank, and seen them bringing up all the women on to the top deck.

I don't see how some of the people took it so calmly; how Mr. Smith, for instance, could have gone on smoking and telling how he'd had a steamer "sink on him" on Lake Nipissing and a still bigger one, a side-wheeler, sink on him in Lake Abbitibbi.

Then, quite suddenly, with a quiver, down she went. You could feel the boat sink, sink—down, down—would it never get to the bottom? The water came flush up to the lower deck, and then—thank heaven—the sinking stopped and there was the Mariposa Belle safe and tight on a reed bank.

Really, it made one positively laugh! It seemed so queer and, anyway, if a man has a sort of natural courage, danger makes him laugh. Danger? pshaw! fiddlesticks! everybody scouted the idea. Why, it is just the little things like this that give zest to a day on the water.

Within half a minute they were all running round looking for sandwiches and cracking jokes and talking of making coffee over the remains of the engine fires.

* * *

I don't need to tell at length how it all happened after that. I suppose the people on the Mariposa Belle would have had to settle down there all night or till help came from the town, but some of the men who had gone forward and were peering out into the dark said that it couldn't be more than a mile across the water to Miller's Point. You could almost see it over there to the left—some of them, I think, said "off on the port bow", because you know when you get mixed up in these marine disasters, you soon catch the atmosphere of the thing.

So pretty soon they had the davits swung out over the side and were lowering the old lifeboat from the top deck into the water.

There were men leaning out over the rail of the Mariposa Belle with lanterns that threw the light as they let her down, and the glare fell on the water and the reeds. But when they got the boat lowered, it looked such a frail, clumsy thing as one saw it from the rail above, that the cry was raised: "Women and children first!" For what was the sense, if it should turn out that the boat wouldn't even hold women and children, of trying to jam a lot of heavy men into it?

So they put in mostly women and children and the boat pushed out into the darkness so freighted down it would hardly float.

In the bow of it was the Presbyterian student who was relieving the minister, and he called out that they were in the hands of Providence. But he was crouched and ready to spring out of them at the first moment.

So the boat went and was lost in the darkness except for the lantern in the bow that you could see bobbing on the water. Then presently it came back and they sent another load, till pretty soon the decks began to thin out and everybody got impatient to be gone.

It was about the time that the third boat-load put off that Mr. Smith took a bet with Mullins for twenty-five dollars, that he'd be home in Mariposa before the people in the boats had walked round the shore.

No one knew just what he meant, but pretty soon they saw Smith disappear down below into the lowest part of the steamer with a mallet in one hand and a big bundle of marline in the other.

They might have wondered more about it, but it was just at this time that they heard the shouts from the rescue boat —the big Mackinaw lifeboat—that had put out from the town with fourteen men at the sweeps when they saw the first rockets go up.

I suppose there is always something inspiring about a rescue at sea, or on the water.

After all, the bravery of the lifeboat man is the true bravery—expended to save life, not to destroy it.

Certainly they told for months after of how the rescue boat came out to the Mariposa Belle.

I suppose that when they put her in the water the lifeboat touched it for the first time since the old Macdonald Government placed her on Lake Wissanotti.

Anyway, the water poured in at every seam. But not for a moment—even with two miles of water between them and the steamer—did the rowers pause for that.

By the time they were half-way there the water was almost up to the thwarts, but they drove her on. Panting and exhausted (for mind you, if you haven't been in a fool boat like that for years, rowing takes it out of you), the rowers stuck to their task. They threw the ballast over and chucked into the water the heavy cork jackets and lifebelts that encumbered their movements. There was no thought of turning back. They were nearer to the steamer than the shore.

"Hang to it, boys," called the crowd from the steamer's deck, and hang they did.

They were almost exhausted when they got them; men leaning from the steamer threw them ropes and one by one every man was hauled aboard just as the lifeboat sank under their feet.

Saved! by Heaven, saved by one of the smartest pieces of rescue work ever seen on the lake.

There's no use describing it; you need to see rescue work of this kind by lifeboats to understand it.

Nor were the lifeboat crew the only ones that distinguished themselves.

Boat after boat and canoe after canoe had put out from Mariposa to the help of the steamer. They got them all.

Pupkin, the other bank teller with a face like a horse, who hadn't gone on the excursion—as soon as he knew that the boat was signalling for help and that Miss Lawson was sending up rockets—rushed for a row boat, grabbed an oar (two would have hampered him)—and paddled madly out into the lake. He struck right out into the dark with the crazy skiff almost sinking beneath his feet. But they got him. They rescued him. They watched him, almost dead with exhaustion, make his way to the steamer, where he was hauled up with ropes. Saved! Saved!

*   *   *

They might have gone on that way half the night, picking up the rescuers, only, at the very moment when the tenth load of people left for the shore—just as suddenly and saucily as you please, up came the Mariposa Belle from the mud bottom and floated.

Floated?

Why, of course she did. If you take a hundred and fifty people off a steamer that has sunk, and if you get a man as shrewd as Mr. Smith to plug the timber seams with mallet and marline, and if you turn ten bandsmen of the Mariposa band on to your hand pump on the bow of the lower decks—float? why, what else can she do?

Then, if you stuff in hemlock into the embers of the fire that you were raking out, till it hums and crackles under the boiler, it won't be long before you hear the propeller thud—thudding at the stern again, and before the long roar of the steam whistle echoes over to the town.

And so the Mariposa Belle, with all steam up again and with the long train of sparks careering from the funnel, is heading for the town.

But no Christie Johnson at the wheel in the pilot house this time.

"Smith! Get Smith!" is the cry.

Can he take her in? Well, now! Ask a man who has had steamers sink on him in half the lakes from Temiscaming to the Bay, if he can take her in? Ask a man who has run a York boat down the rapids of the Moose when the ice is moving, if he can grip the steering wheel of the Mariposa Belle? So there she steams safe and sound to the town wharf!

Look at the lights and the crowd! If only the federal census taker could count us now! Hear them calling and shouting back and forward from the deck to the shore! Listen! There is the rattle of the shore ropes as they get them ready, and there's the Mariposa band—actually forming in a circle on the upper deck just as she docks, and the leader with his baton—one—two—ready now—

"O CAN-A-DA!"

In the clearings

Susanna Moodie

ON A JOURNEY TO THE WOODS

> 'Tis well for us poor denizens of earth
> That God conceals the future from our gaze;
> Or Hope, the blessed watcher on Life's tower,
> Would fold her wings, and on the dreary waste
> Close the bright eye that through the murky clouds
> Of blank Despair still sees the glorious sun.

It was a bright frosty morning when I bade adieu to the farm, the birthplace of my little Agnes, who, nestled beneath my cloak, was sweetly sleeping on my knee, unconscious of the long journey before us into the wilderness. The sun had not as yet risen. Anxious to get to our place of destination before dark, we started as early as we could. Our own fine team had been sold the day before for forty pounds; and one of our neighbours, a Mr. D——, was to convey us and our household goods to Douro for the sum of twenty dollars. During the week he had made several journeys, with furniture and stores; and all that now remained was to be conveyed to the woods in two large lumber sleighs, one driven by himself, the other by a younger brother.

It was not without regret that I left Melsetter, for so my husband had called the place, after his father's estate in Orkney. It was a beautiful, picturesque spot; and, in spite of the evil neighbourhood, I had learned to love it; indeed, it was much against my wish that it was sold. I had a great dislike to removing, which involves a necessary loss, and is apt to give to the emigrant roving and unsettled habits. But all regrets were now useless; and happily unconscious of the life of toil and anxiety that awaited us in those dreadful woods, I tried my best to be cheerful, and to regard the future with a hopeful eye.

Our driver was a shrewd, clever man for his opportunities. He took charge of the living cargo, which consisted of my husband, our maid-servant, the two little children, and myself—besides a large hamper full of poultry, a dog, and a cat. The lordly sultan of the imprisoned seraglio thought fit to conduct himself in a very eccentric manner, for at every barn-yard we happened to pass, he clapped his wings, and crowed so long and loud that it afforded great amusement to the whole party, and doubtless was very edifying to the poor hens, who lay huddled together as mute as mice.

"That 'ere rooster thinks he's on the top of the heap," said our driver, laughing. "I guess he's not used to travelling in a close conveyance. Listen! How all the crowers in the neighbourhood give him back a note of defiance! But he knows that he's safe enough at the bottom of the basket."

The day was so bright for the time of year (the first week in February), that we suffered no inconvenience from the cold. Little Katie was enchanted with the jingling of the sleigh-bells, and, nestled among the packages, kept singing or talking to the horses in her baby lingo. Trifling as these little incidents were, before we had proceeded ten miles on our long journey, they revived my drooping spirits, and I began to feel a lively interest in the scenes through which we were passing.

The first twenty miles of the way was over a hilly and well-cleared country; and as in winter the deep snow fills up the inequalities, and makes all roads alike, we glided as swiftly and steadily along as if they had been the best highways in the world. Anon, the clearings began to diminish, and tall woods arose on either side of the path; their solemn aspect, and the deep silence that brooded over their vast solitudes, inspiring the mind with a strange awe. Not a breath of wind stirred the leafless branches, whose huge shadows

—reflected upon the dazzling white covering of snow—lay so perfectly still, that it seemed as if Nature had suspended her operations, that life and motion had ceased, and that she was sleeping in her winding-sheet, upon the bier of death.

"I guess you will find the woods pretty lonesome," said our driver, whose thoughts had been evidently employed on the same subject as our own. "We were once in the woods, but emigration has stepped ahead of us, and made our'n a cleared part of the country. When I was a boy, all this country, for thirty miles on every side of us, was bush land. As to Peterborough, the place was unknown; not a settler had ever passed through the great swamp, and some of them believed that it was the end of the world."

"What swamp is that?" asked I.

"Oh, the great Cavan swamp. We are just two miles from it; and I tell you that the horses will need a good rest, and ourselves a good dinner, by the time we are through it. Ah! Mrs. Moodie, if ever you travel that way in summer, you will know something about corduroy roads. I was 'most jolted to death last fall; I thought it would have been no bad notion to have insured my teeth before I left C——. I really expected that they would have been shook out of my head before we had done manoeuvring over the big logs."

"How will my crockery stand it in the next sleigh?" quoth I. "If the road is such as you describe, I am afraid that I shall not bring a whole plate to Douro."

"Oh! the snow is a great leveller—it makes all rough places smooth. But with regard to this swamp I have something to tell you. About ten years ago, no one had ever seen the other side of it, and if pigs or cattle strayed away into it, they fell a prey to the wolves and bears, and were seldom recovered.

"An old Scotch emigrant, who had located himself on this side of it, so often lost his beasts that he determined during the summer season to try and explore the place, and see if there were any end to it. So he takes an axe on his shoulder, and a bag of provisions for a week, not forgetting a flask of whiskey, and off he starts all alone, and tells his wife that if he never returned, she and little Jock must try and carry on the farm without him; but he was determined to see the end of the swamp, even if it led to the other world. He fell upon a fresh cattle tract which he followed all that day; and towards night he found himself in the heart of a tangled wilderness of bushes, and himself half eaten up with mosquitoes and black flies. He was more than tempted to give in and return home by the first glimpse of light.

"The Scotch are a tough people; they are not easily daunted—a few difficulties only seem to make them more eager to get on; and he felt ashamed the next moment, as he told me, of giving up. So he finds out a large thick cedar-tree for his bed, climbs up, and coiling himself among the branches like a bear, he was soon fast asleep.

"The next morning, by daylight, he continued his journey, not forgetting to blaze with his axe the trees to the right and left as he went along. The ground was so spongy and wet that at every step he plunged up to his knees in water, but he seemed no nearer the end of the swamp than he had been the day before. He saw several deer, a racoon, and a ground-hog, during his walk, but was unmolested by bears or wolves. Having passed through several creeks, and killed a great many snakes, he felt so weary towards the close of the second day that he determined to go home the next morning. But just as he began to think his search was fruitless, he observed that the cedars and tamaracks which had obstructed his path became less numerous, and were succeeded by bass and soft maple. The ground, also, became less moist, and he was soon ascending a rising slope, covered with oak and beech, which shaded land of the very best quality. The old man was now fully convinced that he had cleared the great swamp, and that, instead of leading to the other world, it had conducted him to a country that would yield the very best returns for cultivation. His favourable report led to the formation of the road that we are about to cross, and to the settlement of Peterborough, which is one of the most promising new settlements in this district, and is surrounded by a splendid back country."

We were descending a very steep hill, and encountered an ox-sleigh, which was crawling slowly up it in a contrary direction. Three people were seated at the bottom of the vehicle upon straw, which made a cheap substitute for buffalo-robes. Perched, as we were, upon the crown of the height, we looked completely down into the sleigh, and during the whole course of my life I never saw three uglier mortals collected into such a narrow space. The man was blear-eyed, with a hare-lip, through which protruded two dreadful yellow teeth that resembled the tusks of a boar. The woman was long-faced, high cheek-boned, red-haired, and freckled all over like a toad. The boy resembled his hideous mother, but with the addition of a villainous obliquity of vision which rendered him the most disgusting object in this singular trio.

As we passed them, our driver gave a knowing nod to my husband, directing, at the same time, the most quizzical glance towards the strangers, as he exclaimed, "We are in luck, sir! I think that 'ere sleigh may be called Beauty's egg-basket!"

We made ourselves very merry at the poor people's expense, and Mr. D——, with his odd stories and Yankeefied expressions, amused the tedium of our progress through the great swamp, which in summer presents for several miles one uniform bridge of rough and unequal logs, all laid loosely across huge sleepers, so that they jump up and down, when pressed by the wheels, like the keys of a piano. The rough motion and jolting occasioned by this collision is so distressing, that it never fails to entail upon the traveller sore bones and an aching head for the rest of the day. The path is so narrow over these logs that two waggons cannot pass without great difficulty, which is rendered more dangerous by the deep natural ditches on either side of the bridge, formed by broad creeks that flow out of the swamp, and often terminate in mud-holes of very ominous dimensions. The snow, however, hid from us all the ugly features of the road, and Mr. D—— steered us through in perfect safety, and landed us at the door of a little log house which crowned the steep hill on the other side of the swamp, and which he dignified with the name of a tavern.

It was now two o'clock. We had been on the road since seven; and men, women, and children were all ready for the good dinner that Mr. D—— had promised us at this splendid house of entertainment, where we were destined to stay for two hours, to refresh ourselves and rest the horses.

"Well, Mrs. J——, what have you got for our dinner?"

said our driver, after he had seen to the accommodation of his teams.

"Pritters* and pork, sir. Nothing else to be had in the woods. Thank God, we have enough of that!"

D—— shrugged up his shoulders, and looked at us.

"We've plenty of that same at home. But hunger's good sauce. Come, be spry, widow, and see about it, for I am very hungry."

I inquired for a private room for myself and the children, but there were no private rooms in the house. The apartment we occupied was like the cobbler's stall in the old song, and I was obliged to attend upon them in public.

"You have much to learn, ma'am, if you are going to the woods," said Mrs. J——.

"To unlearn, you mean," said Mr. D——. "To tell you the truth, Mrs. Moodie, ladies and gentlemen have no business in the woods. Eddication spoils man or woman for that location. So, widow (turning to our hostess), you are not tired of living alone yet?"

"No, sir; I have no wish for a second husband. I had enough of the first. I like to have my own way—to lie down mistress, and get up master."

"You don't like to be put out of your *old* way," returned he, with a mischievous glance.

She coloured very red; but it might be the heat of the fire over which she was frying the pork for our dinner.

I was very hungry, but I felt no appetite for the dish she was preparing for us. It proved salt, hard, and unsavoury.

D—— pronounced it very bad, and the whiskey still worse, with which he washed it down.

I asked for a cup of tea and a slice of bread. But they were out of tea, and the hop-rising had failed, and there was no bread in the house. For this disgusting meal we paid at the rate of a quarter of a dollar a-head.

I was glad when the horses being again put to, we escaped from the rank odour of the fried pork, and were once more in the fresh air.

"Well, mister; did not you grudge your money for that bad meat?" said D——, when we were once more seated in

*Vulgar Canadian for potatoes.

the sleigh. "But in these parts the worse the fare the higher the charge."

"I would not have cared," said I, "if I could have got a cup of tea."

"Tea! it's poor trash. I never could drink tea in my life. But I like coffee, when 'tis boiled till it's quite black. But coffee is not good without plenty of trimmings."

"What do you mean by trimmings?"

He laughed. "Good sugar, and sweet cream. Coffee is not worth drinking without trimmings."

Often in after-years have I recalled the coffee trimmings, when endeavouring to drink the vile stuff which goes by the name of coffee in the houses of entertainment in the country.

We had now passed through the narrow strip of clearing which surrounded the tavern, and again entered upon the woods. It was near sunset, and we were rapidly descending a steep hill, when one of the traces that held our sleigh suddenly broke. D—— pulled up in order to repair the damage. His brother's team was close behind, and our unexpected stand-still brought the horses upon us before J. D—— could stop them. I received so violent a blow from the head of one of them, just in the back of the neck, that for a few minutes I was stunned and insensible. When I recovered, I was supported in the arms of my husband, over whose knees I was leaning, and D—— was rubbing my hands and temples with snow.

"There, Mr. Moodie, she's coming to. I thought she was killed. I have seen a man before now killed by a blow from a horse's head in the like manner."

As soon as we could, we resumed our places in the sleigh; but all enjoyment of our journey, had it been otherwise possible, was gone.

When we reached Peterborough, Moodie wished us to remain at the inn all night, as we had still eleven miles of our journey to perform, and that through a blazed forest-road, little travelled, and very much impeded by fallen trees and other obstacles; but D—— was anxious to get back as soon as possible to his own home, and he urged us very pathetically to proceed.

The moon arose during our stay at the inn, and gleamed

upon the straggling frame-houses which then formed the now populous and thriving town of Peterborough. We crossed the wild, rushing beautiful Otonabee River by a rude bridge, and soon found ourselves journeying over the plains or level heights beyond the village, which were thinly wooded with picturesque groups of oak and pine, and very much resembled a gentleman's park at home.

Far below, to our right (for we were upon the Smithtown side) we heard the rushing of the river, whose rapid waters never received curb from the iron chain of winter. Even while the rocky banks are coated with ice, and the frost-king suspends from every twig and branch the most beautiful and fantastic crystals, the black waters rush foaming along, a thick steam rising constantly above the rapids, as from a boiling pot. The shores vibrate and tremble beneath the force of the impetuous flood, as it whirls round cedar-crowned islands and opposing rocks, and hurries on to pour its tribute into the Rice Lake, to swell the calm, majestic grandeur of the Trent, till its waters are lost in the beautiful Bay of Quinté, and finally merged in the blue ocean of Ontario.

The most renowned of our English rivers dwindle into little muddy rills when compared with the sublimity of the Canadian waters. No language can adequately express the solemn grandeur of her lake and river scenery; the glorious islands that float, like visions from fairyland, upon the bosom of these azure mirrors of her cloudless skies. No dreary breadth of marshes, covered with flags, hides from our gaze the expanse of heavy-tinted waters; no foul mud-banks spread the unwholesome exhalations around. The rocky shores are crowned with the cedar, the birch, the alder, and soft maple, that dip their long tresses in the pure stream; from every crevice in the limestone the harebell and Canadian rose wave their graceful blossoms.

The fiercest droughts of summer may diminish the volume and power of these romantic streams, but it never leaves their rocky channels bare, nor checks the mournful music of their dancing waves.

Through the openings in the forest, we now and then caught the silver gleam of the river tumbling on in moonlight splendour, while the hoarse chiding of the wind in the lofty pines above us gave a fitting response to the melancholy cadence of the waters.

The children had fallen asleep. A deep silence pervaded the party. Night was above us with her mysterious stars. The ancient forest stretched around us on every side, and a foreboding sadness sunk upon my heart. Memory was busy with the events of many years. I retraced step by step the pilgrimage of my past life, until, arriving at this passage in the sombre history, I gazed through tears upon the singularly savage scene around me, and secretly marvelled, "What brought me here?"

"Providence," was the answer which the soul gave. "Not for your own welfare, perhaps, but for the welfare of your children, the unerring hand of the Great Father has led you here. You form a connecting link in the destinies of many. It is impossible for any human creature to live for himself alone. It may be your lot to suffer, but others will reap a benefit from your trials. Look up with confidence to Heaven, and the sun of hope will yet shed a cheering beam through the forbidding depths of this tangled wilderness."

The road now became so bad that Mr. D—— was obliged to dismount and lead his horses through the more intricate passages. The animals themselves, weary with their long journey and heavy load, proceeded at footfall. The moon, too, had deserted us, and the only light we had to guide us through the dim arches of the forest was from the snow and the stars, which now peered down upon us, through the leafless branches of the trees, with uncommon brilliancy.

"It will be past midnight before we reach your brother's clearing" (where we expected to spend the night), said D——. "I wish, Mr. Moodie, we had followed your advice and stayed at Peterborough. How fares it with you, Mrs. Moodie, and the young ones? It is growing very cold."

We were now in the heart of a dark cedar swamp, and my mind was haunted with visions of wolves and bears; but beyond the long, wild howl of a solitary wolf, no other sound awoke the sepulchral silence of that dismal-looking wood.

"What a gloomy spot!" said I to my husband. "In the old country, superstition would people it with ghosts."

"Ghosts! There are no ghosts in Canada!" said Mr. D——.

"The country is too new for ghosts. No Canadian is afear'd of ghosts. It is only in old countries, like your'n, that are full of sin and wickedness, that people believe such nonsense. No human habitation has ever been erected in this wood through which you are passing. Until a very few years ago, few white persons had ever passed through it; and the Red Man would not pitch his tent in such a place as this. Now, ghosts, as I understand the word, are the spirits of bad men that are not allowed by Providence to rest in their graves, but, for a punishment, are made to haunt the spots where their worst deeds were committed. I don't believe in all this; but, supposing it to be true, bad men must have died here before their spirits could haunt the place. Now, it is more than probable that no person ever ended his days in this forest, so that it would be folly to think of seeing his ghost."

This theory of Mr. D——'s had the merit of originality, and it is not improbable that the utter disbelief in supernatural appearances which is common to most native-born Canadians, is the result of the same very reasonable mode of arguing. The unpeopled wastes of Canada must present the same aspect to the new settler that the world did to our first parents after their expulsion from the Garden of Eden; all the sin which could defile the spot, or haunt it with the association of departed evil, is concentrated in their own persons. Bad spirits cannot be supposed to linger near a place where crime has never been committed. The belief in ghosts, so prevalent in old countries, must first have had its foundation in the consciousness of guilt.

After clearing the low, swampy portion of the woods, with much difficulty, and the frequent application of the axe to cut away the fallen timber that impeded our progress, our ears were assailed by a low, roaring, rushing sound, as of the falling of waters.

"That is Herriot's Falls," said our guide. "We are within two miles of our destination."

Oh, welcome sound! But those two miles appeared more lengthy than the whole journey. Thick clouds, that threatened a snow-storm, had blotted out the stars, and we continued to grope our way through a narrow, rocky path, upon the edge of the river, in almost total darkness. I now felt the chillness of the midnight hour and the fatigue of the long journey, with double force, and envied the servant and children, who had been sleeping ever since we left Peterborough. We now descended the steep bank, and prepared to cross the rapids.

Dark as it was, I looked with a feeling of dread upon the foaming waters as they tumbled over their bed of rocks, their white crests flashing, life-like, amid the darkness of the night.

"This is an ugly bridge over such a dangerous place," said D——, as he stood up in the sleigh and urged his tired team across the miserable, insecure log bridge, where darkness and death raged below, and one false step of his jaded horses would have plunged us into both. I must confess I drew a freer breath when the bridge was crossed, and D—— congratulated us on our safe arrival in Douro.

We now continued our journey along the left bank of the river, but when in sight of Mr. S——'s clearing, a large pine-tree, which had newly fallen across the narrow path, brought the teams to a standstill.

The mighty trunk which had lately formed one of the stately pillars in the sylvan temple of Nature, was of too large dimensions to chop in two with axes; and after about half an hour's labour, which to me, poor, cold, weary wight! seemed an age, the males of the party abandoned the task in despair. To go round it was impossible; its roots were concealed in an impenetrable wall of cedar-jungle on the right-hand side of the road, and its huge branches hung over the precipitous bank of the river.

"We must try and make the horses jump over it," said D——. "We may get an upset, but there is no help for it; we must either make the experiment, or stay here all night, and I am too cold and hungry for that—so here goes." He urged his horses to leap the log; restraining their ardour for a moment as the sleigh rested on the top of the formidable barrier, but so nicely balanced, that the difference of a straw would almost have overturned the heavily-laden vehicle and its helpless inmates. We, however, cleared it in safety. He now stopped, and gave directions to his brother to follow the same plan that he had adopted; but whether the young man had less coolness, or the horses in his team were more difficult to manage, I cannot tell: the sleigh, as it hung poised upon the top of the log, was overturned with a loud crash, and all my household goods and chattels were scattered over the road.

Alas, for my crockery and stone china! scarcely one article remained unbroken.

"Never fret about the china," said Moodie; "thank God, the man and the horses are uninjured."

I should have felt more thankful had the crocks been spared too; for, like most of my sex, I had a tender regard for china, and I knew that no fresh supply could be obtained in this part of the world. Leaving his brother to collect the scattered fragments, D—— proceeded on his journey. We left the road, and were winding our way over a steep hill, covered with heaps of brush and fallen timber, and as we reached the top, a light gleamed cheerily from the windows of a log house, and the next moment we were at my brother-in-law's door.

My brother-in-law and his family had retired to rest, but they instantly rose to receive the way-worn travellers; and I never enjoyed more heartily a warm welcome after a long day of intense fatigue, than I did that night of my first sojourn in the backwoods.

THE OTONABEE

Dark, rushing, foaming river!
 I love the solemn sound
  That shakes thy shores around,
And hoarsely murmurs, ever,
  As thy waters onward bound,
   Like a rash, unbridled steed
Flying madly on its course;
That shakes with thundering force
  The vale and trembling mead.
So thy billows downward sweep,
 Nor rock nor tree can stay
  Their fierce, impetuous way;
Now in eddies whirling deep,
 Now in rapids white with spray.

I love thee, lonely river!
 Thy hollow restless roar,

Thy cedar-girded* shore;
The rocky isles that sever
    The waves that round them pour.
        Katchawanook† basks in light,
But thy currents woo the shade
By the lofty pine-trees made,
        That cast a gloom like night,
    Ere day's last glories fade.
    Thy solitary voice
The same bold anthem sung
When Nature's frame was young.
    No longer shall rejoice
The woods where erst it rung.

Lament, lament, wild river!
    A hand is on thy mane‡
    That will bind thee in a chain
No force of thine can sever.
    Thy furious headlong tide,
In murmurs soft and low,
    Is destined yet to glide
To meet the lake below;
    And many a bark shall ride
Securely on thy breast,
    To waft across the main
    Rich stores of golden grain
From the valleys of the West.

*The banks of the river have since been denuded of trees. The
rocks that formed the falls and rapids have been blasted out. It is
tame enough now.
†This is the Indian name for one of the many expansions of this
beautiful river.
‡Some idea of the rapidity of this river may be formed from the
fact that heavy rafts of timber are floated down from Herriot's
Falls, a distance of nine miles from Peterborough, in less than an
hour. The shores are bold and rocky, and abound in beautiful and
picturesque views.

Patrick Slater　　　ADRIFT

Jack Trueman's dog was a black and tan collie with a bobtail. His was the general-purpose breed of a drover's tyke; and he was all dog. Jack claimed to own the sharp-eyed, self-reliant fellow—but that was a matter of opinion, merely. In the dog's way of looking at things, Rover owned Jack Trueman; and Trueman—he owned me. When a smart, clever dog has something of his very own, you understand—say a smelly bone or an unruly boy—naturally he thinks highly of his own property. And he puts up with the smell of his own bone and the kicks of his own boy as one of the inconveniences of proprietorship, just the same as you and I put up with taxes.

Rover liked, at times, to have his boy throw sticks for him; and, of course, sticks can not be thrown if they are not fetched. But he only fancied that sort of thing in moderation. When the sport ceased to amuse him, he would cock his leg against a post, and then run away on business of his own. This was clear evidence, you will agree, that Rover was the chief executive.

Jack Trueman had not bought the dog; nor had he been given the dog. One day, Rover had left the drover's team he was looking after, and had dropped in, casual-like, to inspect the alley at the side and the stable in the rear of the Tavern Tyrone. He fancied the look of the place and the smell of the slop-bucket. Off-hand, he decided he would like to own a boy who lived round an interesting place like that. So the two of them struck up a bargain on the spot—at least they thought they did. There was a mutual misunderstanding so complete that things worked out all right.

Rover was old enough to have sense, but young enough to be full of devilment. He was a regular fellow. He never got into any squabbles with girl dogs; but the body-odours of any gent of his own kind who strayed within a block of the Tavern Tyrone seemed very displeasing to him. And, when he fought another dog, Rover stuck right at the job till he gave a thrashing to the son of a bitch, or enough silly humans ran together to make it a draw. Jack and his collie got into street fights daily. I was their partisan and did a lot of grunting for them. The three of us skylarked that spring about the streets of Toronto.

One June day, we were down to the foot of Berkeley Street to see a double hanging; and that surely was one glorious, well-filled day. There was a high stone wall clear around the prison which stood close to the bay-shore; and the Fair Grounds lay open to the west. Two men, Turney and Hamilton, were to be hanged on a Tuesday morning. To give the public a tidy view of the drops, both before and after taking, a double gallows had been built facing the Fair Grounds and high on top of the prison wall.

Before the early-risers were abroad, hundreds of heavy farm carts and lumbering wains came creaking into town with their loads of merry, holiday-making country folk from far and near. Along the muddy roads came also bands of stalky farm lads, faring stoutly on foot, with stick in hand and bag on back, stepping down thirty miles or so to see the doings. Two men were to be killed by the law in the morning as an example to the public; and the schools throughout the district were closed that the children might benefit by so valuable a lesson in morals and good living. That day the taverns of Toronto did a stirring business.

"Your soul to the devil!" said young Jack to me. "Let us hooray down and see the necks stretched."

The hangings had been set for ten o'clock in the morning; but an hour ahead of time there was a good-natured throng of thousands jostling one another before the grim prison walls. It was the sort of crowd one sees nowadays at a big country fall fair. Neighbours were greeting neighbours, and joshing over local affairs. Men carried their liquor well in those days; and, of course, mothers had brought the young children in their arms. What else could the poor dears do?

A stir among the men on the prison walls told us the death procession was coming. A hush of awed expectancy fell upon the great throng. And this gaping crowd, stirred with thoughts of human slaughter, was standing in the most humane and tolerant colony Europe ever established beyond the seas! New England had been developed by the labour of convicts transported to be sold as serfs on an auction-block. We are often told of the *Mayflower* landing the Pilgrim Fathers on the Plymouth Rock. Oh yes! But we hear little of the fact that for a century every other merchant ship touching a New England port landed a cargo of convicts on the Pilgrim Fathers. The outposts of those colonies were pushed westward by rough frontiersmen who murdered as they went on frolics of their own. The southern colonies were developed by slave labour, and the full wages of that slavery have not yet been paid. One of the first laws passed in Upper Canada, in 1793, provided for the abolition of slavery; and, in dealing with another human, there has never been a time or place in Canada, save in her wretched prisons, that any man could with impunity make his will a law to itself.

You ask what brought thousands of people together to see such a terrible sight as a double hanging; and I answer you that fifty thousand of the likes of you would turn out any morning to view a well-bungled hanging today. A murderer is a celebrity; and people run open-mouthed to see a celebrity, to hear him speak and see him decorated—or hanged—as the case may be. Every crowd hungers for excitement and is looking for a thrill. Every mob is by nature cruel and bloodthirsty. With all his clothing and culture, man remains a savage, a fact that becomes obvious when a few of them run together.

The breath going out of thousands of throats made a low murmur as the murderer William Turney, in his grave clothes and pinioned, came into public view and stoutly mounted the stairs of the scaffold platform. A priest walked beside him. Behind them strode a hangman, who was closely masked.

It was a matter of good form—and decently expected in those days—that a murderer make a speech and exhort the public. A lusty cheer went up as William Turney stepped smartly forward to make his speech from the gallows. His was an Irish brogue; and his voice was loud and clear.

"Die—like—a—man!" shouted loud-voiced Michael, the smuggler.

Turney had been working the fall before as a journeyman tailor at Markham Village. He dropped into a local store one dark night to get a jug of whisky to take to an apple-paring bee. As the clerk, McPhillips, was bending over the liquor-barrel, Turney stove the man's skull in with a hammer, and then rifled the till. He turned off the spigot, blew out the candles, closed the wooden shutters, and quietly went home to bed. The dead body was not found till the morning after. No one had seen Turney abroad the night before. He came under suspicion the next day because he rode to Toronto on a borrowed horse, and bought himself for cash money a pair of boots and a leather jacket. But that, you'll agree, was not hanging evidence.

Turney, however, needed money for his defence; and while lying in gaol at Toronto he got a letter smuggled out to his wife. The poor simple woman was no scholar; and she asked a neighbour to read it for her. The letter told her the sack of money was hidden under a loose board in the floor of their back-house at Markham Village. He bade her get the money and give it to the lawyer-man. So the damaging evidence leaked out. How much wiser to have let the solicitor's clerk visit the privy!

On the scaffold, Turney made a rousing speech. He shouted to us that he had been a British soldier in his day, and was not afeared of death. Turney thanked us all kindly for the compliment of coming to his hanging. It was sorry he was for killing the poor man, McPhillips, who had never hurted him and had treated him as a friend. The crime, he told us, had not been planned, but was done on the spur of the moment. The devil had tempted him, and he fell. He had run home that dark night in a terrible fear. The wind in the trees sounded in his ears like the groans of poor tortured souls in hell. Hanging, he told us, was what he deserved. Let it be a lesson to us all.

Turney's feelings then got the better of him. He broke down and wailed loudly, praying that God would prove a guardian to his poor wife and fatherless child. The crowd did not like the tears. The high-pitched cries of women jeering at the miserable creature mixed with the heavy voices of men urging him to keep his spirits up.

"Doo—ye—loo-ike—a—maa-hun!" boomed Michael, the leather-lunged.

In the pause, Turney got a fresh holt on his discourse. He went on to tell us he had been a terrible character in his day. He had started serving the devil by robbing his mother of a shilling; and, in after years, while plundering a castle, he had helped wipe out an entire family in Spain. He explained that a full account of his high crimes was in the printer's hands. He beseeched everyone to buy a copy for the benefit of his poor wife and child. In the hope of getting a few shillings for them, Turney stepped back to his death with these great lies ringing in our ears.

At the foot of the scaffold stairs, the other felon requested the Protestant minister who walked beside him to kneel and have a session in prayer. The murderer seemed in no hurry to be up to finish his journey. The clergyman tried the stairs carefully, stepping up and down to prove them solid and sound. But it is hard to convince a man against his will. The hangman waited a tidy space, and then spit on his fist. He took the victim by the scuff of his neck and the waist-band and hoisted him up the stairs, the clergyman lending a helping hand. The crowd jeered loudly; but, once up in open public view, the felon's courage revived. Hamilton came forward with stiff, jerky little steps; and, in a high-pitched voice, he admonished us all to avoid taverns, particularly on the Sabbath.

Then the serious business began. The executioners hurried around, strapping the legs of their victims and adjusting the caps and halters. The culprits assumed a kneeling position over the traps and prayed to God for mercy.

A loud murmur went up from the thousands of throats—"Aw!"—as the bolts were shot. The two bodies tumbled down to dangle on the ropes and pitch about. It took Turney quite a while to choke to death. The other body seemed to drop limp.

This business of hanging folk should be intensely interesting to every Canadian of old-country British stock. The blood strain of every one of us leads back to the hangman's noose. Many a man was smuggled out of Ireland to save his neck from stretching for the stealing of a sheep.

And public hanging had something to justify it. In the olden days, human life was of little more account than it is today; and hoisting bodies in the air, and leaving them to rot on gibbets, was thought to be a rough-and-ready warning to evil-doers. What a pity public hangings were ever done away with! Had they continued a few years longer, the horrible practice of hanging men would have passed away under the pressure of public opinion.

At any rate, Jack Trueman and I profited greatly as a result of William Turney's speech from the gallows. We ran off at once for copies of his "confessions" to the office of the *British Colonist*, a paper printed on King Street; and we spent the rest of the day crying our wares on the streets and in the taverns of Toronto. We refreshed ourselves with peppermint bull's-eyes made by Sugar John, who combined a tavern with a candy shop on the east side of Church Street.

To make it a perfect day, a fire broke out that evening in a row of frame dwellings at the north-west corner of Richmond and Yonge streets. The flames shot up quickly, cutting into heavy clouds of smoke. Away everyone ran to the scene of the fire. The city had a paid fire marshal and several volunteer fire companies; but fires were frequent that summer, and only heaps of smouldering ashes usually marked their battle-scenes.

The engagement opened that evening with a wild charge of one-horse carts. Drunken drivers whipped their old horses into action hell-split, wheeling batteries of water-barrels. The first carter with a civic licence arriving at a scene of a fire with a puncheon of water got a municipal grant of £3, Halifax currency. Subsequent hauling was done, however, on a time basis; and the second fillings arrived in a more leisurely fashion.

After a time, the municipal fire-pump came on the scene. The hose was reeled off in lively fashion, and attached to a fire-plug on the water-main at Yonge Street. The volunteers rushed to man the pumps. They speedily discovered what everyone else already knew—that there was no pressure in the water-mains after nightfall. A meeting of excited rate-payers was held on the spot to protest against the wickedness of Mr. Furniss of the gas and water company. But he was there himself to tell them, good and plenty, he gave the town all that £250 had paid for. There was a great running together of newspaper editors and a deputation was finally dispatched to measure the depth of water in the company's tank. Meanwhile the flames licked up frame buildings at their pleasure; and things got so hot that the municipal pumping equipment itself caught fire. An enthusiastic detail of volunteers were busy pitching furniture out of upstairs windows, and smashing and rifling the contents of dwellings in and near the general direction of the blaze. People grabbed small things and ran home with them to save them from the fire.

I was watching a tipsy carter in a dispute with an open-headed barrel of water, when the scene closed so far as I was concerned. Something had apparently lost its balance in the two-wheeled cart. The puncheon upset and won the argument. The carter disappeared in an avalanche of water. He emerged spluttering and talking loudly to God. At that moment a flying bed-mattress caught me fair on; and I went to earth beneath its enfolding arms. I wiggled out, only to dodge a flying jerry mug. I have not crossed the briny ocean, thought I, to have my head cracked with a dirty old thing like that. So I went off home and called it a day.

A large number of negro families were living in Toronto at that time; and their shining black faces and rolling white eyeballs startled my young Irish mind and held me in a pop-eyed fascination. For years previously, fugitive slaves had been drifting northward by undercover routes; and many of the more resourceful and enterprising of them reached the British line and settled in southern Ontario. Public opinion was such in Canada, at that time, that negroes were permitted to cross the border freely, and, while slavery continued to exist on the continent, it remained practically impossible to extradite a black man out of Canada on any charge whatever. Among the cabins in the southern plantations, there had grown up a tradition that far away under the North Star could be found a paradise of freedom over which a great queen reigned. On first setting foot on Canadian soil, the fugitive slave kneeled to kiss the bosom of a kindly mother; and all would be well with her soul had every other immigrant to Canada had within him the spirit to do likewise.

Just across the way from Mr. O'Hogan's, there was a coloured tavern run by Jim Henderson, a big, black, deepvoiced negro who told thrilling tales of slavery in the south. Jim had a weakness for fatty fried meats, and, to regulate his system, he made a practice, every Friday night, of gurgling down the full of a big bottle of castor oil to the delight of sundry urchins who assembled for the occasion. Rolling his eyes and smacking his lips, Henderson would then shuffle off back for a glass of gin to cut oil out of his gullet. The negroes in Toronto were a harmless, law-abiding body of simpleminded people. These ex-slaves worked as labourers and teamsters; and a few of them were already property-holders, and took part in the stormy elections of the day. Some of their descendants have risen to important positions in Canada; but the climate has proven too rigorous for the majority of them.

Everything is relative in this life, and especially so the element of time. A summer takes longer to pass in the inquiring days of childhood than does an entire decade further along life's journey. As that long summer dragged on, the plague came and hung over the town like the dread, intangible wraith that chokes one in a nightmare. There was fear and dread in everyone's heart; and it was the deep, smothering fear of utter helplessness. We all wore little bags of camphor about the neck. The angel of death seemed to mark at random the door-lintels of the chosen ones. Perhaps the death toll of 1847 has been exaggerated; but, in a literal sense, the poor died by the hundred. In the summer and early fall of 1847, 863 poor Irish died in Toronto, and, of the 97,933 emigrants who sailed from Irish ports for Canada in the spring and summer of that year, 18,625 souls did not live to feel the frosts of a Canadian winter.

The plague was a terrible thing, but kindly in its way because it was swift about its business. One afternoon my poor young mother fell ill. She was lying on an old straw tick in the corner of the room upstairs. When I found her, she was cold and clammy and in frightful distress. I threw her old shawl over her and ran for water. Within five minutes every other occupant of the house had cleared out. Mr. O'Hogan set off post-haste to bespeak the death-cart to take her body away. I ran around to get Mistress Kitty O'Shea. I knew she would help me, because she was out night and day nursing the sick. She came right over, and stayed till my mother's body stiffened with the rigor. Poor Kitty O'Shea! She died herself the day the plague struck down Michael Power, the first Catholic bishop of Toronto; and they both laid down their lives ministering to the sick on the streets of Toronto. Perhaps He that sitteth in the heavens has found a place among His many mansions for the soul of Kitty O'Shea!

My mother begged for the priest. He put the holy oil on her, and her mind was comforted.

"Sit over by the window," Mistress O'Shea said to me. "Your mother doesn't want you to be looking at her, Paddy. She doesn't want you to remember the look of her face in the sickness."

The dip-candle stuck in a bottle guttered and spent itself during the watches of that terrible night. The agonies of the destroying disease were distressing.

As the sky began to brighten with the dawn, the stiffening collapse of the disease overcame my mother's body. Mistress O'Shea crossed herself as she covered the rigid face.

I hoisted the window to let the soul get out.

Two rough-looking men with a one-horse cart came in the forenoon to take my mother's body away. They were gathering bodies of the Catholic poor for burial in a potter's field at the east side of the city. They had started off with a load of empty board coffins, and Mr. O'Hogan's place was the final call on that trip. They placed an empty coffin on the street. They came upstairs with a heavy bag made of ducking.

I knew my mother was not yet dead because only one eye was closed. But they shoved her stiff body into their bag and tied the mouth of it with a stout cord. One of the men shouldered the burden and bore it to the street. The lid of the coffin was hammered on. It was hoisted up into its place on the cart. The cart trundled off up York Street. And I followed after.

As we rounded the corner of Richmond Street, Dick Crispin was opening the bar-room door of his yellow tavern. Mr. Crispin had been in service with Sir John Colborne, the governor; and his public house was much frequented by official gentry from below stairs. The carter hollered to him for a drink. Coachman Dick brought out a generous flask of whisky, and set it on the roadway. The body-gatherers drank to the souls of the departed, and emptied the bottle. Of course, they had been tight already. But they were brave men, doing a necessary and dangerous duty. Drinking heavily was the only precaution they knew.

It was a curious funeral procession that wended its way along Richmond Street, up Church, and east on Queen Street —an old cart full of corpses, two drunken carters, a dirty, ragged little urchin with tear-stained face, and a bob-tailed collie that did not understand. The road cleared in front of us; and people closed doors and ducked up alleys as we passed along.

Anyway, there was one sincere mourner present, which is more than some great funeral processions have. The whole affair had been sudden, and it seemed terrible to me. I felt sick. There was a strange co-rumbling in my belly. The essence of true sorrow is always self-pity. I was not so much sorry for my poor mother. I felt helpless and utterly lonely; and I was sorry for myself because they were taking her away from me.

I followed along after the cart, blubbering and poking my grimy knuckles into my eyes. Rover knew I was in distress, and he wanted to help me.

I was bothered that the old cart made so much noise. They might be hurting her.

I got to thinking that prayers should be said for her. I sobbed out what I could:

> *Hail, Mary, full of grace!*
> *The Lord is with thee;*
> *Blessed art thou among women,*
> *And blessed is the fruit of thy womb, Jesus.*

The cart rattled on to Queen Street.

> *Holy Mary, Mother of God,*
> *Pray for us sinners, now and*
> *At the hour of our death. Amen.*
>
> . . . .
>
> *May the souls of the departed*
> *Repose in peace. Amen.*

They put the load of bodies into one great hole. The cold of the grave was in my heart.

When I got back home, they were fumigating the house and Mr. O'Hogan told me to clear out—I was not wanted there. I asked for my mother's things. They had all been burnt —so he said; but I didn't believe him.

"And there," I accused him, "you liar, you have my father's own stick in your hand!"

Mr. O'Hogan chased me out onto the street and threw the stick after me.

I faulted him roundly in Irish as I ran to pick it up; and the man crossed himself.

"What were you saying to the man, little boy?" an old gentleman inquired of me.

"I was putting a curse on him," I explained. "I was blasting his soul to the devil for a dirty, lying thief."

I still keep that stick by me, for I hold it very dear. It reminds me of the old, unhappy, far-off days when my father died 'evic' and left me as his whole estate his Irish blackthorn stick.

So not a stitch nor token have I to remind me of my mother. But when the sunbeams strike down sudden-like through the storm-clouds, I think of the glint in her fun-loving eyes. And, when the rain-thrush flutes his neat little tune to the clearing sky, I hear again the soft, lovable brogue of that poor little, forgotten, black Irish mother of mine.

When night set in, I slipped down the alley to the east of the Tavern Tyrone. Rover whined a welcome from the stable door. It is a quality of a dog's friendship that he knows all your secret faults, yet remains loving and kind to be sure; and he will never despitefully use you. I was sick and tired as a child

is after hysteria of any kind; and I was actually weak, because
I had fasted the livelong day, which is sore against the grain
of a little boy's belly. I laid me down in the sweet, crisp hay,
and Rover snuggled over beside me. In my utter loneliness,
the dog's sympathy and loving-kindness refreshed me, and
my body felt warmer. Sobbing, I fell asleep.

Morley Callaghan

LAST
SPRING
THEY
CAME
OVER

Alfred Bowles came to Canada from England and got a job
on a Toronto paper. He was a young fellow with clear, blue
eyes and heavy pimples on the lower part of his face, the son
of a Baptist minister whose family was too large for his
salary. He got thirty dollars a week on the paper and said it
was surprisingly good screw to start. For five a week he got
an attic room in a brick house painted brown on Mutual
Street. He ate his meals in a quick-lunch near the office. He
bought a cane and a light-gray fedora.

He wasn't a good reporter but was inoffensive and obliging.
After he had been working two weeks the fellows took it for
granted he would be fired in a little while and were nice to
him, liking the way the most trifling occurrences surprised
him. He was happy to carry his cane on his arm and wear the
fedora at a jaunty angle, quite the reporter. He liked to explain
that he was doing well. He wrote home about it.

When they put him doing night police he felt important,
phoning the fire department, hospitals, and police stations,
trying to be efficient. He was getting along all right. It was
disappointing when after a week the assistant city editor,

Mr. H. J. Brownson, warned him to phone his home if anything important happened, and he would have another man cover it. But Bowles got to like hearing the weary, irritable voice of the assistant city editor called from his bed at three o'clock in the morning. He liked to politely call Mr. Brownson as often and as late as possible, thinking it a bit of good fun.

Alfred wrote long letters to his brother and to his father, the Baptist minister, using a typewriter, carefully tapping the keys, occasionally laughing to himself. In a month's time he had written six letters describing the long city room, the fat belly of the city editor, and the bad words the night editor used when speaking of the Orangemen.

The night editor took a fancy to him because of the astounding puerility of his political opinions. Alfred was always willing to talk pompously of the British Empire policing the world and about all Catholics being aliens, and the future of Ireland and Canada resting with the Orangemen. He flung his arms wide and talked in the hoarse voice of a bad actor, but no one would have thought of taking him seriously. He was merely having a dandy time. The night editor liked him because he was such a nice boy.

Then Alfred's brother came out from the Old Country and got a job on the same paper. Some of the men started talking about cheap cockney labourers crowding the good guys out of the jobs, but Harry Bowles was frankly glad to get the thirty a week. It never occurred to him that he had a funny idea of good money. With his first pay he bought a derby hat, a pair of spats, and a cane, but even though his face was clear and had a good colour he never looked as nice as his younger brother because his heavy nose curved up at the end. The landlady on Mutual Street moved a double bed into Alfred's room and Harry slept with his brother.

The days passed with many good times together. At first it was awkward that Alfred should be working at night and his brother in the day-time, but Harry was pleased to come down to the office every night at eleven and they went down the street to the hotel that didn't bother about Prohibition. They drank a few glasses of good beer. It became a kind of rite that had to be performed carefully. Harry would put his left foot and Alfred his right foot on the rail and leaning a elbow on the bar they would slowly survey the zigzag line of frothing glasses the length of the long bar. Men jostled them for a place at the foot-rail.

And Alfred said: "Well, a bit of luck."

Harry grinning and raising his glass said: "Righto."

"It's the stuff that heals."

"Down she goes."

"It helps the night along."

"Fill them up again."

"Toodleoo."

Then they would walk out of the crowded bar-room, vaguely pleased with themselves. Walking slowly and erectly along the street they talked with assurance, a mutual respect for each other's opinion making it merely an exchange of information. They talked of the Englishman in Canada, comparing his lot with that of the Englishman in South Africa and India. They had never travelled but to ask what they knew of strange lands would have made one feel uncomfortable; it was better to take it for granted that the Bowles boys knew all about the ends of the earth and had judged them carefully, for in their eyes was the light of far-away places. Once in a while, after walking a block or two, one of the brothers would say he would damn well like to see India and the other would say it would be simply topping.

After work and on Sundays they took a look at the places they had heard about in the city. One Sunday they got up in good time and took the boat to Niagara. Their father had written asking if they had seen the Falls and would they send some souvenirs. That day they had as nice a time as a man would want to have. Standing near the pipe-rail a little way from the hotel that overlooks the Falls they watched the water-line just before the drop, smooth as a long strip of bevelled glass, and Harry compared it favourably with a cataract in the Himalayas and a giant waterfall in Africa, just above the Congo. They took a car along the gorge and getting off near the whirlpool, picked out a little hollow near a big rock at the top of the embankment where the grass was lush and green. They stretched themselves out with hats tilted over their eyes for sunshades. The river whirled below. They talked about the funny ways of Mr. Brownson and his short fat legs and about the crazy women who fainted at the lifted hand of the faith healer who was in the city for the week. They liked the distant rumble of the Falls. They agreed to try and save a lot of money and go west to the Pacific in a year's time. They never mentioned trying to get a raise in pay.

Afterwards they each wrote home about the trip, sending the souvenirs.

Neither one was doing well on the paper. Harry wasn't much good because he hated writing the plain copy and it was hard for him to be strictly accurate. He liked telling a good tale but it never occurred to him that he was deliberately lying. He imagined a thing and straightway felt it to be true. But it never occurred to Alfred to depart from the truth. He was accurate but lazy, never knowing when he was really working. He was taken off night police and for two weeks helped a man do courts at the City Hall. He got to know the boys at the press gallery, who smiled at his naïve sincerity and thought him a decent chap, without making up their minds about him. Every noon-hour Harry came to the press gallery and the brothers, sitting at typewriters, wrote long letters all about the country and the people, anything interesting, and after exchanging letters, tilted back in their swivel chairs, laughing out loud. Heaven only knows who got the letters in the long run. Neither one when in the press gallery seemed to write anything for the paper.

Some of the men tried kidding Alfred, teasing him about women, asking if he found the girls in this country to his liking; but he seemed to enjoy it more than they did. Seriously he explained that he had never met a girl in this country, but they looked very nice. Once Alfred and Bun Brophy, a redheaded fellow with a sharp tongue who did City Hall for the paper, were alone in the gallery. Brophy had in his hands a big picture of five girls in masquerade costumes. Without explaining that he loved one of the girls Brophy asked Bowles which of the lot was the prettiest.

"You want me to settle that," said Alfred, grinning and waving his pipe. He very deliberately selected a demure little girl with a shy smile.

Brophy was disappointed. "Don't you think this one is pretty?"—a colourful, bold-looking girl.

"Well, she's all right in her way, but she's too vivacious. I'll take this one. I like them kittenish," Alfred said.

Brophy wanted to start an argument but Alfred said it was neither here nor there. He really didn't like women.

"You mean to say you never step out?" Brophy said.

"I've never seemed to mix with them," he said, adding that the whole business didn't matter because he liked boys much better.

The men in the press room heard about it and some suggested nasty things to Alfred. It was hard to tease him when he wouldn't be serious. Sometimes they asked if he took Harry out walking in the evenings. Brophy called them the heavy lovers. The brothers didn't mind because they thought the fellows were having a little fun.

In the fall Harry was fired. The editor in a nice note said that he was satisfied Mr. H. W. Bowles could not adapt himself to their methods. But everybody wondered why he hadn't been fired sooner. He was no good on the paper.

The brothers smiled, shrugged their shoulders and went on living together. Alfred still had his job. Every noon-hour in the City Hall press room they were together, writing letters.

Time passed and the weather got cold. Alfred's heavy coat came from the Old Country and he gave his vest and a thin sweater to Harry, who had only a light spring coat. As the weather got colder Harry buttoned his coat higher up on his throat and even though he looked cold he was neat as a pin with his derby and cane.

Then Alfred lost his job. The editor, disgusted, called him a fool. For the first time since coming over last spring he felt hurt, something inside him was hurt and he told his brother about it, wanting to know why people acted in such a way. He said he had been doing night police. On the way over to No. 1 station very late Thursday night he had met two men from other papers. They told him about a big fire earlier in the evening just about the time when Alfred was accustomed to going to the hotel to have a drink with his brother. They were willing to give all the details and Alfred thankfully shook hands with them and hurried back to the office to write the story. Next morning the assistant city editor phoned Alfred and asked how it was the morning papers missed the story. Alfred tried to explain but Mr. Brownson said he was a damn fool for not phoning the police and making sure instead of trying to make the paper look like a pack of fools printing a fake story. The fellows who had kidded him said that too. Alfred kept asking his brother why the fellows had to do it. He seemed to be losing a good feeling for people.

Still the brothers appeared at noontime in the press room. They didn't write so many letters. They were agreeable, cheerful, on good terms with everybody. Bun Brophy every day asked how they were doing and they felt at home there. Harry would stand for a while watching the checker game always in progress, knowing that if he stood staring intently at the black and red squares, watching every deliberate move, he would be asked to sit in when it was necessary that one of the players make the rounds in the hall. Once Brophy gave Harry his place and walked over to the window where Alfred stood watching the fleet of automobiles arranged in a square in the courtyard. The police wagon with a load of drunks was backing toward the cells.

"Say, Alfie, I often wonder how you guys manage," he said.

"Oh, first rate."

"Well, you ought to be in a bad way by now."

"Oh no, we have solved the problem," said Alfred in a grand way, grinning, as if talking about the British Empire.

He was eager to tell how they did it. There was a store in their block where a package of tobacco could be got for five cents; they did their own cooking and were able to live on five dollars a week.

"What about coming over and having tea with us sometimes?" Alfred said. He was decidedly on his uppers but he asked Brophy to visit them and have tea.

Brophy, abashed, suggested the three of them go over to the café and have a little toast. Harry talked volubly on the way over and while having coffee. He was really a better talker than his brother. They sat in an arm-chair lunch, gripped the handles of their thick mugs, and talked about religion. The brothers were sons of a Baptist minister but never thought of going to church. It seemed that Brophy had travelled a lot during war-time and afterward in Asia Minor and India. He was telling about a great golden temple of the Sikhs at Amritsar and Harry listened carefully, asking many questions. Then they talked about newspapers until Harry started talking about the East, slowly feeling his way. All of a sudden he told about standing on a height of land near Amritsar, looking down at a temple. It couldn't have been so but he would have it that Brophy and he had seen the same temple and he described the country in the words Brophy had used. When he talked that way you actually believed that he had seen the temple.

Alfred liked listening to his brother but he said finally: "Religion is a funny business. I tell you it's a funny business." And for the time being no one would have thought of talking seriously about religion. Alfred had a casual way of making a cherished belief or opinion seem unimportant, a way of dismissing even the bright yarns of his brother.

After that afternoon in the café Brophy never saw Harry. Alfred came often to the City Hall but never mentioned his brother. Someone said maybe Harry had a job but Alfred laughed and said no such luck in this country, explaining casually that Harry had a bit of a cold and was resting up. In the passing days Alfred came only once in a while to the City Hall, writing his letter without enthusiasm.

The press men would have tried to help the brothers if they had heard Harry was sick. They were entirely ignorant of the matter. On a Friday afternoon at three-thirty Alfred came into the gallery and, smiling apologetically, told Brophy that his brother was dead; the funeral was to be in three-quarters of an hour; would he mind coming? It was pneumonia, he added. Brophy, looking hard at Alfred, put on his hat and coat and they went out.

It was a poor funeral. The hearse went on before along the way to the Anglican cemetery that overlooks the ravine. One old cab followed behind. There had been a heavy fall of snow in the morning, and the slush on the pavement was thick. Alfred and Brophy sat in the old cab, silent. Alfred was leaning forward, his chin resting on his hands, the cane acting as a support, and the heavy pimples stood out on the lower part of his white face. Brophy was uncomfortable and chilly but he mopped his shining forehead with a big handkerchief. The window was open and the air was cold and damp.

Alfred politely asked how Mrs. Brophy was doing. Then he asked about Mr. Brownson.

"Oh, he's fine," Brophy said. He wanted to close the window but it would have been necessary to move Alfred so he sat huddled in the corner, shivering.

Alfred asked suddenly if funerals didn't leave a bad taste in the mouth and Brophy, surprised, started talking absently about that golden temple of the Sikhs in India. Alfred appeared interested until they got to the cemetery. He said suddenly he would have to take a look at the temple one fine day.

They buried Harry Bowles in a grave in the paupers' section on a slippery slope of the hill. The earth was hard and chunky and it thumped down on the coffin case. It snowed a little near the end.

On the way along the narrow, slippery foot-path up the hill Alfred thanked Brophy for being thoughtful enough to come to the funeral. There was little to say. They shook hands and went different ways.

After a day or two Alfred again appeared in the press room. He watched the checker game, congratulated the winner and then wrote home. The men were sympathetic and said it was too bad about his brother. And he smiled cheerfully and said they were good fellows. In a little while he seemed to have convinced them that nothing important had really happened.

His last cent must have gone to the undertaker, for he was particular about paying bills, but he seemed to get along all right. Occasionally he did a little work for the paper, a story from a night assignment when the editor thought the staff was being overworked.

One afternoon at two-thirty in the press gallery Brophy saw the last of Alfred, who was sucking his pipe, his feet up on a desk, wanting to be amused. Brophy asked if anything had turned up. In a playful, resigned tone, his eye on the big clock, Alfred said he had until three to join the Air Force. They wouldn't take him, he said, unless he let them know by three.

Brophy said, "How will you like that?"

"I don't fancy it."

"But you're going through."

"Well, I'm not sure. Something else may come along." It was a quarter to three and he was sitting there waiting for a job to turn up before three.

No one saw him after that, but he didn't join the Air Force. Someone in the gallery said that wherever he went he probably wrote home as soon as he got there.

Austin Clarke   # THEY HEARD A RINGING OF BELLS

"What is them I hearing?" Estelle asked, looking up at the skies.

"Them is bells, darling," Ironhorse said.

"It is a man up there playing pon them bells," Sagaboy explained. "They is bells that you and me, and Ironhorse Henry hearing play so nice."

"Bells playing hymns? God bless my eyesight! Boy, this Canada is a damn great country, in truth!" she exclaimed.

"It don't have nothing like this back in them islands, eh, old man?" Ironhorse said, really teasing Sagaboy, who was a Trinidadian.

"Well, let the three o' we sit down right here pon this piece o' grass, and listen to that man up there in the skies playing them bells." And they did what Sagaboy suggested. They sat on the grass, in front of the tower which seemed to become more powerful and mysterious with each ring of the bells that resounded in the hearts of these three West Indians. Estelle spread her dress around her like an umbrella. Sagaboy and Ironhorse Henry took off their jackets, and without offering her one of them they sat down. Estelle was sitting on the bare grass. But the grass wasn't cold.

The bells were ringing hymns. And the voice of the bells swept a tide of freshness through Estelle's heart, and washed out the heaviness of deportation that had been lingering there. The immigration department had given her one week to leave the country.

Looking up at the bells, she said, "I am too glad the Lord open up this door, boy! Imagine me, nuh, imagine me up in this big-able country. I can't imagine it is really me, Estelle, sitting down here! I sitting down here, this bright Sunday afternoon, listening to some damn man up there, saying he playing hymns on bells! Well well well, what the hell's next? Who would have think that I would ever live to see a thing so nice? I can't believe my ears at all, at all. It is the wonders o' God, boy, the wonders of the good God, cause I poor as a bird's arse and I am still up here in Canada. And I *know* that a good time can't happen to any and every man, saving that man stand in possession of money. If he have a piece of change in his pockets, he could get in a plane, God! and he could be taken to the ends of this earth, *swoosh!* in the twinkling of an eye! Man, I barely had time to swallow a mouth-ful o' hot-water tea back in Barbados, before, bram! I wasn't in a different place. And now, look me! . . . I am up in this big-able Canada. From a little little village somewhere behind God back I come up here, and now enjoying a little goodness o' life. Little good living that only the white people and the rich black people back home does enjoy. And now, ha-dai! the thing turn round, boy! It turn round as good as a cent. This is what I calls *living*. This is the way *every* black person should live! Look, I putting my hand pon a blade of grass ...look, Henry, look Saga, man, this blade of grass is the self-same grass as what I left back in Barbados. The said grass that I now sitting down pon, the same grass, man; but only *different*. And it is different only becausing it situated in a different place. A different, but a more better, more advance place than where I come from; and because o' this I am telling you now, this blessed Sunday afternoon, that I glad glad as hell that life still circulating through this body o' mine."

Neither Ironhorse Henry nor Sagaboy could find words of comment for this waterfall of feeling. Ironhorse had not heard anything like it since he left Barbados, more years ago than he cared to remember. But as Estelle talked he had watched her; and, with her, he had listened to the bells singing in his heart. And there he found a deep love for her. A love so great that he could not find words to express it. But he knew he had to remain silent; that he might never get the opportunity to tell it to her. She was Sagaboy's woman. And she was going to be deported next week. There she was, so near to him now; in a few days, so far away; and he could do nothing, nothing except wish that something would happen to his good friend Sagaboy, that he would cough his guts through his mouth, that he would die from the tuberculosis that rackled in his chest like stones in a can. And Sagaboy, sitting on the other side of Estelle, remained very quiet as if he was in a dream. Then, it seemed, the bubble of his dream burst, and he tugged at a blade of grass near his feet, and exploded, "It ain't no wonders of no blasted God, woman! You have just start to live like you should have been living from the day you born. But instead, you been spending your lifetime down in Barbados, the same way as your forefathers and foremothers been spending it . . . in the kiss-me-arse cane-field, and in slavery. Down there you didn't have food to eat, nor proper clothes to put on your back, and you didn't comprehend the piece o' histries involve in that kinda life, till one morning, bright and early, Satan get in your behind, and you look round, and bram! your eyes see that topsy-turvy world down there, and you turned round and look at yourself, and you didn't see nothing but rags and lice and filth and misery and the blasted British. And what happen? Revolutions run up inside your head, child, and you start to put two and two together. And you say, be-Christ, it ain't true, pardner, that is not true, at all! So what happen next? You pull up stakes and run abroad. You come up here in a more progressive country, but you still going exist in a worser life than what you was accustomed to back home. Look, every one o' we, you, me, Ironhorse here, we get so damn tired, we get so damn vexed . . . you down there in Barbados, and I in Trinidad, and brisk-brisk! it is pulling out, for so! Setting sail. Pawning things that we never own and possess, borrowing and thiefing, and we sail for Canada. It have millions o' men and women from the islands who set sail already for Britain.

And that situation is a funny funny piece o' histries, too. I sits down in my bed over on Spadina Avenue, and I laugh hard hard as hell, hee-hee-hee! at all them people who say we shouldn't make Great Britain more blacker than she is or was, in the first Elizabethan era. And all the time I does be laughing, I does be thinking of long long ago when the Queen o' Britain send all them convicts and whores and swivilitic men and women overseas, to *fuck-up* and populate the islands! Well, darling, now the tables turn round, because this is the *second* Elizabethan era! And it is the islands who sending black people, *all kinds*, the good and the bad, the godly and the ungodly, and we intend to fuck-up the good old Mother Country like rass, as my Jamaican friend would say. Man, I hear if you look round in Britain this afternoon you swear to God that you ain't in Britain no longer, but that you back in the islands. Black people? Oh rass!" And straightway, he broke into the popular calypso, *Yankees Gone And Sparrow Take Over Now*.

"God, that boy does talk as if he have a mouthful o' honey inside his mouth," Ironhorse said, appreciatively.

"Sagaboy, you talking the truth. You have just talk a piece o' truth . . . you call it histries, but I haven't heard nobody talk it that way, yet!" Estelle said, agreeing.

And then they stopped talking, and listened. The bells were ringing. You could see how the bells changed the tense expression on Estelle's face, an expression which emigration had placed there; and how they brought fear, a fear for the wondrous works of God, in its place. And looking more closely, you could see a primitive beauty painted on the sharp cheekbones and on the large mouth which gave her the haughtiness of a black princess.

"What hymn that is, what hymn he playing there?" she asked. "Ain't that hymn name *The Day Thou Gavest Lord Is Ending*? Ain't it that said hymn? The selfsame tune, Henry, the same tune, Sagaboy. And that is the very-same song they took my father, God rest his soul, to the grave with! You should have seen him when they pull him outta the sea, drown, and with the water in his body, making him big like a whale, and still looking powerful and strong as he use to be when he was living and in the flesh. Lord! and when they come and tell me that my father *dead*, oh God, Henry, Saga-boy, I cry and I cry till I couldn't find water to cry with no more. And the people in the neighbourhood come and look in at the oval hole in the top o' the mahogany coffin when the undertaker-man had bring him home. And the whole village bow down their heads in respects o' the dead, in Pappy behalfs, cause my father was a man who had lots o' respects in the whole entire village and in the districts round our village. And the old women in our village bow down their heads low low low, and say, Thank God that at least He make a good dead outta Nathan. Nathan look nice as a dead. God go with thee, son, they say. And when they say that, all the men with their big bass voices start up singing this very hymn that you and me hearing coming outta that tall tower-thing. And Lord! water come to everybody's eye. The weeping and the crying and the singing. When they was weeping all that weeping, I had a funny feeling that they wasn't weeping only for my father, but for all the fathers that was ever killed by the cruel hands of the waves in the sea. And then they start filing past the coffin, singing; and the women were wringing their hands, like they was ringing out clothes, earlier that very-same day . . . God! I think I seeing it now, clear clear before my two eyes, as I listen to the magic and poetry coming outta that bell up there, this Sunday afternoon. And to think, just think that the first time I going to call back all this to mind is now that I have escape from that blasted past-tense village in Barbados to come up here, in Canada. Man, it is a long long time ago now, cause my father dead, when he dead, he left me a little girl in pigtails."

The bells were ringing still, ringing loud and clear in the quiet Toronto afternoon. Estelle's voice broke down, and she started to hum along with the carilloneur. It was a clear voice, a soft voice. A voice like a stream of crystal water fighting to reach the sea.

"A lot o' salt water separating me from the place where my father drown. And I still remember it to this day," she went on. "I even remember the dress I wear, which was the said white dress that my half-sister Bernice wore when she got baptise in the Church o' the Nazarene. A white shark skin piece o' material that Mammy had bought at a sale. And when we reach Westbury Cemetery, shadows was walking through the evergreen trees, round the graveyard. And a man come, a big, fat, ugly black man dressed down in black, come and put dirt on top o' the coffin, and then he pull off the silver things that was screwed-on to the coffin, and as quick as a fly he push them inside his pocket; and then sudden so, like how you see dusk does fall outta the skies and nobody don't know, sudden so, that same man drop my father contained in that coffin-box in the hole, and Lord! I couldn't see my father's face no more. Such a mighty screeling went up, such a terrible crying escape from the women that you would have thought the heavens was collapsing, and it weren't just a poor fisherman that was taken to his resting place under a sandbox tree. And I remember that the people in the village was so poor, most of them, that only a handful could afford to rent a motor car from Johnson's Stables to follow my father in. Most of the men had was to follow on bicycles, and some even had to carry their women and their wives on the bicycle bars." She paused for a while, it seemed, to permit the bells to return the sadness of the funeral to her mind, and stir up the memories lurking there. She went on, "I can see his face now. I can see Pappy face before my two eyes right now. And I swear then, as I take the oath now, I swear blind that he wasn't dead in truth, cause I thought I could see his lips move, or did want to move and open, and whisper something to me from the grave. And I sorry sorry that up till now I don't know, and I can't imagine what the hell it was Pappy wanted to leave with me in the way of wisdom or advice, as he parted from me in the quick. I am the onliest living soul who see the dead attempt to talk. The only one who see that happen. And because o' that, I swear blind that they put my father to rest before his time was up. You understand what I mean? What I mean to affirm and state is this: down there in that damn island, the people don't have no lot o' respect, and a undertaker-man could make a mistake like nothing and put a person in a coffin and nail up that coffin and lower him in a grave be-Christ, before that dead-man is really a dead-man, before he stop breathing. Because them undertakers is really sharks and barracudas.

Once they *suspect* that you will soon be a dead-man, that you are in a poor state o' health, that you are passing away, and they know they stand to get a few coppers for burying you, well, boy, they rushes like bloody-hell and they would *kill* you and turn you into a dead person if they think you ain't deading fast enough. Some stupid old women say it is a good thing, becausing God did love Pappy, and that is why He take my only father to His grave. But I don't believe that. Even now, at my age, I still don't think that God could say He is in love with a man, and then turn round and put His hand pon that man, strangulate him, and drop him dead, and in the quick, and still say He *love* him? Standing up by that grave that evening I hold up my two hands, high high in the air, and I screamed so bloody hard that they get frightened and they had to drag me, still screaming and twirling pon the ground, mind you, to a motor car, and administer smelling salts to my nose to revive me and pacify me. Cause, don't matter how rough and cruel a father treats you, boy, a father is a father. That happen long long ago. Long ago, the Good Lord lift up my poor father up in the heavens with Him. And that is my testimony to the two o' you, as I sitting down here betwixt the two o' you, this bright Sunday evening in Toronto Canada, hearing this hymn, this selfsame tune that carried Nathan Sobers, my father, to his grave in Westbury Cemetery. Ain't you hearing that same hymn, *The Day Thou Gavest*?"

"I hearing it, Estelle, darling, I hearing it like anything," Sagaboy said, in a whisper, as if his voice had left his body and was now distant, far off, lost in the sea of time. Estelle's words had taken him back to his family and his home, tucked away out of memory in Trinidad; and they had made him think of the recent death of his Karen, his wife from Germany.

"Ain't it strange, ain't it wondrous strange how a person remembers things that happen so long ago? And ain't it strange too, how a simple thing like a bell in a tower could cause that same person to travel miles and miles in memory ..."

"Strange!" Sagaboy told her. Still, his voice was far

away across the ocean, miles away from the grass and the tower and the university campus where they were sitting and from the invisible hand of the carilloneur playing hymns on his bells. And then the bells stopped ringing; and then the three of them became bored with time resting so heavily on them, for they could think of nothing to do, or say, now that the bells had stopped ringing.

All you can hear now is the heavy breathing from Sagaboy, as he chews on a match stick. Henry begins to chew a match stick too. Suddenly he stops chewing, and offers a cigarette to Sagaboy, and to Estelle.

"Back home, I won't be seen dead with one o' these in my mouth, and on a Sunday, to boot!" she said. "What is one man's medicine is a next man's poison."

"You in Canada now, darling, you not back home," Ironhorse Henry reminded her. And with that, the conversation died; and the stillness and the sterility of a Toronto Sunday returned. Estelle blew smoke through her nostrils and her mouth at the same time, looking at the cigarette as if it was a bomb, and shaking her head, and muttering again about one man's medicine being another man's poison. Sagaboy started to cough. Ironhorse Henry looked up at the tower to avoid looking into Estelle's eyes. Sagaboy got up from them, and went aside to cough freely, and to spit. He could hardly control his breathing as the coughing racked his body in two, like a hairpin. A lump came up in his throat. The lump tickled him so much that he almost laughed, that he had to shut his eyes. Water began to spring from his eyes as the lump came nearer to his mouth. Then, as if playing a game with him, it went back down deeper. Sagaboy coughed and coughed, and when he did manage to spit . . . *"Blood!* Is blood I see?" But he wiped his feet on it, and hid the evidence from himself, and from Ironhorse Henry and from Estelle, who did not even look behind them while he was coughing.

Estelle broke the heaviness of the evening with a rasp-like noise of her teeth, and emphasized it by shaking her head from side to side, in despair. "Ain't no fairness in this damn world, you know that?" And when Ironhorse Henry had no comment, she added, "Now, look at me. I been here now, how much weeks? Four weeks going pon five, waiting and waiting pon them bastards at the immigration office, to give me a chance so's I could make a better woman outta myself. And you think they would give me a chance?"

"Your chance going come, love," Sagaboy said, returning to join them; and knowing, of course, that her chance would never come.

"I been hearing that tune since I was a little girl in pigtails. I know a man who waited his chance cause everybody was always telling him his chance going come. And you know how old that man was when his chance come?" She paused for effect; and then she said, "On his blasted death-bed!" And they burst out laughing. It was a tense, joyless, clench-teeth laugh. "I am getting more and more older every day, sweetheart. I don't have time to wait. That is old slave talk. Wait, wait, wait. If the greedy wait, hot going cool! If you patient, God going bring you through in the name o' the Lord. If a enemy hit you in your face, on the right hand side, you must then turn round and present him with the other side o' your fisiogomy, and let him lick-in that too. Christ Almighty, I telling you now that if I could just get one *little* chance, one little opportunity to work as a domestic servant in this place, be-Jesus Christ, I not waiting. I not waiting, nor praying, nor faltering. Not Estelle."

"This is a white man country, woman," Sagaboy teased her. "You want to cause a race riot?"

"I see eye-to-eye with Estelle," Ironhorse Henry said, in a manner which he hoped Estelle would understand, and in a tone of voice which implied more than was said. "Me and you view this situation in the same fashion. It is a shame that only a certain class o' individual could get through the doors o' immigration, and a next class o' people can't even squeeze through, at all!" He cleared his throat while they pondered on his words. He spat, neatly and accurately, on a cigarette box about ten feet away. "Now, you take them Eyetalians. *Them* is people!"

"How they get into this discussion?" Sagaboy wanted to know.

"Now, take them Eyetalians," Ironhorse continued, "them

Eyetalians, man, you does see them Eyetalians coming into this country be-Christ, as if Canada is in Rome and not in Northamerica, and . . ."

"And why the hell you don't turn into a Neyetalian, then? Why you don't learn to talk in the Eyetalian tongue, and become a Neyetalian?"

"I not arguing nor affirming that it have anything particularly wrong with not being a Neyetalian," Ironhorse Henry explained, "and I not saying that as a Westindian man, I am better off, or worse off. All I affirming is that every day you look round in this city . . . now, you take the corner o' College and Spadina where you live! Man, when I first land up in Toronto, you didn't see ten Eyetalians at that corner. Now? All you seeing is Eyetalians Eyetalians and be-Christ, more Eyetalians. You in *Italy* now, old man, you aren't no longer in Toronto."

"God, but I like them Eyetalians too bad, though!" Estelle said. "I like to see them talking and holding up their two hand up in the air, and laughing and crying and shouting for blue-murder as they talks . . . brabba-rabba-brabba-rabba-seenioreeta! God have given that tribe a very pretty tongue and a real sweet language. And I like to see how the women does dress-down in black, from head to toenail, and still manage to look so womanish, in a positive kind o' way, as if a woman was create to always look that way, and in that manner and fashion o' dressing, in order to be a lady. I am only a part-time citizen o' Canada, but I have never see *one* Canadian woman look as if she was glad to be a woman. She want to be a *man*! You understand what I mean? Them Canadian women, particularly the old ones, with their false hair and their false teet' and rimless glasses, Jesus Christ, they don't look as if they is really women at all. And they certainly don't behave as if they is mothers, neither! Everybody always looking as if she come outta a fashion book that gone outta print in the last century."

"Child, don't let nobody hear you say these things! Shut up your mouth tight tight, cause you not born here. Don't criticize the same people that going put bread in your mouth. Keep your tail betwixt thy legs, and live and

let the blasted white people live, too. That is my philosophy
of the histries o' man." It was Sagaboy cautioning her, with
great excitement in his manner. And this brought out a tiny
rackling in his chest. It became louder and noisier until
he had to cough. But the more he coughed, the more
rackling in his chest continued. He got up from them again,
and went behind the small building where he could be at
ease to untie the knots in his chest, until the bulldozers there
smashed up the eruption inside him. And as the cough was
about to break and calm down, a lump wormed its way up
to his mouth. Afraid to spit it out, he closed his eyes and
swallowed hard. But the moment it hit bottom, the coughing
and rackling blew up again, like a storm. The lump returned
to his mouth, and he closed his eyes and spat. He moved
swiftly away from the spot because he did not want to look
at it. Once he did turn, and try to look down, but the memory
of the previous shock made him move away fast; and he
rejoined his friends. But before he could return, and while
his guts were erupting, Ironhorse Henry had placed his hand
on the fat of Estelle's legs, soft as a feather in a breeze; and
he had looked into her eyes, and for a moment, one moment,
had expressed the pain that was in his heart.

"I love you bad as arse," he told her, from the bottom
of his heart.

"Look, man, behave yourself, do," she said, and then
laughed away his profession of love. All this happened while
Sagaboy was coughing; and all the time, Ironhorse Henry
wished he would drop down dead.

"You find it getting chilly here?" Sagaboy asked them.

"You have consumption, or TB, or something?" Ironhorse
asked. He glanced at Estelle to see if she was as revolted
as he. And when he saw that she was not, he added, "You
gotta be careful with that fresh-cold, man."

"Oh, little coughing can't harm him," she said, putting
a pin in Ironhorse's balloon of love.

And then they heard the bells again, loud this time, as
if the man in the tower wanted to drown out their voices.
They did not recognize the tune that the bells were playing
now. And for a long time they sat, silently, arguing in their
minds that they did know the tune, but listening all the

time to the magic in the hands that tolled the bells so beautifully. They listened, wondering how a man could receive such power of beauty, such sweetness, such purity from his hands, and put them into bells . . . bells that were made to call people to church, to toll them to the sides of graves, to drop flowers on the coffin of a friend, or a lover, or a father.

"Jesus Christ, listen. Listen to the poetry in that damn bell, though!" Ironhorse said, raising his head to catch the smallest note, the softest ting. "That man playing that bell like how great Gort used to caress his tenor pan in the steel band, back in the old days. Too blasted sweet. Man, listen to that damn bell."

"What you say this place name?" Estelle asked.

"The campus," Sagaboy told her.

"I got to come back here, again, some time soon, and hear some more o' these white people bell-music."

"You know something? I just realize that Sunday evening is the same all over the blasted world. We sitting down here in Canada, pon the grass, and it is the same thing as when we was little boys back home, sitting down in a place we used to call The Hill," Ironhorse said. Poetry also was coming with his reminiscences. "Every man should sit down on a hill at least once in his lifetime, on a Sunday afternoon or evening, preferably alone, and look at the sea, and think about the past and the present and the future, and learn how to know himself. You gotta be yourself, alone, sitting down pon that hill of time, with the sun sinking behind your back and the moon rising in your face, both at one and the same time, before you is man enough to come to me and affirm that you really know yourself."

"I remember that feeling, old man," Sagaboy said, as if he was really experiencing it again, right in their presence. "I remember that emotion. I remember, how every Sunday night back home, we used to sit down on a hill called Brittons Hill. Me and the rest o' the boys, sitting down pon that damn hill, like if we was in a upstairs house looking down in the sea. And the same feeling, like I was lost, you know, like I wasn't worth nothing like how sometimes the same feeling does overpower me in that blasted five-dollars-a-week rat-trap I lives in, on Spadina, right here in this kiss-me-arse advance country . . ." He took a beaten-up, half-smoked cigarette from his pocket and put a match to its black tip. ". . . and the birds chirping. You know something? I have never see *one* blasted bird in this place yet, and I now remember that, for the first time! Back home, the birds chirping nice songs and then they run off to sleep. And the trees, trees all round where we was sitting down, trees dress-up in a more greener coat o' green than this grass. And then a funny thing would happen. Just at that moment before shadow and darkness take them up in their hands as if they was little children put to bed, be-Christ, they would turn *more greener* still! We would be sitting down in the midst of the evening dusk and shadows, thinking bout what and what we was going to be when we grow up to be big strong men. And if on that particular Sunday we did have a nice feed, like split-pea rice and fry pork, or something nice and heavy in the bowels, well, pardner, everybody want to be something, or somebody great and powerful. Like a doctor, or a police commissioner, or even a plantation manager. And you don't know that one evening, I must have been so blasted full o' black-eye peas and rice that I say I wanted to be the *governor o' the whole blasted West Indies*. Be-Christ, if that ain't dreaming, tell me what is? But one boy, Lester Theophillis Bynoe, all he wanted to be, with a full-belly or no full-belly, was a hangman. And you know something? Be-Christ, that is what he turned out to be! He is the biggest, the blackest, and the best hangman in the whole Caribbean! But if things wasn't so great, kitchen-wise or food-wise, or if our mothers had give us a regular stiff cut-arse with a window stick or with a piece o' bamboo, well, everybody want to jump on a boat and become sailors and buccaneers. And always, after we finish wishing and dreaming, you could hear the church bells from St. Barnabas Church, miles and miles of sugar canes away, over the fields, coming right up to your two earholes. Church bells, old man, *ding-dong-ding-dong!* . . . " His coughing aborted his reverie, and it shook him like a huckster shaking a coconut to see if there is any water inside. Ironhorse Henry rushed to him, and held him around the waist; and Estelle became very alarmed, as Ironhorse Henry beat the coughing man's chest to dislodge the thorns of pain that were inside him. And Ironhorse took out his own handkerchief, and gave it to Sagaboy to put to his mouth. "Let we go home," he said, when the heaving permitted him to form a word. "That damn bell ring till it give me a headache. And it chilly as hell here, too."

And they walked hurriedly away from the campus. Shadows were running slow races across the front lawns, and across the large circle of green grass in front of a large grey building. The bells kept ringing for a while, and then they stopped. And then Estelle pushed her arms through both their arms, through Sagaboy's, on her left, and Ironhorse Henry's, on her right, and like this they walked on in the darkness of the bells.

David Helwig

IN EXILE

He wakes screaming again, climbing upward from the dim confinements of nightmare into the discomforts of being too old to remember how old he is, stiff and sludged among the smells of his body. He opens his eyes. They are blurred with mucus. He rubs them hard with his hands and opens them. Sees. The texture of the thin wood of the packing case. He stares at the straight rough texture of its grain, and wonders what kind of wood it is. Every morning he wonders what kind of wood it is. His eyes engage in a contest with his bladder. Bladder wins. He crawls to the door of the shack because it is too low to stand up in.

When he pushes aside the rags that cover the opening, the sun is bright and hurts him. He crawls out of the shack and stands up. All his bones hurt.

He pisses not much down the hill toward the reeds. He is far-sighted and when he looks across the reeds, he can see clearly the other side of the river where a seagull is flying slowly and a black car moves on the highway, but when he looks down, the old thing that hangs in his hands is blurred.

The air isn't warm in spite of the sun. As he stands there, he looks at the reeds all bending in the same way under the wind and thinks maybe soon it will be getting cold. Dog walks out from his place at the side of the shack, stretches and walks over to him. He rubs Dog's ear.

They'll come again today. He is sure of that but scorns to prepare for them. Like a king always, he proudly puts them out of mind.

As he stands by his shack he hears the sound of cars from the road above. The hill that leads up to the road is rough with clumps of earth in which long grass is rooted, and among these grow wild raspberry canes, small bushes and the stiff stalks of chicory, with a few of the small purple flowers that bloom at this time of year. In a few places where the hill is almost bare of grass, the water has made channels in the mud.

For a moment, he remembers the nightmare that wakened him, but then it is gone, and he is not convinced that it wasn't the memory of some other nightmare from years in the past that had darted out from behind his brain for a moment. Every day it gets harder for him to separate the real memories from the memories of old and repeated dreams. There is a room that he remembers, at the bottom of a staircase with closed doors, and he is afraid to go in, but he can't be sure if this is a memory of his childhood or merely a dream he has dreamed a thousand times. He remembers lumber camps and a farm. Little else.

He walks to the door of his shack, bends himself down and crawls in to get the water cup. Inside it is warm with the heat of his sleep and because the wind doesn't blow in here. It is half dark, and he can hardly see the tin cup beside the mattress. Here the mattress looks grey, but he remembers from the day he dragged it from the dump that it is light blue. He finds the cup and crawls back out of the small doorway.

Once he was careful of the water he drank, but he no longer troubles much about it, only walks along the edge of the reeds to a group of rocks where the water is less muddy. He drinks a cup of the water that he has dipped up then sits on the rock and looks up the river to the distant bridge which carries the big highway across. He sits and watches, counting the cars, but he loses track somewhere before a hundred and climbs off the rock. On the way back, one of his feet slips in the mud, and when he gets back to the shack, he scrapes his muddy foot back and forth over the dry stony earth until it is clean. He throws the cup in the door of the shack.

He looks up the hill toward the road. That is where they will come from, that's where the other one came from. For a few seconds he wonders if that man was a dream, but decides not. The old man is a little hungry now, wonders what he can find or steal or get the money to pay for. He starts up the hill. It is a long climb and, when he reaches the top, he stands still to get his wind back. He is still nearly a hundred feet from the road that curves toward him from the city to the south, and away from him as it reaches toward the country. Across the road is a wrecking yard, behind a high green fence. The gate is open and he can see the jumble of wrecked cars like fish that all died with their mouths and eyes open.

He walks toward the road, and in the ditch beside it sees two pop bottles. Four cents, a good start. He picks up the bottles and puts one in each side pocket of his coat. There are holes in the pockets, but not holes big enough for the bottles to fall through.

Now he walks as a hunter, head down, concentrating on the ground beside his feet. By the time he reaches the new subdivision, he has found several butts worth saving and a penny, and he relaxes his observation a little as he walks down two side streets that lead him toward the Red and White he always goes to. The streets here are neatly kept, and he expects to find nothing, especially no bottles, but on the next street of older houses, half run down, the other half respectably kept, he begins to watch again. Halfway down the street he sees an empty pop bottle, a five-cent one, on a front porch beside a broken wicker chair.

There are children playing on the street, but they are half a block away and concentrating on their game. He bends for a couple of butts, not wanting them, but wanting to stop and look around him. It seems safe, and he walks quickly up to the house, puts the big bottle in his pocket and walks away.

"What have you got there?"

It is the shrill voice of a woman calling out at him from behind. He does not bother to look at her, only moves steadily forward to the corner. He hears her footsteps running after him. She comes up beside him and grabs at his coat. He pulls away from her and keeps walking but she comes again, beside him, her thin face with protruding eyes pushing forward at him.

"What did you take off my porch? I saw you up there."

She is still holding his coat as he tries to pull away from her. Her face beside him has red blotches and bad teeth. He spits in her face, and she lets go of him and begins to swear and cry. As he turns the corner, she is still standing at the same place on the sidewalk.

Ahead of him he sees the red and white sign half a block away. They know him now at this store and suspect him of being a thief. He has stolen a little from them once or twice, but now they watch him whenever he comes in, angry faces following him wherever he goes.

Close to the store he stops and stands waiting. A woman comes out of the store and passes him, then another. He waits again. A man comes, rich, good clothes. The old man steps in front of him and begs a dime. It is the first time in days that he has heard his own voice, and it surprises him. The man gives him the money.

When he walks in the store, the old woman at the checkout stares at him sourly. He puts his three bottles on the counter without speaking and takes the nickel and four pennies she gives him. Instead of going straight back through the store, he crosses to the vegetable counter and starts to squeeze the tomatoes. He sees the manager coming from the back of the store, angry and ready to shout at him, so he turns back and walks up the middle aisle, stopping to pick up boxes and cans, and move them close to him and put them back. The sour woman in the checkout is watching him and so is one of the boys who is filling shelves farther away. He moves toward the back of the store now, around a corner of the shelf and toward the soaps. Nobody can see him here, unless they walk round the same corner. The manager does and begins to move the soap packages, pretending to be busy there. By now the old man is tired of the

game he has been playing and crosses the aisle to the dog
food. There are still a couple of dozen of the kind he wants
on sale cheap so they can get rid of it. One can of this will
last him two or three days. It satisfies his hunger and he keeps
strong and well on it. He takes a can and carries it to the
front of the store where he puts it on the counter with all his
money, except one penny.

He puts the can in his pocket and walks out of the store.
He is hungrier now, but won't be able to open the can until
he gets back to his shack, and he carries the hunger with him
like a small fire hoarded in the round stove of his belly. The
sun is shining in his face, and he squints his eyes almost shut
against it. When he turns his face to avoid the sun, he sees
a young woman in a back yard lying in the sun almost
naked, her woman-fat hips rising bare from a long bare back.
He hasn't looked for a woman for years, not wanted one,
desert now, dry and sand, but once he had been mad for
women, and this nakedness in his sight angers him. He cannot
understand how younger men can look at this and do nothing.
He growls away the moment's anger and walks on. She is
beneath his concern.

The streets unwind before his feet, dull mostly for there is
nothing he cares to see. When he gets close to the hill where
he will find his shack, the hunger is intense, but he doesn't
hurry, for his legs have their own speed, and if he denies
them, they will betray him, trip him on the hill.

When he reaches the shack, he crawls inside and, squatting
in the half light, opens the can with an opener he keeps
there, then throws down the opener and crawls back out
into the light. He leans against the front of the shack and
begins to eat, digging out chunks of the rich strong meat
with his fingers and shoving them into his mouth, then
licking the fingers one at a time before scratching out another
bite.

He has almost finished eating when he hears the truck stop
on the road above. They are coming now. He takes the can
of red meat and puts it in his coat pocket. Other than this he
will not prepare. He sits on the ground and waits for them.

He sees them on the hill above, more this time, as he knew
there would be, the one in uniform leading them as they

blunder through the long grass and scrub bushes. He sits still hardly watching them, simply aware of their coming.

When they reach the bottom of the hill, they talk quietly among themselves, awkward, waiting for the one in uniform to assert his leadership and speak for them.

"Hello there," the one in the uniform says.

The old man waits.

"Told you yesterday, didn't I, that you'd have to move out. There's a statute against any squatters here in the marsh. I told you that, didn't I?"

The old man sits still on the ground. He has no need to speak.

"The council wants all the squatters out of here. For their own protection and so they won't be lighting the marsh on fire again. Last year the reeds got set on fire down here and they had an awful time with them. Do you understand what I'm saying to you, old fellow? You got to go. Go away. No live here."

The man has red under his jaw from shaving.

"These men here are from the Works Department."

The other men nod their heads.

"You go away now. No live here. You go to the Salvation Army. Or the Welfare. No live here. Too cold in winter anyway. OK?"

Dog is watching the men.

"C'mon boys," the one in uniform says, "get to work."

The other men approach the shack slowly. They carry tools and begin to hack and chop, to pry and pull down. Dog moves away, cowardly, with his tail down. The old man watches. He sees a white horse trampling the ruins, a horse ridden by an old woman, she naked, with two little shrivelled breasts like testicles. She bows to the old man, knowing him.

"Sorry about this, old timer," the one in uniform says. "I really hate to do this, but it's my job, you realize that. You want me to give you a ride into town, I will. I don't have to hang around here."

The men are now almost finished with the ruin of his shack. When the wood and rags lie on the ground the men stop and look at their leader.

"We got to burn the material," he says. "Is there anything that you want to take with you?"

The old man thinks of the can opener and the cup, but he will not speak. He looks at the ground beside him. The men are sprinkling gasoline on the fragments of his shack. The policeman takes out a match, lights it, and throws it down into the rags. There is a puff of black smoke and a sudden explosion of fire goes up into the air. The heat is almost painful, but the old man doesn't move. He stares into the flames and sees a lion risen on his hind legs, carving the air with his claws, his head black with smoke, fire in his mouth. Then it changes and is a shapeless unknown fearsome beast of burning places, a dragon perhaps, nuzzling down into the ashes as the fire sinks, acknowledging the old man as it leaves for the cities under the earth.

He looks upward into the sky to see if birds or a winged horse are coming for him, but there is only blue and space and the running light. The men begin to beat the ashes with their shovels, beat out the fire and cover it with earth and pebbles. They walk over the place with their feet stepping heavily, their heads down, the dance of destruction gripping them.

"I can take you in to the Sally Ann if you want, old timer. Or the Welfare."

The men have stopped dancing, except one, who continues to walk and stamp. When he stops, everything is still. It is now the birds should come from the sky. The old man screws up his eyes against the light of the sun, but sees nothing coming down on him.

"You don't want to come with us, eh? No come to town?"

The men begin to move away now, looking back now and then at their work and the old man sitting on the ground. He does not watch them, only looks upward to the sky. When the men disappear over the crest of the hill, Dog comes over to him and licks his hand. The old man grunts at him and stands up. It's not easy after sitting there for so long. He looks at the sky again, but again there is nothing, only the wind that pulls at his coat.

He looks at Dog, at the reeds and the wide river. He begins to walk. Away from the town and out into the open country. Scorns to look back.

"Is this the way to Sunshine?"

Duncan Campbell Scott   EXPIATION

Above the level ground upon which the buildings of the Missanabie Post are erected there rises a point of rock looking westward over the lake. At its foot lies a pool of water, black from its great depth, covered sometimes with gleams of dead colour from glorious sunsets, and sometimes with the fragile streaks of dawn that fly timidly through the mists.

From this point of rock an observer can see the lake to its farthest shores, can note the contour of its islands, and can hear the dulcet sound of all its small waves ringing like the tones of innumerable lute-players sounding their fairy music. The peculiarity of this place is its aloofness; for with the wide expanse before and the clear depth of the water below, it seems far removed from the mean huddle of buildings which is the metropolis of those silent environs of forest. Yet it is distant but the cast of a stone, and from the stockade any person may be seen upon the observation-point, standing or sitting.

The sight of a figure there during the last ten years had become so common that it attracted no attention from Indians or half-breeds, habitués of the post. It seemed part of the landscape, a continuation of the rock itself, rather than a human figure outlined against the sky. But no mass of rocks could express the strength of human feeling as that form expressed it. Something deeper than any simple emotion seemed to emanate from the man's figure.

Hardly anyone noticed when he went there or when he came away. Sometimes a trader from beyond, someone who had heard of the man in his days of power, would stroll by in vulgar curiosity, thinking to hail him. The stranger had, perchance, just bought tobacco of him in the store; why should he not converse with him in the open air? But the inquisitive one passed by without a word. The figure sat there with an inscrutable air, unconsciously expressing itself with such intensity that none dared profane the sacredness of such silence. The mere elements of clothing which he wore, encompassing him, ample and rude, seemed to radiate the feeling, but particularly the fillet formed of three mink-skins, roughly sewn together, which he ever wore about his brow.

Forbes Macrimmon had been the chief trader at Missanabie, and a mighty man. The post was in the centre of a valuable hunting-ground, and three hundred Indians traded there. All went well until opposition came. There are some men who are resourceful only in adversity; there are others in whom rivalry breeds irritation and develops incompetency. Macrimmon was of the latter class. When Pierre Loudet, of the French Company—this was in the year 1808—appeared before his fort, laid peaceful siege to it, and endeavoured to undermine its trade, he was at his wits' end. Forbes was a Highlandman, proud of everything that went to make up the individual Macrimmon—his strength, his stature, his shrewdness in a trade, his ancestry, his power of drinking much rum, his quick temper, his politeness. His pride led him to say many foolish things.

"I'm not afraid of man, God, or devil," he would say. "Nothing touches me, love nor hate nor greed, and I can give up the thing that most men cherish as an Indian gives up an old pack-strap. I never sucked a drop of my mother's milk, and neither woman nor man has any control over me."

Thus he philosophised, knowing not at all what manner of man he was; but when the time was ripe God taught him. Pierre Loudet was polished as a dancing-floor, but was any man to best a Macrimmon in politeness? They exchanged visits, drank quarts of each other's rum, and fought each other for the trade. The contest made Macrimmon anxious, irritable, and despondent, and he imagined that he was losing ground.

His chief hope lay in his servant, Daniel Wascowin. Daniel was almost a pure Indian, but there was a little white blood in him. He was a great hunter, who always took thrice as many skins as any one else, and his prowess gave him a position of control over the other Indians. As long as the Scotsman was sure of Daniel, the balance of trade was certain to be in his favour; and Daniel was firm in his allegiance. He thought that Macrimmon was the greatest of all earthly powers. His knowledge of heavenly powers was but dim and fitful, and of other earthly powers he knew nothing. Macrimmon might be a hard master, sudden, fierce, and inexplicable; but he was to be obeyed, he could do no wrong.

Loudet tried to corrupt Daniel, but he might as well have tried to gain an hour of May sunlight on a December day. He saw that until the power of Macrimmon's faithful henchman was humbled he would have no great success in trade at Missanabie.

Pierre Loudet was a cunning fellow. One evening, when Macrimmon had accepted his hospitality, and they were deep in the French Company's rum, he noticed on the table a little tin pail with a copper bottom, such as the Indians use to make a drawing of tea. Now, he knew that his rival had none of these pails to sell, but an inferior sort, and that those with the copper bottoms were much esteemed by the Indians. As soon as Loudet saw that his guest's eye had caught the pail he began to praise Daniel.

"A fine fellow, that Wascowin!"

"Yes, as faithful as a dog," answered Macrimmon.

"Yes, he is a faithful fellow," said Loudet with an odd inflection; and saying the word, he poured a little water from the pail on the table.

"You have an odd way of speaking, Mr. Loudet," said Macrimmon, angry in a moment.

"Oh, no offence intended," said the Frenchman smoothly. "I was just saying your man was a good man—a very faithful man." But he gave his words such a singsong that Macrimmon did not like the tune.

"I wouldn't stand that from any man whose rum I was not drinking!" cried the trader, dashing down his pannikin, and with that he flared up and walked out of the house in a mighty rage.

The Frenchman had done a very simple thing, but it was full subtle. The fact of his having one of the Hudson's Bay Company's pails, and his peculiar look or accent in praising the faithful Daniel, worked down through Macrimmon's spirit like a drop of acid on a wound.

Next day the trader was very quiet, and very terrible in his quiet. He was watching an opportunity to prove his servant. Too proud, too irritable—in other words, too weak— to be patient, the slightest indication of guilt would serve his purpose. When his passion broke loose he promised himself that he would give them all a fine lesson. Toward evening, when he and Daniel Wascowin were alone in the store, he suddenly roared out:

"What have ye been doing with all the tea-pails?"

The question was so loud and violent that Daniel started. He looked up to where the pails hung, near the ceiling.

"They're not all there," he said slowly.

"No, they're not all there!"

"I haven't been selling any!" continued Daniel, thinking out loud, and wondering who could have taken them; he hardly thought of anyone having stolen them.

Macrimmon watched his servant, his eyes furious and devouring. Daniel had never seen him so angry, and he quailed before him. Macrimmon saw guilt where there was only surprise. His anger was a hasty as fire in grass. He leaped upon the Indian as a lion leaps on a gazelle, caught him by the throat, and forced him back against the wall.

"I'll give you a lesson, you red dog, you and all your red whelps. The like o' you in league with that frogeater—to steal the good tea-pails, and then to lie about it! There was the lie in your eyes." As he pressed Daniel against the wall with his left hand, he whipped out his double-barrelled pistol with the right. "Do you hear this?" he raged. "It'll be the last thing ye hear, and ye'll remember it. Get out of this quick, and when ye come back let it be for a better reason than because ye think I can't get on without ye. There's a charge for each side of your head!"

"Bang!" went the pistol at Daniel's left ear, and the bullet crashed into the wall. "Bang!" went the pistol at his right ear, and the bullet crashed into the wall. Macrimmon drove the hot muzzle against the Indian's forehead.

"Let me set eyes on ye to-morrow, and I'll put a ball *there!*"

Dashing down the pistol, he caught Daniel and cast him through the door into the yard. The Indians, excited by the shots, came curiously forward by one and twos. Daniel's wife, crossing the yard with a pail of water, saw him trying to get to his feet, but reeling and groping, as if he were stricken with a mastering illness. Blood ran from his ears; his face was scorched and blackened by flame and powder. Dropping her pail with a cry, she half carried, half led him away to his wigwam.

A little later, when the evening mist had begun to gather in the long reeds by the shore, a canoe crept through it, gliding in silence, an intensified shadow within the shadow. Then nothing was there but a ripple in the water under the mist.

The bark had been stripped from Daniel's wigwam; the stars looked through the poles. He was obedient. He had departed.

From that time forward things went very badly with Macrimmon. His anger had disappeared, though suspicions of Daniel were still in his thoughts; but Daniel was gone, and a calmer state of mind would not serve to call him back. Without Daniel he was nothing. There had been no one else to trust, and now he must do everything, watch everybody, be everywhere himself. It was an impossible task, and he saw Pierre Loudet profit by his confusion. The continued politeness of the Frenchman maddened him, and he wore down his spirit in the effort to carry himself as urbanely and jauntily as his triumphant opponent.

Without Daniel's restraining influence, the Indians became impudent, ran about, traded where they pleased. In the autumn some of the best hunters took their credits from the French Company; in the following spring Loudet got the best of the furs, and many Indians did not even attempt to repay the advances Macrimmon had given them. The Scotsman's defeat was thorough. His fur-packs were so light that, in shame, he shirked taking them down to the district headquarters himself, and sent them with a crew of Indians. These careless fellows upset one canoe in a rapid; one of them was drowned and part of the load lost.

Unnumbered times Macrimmon wished for Daniel Wascowin, but he had disappeared. The Indians reported that he had deserted his old hunting-grounds. There was a vague rumour that he had been seen somewhere in the far north, but it was only a rumour.

During that spring and summer Macrimmon formed the habit of standing or sitting on the top of the rock and looking forth over the lake. He had learned much about himself, and was deeply conning the lesson. He was like one doomed, expecting some final change, the close of a chapter of his life. The end came when the trading canoes returned. A man had been sent to supersede him at the post; he had been degraded; he was to act as clerk and helper. The fact that his master was an Englishman named Gooderich was the annihilation of his pride.

This Gooderich was a bright, bustling little fellow, and he soon controlled the Indians. By the second spring he had won back so much of the trade that Pierre Loudet thought it best to travel farther westward. When Loudet was gone the truth came out.

"What an ass you were, Macrimmon," Gooderich said one day, "to let this Frenchman deceive you! One of the half-breeds told me just now that Loudet put him up to steal the tea-pails; you must have been drunk!"

"Yes, I was drunk," said Macrimmon quietly.

Through long brooding over his humiliation he came to the knowledge that he had been drunk with pride and arrogance. The intimation that Daniel was innocent fell upon his new mood like a stroke of lightning. His injustice, his violence, rose up against him. He would have recompensed his faithful servant a thousandfold had it been possible.

One evening in May an Indian came into the store and said quietly to Macrimmon:

"Daniel Wascowin has come back."

Gooderich had gone off for the day, and Macrimmon was alone. He gazed at the Indian in a dazed way and walked to the door. But a flash of his old pride sprang up in him.

"Tell him to bring his furs to the store," he said gruffly.

When the messenger had gone, Macrimmon paced to and fro excitedly. Daniel had returned—yes, he had come home. He thought of his servant just as he had been, strong and alert, striding up with a huge bundle of furs on his back, as he had often seen him in the old days when he used to pour out a tot of rum for him and shake his hand.

But Wascowin did not come. Impatient of the delay, Macrimmon went to meet him, forgetful of the last stirring of his pride. Just outside the door he met a woman whom he did not recognise at first. She was gaunt, and her eyes glittered with a famished lustre. The skin was drawn tightly over the bones of her face, and she had no expression except the fixed one of weary hunger. It was Daniel's wife. In her hands she held three mink-skins.

"What's the matter with you?" he cried, fearful of what the figure might portend.

"You sent for Daniel's furs. I am his wife. I have brought them myself."

She held out the three pitiful mink-skins. In days gone by there had been many prime skins of otter and beaver and mink and marten, and of silver fox not a few. She held out three mink-skins!

Macrimmon saw the whole history of three years in those skins. He trembled. He set his teeth.

"Where is Daniel!" he said hoarsely.

She pointed toward the boat-landing.

Daniel had crawled out of his canoe, and lay at the landing-place, unable to move. There was just a spark of spirit left in his body of bone and skin. He tried to smile as Macrimmon bent over him. On his forehead he saw the mark he had put there—the two crescents made by the hot pistol-barrels, blackened by powder as if tattooed.

Yielding up at that moment everything of self there was in him, Macrimmon lifted the Indian in his arms, carried him to the house, and put him in his own bed. Daniel had no strength to tell him that it was impossible to hunt when in one ear there was silence, and in the other a roaring like the rapids on the Missanabie, which the trappers call Hell's Gate. Moreover, no man can hunt with a broken spirit. He was obedient to the last; he had come back for a good reason.

In the dead of night, when they were alone, Macrimmon cried out in the anguish of his soul, and told of his grievous downfall. But Daniel could not hear a word; that was the bitterness of it. He only knew the great honour of lying in that bed; he ventured and put his hand on the white man's arm. That touch, and his confession, purged Macrimmon's spirit. He was not the man he had been. There was a peculiar strength grown up in him, but not the fatal strength of pride.

In the morning light the two men could only look helplessly into each other's eyes; and in a little while two of the eyes were darkened.

Macrimmon tanned the three mink-skins, which seemed to him symbols of the grievous wrong that he had cast upon his servant, and of his own degradation. Roughly he sewed them together; and he wore them ever after like a fillet bound about his brow.

Sara Jeanette Duncan **THE JORDANVILLE MEETING**

Miss Milburn pressed her contention that the suspicion of his desire would be bad for her lover's political prospects till she made him feel his honest passion almost a form of treachery to his party. She also hinted that, for the time being, it did not make particularly for her own comfort in the family circle, Mr. Milburn having grown by this time quite bitter. She herself drew the excitement of intrigue from the situation, which she hid behind her pretty, pale, decorous features, and never betrayed by the least of her graceful gestures. She told herself that she had never been so right about anything as about that affair of the ring—imagine, for an instant, if she had been wearing it now! She would have banished Lorne altogether if she could. As he insisted on an occasional meeting, she clothed it in mystery, appointing it for an evening when her mother and aunt were out, and answering his ring at the door herself. To her family she remarked with detachment that you saw hardly anything of Lorne Murchison now, he was so taken up with his old election; and to Hesketh she confided her fear that politics did interfere with friendship, whatever he might say. He said a good deal, he cited lofty examples; but the only agreement he could get from her was the hope that the estrangement wouldn't be permanent.

"But you are going to say something, Lorne," she insisted, talking of the Jordanville meeting.

"Not much," he told her. "It's the safest district we've got, and they adore old Farquharson. He'll do most of the talking—they wouldn't thank me for taking up the time. Farquharson is going to tell them I'm a first-class man, and they couldn't do better, and I've practically only to show my face and tell them I think so too."

"But Mr. Hesketh will speak?"

"Yes; we thought it would be a good chance of testing him. He may interest them, and he can't do much harm, anyhow."

"Lorne, I should simply love to go. It's your first meeting."

"I'll take you."

"Mr. Murchison, *have* you taken leave of your senses? Really, you are—"

"All right, I'll send you. Farquharson and I are going out to the Crow place to supper, but Hesketh is driving straight there. He'll be delighted to bring you—who wouldn't?"

"I shouldn't be allowed to go with him alone," said Dora, thoughtfully.

"Well, no. I don't know that I'd approve of that myself," laughed the confident young man. "Hesketh is driving Mrs. Farquharson, and the cutter will easily hold three. Isn't it lucky there's sleighing?"

"Mother couldn't object to that," said Dora. "Lorne, I always said you were the dearest fellow! I'll wear a thick veil, and not a soul will know me."

"Not a soul would in any case," said Lorne. "It'll be a Jordanville crowd, you know—nobody from Elgin."

"We don't visit much in Jordanville, certainly. Well, Mother mayn't object. She has a great idea of Mrs. Farquharson, because she has attended eleven Drawing-Rooms at Ottawa, and one of them was given—held, I should say—by the Princess Louise."

"I won't promise you eleven," said Lorne, "but there seems to be a pretty fair chance of one or two."

At this she had a tale for him which charmed his ears. "I didn't know where to look," she said. "Aunt Emmie, you know, has a very bad trick of coming into my room without knocking. Well, in she walked last night, and found me before the glass *practising my curtsey!* I could have killed her. Pretended she thought I was out."

"Dora, would you like *me* to promise something?" he asked, with a mischievous look.

"Of course, I would. I don't care how much *you* promise. What?"

But already he repented of his daring, and sat beside her suddenly conscious and abashed. Nor could any teasing prevail to draw from him what had been on his audacious lips to say.

Social precedents are easily established in the country. The accident that sent the first Liberal canvasser for Jordanville votes to the Crow place for his supper would be hard to discover now; the fact remains that he has been going there ever since. It made a greater occasion than Mrs. Crow would ever have dreamed of acknowledging. She saw to it that they had a good meal of victuals, and affected indifference to the rest; they must say their say, she supposed. If the occasion had one satisfaction which she came nearer to confessing than another, it was that the two or three substantial neighbours who usually came to meet the politicians left their wives at home, and that she herself, to avoid giving any offence on this score, never sat down with the men. Quite enough to do it was, she would explain later, for her and the hired girl to wait on them and to clear up after them. She and Bella had their bite afterward when the men had hitched up, and when they could exchange comments of proud congratulation upon the inroads on the johnny-cake or the pies. So there was no ill feeling, and Mrs. Crow, having vindicated her dignity by shaking hands with the guests of the evening in the parlour, solaced it further by maintaining the masculine state of the occasion, in spite of protests or entreaties. To sit down opposite Mr. Crow would have made it ordinary "company"; she passed the plates and turned it into a function.

She was waiting for them on the parlour sofa when Crow brought them in out of the nipping early dark of December, Elmore staying behind in the yard with the horses. She sat on the sofa in her best black dress with the bead trimming on the neck and sleeves, a good deal pushed up and wrinkled across the bosom, which had done all that would ever be required of it when it gave Elmore and Abe their start in life. Her wiry hands were crossed in her lap in the moment of waiting: you could tell by the look of them that they were not often crossed there. They were strenuous hands; the whole worn figure was strenuous, and the narrow set mouth, and the eyes which had looked after so many matters for so long, and even the way the hair was drawn back into a knot in a fashion that would have given a phrenologist his opportunity. It was a different Mrs. Crow from the one that sat in the midst of her poultry and garden-stuff in the Elgin market square; but it was even more the same Mrs. Crow, the sum of a certain measure of opportunity and service, an imperial figure in her bead trimming, if the truth were known.

The room was heated to express the geniality that was harder to put in words. The window was shut; there was a smell of varnish and whatever was inside the "suite" of which Mrs. Crow occupied the sofa. Enlarged photographs—very much enlarged—of Mr. and Mrs. Crow hung upon the walls, and one other of a young girl done in that process which tells you at once that she was an only daughter and that she is dead. There had been other bereavements; they were written upon the silver coffin-plates which, framed and glazed, also contributed to the decoration of the room; but you would have had to look close, and you might feel a delicacy.

Mrs. Crow made her greetings with precision, and sat down again upon the sofa for a few minutes' conversation.

"I'm telling them," said her husband, "that the sleighin's just held out for them. If it 'ud been tomorrow they'd have had to come on wheels. Pretty soft travellin' as it was, some places, I guess."

"Snow's come early this year," said Mrs. Crow. "It was an open fall, too."

"It has certainly," Mr. Farquharson backed her up. "About as early as I remember it. I don't know how much you got out here; we had a good foot in Elgin."

" 'Bout the same, 'bout the same," Mr. Crow deliberated, "but it's been layin' light all along over Clayfield way—ain't had a pair of runners out, them folks."

"Makes a more cheerful winter, Mrs. Crow, don't you

think, when it comes early?" remarked Lorne. "Or would you rather not get it till after Christmas?"

"I don't know as it matters much, out here in the country. We don't get a great many folks passin', best of times. An' it's more of a job to take care of the stock."

"That's so," Mr. Crow told them. "Chores come heavier when there's snow on the ground, a great sight, especially if there's drifts."

And for an instant, with his knotted hands hanging between his knees, he pondered this unvarying aspect of his yearly experience. They all pondered it, sympathetic.

"Well, now, Mr. Farquharson," Mrs. Crow turned to him. "An' how reely *be* ye? We've heard better, an' worse, an' middlin'—there's ben such contradictory reports."

"Oh, very well, Mrs. Crow. Never better. I'm going to give a lot more trouble yet. I can't do it in politics, that's the worst of it. But here's the man that's going to do it for me. Here's the man!"

The Crows looked at the pretendant, as in duty bound, but not any longer than they could help.

"Why, I guess you were at school with Elmore?" said Crow, as if the idea had just struck him.

"He may be right peart, for all that," said Elmore's mother, and Elmore, himself, entering with two leading Liberals of Jordanville, effected a diversion, under cover of which Mrs. Crow escaped, to superintend, with Bella, the last touches to the supper in the kitchen.

Politics in and about Jordanville were accepted as a purely masculine interest. If you had asked Mrs. Crow to take a hand in them she would have thanked you with sarcasm, and said she thought she had about enough to do as it was. The school-house, on the night of such a meeting as this, was recognized to be no place for ladies. It was a man's affair, left to the men, and the appearance there of the other sex would have been greeted with remark and levity. Elgin, as we know, was more sophisticated in every way, plenty of ladies attended political meetings in the Drill Shed, where seats as likely as not would be reserved for them; plenty of handkerchiefs waved there for the encouragement of the hero of the evening. They did

not kiss him; British phlegm, so far, had stayed that demon-
stration at the southern border.

The ladies of Elgin, however, drew the line somewhere,
drew it at country meetings. Mrs. Farquharson went with her
husband because, since his state of health had handed him
over to her more than ever, she saw it a part of her wifely
duty. His retirement had been decided upon for the spring,
but she would be on hand to retire him at any earlier moment
should the necessity arise. "We'll be the only female creatures
here, my dear," she had said to Dora on the way out, and
Hesketh had praised them both for public spirit. He didn't
know, he said, how anybody would get elected in England
without the ladies, especially in the villages, where the people
were obliged to listen respectfully.

"I wonder you can afford to throw away all the influence
you get in the rural districts with soup and blankets," he said;
"but this is an extravagant country in many ways." Dora kept
silence, not being sure of the social prestige bound up with the
distribution of soup and blankets, but Mrs. Farquharson set
him sharply right.

"I guess we'd rather do without our influence if it came to
that," she said.

Hesketh listened with deference to her account of the rural
district which had as yet produced no Ladies Bountiful, made
mental notes of several points, and placed her privately as a
woman of more than ordinary intelligence. I have always
claimed for Hesketh an open mind; he was filling it now, to
its capacity, with care and satisfaction.

The schoolroom was full and waiting when they arrived.
Jordanville had been well billed, and the posters held, in addition to the conspicuous names of Farquharson and Murchison, that of Mr. Alfred Hesketh (of London, England). There
was a "send-off" to give to the retiring member, there was
a critical inspection to make of the new candidate, and there
was Mr. Alfred Hesketh, of London, England, and whatever
he might signify. They were big, quiet, expectant fellows, with
less sophistication and polemic than their American counter-
parts, less stolid aggressiveness than their parallels in England,
if they have parallels there. They stood, indeed, for the
development between the two; they came of the new country

but not of the new light; they were democrats who had never
thrown off the monarch—what harm did he do there overseas?
They had the air of being prosperous, but not prosperous
enough for theories and doctrines. The Liberal vote of South
Fox had yet to be split by Socialism or Labour. Life was a
decent rough business that required all their attention; there
was time enough for sleep but not much for speculation.
They sat leaning forward with their hats dropped between
their knees, more with the air of big schoolboys expecting an
entertainment than responsible electors come together to
approve their party's choice. They had the uncomplaining
bucolic look, but they wore it with a difference; the difference
by this time, was enough to mark them of another nation.
Most of them had driven to the meeting; it was not an adjourn-
ment from the public house. Nor did the air hold any hint
of beer. Where it had an alcoholic drift the flavour was of
whisky; but the stimulant of the occasion had been tea or
cider, and the room was full of patient good will.

The preliminaries were gone through with promptness; the
Chair had supped with the speakers, and Mr. Crow had given
him a friendly hint that the boys wouldn't be expecting much
in the way of trimmings from *him*. Stamping and clapping
from the back benches greeted Mr. Farquharson. It diminish-
ed, grew more subdued, as it reached the front. The young
fellows were mostly at the back, and the power of demon-
stration had somehow ebbed in the old ones. The retiring
member addressed his constituents for half an hour. He was
standing before them as their representative for the last time,
and it was natural to look back and note the milestones behind, the changes for the better with which he could fairly
claim association. They were matters of Federal business
chiefly, beyond the immediate horizon of Jordanville, but
Farquharson made them a personal interest for that hour at
all events, and there were one or two points of educational
policy which he could illustrate by their own schoolhouse. He
approached them, as he had always done, on the level of
mutual friendly interest, and in the hope of doing mutual
friendly business. "You know and I know," he said more than
once; they and he knew a number of things together.

He was afraid, he said, that if the doctors hadn't chased him out of politics, he never would have gone. Now, however, that they gave him no choice, he was glad to think that though times had been pretty good for the farmers of South Fox all through the eleven years of his appearance in the political arena, he was leaving it at a moment when they promised to be better still. Already, he was sure, they were familiar with the main heads of that attractive prospect and, agreeable as the subject, great as the policy was to him, he would leave it to be further unfolded by the gentleman whom they all hoped to enlist in the cause, as his successor for this constituency, Mr. Lorne Murchison, and by his friend from the old country, Mr. Alfred Hesketh. He, Farquharson, would not take the words out of the mouths of these gentlemen, much as he envied them the opportunity of uttering them. The French Academy, he told them, that illustrious body of literary and scientific men, had a custom, on the death of a member and the selection of his successor, of appointing one of their number to eulogize the newcomer. The person upon whom the task would most appropriately fall, did circumstances permit, would be the departing academician. In this case, he was happy to say, circumstances did permit—his political funeral was still far enough off to enable him to express his profound confidence in and his hearty admiration of the young and vigorous political heir whom the Liberals of South Fox had selected to stand in his shoes. Mr. Farquharson proceeded to give his grounds for this confidence and admiration, reminding the Jordanville electors that they had met Mr. Murchison as a Liberal standard-bearer in the last general election, when he, Farquharson, had to acknowledge very valuable services on Mr. Murchison's part. The retiring member then thanked his audience for the kind attention and support they had given him for so many years, made a final cheerful joke about a Pagan divinity known as Anno Domini, and took his seat.

They applauded him, and it was plain that they regretted him, the tried friend, the man there was never any doubt about, whose convictions they had repeated, and whose speeches in Parliament they had read with a kind of proprietorship for so long. The Chair had to wait, before introducing Mr. Alfred Hesketh, until the backbenchers had got through with a double rendering of "For He's a Jolly Good Fellow,"

which bolder spirits sent lustily forth from the anteroom
where the little girls kept their hats and comforters, inter-
spersed with whoops. Hesketh, it had been arranged, should
speak next, and Lorne last.

Mr. Hesketh left his wooden chair with smiling ease, the
ease which is intended to level distinctions and put everybody
concerned on the best of terms. He said that though he was no
stranger to the work of political campaigns, this was the first
time that he had had the privilege of addressing a colonial
audience. "I consider," said he handsomely, "that it is a privilege." He clasped his hands behind his back and threw out his
chest.

"Opinions have differed in England as to the value of the
colonies, and the consequence of colonials. I say here with
pride that I have ever been among those who insist that the
value is very high and the consequence very great. The fault is
common to humanity, but we are, I fear, in England, too
prone to be led away by appearances, and to forget that under
a rough unpolished exterior may beat virtues which are the
brightest ornaments of civilization, that in the virgin fields of
the possessions which the good swords of our ancestors wrung
for us from the Algonquins and the—and the other savages—
may be hidden the most glorious period of the British race."

Mr. Hesketh paused and coughed. His audience neglected
the opportunity for applause, but he had their undivided
attention. They were looking at him and listening to him, these
Canadian farmers, with curious interest in his attitude, his
appearance, his inflection, his whole personality as it offered
itself to them—it was a thing new and strange. Far out in the
Northwest, where the emigrant trains had been unloading all
the summer, Hesketh's would have been a voice from home;
but here, in long-settled Ontario, men had forgotten the sound
of it, with many other things. They listened in silence, weighing with folded arms, appraising with chin in hand; they were
slow, equitable men.

"If we in England," Hesketh proceeded, "required a lesson
—as perhaps we did—in the importance of the colonies, we
had it, need I remind you? in the course of the late protracted
campaign in South Africa. Then did the mother country in
deed prove the loyalty and devotion of her colonial sons. Then

were envious nations compelled to see the spectacle of Canadians and Australians rallying about the common flag, eager
to attest their affection for it with their life-blood, and to
demonstrate that they, too, were worthy to add deeds to
British traditions and victories to the British cause."

Still no mark of appreciation. Hesketh began to think them
an unhandsome lot. He stood bravely, however, by the note he
had sounded. He dilated on the pleasure and satisfaction it had
been to the people of England to receive this mark of attach-
ment from far-away dominions and dependencies, on the
cementing of the bonds of brotherhood by the blood of the
alien, on the impossibility that the mother country should
ever forget such voluntary sacrifices for her sake, when, unexpectedly and irrelevantly, from the direction of the cloak-
room, came the expressive comment—"Yah!"

Though brief, nothing could have been more to the purpose, and Hesketh sacrificed several effective points to hurry
to the quotation—

> *What should they know of England*
> *Who only England know?*

which he could not, perhaps, have been expected to forbear.
His audience, however, were plainly not in the vein for compliment. The same voice from the anteroom inquired iron-
cally, "That so?" and the speaker felt advised to turn to more
immediate considerations.

He said he had had the great pleasure on his arrival in this
country to find a political party, the party in power, their
Canadian Liberal party, taking initiative in a cause which he
was sure they all had at heart—the strengthening of the bonds
between the colonies and the mother country. He congratulated the Liberal party warmly upon having shown themselves
capable of this great function— a point at which he was again
interrupted; and he recapitulated some of the familiar arguments about the desirability of closer union from the point
of view of the army, of the Admiralty, and from one which
would come home, he knew, to all of them, the necessity of a
dependable food supply for the mother country in time of
war. Here he quoted a noble lord. He said that he believed
no definite proposals had been made, and he did not understand how any definite proposals could be made; for his part,

if the new arrangement was to be in the nature of a bargain, he would prefer to have nothing to do with it.

"England," he said, loftily, "has no wish to buy the loyalty of her colonies, nor, I hope, has any colony the desire to offer her allegiance at the price of preference in British markets. Even proposals for mutual commercial benefit may be under pinned, I am glad to say, by loftier principles than those of the market-place and the counting-house."

At this one of his hearers, unacquainted with the higher commercial plane, exclaimed, "How be ye goin' to get 'em kept to, then?"

Hesketh took up the question. He said a friend in the audience asked how they were to ensure that such arrange ments would be adhered to. His answer was in the words of the Duke of Dartmoor, "By the mutual esteem, the inherent integrity, and the willing compromise of the British race."

Here someone on the back benches, impatient, doubtless, at his own incapacity to follow this high doctrine, exclaimed in temperately, "Oh, shut up!" and the gathering, remembering that this, after all, was not what it had come for, began to hint that it had had enough in intermittent stamps and uncom promising shouts for "Murchison!"

Hesketh kept on his legs, however, a few minutes longer. He had a trenchant sentence to repeat to them which he thought they would take as a direct message from the distinguished nobleman who had uttered it. The Marquis of Aldeburgh was the father of the pithy thing, which he had presented, as it happened, to Hesketh himself. The audience received it with respect—Hesketh's own respect was so marked—but with misapprehension; there had been too many allusions to the nobility for a community so far removed from its soothing influence. "Had ye no friends among the commoners?" suddenly spoke up a dry old fellow, stroking a long white beard and the roar that greeted this showed the sense of the meeting. Hesketh closed with assurances of the admiration and confidence he felt toward the candidate proposed to their suffrages by the Liberal party that were quite inaudible, and sought his yellow pinewood schoolroom chair with rather forced smile. It had been used once before that day to isolate conspicuous stupidity.

They were at bottom a good-natured and a loyal crowd, and they had not, after all, come there to make trouble, or Mr. Alfred Hesketh might have carried away a worse opinion of them. As it was, young Murchison, whose address occupied the rest of the evening, succeeded in making an impression upon them distinct enough, happily for his personal influence, to efface that of his friend. He did it by the simple expedient of talking business, and as high prices for produce and low ones for agricultural implements would be more interesting there than here, I will not report him. He and Mr. Farquharson waited, after the meeting, for a personal word with a good many of those present, but it was suggested to Hesketh that the ladies might be tired, and that he had better get them home without unnecessary delay. Mrs. Farquharson had less comment to offer during the drive home than Hesketh thought might be expected from a woman of her intelligence, but Miss Milburn was very enthusiastic. She said he had made a lovely speech, and she wished her father could have heard it.

A personal impression, during a time of political excitement, travels unexpectedly far. A week later Mr. Hesketh was concernedly accosted in Main Street by a boy on a bicycle.

"Say, mister, how's the dook?"

"What duke?" asked Hesketh, puzzled.

"Oh, any dook," responded the boy, and bicycled cheerfully away.

Harvey O'Higgins   **SIR**
                              WATSON
                              TYLER

Tyler, Sir Watson, K.C.B. *b.* Coulton, Ont., May 24, 1870;
ed. pub. schools, Univ. of Toronto, grad. 1891; *m.* Alicia
Janes, 1893; Pres. Coulton Street Ry. Co., Coulton Gas
and Electric Co., Farmers' Trust Co., Mechanics' Bank of
Canada, Janes Electric Auto Co., etc. Donor Coulton
Conservatory of Music, Mozart Hall, etc. Founder Coulton
Symphony Orchestra, Beethoven Choir, etc. Conservative
leader. Senate, 1911. Privy Council, Minister without port-
folio, 1912. Knighted 1915 for services to the Empire.—
Canada's Men of Mark.

1

The stairs that Wat descended—
(He had been christened "Wat," not "Watson." He made it
"Watson" later. I am writing of the fall of 1892, when he was
twenty-odd years old.)
The stairs that Wat descended on that crucial Sunday
morning had been designed by an architect who had aspired
to conceal the fact that they were, after all, stairs. He had
disguised them with cushioned corner-seats and stained-glass
windows, with arches of fretwork and screens of spindles, with
niches and turns and exaggerated landings, until they were

almost wholly ornamental and honorific. They remained, however, stairs—just as the whole house remained a house, in spite of everything that had been done to make it what *The Coulton Advertiser* called a "prominent residence." And to Wat, that morning, those stairs were painfully nothing but stairs, leading him directly from a bedroom which he had been reluctant to leave down to a dining-room which he was loath to enter. In the bedroom, since daylight, he had been making up his mind to tell his family something that must soon be told to them. He had decided to tell them at the breakfast-table; and he could have forgiven the architect if the stairs had been a longer respite than they were.

In a dining-room that had been made as peevish with decoration as the stairs he found his father, his mother, and his two sisters already busy with breakfast and a Sunday paper, which, in those early days of Coulton, was imported across the border from Buffalo. His sisters were both younger than he and both pertly independent of their elders, and they did not look up from the illustrated sections of fashion and the drama which they were reading, aside, as they ate. His father seemed always to seize on his hours of family leisure to let his managerial brain lounge and be at rest in the comfortable corpulence of his body; he was stirring his coffee in a humorous reflectiveness that was wholly self-absorbed. Mrs. Tyler smiled apprehensively at her son, but she did not speak. She did not care to disturb the harmony of the domestic silence. Both the harmony and the silence were rare and pleasant to her.

Wat sat down, and humped himself over his fruit, and began to eat with an evident lack of zest. The dining-room maid came and went rustling by. Mrs. Tyler brushed at a persistent crumb among the ribbons on the ample bosom of her morning wrapper, and regarded Wat from time to time with maternal solicitude.

He had once been a delicate, fat boy—before he took a four years' college course in athletics—and she had never been quite convinced of the permanency of his conversion to health. He had come home late the previous night, and he looked pale to her. His lack of appetite was unusual enough to be alarming. He did not begin his customary Sunday morning dispute with his sisters about "hogging" the picture pages of the newspaper.

She broke out at last: "What is it, Wat? Aren't you well?"

"N-no," he stammered, taken by surprise. "I'm all right."

His sisters glanced at him. He was unthinkingly afraid that they might see his secret in his eyes. They had all the devilish penetration of the young female. And he looked down his nose into his coffee-cup with an ostentatious indifference to them as he drank.

Naturally they accepted his manner as a challenge to them. Millie remarked to Ollie that he seemed thin—which was far from true. Ollie replied, with her eyes in her newspaper, that he was probably going into a "decline." He pretended to pay no attention to them; but his mother interfered, as they had expected her to.

"You've no business, now, making fun of Wat about his health," she said. "You know he isn't strong. He's big— but he's soft."

"Soft!" the girls screamed. "Paw, Maw says Wat's soft!"

It *is* incredible, but—at that day, to everybody in the household except his mother—Sir Watson Tyler was a joke. And it *is* incredible, but—in spite of all the honourable traditions of convention to the contrary—these were the family relations in the Tyler home.

Mr. Tyler turned an amused eye on his wife, and she appealed to him with her usual helpless indignation. "Well, I think you ought to speak to the girls, Tom. I don't think it's very nice of them to make fun of their mother."

"But, Maw!" Millie laughed. "You say such funny things we can't help it."

"I don't. You twist everything I say. Wat *isn't* strong. You ought to be ashamed of yourselves."

She scolded them in a voice that was unconvincing, and they replied to her as if she were an incompetent governess for whom they had an affectionate disrespect.

Wat began to fortify himself with food for the announcement which he had to make. He ate nervously—determinedly —even, at last, doggedly. His mother retired into silence. His sisters continued to read.

When they got to discussing some of the society news he

saw an opportunity of leading up to his subject; and when they were talking of a girl whom they had met during the summer, at the lake shore, he put in, "Did you ever meet Miss Janes there?"

They turned their heads without moving their shoulders. "*Lizzie* Janes?"

The tone was not enthusiastic. He cleared his throat before he answered, "Yes."

Millie said, superbly casual: "Uh-huh. Isn't she a *freak*!"

His face showed the effort he made to get that remark down, though he swallowed it in silence. His mother came to his rescue. "Who is she, Wat?"

"A girl I met this summer. I went over there with Jack Webb."

His sisters found his manner strained. They eyed him with suspicion. His mother asked, "What is she like?"

"Well," Millie put in, "she has about as much style—!"

Wat reddened. "She hasn't *your* style, anyway. She doesn't look as if her clothes—"

He was unable to find words to describe how his sisters looked. They looked as if their limp garments had been poured cold over their shoulders and hung dripping down to their bone-thin ankles.

"I'm glad you like her," Millie said. "She's a sight."

He had determined to be politic. It was essential that he should be politic. Yet he, the future leader of a Conservative party, retorted: "It'd do you good to know a few girls like her. The silly crowd *you* go with!"

"Lizzie Janes! That frump!"

He appealed to his mother. "I certainly think *you* ought to call on them, mother. They've been mighty good to me this summer while you were away."

"Well, Wat," she said, "if you wish it—"

"You'll do no such thing!" Millie cried.

The squabble that followed did not end in victory for Wat. It was Millie's contention that they were not bound to receive every "freak" that he might "pick up"; and Mrs. Tyler—who, in social matters, was usually glad to remain in the quiet background of the family—put herself forward inadequately in Wat's behalf. She succumbed to her husband's decision that she "had better leave it to the girls"; he ended the dispute in-differently by leaving the table; and Wat realized, with des-peration, that he had failed in his diplomatic attempt to engage the family interest for Miss Janes by introducing mention of her and her virtues into the table talk.

2

He went back up-stairs to his bedroom and locked himself in with his chagrin and his sentimental secret. It was a secret that showed in a sort of gloomy wistfulness as he stood gazing out the glass door that opened, from one angle of his room, upon a little balcony—an ornamental balcony whose turret top adorned a corner of the Tyler roof with an aristocratically useless excrescence. You will notice it in the picture of "Sir Watson Tyler's Boyhood Home" in *The Canadian Maga-zine*'s article about him. From the door of this balcony, look-ing over the autumn maples of the street, through a gap be-tween the opposite houses, Wat could see the chimney of the Janes house.

It was a remarkable pile of bricks, that chimney. All around it were houses that existed only as neighbours to that one supreme house. And around those were still others, less and less important, containing the undistinguished mass of lives that made up the City of Coulton in which she lived. The heart of interest in Coulton had once been his own home—as, for example, when he came back to it from college for his holidays. Now, when he returned in the evenings from his father's office he found himself on the circumference of a circle of which Miss Janes' home was the vital centre. He saw his own room merely as a window looking toward hers. And this amazing displacement had been achieved so im-perceptibly that he had only just become acutely conscious of it himself.

His mother and his sisters had spent the summer on the clay-lipped lake shore that gave the name of "Surfholm" to the Tyler cottage in the society news of *The Coulton Ad-vertiser*; and Wat and his father had remained in town, from Mondays to Saturdays, to attend to the real-estate and invest-ment business that supplied the Tyler income. (They also

owned the Coulton horse-car line, but it supplied no income
for them.) On a memorable Tuesday evening Wat had
"stopped in" at the Janeses' on his way down-town with his
friend Webb, to let Webb return to Miss Janes some music
that he had borrowed. And, by a determining accident of fate,
as they approached the lamplit veranda of the Janes cottage,
Alicia Janes was sitting behind the vine-hung lattice, reading
a magazine, while her mother played the piano.

Observe: There was no veranda on the Tyler "residence";
no one ever sat outdoors there; and no one ever played anything but dance-music on the Tyler piano. Alicia Janes
looked romantic under the yellow light, in the odour of
flowers, with the background of green leaves about her. Her
mother had more than a local reputation as a teacher of
music, and the melody that poured out of the open French
windows of the parlour was eloquent, impassioned, uplifting.
The introductions were made in a low voice, so as not to
disturb the music, and it was in silence that Alicia put out a
frank hand to Wat and welcomed him with the strong grasp of
a violinist's fingers.

Wat's ordinary tongue-tied diffidence went unnoticed
under these circumstances. He was able to sit down without
saying anything confused or banal. The powerful music,
professionally interpreted, filled him with stately emotions, to
which he moved and sat with an effect of personal dignity and
repose.

These may seem to be details of small importance. But life
has a way of concealing its ominous beginnings and of being
striking only when its conclusions are already foregone. So
death is more dramatic, but less significant, than the un-
perceived inception of the fatal incidents that end in death.
And in the seemingly trivial circumstances of Wat's introduction to the Janes veranda there were hidden the germs of
vital alterations for him—alterations that were to affect the life
of the whole community of Coulton, and, if the King's birthday list is to be believed, were to be important even to the
British Empire.

Alicia Janes was dressed in a belted black gown, like an art
student, with a starched Eton collar and cuffs. Instead of the
elaborate coiffure of the day's style she wore her dark hair

simply parted and coiled low on her neck in a Rossetti mode.
Her long olive face would have been homely if it had not been
for her eyes. They welcomed Wat with the touching smile of
a sensitive independence, and he did not notice that her lips
were thin and her teeth prominent. In dress and manner she
was unlike any of the young women whom he had met in the
circle of his sisters' friends; if she had been like them, the
memory of past embarrassments would probably have inhi-
bited every expression of his mind. Her surroundings were
different from any to which he had been accustomed; and, as a
simple consequence, he was quite unlike himself in his
accustomed surroundings. Perhaps it was the music most of
all that helped him. It carried him as a good orchestra might
carry an awkward dancer, uplifted into a sudden confident
grace.

When she asked him some commonplace questions in an
undertone he replied naturally, forgetting himself. He listened
to the music and he looked at her, seriously thrilled. When
Webb asked her if she wouldn't play the violin, and she
replied that she always played badly before strangers, Wat
begged her in a voice of genuine anxiety not to consider him
a stranger. She said, "I'll play for you the next time you
come." And he was so grateful for the implied invitation to
come again that his "Thank you" was sincere beyond elo-
quence. He even met her mother without embarrassment,
although Mrs. Janes was an enigmatic-looking, dark woman
with a formidable manner. She became more friendly when
she understood that he was the son of the Tylers of Queen's
Avenue, and he felt that he was accepted as a person of some
importance, like herself. That was pleasant.

After a half-hour on the veranda he went on down-town
with Webb, as calm outwardly as if he had parted from old
friends, and so deeply happy in the prospect of seeing her
again that he was quite unaware of what had happened to
him. The following afternoon he telephoned to her eagerly.
And he was back with her that night for hours in the lamplight, among the vines—without Webb— talking, smiling, and
listening with profound delight while she played the violin to
her mother's piano.

And there was an incredible difference between Wat on the

veranda and Wat at home. Under his own roof he was a large-headed, heavy-shouldered, apparently slow-witted, shy youth, who read in his room, exercised alone in a gymnasium which he had put in his attic during a college vacation, wrote long letters to former classmates in other cities, and, going out to the post-box, mooned ponderously around the streets till all hours. He had never anything much to say. Although he never met any one if he could avoid it, and suffered horribly in a drawing-room, he was—like most shy men—particular to the point of effeminacy about his appearance. He bathed and shaved and brushed his hair and fussed over his clothes absurdly, morning and night. He was, in fact, in many ways ridiculous.

On the Janes veranda he was nothing of the sort. As the son of the owner of the Coulton street-car line and the Tyler real estate, he was a young man of social importance in a home where the mother earned a living by teaching music and the daughter had only the prospect of doing the same. He was a man of the practical world, whose opinions were authoritative. He was well dressed and rather distinguished-looking, with what has since been called "a brooding forehead." He was fond of reading, and he had the solid knowledge of a slow student who assimilated what he read. Alicia deferred to him with an inspiring trust in his wisdom and his experience. She deferred even to his judgment in music—for which, it transpired, he had an acute ear and a fresh appreciation. She played to him as eagerly as a painter might show his sketches to a wealthy enthusiast who was by way of becoming a collector. Their evenings together were full of interest, of promise, of talk and laughter, of serious converse and melodic emotion.

There was in those days, in Coulton, no place of summer amusement to which a young pair could make an excuse of going in order to be together, so that Wat was never called on to make a public parade of his devotion. The best that he could do was to take Alicia to her church. But it was not *his* church. He was not known there. Mrs. Janes was the church organist; Alicia often added the music of her violin; and she sat always in the choir. Wat, in a back pew downstairs was inconspicuous and not coupled with her. It was for these

reasons that his interest in Miss Janes was not at once generally known. That was entirely accidental.

But it was not an accident that he did not make it known to
his family. At first he foresaw and dreaded only the amusement of his sisters. Wat "girling"! What next! And then he
shrank from the effect on Alicia Janes of getting the family
point of view on him. It was almost as if he had been roman-
ticizing about himself and knew that his family would tell her
the truth. And finally, as guilty as if he were leading a double
life, he confronted the problem that haunts all double lives—
the problem of either keeping them apart or of uniting them in
any harmony. As long as his family had been at "Surfholm" it
had not been necessary that they should recognize Miss Janes,
but, now that they were back in town, every day that they
ignored her was an insult to her and an accusation of him.

He had to tell them. He had to put into words the beautiful
secret of his feeling for her. "That freak!" He had to introduce
Alicia to his home and to the shame of his belittlement in his
home, and let his contemptuous sisters disillusion her about
him.

A horrible situation! Believe me or not, of a career so
distinguished as Sir Watson's this was the most crucial point,
the most agonized moment. It is not even hinted at in the
official accounts of his career, yet never in his life afterward
was he to be so racked with emotion, so terrified by the real
danger of losing everything in the world that could make the
world worth living in. And never afterward was he forced to
choose a course that meant so much not only to himself, but to
the world in which he lived.

3

That is why I have chosen this autumn Sunday of 1892
as the most notable day to scrutinize and chronicle in a char-
acter-study of Sir Watson Tyler. I should like to commemo-
rate every moment of it, but, as the memoir-writers say—
when their material is running short—space forbids. You will
have to imagine him trying to dress in order to take Miss
Janes to church: struggling through a perspiring ecstasy of
irresolution in the choice of a necktie, straining into a Sunday

coat that made him look round-shouldered because of the bulging muscularity of his back, cursing his tailor, hating his hands because they hung red and bloated below his cuffs, hating his face, his moon face, his round eyes, his pudding of a forehead, and all those bodily characteristics that were to mark him, to his later biographers, as a born leader among men, "physically as well as mentally dominant."

He never went to church, to his family's knowledge, so he had to wait until they had gone in order to avoid inconvenient questions. They were always late. He watched them, behind the curtains of his window, till they rounded the circular driveway and reached the street. Five minutes later he was cutting across the lawn, scowling under a high hat that always pinched his forehead, on his way to the Janeses'.

He did not arrive there. He decided that he was too late. He decided he could not arrive there without having first made up his mind what to do. And he turned aside to wander through the residential streets of Coulton, pursued by the taunts of the church-bells. He came to the weed-grown vacant lots and the withered fields of market-gardeners in a northern suburb that was yet to be nicknamed "Tylertown." He ended beside Smith's Falls, where the Coulton River drops twenty feet over a ridge into the Coulton Valley; and he sat down on a rock, in his high hat, on the site of the present power-house— his power-house—that has put the light and heat of industrial life into the whole community. He resolved to see his mother privately, tell her the truth, get her to help him with his father, and let his sisters do their worst.

But it was not easy to see Mrs. Tyler privately in her home on Sunday. They had a long and solemn noon dinner that was part of the ritual of the day, and after dinner she always sat with her husband and her daughters in the sitting-room upstairs, indulging her domestic soul in the peace of a family reunion that seemed only possible to the Tylers on Sunday afternoon when they were gorged like a household of pythons. Wat retired to his bedroom. Every twenty minutes he wandered downstairs, passed the door of the sitting-room slowly, and returned up the back stairs by stealth. They heard him pacing the floor overhead. Millie listened to him thoughtfully. The younger sister, Ollie, was trying to write letters on notepaper of robin's-egg blue, and she blamed him for all the difficulties of composition; it was so distracting to have him paddling around like that. Finally, when his mother heard him creaking down the stairs for the fourth time, she called out: "Wat! What *is* the matter with you? If you're restless, why don't you go for a walk?"

He answered, hastily, "I'm going," and continued down to the lower hall. Millie waited to hear the front door shut behind him. She had just remembered what he said at breakfast about Jack Webb taking him to see the Janes girl. She went at once to the library to telephone.

And she came flying back with the news that while they had been away Wat had been spending almost every evening with Lizzie Janes; that he had been going to see her since their return; that Jack Webb thought they were engaged. "And the first thing *we* know," she said, "he'll be married to her."

Mr. Tyler tilted one eyebrow. He thought he understood that there were things that were not *in* Wat.

"Well, what's the matter with him, then?" Millie demanded. "Why has he been hiding it, and sneaking off to see her and never saying a word about it, if he isn't ashamed of it and afraid to tell us? They've roped him in. That's what I think. Lizzie Janes is a regular old maid now. If she isn't engaged to Wat, she intends to be. No one else would ever marry her. I bet they've been working Wat for all they're worth. They're as *poor*—"

Her father continued incredulous.

"Well," she cried, "Jack Webb says Wat's been going to church with her twice a Sunday."

Wat's indolent aversion to church-going being well known, this was the most damning piece of evidence she could have produced against him.

Mrs. Tyler pleaded, "She can't be a *bad* girl if she goes to church twice a—"

"What difference does that make?" Millie demanded. "It doesn't make it any better for *us*, does it?"

"I'll speak to Wat," Mrs. Tyler promised, feebly.

"It's no use speaking to Wat! *He* has nothing to do with it. Any one can turn Wat around a little finger."

"Do you know her?" Mr. Tyler asked.

"I used to know her—before she went to—when she was at school here. She used to wear thick stockings, and woollen mitts."

Ollie added, as the final word of condemnation, "Home-made!"

Mr. Tyler may have felt that he did not appreciate the merit of these facts. He made a judicial noise in his throat and said nothing.

"She's older than any of us—than Wat, too."

"Well," he said, reaching for his newspaper, "I suppose Wat'll do what he likes. He's not likely to do anything remarkable one way or the other."

"He's not going to marry Lizzie Janes," Millie declared. "Not if *I* can help it."

"Millie," her mother scolded, "you've no right interfering in Wat's affairs. He's older than you are—"

"It isn't only Wat's affair," she cried. "She isn't only going to marry Wat. We're thrown in with the bargain. I guess we have something to say."

"Tom!" Mrs. Tyler protested. "If you let her—"

"Well," he ruled, "Wat hasn't even taken the trouble to ask us what we thought about it. I don't feel called on to help him. It means more to the girls than it does to us, in any case. They'll have to put up with her for the rest of her life."

"I guess *not!*" Millie said, confidently.

"Now, Millie!" her mother threatened. "If you—"

"If you want Lizzie Janes and her mother in this family," Millie said, "*I* don't. I guess it won't be hard to let Wat and them know it, either. And if *you* won't," she ended, defiantly, as she turned away, "*I will!*"

She went out and Ollie followed. Mrs. Tyler dropped back in her chair, gazing speechlessly at her husband. He caught her eye as he turned a page of his paper "All right, now," he said. "Wait till Wat comes."

They waited. Millie did not. She distrusted her mother's partiality for Wat, and she distrusted her father's distaste for interfering in any household troubles. She trusted herself only, assured that if Wat's ridiculous misalliance was to be prevented it must be prevented by her; and she felt that it could be easily prevented, because it *was* ridiculous, because Wat

was ridiculous, because Lizzie Janes was absurd. What was
Wat's secrecy in the affair but a confession that he was
ashamed of it? What was Lizzie Janes' sly silence but an evidence
that she had hoped to hook Wat before his family
knew what was going on?

What indeed? She asked it of Ollie, and Ollie asked it of
her. They had locked themselves in Millie's bedroom to consult
together—Ollie sitting, tailor-wise, cross-legged on the
bed, and Millie gesticulating up and down the room—in one
of those angry councils of war against their elders in which
they were accustomed to face the cynical facts of life with
a frankness that would have amazed mankind.

4

And Wat, meantime, arrived at the door of the Janes house
because it was impossible for him *not* to arrive there. Alicia
greeted him with her usual unchanging, gentle smile. He
began to explain why he had not come that morning to take
her to church; that his family—

"There's some one here," she said, unheeding. "Some one
who wants to meet you. My brother!" And touching him
lightly on the shoulder, she turned him toward the parlour
and ushered him in to meet his future in the shape of Howard
Janes.

Janes was then a tall, gaunt, feverish-eyed, dark enthusiast
of an extraordinary mental and physical restlessness—a man
who should have been a visionary, but had become an electrical
engineer. He had been working on the project to develop
electrical power at Niagara Falls, and in ten minutes
he was describing to Wat the whole theory and progress of
the work, past, present, and future. "In ten years," he said,
"Niagara power will be shot all through this district for a
hundred miles around, and here's Coulton asleep, with one of
the best power projects in Canada right under its nose. Where's
Smith's Falls. And here *you* are, with a dead town, a dead
street-car line, a lot of dead real estate, and the power to make
the whole thing a gold-mine running to waste over that hill.
Why, man, if it was an oil-field you'd be developing it like
mad. Because it's electricity no one seems to see it. And in
ten years it will be too late."

He talked to Wat as if Wat owned the car line, the real estate, the town itself, and when Wat glanced at Alicia she was *looking* at him as if he owned them. The power of that look was irresistible—hypnotic. He began to listen as if he owned the car lines and the real estate, to think as if he owned them, to ask questions, and finally to reply as if he owned them. Very grave, with his eyes narrowed, silent, he became a transportation magnate considering a development scheme proposed by an industrial promoter.

They were interrupted by the telephone in the hall. Alicia answered it. "It's for you," she said to Wat, looking at him significantly. "Your sister."

He went to the phone, puzzled. It was Millie's voice. "You're to come home at once," she said.

Wat asked, "What's the matter?"

"You know what's the matter," she snapped, "as well as I do. You're wanted home here at once." And while the meaning of that was slowly reaching him, through the pre-occupied brain of the railroad magnate, she added, "I don't wonder you were ashamed to tell us!" and slapped up the receiver.

He stood a moment at the phone, pale. And in that moment history was made. He went back to Alicia, face front, head up. She looked at him expectantly. "They want me to bring you to see them," he said.

It was what she had expected, he supposed. Mark it as the beginning of his great career. What she expected! There's the point. That's the secret, as I see it, of the making of Sir Watson Tyler.

After a moment's hesitation she went to put on her hat. He said to her brother: "Can you wait till we get back? We'll be only a few minutes. I want to go into this thing with you in detail." And when he was on the street with her he explained, merely: "I want you to meet mother. I don't suppose we'll see dad. He's always so busy he doesn't pay much attention to what goes on at home."

"I don't think I've ever seen any of your family," she said, "except your sisters." She was thinking of them as she used to see them in their school-days, in short dresses, giggling, and chewing candy in the street-cars.

"They're very young," Wat warned her, "and they've been
spoiled. You mustn't mind if Millie— She's been allowed to
do pretty much as she likes. Our life at home isn't like yours,
you know. I think our house is too big. We seem to be—sort
of separated in our rooms."

Strange! He appeared apologetic. She did not understand
why—unless it was that he was fearful of her criticism of his
family. She knew that they were not socially distinguished,
except by newspaper notice; but she thought she had no rev-
erence for social position. And he could hardly be apologizing
for their income.

5

The house, as they approached it, was pretentious, but that
was probably the architect's fault. It was modestly withdrawn
behind its trees, its flower-beds, and its lawns. For a moment
she saw herself, in her simple costume, coming to be passed
upon by the eyes of an alien wealth. Wat was silent, occupied
with his own thoughts. He rang absent-mindedly.

A maid opened a door on a hall that was architecturally
stuffy and not furnished in the rich simplicity that Alicia had
expected. And the sight of the drawing-room was a shock. It
was overcrowded with pink-upholstered shell-shaped furniture
that gave her a note of overdressed bad taste. The carpet was
as richly gaudy as a hand-painted satin pincushion. The bric-a-
brac, of a florid costliness, cluttered the mantelpieces and the
table-tops like a tradesman's display. The pictures on the wall
were the family photographs and steel engravings of an
earlier home. It was a room of undigested dividends, and she
thought that she began to see why Wat had been apologetic.
To his credit he seemed uncomfortable in it. "I'll just tell
them you're here," he said.

He left her there and went out to the stairs. Millie was
coming down to see who had rung. "Well," she cried from a
landing above him as he ascended resolutely, "will you tell
us what you think you're doing with that Lizzie Janes?"

He caught her by the arm. He said in a voice that was new
to her: "I've brought her to call on mother. Tell her she's
here."

"You've brought her to—! I'll do nothing of the kind. You can just take her away again. *I* don't want her, and *they* don't want her." She had begun to raise her voice, with the evident intention of letting any one hear who would. "If she thinks she can—"

"That's enough!" He stopped her angrily, with his hand over her mouth. "You ought to be—"

She struggled with him, striking his hand away. "How *dare* you! If you think that Lizzie Janes—"

He was afraid that Alicia might hear it. He grabbed her up roughly and began to carry her upstairs, fighting with him, furious at the indignity—for he had caught her where he could, with no respect for her body or her clothes. No one, in years, had dared to lay hands on her, no matter what she did; the sanctity of her fastidious young person was an inviolable right to her; and Wat's assault upon it was brutal to her, degrading, atrocious. She became hysterical, in a clawed and tousled passion of shame and resentment. He carried her to her room, tossed her on to her bed, and left her, face down on her pillows, sobbing, outraged. She could have killed him— or herself.

He straightened his necktie and strode into the sitting-room.

"Why, Wat!" his mother cried. "What's the matter?"

"Miss Janes," he said, "is downstairs. I've brought her to call on you."

She rose, staring. His father looked at him, surprised, over the top of his paper. "Well," he demanded, "what's all this about Miss Janes, anyway?"

Wat gave him back his look defiantly. "She's the finest girl I've ever met. And I'm going to marry her, if I can."

"Oh," Mr. Tyler said, and returned to his news.

Ollie rushed out to find her sister.

Wat turned his amazing countenance on his mother.

"Yes, Wat," she replied to it—and went with him obediently.

6

Of the interview that followed in the drawing-room there were several conflicting reports made. Ollie slipped down quietly to hear the end of it—after a stupefying account from

Millie of what had happened—but *her* report to Millie is negligible. From that night both the girls ceased to exist as factors in Wat's life; he saw them and heard them thereafter only absent-mindedly.

Mrs. Tyler's report was made in voluble excitement to her husband, who listened, frowning, over his cigar. "And, Tom, you wouldn't have known him," she said. "He wasn't like—like himself at all! It was so pretty. They're so in love with each other. She's such a sweet girl."

"Well," he grumbled, "I'll have nothing to do with it. It's in your department. If it was one of the girls it'd be different. I suppose Wat'll have to do his own marrying. He's old enough. I hope she'll make a man of him."

" 'A man of him!' She! Why, she's as—No, indeed! You ought to see the way *she* defers to *him*. She's as proud of him! And he's as *different*!"

He was unconvinced. "I'm glad to hear it. You'd better go and look after Millie. She accuses him of assault and battery."

"It serves her right. I'll not go near her. And, Tom," she said, "he wants to talk to you about a plan he has for the railway—for using electric light to run it, or something like that."

"Huh! Who put that in his head?"

"Oh, he made it up himself. Her brother's an engineer, and they've been talking about it."

"I suppose!" he said. "She'll be working the whole Janes family in on us." He snorted. "I'm glad someone's put something into his head besides eating and sleeping."

"Now, Tom," she pleaded, "you've got to be fair to Wat!"

"All right, Mary," he relented. "Run along and see Millie. I've had enough for *one* Sunday."

As for Alicia Janes, it was late at night when she made her report to her mother in a subdued tremble of excitement. She had overheard something of Wat's scuffle with Millie on the stairway, but she did not speak of it except to say: "I'm afraid the girls are awful. The youngest, Ollie, is overdressed and silly—with the manners of a spoiled child of ten. It's her mother's fault. She's one of those helpless big women. Wat must have got his qualities from his father."

"Did you find out why they hadn't called?"

"No-o. But I can guess."

"Yes?"

"Well, it isn't a nice thing to say, but I really think Wat's rather—as if he were ashamed of them. And I don't wonder, mother! Their front room's furnished with that— Oh, and such bric-a-brac!" She paused. She hesitated. She blushed. "Wat asked me if I'd— You know he had never really spoken before, although I knew he—"

Her mother said, softly, "Yes?"

She looked down at the worn carpet. "And I really felt so sorry for him— The family's awful, I know, but he's so— I said I would."

7

She had said she would. And Wat, long after midnight, lying on his back in bed, staring up at the darkness, felt as if he were afloat on a current that was carrying him away from his old life with more than the power of Niagara. His mind was full of Howard Janes's plans for harnessing Smith's Falls, of electrifying the street railway, of lighting Coulton with electricity and turning the vacant Tyler lots of the northern suburb into factory sites. He was thinking of incorporations, franchises, capitalizations, stocks, bonds, mortgages, and loans. He had been talking them over with Janes for hours on the veranda, at the supper-table, on the street. There had been no music. As Wat was leaving he had spoken to Alicia hastily in the hall—asking her to marry him in fact—and she had said, "Oh, Wat!" clinging to his hands as he kissed her. He could still feel that tremulous confiding grasp of her strong fingers as she surrendered her life to him, depending on him, proud of him, humble to him. He shivered. He was afraid.

And that was to be only the first of many such frightened midnights. A thousand times he was to ask himself: "What am I doing? Why have I gone into this business? It'll kill me! It'll worry me to death!" He had gone into it because Alicia had expected him to; but he did not know it. The maddest thing he ever did—

It was when the power scheme had been successfully

floated, the street railway was putting out long radial lines along the country roads, and the gas company was willing to sell out to him in order to escape the inevitable clash of competition with his electric light. The banks suddenly began to make trouble about carrying him. He was in their debt for an appalling amount. He felt that he ought to prepare his wife for the worst. "Well, Wat," she said, reproachfully, when she understood him, "if the banks are going to bother you, I don't see why you don't get a bank of your own."

It was as if she thought he could buy a bank in a toy-shop. She expected it of him. Miracles! nothing but miracles! And it was the maddest thing he ever did, but he went after the moribund Farmers' Trust Company, got it with his father's assistance, reorganized it and put it on its feet, while he held up the weak-kneed power projects and Janes talked manufacturers into buying power sites. The Mechanics' Bank of Canada passed to him later, but by that time he was running, at "Tylertown," an automobile factory, a stone-crusher, a carborundum works, and the plant of Coulton's famous Eleco Breakfast Food, cooked by electricity, and the success of the whole city of Coulton was so involved with his fortunes that he simply could not be allowed to fail.

And here was the fact that made the whole thing possible: Janes had the vision and the daring necessary to attempt their undertakings, but he could not have carried them out; whereas Wat would never have gone beyond the original power-house; but with Janes talking to him and Alicia looking at him he moved ahead with a stolid, conservative caution and a painstaking care of detail that made every move as safe and deliberate as a glacial advance. He worked day and night, methodically, with a ceaseless application that would have worn out a less solid and lethargic man. It was as if, having eaten and slept—and nothing else—for twenty years, he could do as he pleased about food now, and never rest at all. He was wonderful. His mind digested everything, like his stomach, slowly, but without distress. His shyness, now deeply concealed, made him silent, unfathomable. He had no friends, because he confided in no one; he was too diffident to do it. Behind his inscrutable silence he studied and watched the men with whom he had to work, moving like a quiet engineer among the machinery which he had started, and the uproar of it. And the moment he decided that a man was wrong he took him out and dropped him clean, without feeling, without any friendly entanglement to deter him, silently.

He had to go into politics to protect his franchises, and he became the "Big Business Interests" behind the local campaign; but he never made a public appearance; he managed campaign funds, sat on executive committees, was consulted by the party leaders, and passed upon policies and candidates. *The Coulton Advertiser* annoyed him, and he bought it. His wife had gathered about her a number of music-lovers, and they formed a stringed orchestra that studied and played in the music-room of Wat's new home on the hill above "Tylertown." She expected him to be present, and he rarely failed. As a matter of fact, he seldom heard more than the first few bars of a composition, then, emotionalized, his brain excited, he sat planning, reviewing, advancing, and reconsidering his work. Music had that effect on him. It enlivened his lumbering mind. He became as addicted to it as if it were alcohol.

He followed his wife into a plan for the formation of a symphony orchestra, which he endowed. When there was no proper building for it he put up Mozart Hall and gave it to the city. She wanted to hear Beethoven's Ninth Symphony, so the orchestra had to be supplemented with a choir. He endowed the Coulton Conservatory of Music when she objected that she could not get voices or musicians because there was no way in Coulton to educate or train them. And in doing these things he gave Coulton its fame as a musical centre. (Lamplight on the veranda, and Mrs. Janes playing the piano behind the open French windows!)

It was the campaign against reciprocity that put him in the Senate. He believed that reciprocity with the United States would ruin his factories. He headed the committee of Canadian manufacturers that raised the funds for the national campaign against the measure. The consequent defeat of the Liberal party put his friends in power. They rewarded him with a Senatorship. He was opposed to taking it, but his wife expected him to. He went into the Cabinet, as Minister without portfolio, a year later. It was inevitable. He was the financial head of the party; they had to have him at their government councils. When the war with Germany broke out he gave full pay to all of his employees that volunteered. He endowed a battery of machine-guns from Coulton. Every factory that he controlled he turned into a munition-works. He contributed lavishly to the Red Cross. And, of course, he was knighted.

It is an open secret that he will probably be made Lord Coulton when the readjustment of the colonial affairs of the Empire takes him to London. He will be influential there; he has the silent, conservative air of ponderous authority that England trusts. And Lady Tyler is a poised, gracious, and charming person who will be popular socially. She, of course, is of no importance to the Empire. She still looks at Wat worshipfully, without any suspicion that it was she who made him—not the slightest.

I do not know how much of the old Wat is left in him. His silence covers him. It is impossible to tell how greatly the quality and texture of his mind may have changed under the exercise and labour of his gigantic undertakings. I saw him when he was in New York to hear the Coulton orchestra and choir give the Ninth Symphony, to the applause of the most critical. ("The scion of a noble house," one of the papers called him.) And it certainly seemed impossible—although I swear I believe it is true—that the solid magnificences of the man and his achievements were all due to the fact that when he came back from the Janes telephone to confront the expectancy of Alicia Janes, on that Sunday night in 1892, he said, "They want me to bring you to see them," instead of saying, "They want me at home."

Raymond Knister　　　　**THE LOADING**

Jesse Culworth's air that morning announced that he did not even wish to seem tranquil. His wife, sensitive, as always, to his temper, felt that. So did Garland, his son. When he came in at half-past six from the before-breakfast chores he glowered silently half-sitting, half-leaning with folded arms against the sewing machine, toward the boy, who was washing at the kitchen sink. "Come, Ma," he said to his wife, "dish the porridge up! We're just ready."

When he had washed they sat down. The room was dimly lit by vine-covered windows. Sunbeams made numerous rays through the leaves of virginia creeper, targetting at bright spots on the fading dark paper of the opposite wall. The table at which they sat seemed to half-fill the kitchen. Jesse, strong-looking and unbent of shoulders at forty, ate his oatmeal with melancholy gusto, at times heavily regarding his wife at the other end of the table. He held out his cup and saucer in silence for more tea. As Nettie filled the cup he said, "Whoa!", his use of the accustomed word so abrupt and morose that, startled, his wife passed the cup back. He drank the tea slowly. On his regular thick features a slight moisture could be seen in the dim light of the warm kitchen.

"Going to take them hogs in to town this morning," he

announced to his son as he leaned back in his chair after finishing the tea. "Old Gus told me last night he guessed he'd take 'em."

The good humours of Jesse rather preceded than followed his visits to town. He would see Charlie Alten, or some others of his early friends driving about the village in their motors after the closing of their stores. Always after greeting one of them he would bite his lip and mutter to himself, drawing back his shoulders, "What a fool I was, what a fool! They didn't have any more schooling than I did. To go out on that blasted unearthly farm!" His mother who was living in the village after the death of her husband persuaded him into taking a farm as soon as he had finished high-school. She was intolerably afraid that he would not "settle down," for until his death her husband had not. Jesse stuck to the farm during good years because they might continue, and he wouldn't quit in a poor year because then it and the stock could not be sold for what they were worth. Of late the years seemed mostly alike. The details of his ill-luck became to him of less and less interest except as a subject for objurgation. To heavy rains and droughts he resigned himself almost with enjoyment. If anyone's clover failed to "catch," it was his; if anyone's wheat winter-killed, his did. Hoof and mouth disease broke out miles away to head straight to his stable.

"I should guess he would take 'em, the price he's paying now!" Culworth grunted, looking to his wife for approval of the wit.

There was silence. Like most men he had made a phrase of his own, which he liked to use. His was, "the devilishness of things in general." He took pleasure in using it in the presence of his wife. Aside from her feeling of a discomfortable approach to blasphemy Nettie Culworth did not like such words to be said before her son. Now Jesse eschewed it in a feeling of deprivation. Yet he came down hard on the boy if inadvertently he used any of such gross terms as naturally he would pick up. Jesse seemed to think that no one else was justified in such behaviour.

Without speaking Garland finished his glass of milk and rose. Lifting his chair back from the table he set it against the wall.

"Load 'em in the wagon, eh?" he asked.

"Yes, but the darn horses haven't come up from the bush yet. You'll have to go after them. They'll stay all day."

"It's too bad they can't learn to come up in the mornings," said Nettie, looking at her fifteen-year-old son. "It's a long walk back there."

The boy had taken his broad curling hat from the nail. "Oh, I don't mind it," he mumbled as he let the screen-door swing to behind him.

II

It was the beginning of a June day, warm yet fresh. The young boy walked down the rail-fenced lane to the back of the farm; and the surrounding grass and corn, the weeds in the fence-corners, the inadvertent sounding of insects, a bird alighting on a top rail, the mist hanging in the middle distance and opening a horizon about him as he went, made a whole which was more to him than the vague thoughts which came to his mind. He was at peace. He kept steadily on his way toward the bush, still a wide hidden shape before him in the morning.

The bush was beautiful in its attempted negation of colour, its fragrance and a kind of reserve of warmth. The trees stood dozing, or whispering a little softly so as not to rouse the others. Near the front of the lot, where they were fewer, some of them had always had each a character of its own for Garland. One, he could not tell why, reminded him of an old calm church elder as he stood outside the church after service and greeted the people, his long beard moving. Another one was like a statue of a lion. It was strong-rooted and gnarled. Another was some slender fleet animal, he knew not what, and he wondered, before pausing in the wake of phantasies of his earlier childhood, why it had not sprung away and left the bush since he had been there last.

The boy began calling through the thin woods as he walked. He was at a loss in what direction to go that he might find the horses. He began to walk around the edge of the bush within a few rods of the line fence. The echo of his voice seemed muffled distantly, and to come back about him through the trees and the mist. The near trees became columns upholding clouds as he moved toward them. He had made almost a complete circuit when he decided to strike in to the centre of the wood and to finish examination of the outskirts if necessary afterward.

Now uneasiness came to him, as he thought of his father's waiting, and he walked more quickly.

III

Jesse was growing more and more impatient as the time passed. When he had fed the hogs generously he greased the wagon and put the sides on the rack which was used to haul livestock to market. He could have found plenty of odd jobs for an hour yet, but he did not think of them in his increasing disquiet. He would go to the head of the lane and look down it for the string of horses which should be coming. "Blame the boy, what's ailin' him?" he muttered. The sun was beginning to shine out warmly, and to Jesse as he came forth from pitching down hay for noon from the loft to the stable below it seemed as though the morning were half gone. His annoyance was not lessened when he considered that probably he might not with a show of justice reproach the boy.

He went to the house. After he had taken a drink of water, he breathed heavily, glanced at himself in the mirror above the sink, and stood over the bare cleared wooden table a moment, his hands on each side of yesterday's paper.

Nettie Culworth came from the pantry to look into the oven.

"I wonder what on earth can be keeping that boy! There's no get-up about him. He's been gone for hours. Lot of help he is!" The back of his hand bristled across his mouth.

"He's likely doing the best he can, Jesse," his wife replied, not pausing in her work. "Don't scold him when he comes up. It's a long way back there."

He grunted as he started up from the table and the screen-door cracked to behind him, but made no answer in words. A little relieved by this passage he strode to the corner of the barn. The horses were coming up the lane, old Dan leading them, and Garland behind. Impatiently the father waited.

"Well, you've been long enough!" he called as they came nearer. "You had to run them all over the bush before you could get hold of them, eh?" He was smiling.

"No. . . . I couldn't find them, father."

"Oh! —Well, round 'em up there, hurry up, don't be all day." He slid the door open and stood back at one side of it.

But the other horses were not inclined to follow old Dan into the stable. They swerved away from Jesse and around the small strawstack in the middle of the barn-yard.

"Git after them!" he called to his son. "*Be* quick! Bring them around the stack and I'll watch here."

The boy was already gone, and there was a moment of rustling through the straw and a dry musty smell, then the horses came tearing and plunging from around the stack. Jesse shouted and waved his arms, but he had nothing in his hands to frighten them back. They passed him and went down the lane. Garland leaped the fence and headed them off there, while Jesse strode to the stable door, "Show 'em next time," he muttered, gripping a fork-handle firmly. His impatience, or whatever it was, was augmented by the failure to stay the horses in the presence of his son.

This time one of the horses, head and tail up, came alone from behind the stack. The man ran forward to steer it into the door, but it darted away, leaving him beside the wall when a second one came toward him. He ran swiftly to the gate, growling between his clenched teeth, "Who-oah, *you*!" He thought for an instant he had it, but it was passing him. He unconsciously swerved a little when he saw that they were going through the gate together and did not see protruding at an angle from the post a stiff wire, which grazed his cheek. He stopped and held one hand to his face intently a moment, not looking around, then with set jaw and without a word twisted the wire violently until it was broken off.

Garland looked on at this a moment, then remembered the horses, and went to drive them up a third time. The animals appeared to realize that their mischief had gone far enough for that morning, and came around quietly.

Jesse and his son entered the stable in silence. The boy was making for the box containing the curry-combs and brushes, when he saw that his father took down a collar from the peg. He also lifted down a collar and began to unbuckle its top. Jesse went to a stall.

"Get over here!" he said.

The animal seemed to hesitate, and did not move, so he quietly laid the collar down and bracing his powerful frame against the planks pushed the back part of the horse violently against the opposite wall. Then he seized and held it by the halter and began to kick its stomach. "Show—you!" he grunted between the blows. After that he put on the collar.

Garland stood looking on, pale, for a few seconds, then he entered the stall of the other horse. When he had buckled the collar about its neck his father was waiting with its harness, instead of that of the horse which he had just been abusing. The animal started, knocking its knees in a tattoo against the manger, as he flung upon it the heavy harness which hung down over it behind. Jesse lifted the harness again, and came farther forward in the stall before again flinging it on the horse's back.

"What's the matter with *you*?" he asked tensely, seizing its halter and backing it in order to get at the hames. "You won't eh?" he continued as the horse made a convulsive movement forward, and struck it on the side of the muzzle.

"Father!" cried Garland.

"What's ailin' you?" asked Jesse, looking at his son for a second.

The latter said nothing, but looked shamefacedly away toward the strong glare of sunlight on the rhomboid of dirty stained cement within the door, which made the rest of the interior of the stable still more dim. Outside the sun shone fiercely on the ragged edge of the tarnished strawstack and made each straw where a forkful had been freshly taken look like a precious bit of gold. A dry stifling smell came from the hot barnyard.

"What d'you have to start them running around the stack for then? You knew too well! Or else you'll never learn." The unshaven face was yellow-black in the dim light as the man wrenched the straps into place. "What are you standing there for?" he exclaimed, raising his voice. "Haven't you lost enough time yet, eh?"

The boy reached up the pegs, standing on his toes, and with an effort swung a heavy harness down from them. It was dankly coated with greasy sweat. Holding the front of it in his hands he moved toward the stall. Jesse came and seizing the rear of the harness swung it to the horse's back. The animal pranced and nearly trampled the boy's feet.

"What d'you got to drag it over the floor for? If you can't pick it up, leave it alone."

They went out into the heat of the sun a short distance along the dry lane to the pig yard. The enclosure was meant for a paddock but was long since beaten to a dust by the little hoofs, and only straggling unpalatable weeds stood yet, gray with dust. It was necessary to get the hogs into the pen in order to load them. Finally after a protracted hot struggle this end was accomplished. Each one demanded individual cornering and persuasion, but the last one of all required them after a few minutes' chasing to capture him. Seizing his short hind legs they dragged him raucously complaining to the pen.

When the door was closed on him and his comrades rallying around to welcome with excited gruntings his escape, Jesse had begun to accede to a grim good-humour. He had shown them! And Garland had employed quickness and a good deal of wiry strength.

"You'll make a farmer yet," he said, as though unbendingly. He took off his hat and rubbed his brow with a coloured handkerchief. Then he thought of the scratch from the wire which unaccountably he had forgotten. "I'll go put something on my face," he added, glancing at Garland. "You hitch up on the wagon and we'll go over to Crampton's for their chute." He went to the house hastily.

IV

Coming home the boy remarked, referring to the neighbour whom they had just left, "So Andrew is going to retire?" though Crampton had just been informing them of his intention.

"Yes, the old sucker. After being as stingy as sin all his life and drudging night and day all his life like a slave he can to to town to die of bein' afraid he'll last longer than his money will, and wanting to work out on some farm, even somebody's else, since he's left his own; and being ashamed to."

Without enthusiasm the old man had made his announcement, but he had thought the consummation worthy of a pride which he did not care to show, it was clear His son, who was to have the running of the farm thenceforth, was not so well able to conceal his feeling. Turning aside from them talking together in the stable to hide his uncontrollable grin, he had shouted gruffly at a horse, putting back into its manger some hay which it had turned out.

Garland was silent as he looked absently at the surrounding fields, ashen and green rectangles in the violent sunlight. He sat on the low rear ladder of the wagon, and the irregular cackling rattle of the wheels lulled him. A lazy bit of dust hung alongside the wagon as they drove. The long road was empty, and seemed to hold, more than the farmyard they had just left, the hush and warmth of noon.

"Never be a farmer," said Jesse, brooding. "It's one thing or another. Either you have a heavy crop and everybody else has the same, and you take what they give you for it, or else if the price is decent you've got but little or none. And it's always work, work,—more work than if you did have a good crop. We'll have to go into business, you and I. Hardware business out West, eh? If I'm ever able to get shut of this farm," he added with an intonation of bitterness. He brought this out as though it had long since been formed in his mind.

"Maybe we'll find a buyer," said Garland. Lolling against the rear ladder he was again in the green woods of the morning, peering through the soft air cobwebbed with mist for the shapes of the horses showing through it vaguely in the depths. His calls rang on the thick air, but farther in the wood echoes were muffled, somehow. The horses made no movement or sound in answer, but did not try to escape when he came up to them. Dan raised a sleepy eye as he heard him coming. "You old rascal!" Garland said when he had caught hold of his forelock. "You brought them here, you know you did." The wise old boy shook the end of his long nose from side to side and snored. They all blinked at him lazy-eyed, enjoying their truancy, but not then interested

nough to attempt to make a get-away. Slowly they twined
ut of the bush and up the long lane. For a distance he held
Dan by the damp forelock of his lowered head, old Mack and
he others following. But when they came to the foot of the
ane Garland slipped back behind them all, so that his father
might not scold him for taking the risk of their getting away
rom him; and followed whistling in the sun and the light
olling waves of fog past large maples and oaks that overhung
he lane. Broad circles of ground beneath the trees were
eaten to a finer dust by the hoofs of the horses and cattle.
Even then the mist was spreading and thinning. There was
romise of a very warm day. . . .

"I want you to be something better than a farmer," his
ather was saying impressively.

"Oh, I don't know," Garland answered uncertainly.

"Get along, Dan!" shouted Jesse, slashing with the lines.
They rattled on a few hundred yards and came to the
ome gate. They swung out widely to enter it. Garland
uddenly cried out, and his father turning saw the heavy
hute which protruded from the rack about to strike the
ate-post and slide back, crushing the boy's legs. He pulled
nd shouted at the horses, and at that instant gate post and
hute caught, but slightly, and the structure was moved only
few inches back from its place.

The boy's face was pink and sheepish, but his father was
ale. "Well, what *are* you thinking of this morning?" he
houted as the wagon went down the lane. "Will you never
arn? How often have I told you to look out for things like
at? You could see blame well what was coming. But I've
ot to watch you like a baby. Ever *see* such a boy! *I* haven't
ough to do, I must always be turning around and watching
im. I'll have to have his mother out to help me take care
him. A great lot of good—! Whoa!"

They drove into the bare yard and reached the pig pen.
esse jumped down indignant. Garland continued to stand
amefaced by the back ladder of the wagon. How had he
ome to make such a blunder? It was true that his father had
equently warned him about such things. He must have
en asleep. Still, he might have been able to jump off the
ack of the wagon if the chute had come any farther toward

him, if the wagon were not going too rapidly. Well, another
time—.

He was roused by hearing his father say, "Well, are you
going to help me take this thing off, or aren't you?"

At that he stepped quickly forward and began lifting
the heavy bulk. Slowly it was twisted back and forth and
eased to the ground. Then he jumped down and helped to drag
it into place inside the door of the pen.

"Go get some chunks to block the wheels—the damn
horses won't stand, I know—while I back the wagon into
position."

Garland went away to a pile of rubbish outside the barnyard
fence. He was in a sort of daze of which he was scarcely
half aware. He kept thinking of his first whiff of the sweet and
gauzy-aired day from the little open window of his bedroom
of his mother's cheerful greeting, and the strange sadness
he had felt at his father's early ill-temper; again, of the beauty
of the morning bush, and sense of a myriad mist-thralled
birds when one of them broke silence for an instant, for a
note. Inappositely he began thinking of evenings when he
rode down the lane home on the disks musically tinkling
grating or clanging over the stones as the hungry and tired
horses made for the barn; of the wonderful pleasure it now
seemed to come in at dusk to the warm supper in the little
bright-windowed house. The wind would rustle the vine dryly
against the clapboards and the panes, but he would be warm
and replete and in the light. . . . Poor Mother! Poor Dan, the
old slave! Unaccountable pity for everyone and everything
enwrapped him.

In that instant he was fumbling about among old sticks
and rubbish and pieces of rusty fence-wire for the blocks of
wood. A call from his father roused him and he started up
to come bringing them. He saw over in the green wheat field
a horse with its head down. "It's old Mack," he thought.
"We couldn't have tied him up with the others. . . . But how
did he get there, how will we catch him?"

The rear of the wagon was about three feet from the
building. "I haven't got it just in position," said Jesse. "I
thought it was no use until you brought the blocks, the
fidget so."

He went forward, and Garland, taking no account of his movements, went in behind the wagon and looked down the slope of the chute at the pigs. He leaned over the straight lip of the frame. They were peaceful about the trough eating another meal before they died. The boy considered them with a strange pain at his heart. He could not understand his sorrow, and he was turning away silently when he heard a shout.

V

His father had gone to one side to consider the way in which the wagon would have to be manoeuvred in order to bring it to just the right position in relation with the chute. He saw that it must be moved forward to get it in line for backing. He stepped quickly to the heads of the horses to lead them up by the bridles. With straining eyes and forward-sloping ears they both shied back from him, their powerful braced legs pushing the wagon back with a terrible inexorable swiftness, like the piston-swing of a great engine, it seemed. Yet it was a long moment. . . .

Jesse found himself on his knees, his arm reaching up to a horse's rein. If there had been a sound he had not heard it. In silence the sun was beating down on the dirty yard about him, on the scattered grimy weeds which had withstood the browsing hogs. A little cloud of dust lazily wandered away, twisting slowly across the ground. Then he heard the guzzling of the hogs at the feed he had given them—how long?—five minutes ago. And somewhere a bob-white was calling, portent of a day of rain.

Trying to hold his eyes shut, on his hands and knees he crept around to the back of the wagon.

Hugh Garner **ONE-TWO-THREE LITTLE INDIANS**

After they had eaten, Big Tom pushed the cracked and dirty supper things to the back of the table and took the baby from its high chair carefully, so as not to spill the flotsam of bread crumbs and boiled potatoes from the chair to the floor.

He undressed the youngster, talking to it in the old dialect, trying to awaken its interest. All evening it had been listless and fretful by turns, but now it seemed to be soothed by the story of Po-chee-ah, and the Lynx, although it was too young to understand him as his voice slid awkwardly through the ageless folk-tale of his people.

For long minutes after the baby was asleep he talked on, letting the victorious words fill the small cabin so that they shut out the sounds of the Northern Ontario night: the buzz of mosquitoes, the far-off bark of a dog, the noise of the cars and transport trucks passing on the gravelled road.

The melodious hum of his voice was like a strong soporific, lulling him with the return of half-forgotten memories, strengthening him with the knowledge that once his people had been strong and brave, men with a nation of their own, encompassing a million miles of teeming forest, lake and tamarack swamp.

When he halted his monologue to place the baby in the

big brass bed in the corner the sudden silence was loud in his ears, and he cringed a bit as the present suddenly caught up with the past.

He covered the baby with a corner of the church-donated patchwork quilt, and lit the kerosene lamp that stood on the mirrorless dressing table beside the stove. Taking a broom from a corner he swept the mealtime debris across the doorsill.

This done, he stood and watched the headlights of the cars run along the trees bordering the road, like a small boy's stick along a picket fence. From the direction of the trailer camp a hundred yards away came the sound of a car engine being gunned, and the halting note-tumbles of a clarinet from a tourist's radio. The soft summer smell of spruce needles and wood smoke blended with the evening dampness of the earth, and felt good in his nostrils, so that he filled his worn lungs until he began to cough. He spat the resinous phlegm into the weed-filled yard.

It had been this summer smell, and the feeling of freedom it gave, which had brought him back to the woods after three years in the mines during the war. But only part of him had come back, for the mining towns and the big money had done more than etch his lungs with silica: they had also brought him pain and distrust, and a wife who had learned to live in gaudy imitation of the boomtown life.

When his coughing attack subsided he peered along the path, hoping to catch a glimpse of his wife Mary returning from her work at the trailer camp. He was becoming worried about the baby, and her presence, while it might not make the baby well, would mean that there was someone else to share his fears. He could see nothing but the still blackness of the trees, their shadows interwoven in a sombre pattern across the mottled ground.

He re-entered the cabin and began washing the dishes, stopping once or twice to cover the moving form of the sleeping baby. He wondered if he could have transmitted his own wasting sickness to the lungs of his son. He stood for long minutes at the side of the bed, staring, trying to diagnose the child's restlessness into something other than what he feared.

His wife came in and placed some things on the table. He picked up a can of pork-and-beans she had bought and weighed it in the palm of his hand. "The baby seems pretty sick," he said.

She crossed the room, and looked at the sleeping child. "I guess it's his teeth."

He placed the pork-and-beans on the table again and walked over to his chair beside the empty stove. As he sat down he noticed for the first time that his wife was beginning to show her pregnancy. Her squat form had sunk lower, and almost filled the shapeless dress she wore. Her brown ankles were puffed above the broken-down heels of the dirty silver dancing pumps she was wearing.

"Is the trailer camp full?" he asked.

"Nearly. Two more Americans came about half an hour ago."

"Was Billy Woodhen around?"

"I didn't see him, only Elsie," she answered. "A woman promised me a dress tomorrow if I scrub out her trailer."

"Yeh." He saw the happiness rise over her like a colour as she mentioned this. She was much younger than he was— twenty-two years against his thirty-nine—and her dark face had a fullness that is common to many Indian women. She was no longer pretty, and as he watched her he thought that wherever they went the squalor of their existence seemed to follow them.

"It's a silk dress," Mary said, as though the repeated mention of it brought it nearer.

"A silk dress is no damn good around here. You should get some overalls," he said, angered by her lack of shame in accepting the cast-off garments of the trailer women.

She seemed not to notice his anger. "It'll do for the dances next winter."

"A lot of dancing you'll do," he said pointing to her swollen body. "You'd better learn to stay around here and take care of the kid."

She busied herself over the stove, lighting it with newspapers and kindling. "I'm going to have some fun. You should have married a grandmother."

He filled the kettle with water from an open pail near the door. The baby began to cough, and the mother turned it on its side in the bed. "As soon as I draw my money from Cooper

I'm going to get him some cough syrup from the store," she said.

"It won't do any good. We should take him to the doctor in town tomorrow."

"I can't. I've got to stay here and work."

He knew the folly of trying to reason with her. She had her heart set on earning the silk dress the woman had promised.

After they had drunk their tea he blew out the light, and they took off some of their clothes and climbed over the baby into the bed. Long after his wife had fallen asleep he lay in the darkness listening to a ground moth beating its futile wings against the glass of the window.

They were awakened in the morning by the twittering of a small colony of tree sparrows who were feasting on the kitchen sweepings of the night before. Mary got up and went outside, returning a few minutes later carrying a handful of birch and poplar stovewood.

He waited until the beans were in the pan before rising and pulling on his pants. He stood in the doorway scratching his head and absorbing the sunlight through his bare feet upon the step.

The baby awoke while they were eating their breakfast.

"He don't look good," Big Tom said as he dipped some brown sauce from his plate with a hunk of bread.

"He'll be all right later," his wife insisted. She poured some crusted tinned milk from a tin into a cup and mixed it with water from the kettle.

Big Tom splashed his hands and face with cold water, and dried himself on a soiled shirt that lay over the back of a chair. "When you going to the camp, this morning?"

"This afternoon," Mary answered.

"I'll be back by then."

He took up a small pile of woven baskets from a corner and hung the handles over his arm. From the warming shelf of the stove he pulled a bedraggled band of cloth, into which a large goose feather had been sewn. Carrying this in his hand he went outside and strode down the path toward the highway.

He ignored the chattering sauciness of a squirrel that

hurtled up the green ladder of a tree beside him. Above the small noises of the woods could be heard the roar of a transport truck braking its way down the hill from the burnt-out sapling covered ridge to the north. The truck passed him as he reached the road, and he waved a desultory greeting to the driver, who answered with a short blare of the horn.

Placing the baskets in a pile on the shoulder of the road he adjusted the corduroy band on his head so that the feather stuck up at the rear. He knew that by so doing he became a part of the local colour, "a real Indian with a feather'n everything," and also that he sold more baskets while wearing it. In the time he had been living along the highway he had learned to give them what they expected.

The trailer residents were not yet awake, so he sat down on the wooden walk leading to the shower room, his baskets resting on the ground in a half circle behind him.

After a few minutes a small boy descended from the door of a trailer and stood staring at him. Then he leaned back inside the doorway and pointed in Big Tom's direction. In a moment a man's hand parted the heavy curtains on the window and a bed-mussed unshaven face stared out. The small boy climbed back inside.

A little later two women approached on the duckboard walk, one attired in a pair of buttock-pinching brown slacks, and the other wearing a blue chenille dressing gown. They circled him warily and entered the shower room. From inside came the buzz of whispered conversation and the louder noises of running water.

During the rest of the morning several people approached and stared at Big Tom and the baskets. He sold two small ones to an elderly woman. She seemed surprised when she asked him what tribe he belonged to, and instead of answering in a monosyllable he said, "I belong to the Algonquins, Ma'am." He also got rid of one of his big forty-five cent baskets to the mother of the small boy who had been the first one up earlier in the day.

A man took a series of photographs of him with an expensive-looking camera, pacing off the distance and being very careful in setting his lens openings and shutter speeds.

"I wish he'd look into the camera," the man said loudly to

a couple standing nearby, as if he were talking about an animal in a cage.

"You can't get any good picshus around here. Harold tried to get one of the five Dionney kids, but they wouldn't let him. The way they keep them quints hid you'd think they was made of china or somep'n," a woman standing by said.

She glanced at her companion for confirmation.

"They want you to *buy* their picshus," the man said. "We was disappointed in 'em. They used to look cute before, when they was small, but now they're just five plain-looking kids."

"Yeah, My Gawd, you'd never believe how homely they got, would you, Harold? An' everything's pure robbery in Callander. You know, Old Man Dionney's minting money up there. Runs his own souvenir stand."

"That's durin' the day, when he's got time," her husband said.

The man with the camera, and the woman, laughed.

After lunch Big Tom watched Cooper prepare for his trip to North Bay. "Is there anybody going fishing, Mr. Cooper?" he asked.

The man took the radiator cap off the old truck he was inspecting, and peered inside.

"Mr. Cooper!"

"Hey?" Cooper turned and looked at the Indian standing behind him, hands in pockets, his manner shy and deferential. He showed a vague irritation as though he sensed the overtone of servility in the Indian's attitude.

"Anybody going fishing?" Big Tom asked again.

"Seems to me Mr. Staynor said he'd like to go," Cooper answered. His voice was kind, with the amused kindness of a man talking to a child.

The big Indian remained standing where he was, saying nothing. His old second-hand army trousers drooped around his lean loins, and his plaid shirt was open at the throat, showing a grey high-water mark of dirt where his face washing began and ended.

"What's the matter?" Cooper asked. "You seem pretty anxious to go today."

"My kid's sick. I want to make enough to take him to the doctor."

Cooper walked around the truck and opened one of the doors, rattling the handle in his hand as if it was stuck. "You should stay home with it. Make it some pine-sap syrup. No need to worry, it's as healthy as a bear cub."

Mrs. Cooper came out of the house and eased her bulk into the truck cab. "Where's Mary?" she asked.

"Up at the shack," answered Big Tom.

"Tell her to scrub the washrooms before she does anything else. Mrs. Anderson, in that trailer over there, wants her to do her floors." She pointed across the lot to a large blue and white trailer parked behind a Buick.

"I'll tell her," he answered.

The Coopers drove between the whitewashed stones marking the entrance to the camp, and swung up the highway, leaving behind them a small cloud of dust from the pulverized gravel of the road.

Big Tom fetched Mary and the baby from the shack. He gave his wife Mrs. Cooper's instructions, and she transferred the baby from her arms to his. The child was feverish, its breath noisy and fast.

"Keep him warm," she said. "He's been worse since we got up. I think he's got a touch of the 'flu."

Big Tom placed his hand inside the old blanket and felt the baby's cheek. It was dry and burning to his palm. He adjusted the baby's small weight in his arm and walked across the camp and down the narrow path to the shore of the lake where the boats were moored.

A man sitting in the sternsheets of a new-painted skiff looked up and smiled at his approach. "You coming out with me, Tom?" he asked.

The Indian nodded.

"Are you bringing the papoose along?"

Big Tom winced at the word "papoose," but he answered, "He won't bother us. The wife is working this afternoon."

"O.K. I thought maybe we'd go over to the other side of the lake today and try to get some of them big fellows at the creek mouth. Like to try?"

"Sure," the Indian answered, placing the baby along the wide seat in the stern, and unshipping the oars.

He rowed silently to the best part of an hour, the sun beating through his shirt causing the sweat to trickle coldly down his back. At times his efforts at the oars caused a constriction in his chest, and he coughed and spat into the water.

When they reached the mouth of the creek across the lake, he let the oars drag and leaned over to look at the baby. It was sleeping restlessly, its lips slightly blue and its breath laboured and harsh. Mr. Staynor was busy with his lines and tackle in the bow of the boat.

Tom picked the child up and felt its little body for sweat.

The baby's skin was bone dry. He picked up the bailing can from the boat bottom and dipped it over the side. With the tips of his fingers he brushed some of the cold water across the baby's forehead. The child woke up, looked at the strange surroundings, and smiled up at him. He gave it a drink of water from the can. Feeling reassured now he placed the baby on the seat and went forward to help the man with his gear.

Mr. Staynor fished for a half hour or so, catching some small fish and a large black bass, which writhed in the bottom of the boat. Big Tom watched its gills gasping its death throes, and noted the similarity between the struggles of the fish and those of the baby lying on the seat in the blanket.

He became frightened again after a time, and he turned to the man in the bow and said, "We'll have to go pretty soon. I'm afraid my kid's pretty sick."

"Eh! We've hardly started," the man answered. "Don't worry, there's not much wrong with the papoose."

Big Tom lifted the child from the seat and cradled it in his arms. He opened the blanket, and shading the baby's face, allowed the warm sun to shine on its chest. He thought, if I could only get him to sweat; everything would be all right then.

He waited again as long as he dared, noting the blueness creeping over the baby's lips, before he placed the child again on the seat and addressed the man in the bow. "I'm going back now. You'd better pull in your line."

The man turned and felt his way along the boat. He stood

over the Indian and parted the folds of the blanket, looking at the baby. "My God, he is sick, Tom! You'd better get him to a doctor right away!" He stepped across the writhing fish to the bow and began pulling in the line. Then he busied himself with his tackle, stealing glances now and again at the Indian and the baby.

Big Tom turned the boat around, and with long straight pulls on the oars headed back across the lake. The man took the child in his arms and blew cooling drafts of air against its fevered face.

As soon as they reached the jetty below the tourist camp, Tom tied the boat's painter to a stump and took the child from the other man's arms.

Mr. Staynor handed him the fee for a full afternoon's work. "I'm sorry the youngster is sick, Tom," he said. "Don't play around. Get him up to the doctor in town right away. We'll try her again tomorrow afternoon."

Big Tom thanked him. Then, carrying the baby and unmindful of the grasping hands of the undergrowth, he climbed the path through the trees. On reaching the parked cars and trailers he headed in the direction of the large blue and white one where his wife would be working.

When he knocked, the door opened and a woman said, "Yes?" He recognized her as the one who had been standing nearby in the morning while his picture was being taken.

"Is my wife here?" he asked.

"Your wife; Oh, I know now who you mean. No, she's gone. She went down the road in a car a few minutes ago."

The camp was almost empty, most of the tourists having gone to the small bathing beach farther down the lake. A car full of bathers was pulling away to go down to the beach. Big Tom hurried over and held up his hand until it stopped. "Could you drive me to the doctor in town?" he asked. "My baby seems pretty sick."

There was a turning of heads within the car. A woman in the back seat began talking about the weather. The driver said, "I'll see what I can do, Chief, after I take the girls to the beach."

Big Tom sat down at the side of the driveway to wait. After a precious half hour had gone by and they did not return, he got to his feet and started up the highway in the direction of town.

His long legs pounded on the loose gravel of the road, his anger and terror giving strength to his stride. He noticed that the passengers in the few cars he met were pointing at him and laughing, and suddenly he realized that he was still wearing the feather in the band around his head. He reached up, pulled it off, and threw it in the ditch.

When a car or truck came up from behind him he would step off the road and raise his hand to beg a ride. After several passed without pausing he stopped this useless timewasting gesture and strode ahead, impervious to the noise of their horns as they approached him.

Now and again he placed his hand on the baby's face as he plodded along, reassuring himself that it was still alive. It had been hours since it had cried or shown any other signs of consciousness.

Once, he stepped off the road at a small bridge over a stream, and making a crude cup with his hands, tried to get the baby to drink. He succeeded only in making it cough, harshly, so that its tiny face became livid with its efforts to breathe.

It was impossible that the baby should die. Babies did not die like this, in their fathers' arms, on a highway that ran fifteen miles north through a small town, where there was a doctor and all the life-saving devices to prevent their deaths.

The sun fell low behind the trees and the swarms of black flies and mosquitoes began their nightly forage. He waved his hand above the fevered face of the baby, keeping them off, while at the same time trying to waft a little air into the child's tortured lungs.

But suddenly, with feelings as black as hell itself, he knew that the baby was dying. He had seen too much of it not to know now, that the child was in an advanced stage of pneumonia. He stumbled along as fast as he could, his eyes devouring the darkening face of his son, while the hot tears ran from the corner of his eyes.

With nightfall he knew that it was too late. He looked up at the sky where the first stars were being drawn in silver on a burnished copper plate, and he cursed them, and cursed what made them possible.

To the north-west the clouds were piling up in preparation for a summer storm. Reluctantly he turned and headed back down the road in the direction he had come.

It was almost midnight before he felt his way along the path through the trees to his shack. It was hard to see anything in the teeming rain, and he let the water run from his shoulders in an unheeded stream, soaking the sodden bundle he still carried in his arms.

When he reached the shanty he opened the door and fell inside. He placed the body of his son on the bed in the corner. Then, groping around the newspaper-lined walls, he found some matches in a pocket of his mackinaw and lit the lamp. With a glance around the room he knew that his wife had not yet returned, so he placed the lamp on the table under the window and headed out again into the rain.

At the trailer camp he sat down on the rail fence near the entrance to wait. Some lights shone from the small windows of the trailers and from Cooper's house across the road. The illuminated sign said: COOPER'S TRAILER CAMP—Hot And Cold Running Water, Rest Rooms. FISHING AND BOATING—INDIAN GUIDES.

One by one, as he waited, the lights went out, until only the sign lit up a small area at the gate. He saw the car's headlights first, about a hundred yards down the road. When it pulled to a stop he heard some giggling, and Mary and another Indian girl, Elsie Woodhen, staggered out into the rain.

A man's voice shouted through the door, "See you again, sweetheart. Don't forget next Saturday night." The voice belonged to one of the French-Canadians who worked at a creosote camp across the lake.

Another male voice shouted, "Wahoo!"

The girls clung to each other, laughing drunkenly, as the car pulled away.

They were not aware of Big Tom's approach until he grasped his wife by the hair and pulled her backwards to the ground. Elsie Woodhen screamed, and ran away in the direction of the Cooper house. Big Tom bent down as if he was going to strike at Mary's face with his fist. Then he changed his mind and let her go.

She stared into his eyes and saw what was there. Crawling to her feet and sobbing hysterically she left one of her silver shoes in the mud and limped along towards the shack.

Big Tom followed behind, all the anguish and frustration drained from him, so that there was nothing left to carry him into another day. Heedless now of the coughing that tore his chest apart, he pushed along in the rain, hurrying to join his wife in the vigil over their dead.

Men and Women

Gregory Clark

MAY YOUR FIRST LOVE BE YOUR LAST

By and large, I have had little trouble with the fair sex.

I mean, of course, that they have troubled little with me.

Being the first-born of my family, I was naturally a Mamma's Boy. By the time I was five, I already realized, dimly, my responsibility to demonstrate to the younger members of the family, arriving, how to behave. By the time I was eight, I did not have to be told about Tuesdays and Fridays. On Tuesdays and Fridays I put out the ash cans and garbage cans as a matter of course. I wrestled them out to the curb, though I was a shrimp, or whiffet (as we small ones were called). By the age of ten my senses were so acute that at six o'clock in the morning, I could hear the soft snowflakes beating upon the attic bedroom window. Softly I would rise. Softly I would dress, waking neither my young brother and sister, nor my parents. And the first shovel you heard on Howland avenue, at 7 A.M., was mine. All the mothers of Howland avenue admired me.

They pointed me out as a model to their sons. And I was beaten up as a matter of course and frequently had a bloody nose. I was an object of contempt to my generation.

By the time I was twelve, I was so covered with freckles —face, shoulders, arms, hands—that you could hardly see me. From amidst the freckles, my piggy blue eyes looked out eagerly. But nobody looked back. Especially the fair sex. I was spared those grim years of adolescence. No girls troubled me.

Now, do not think I was lonely. Forlorn? Well, maybe a little; but we all must feel forlorn one time or another in our lives. Fortunately, on the next street, Albany avenue, lived two older boys named Hoyes Lloyd and Stuart Thompson who became in their time two of the greatest field naturalists of Canada. They were glad of a queue of younger boys to follow them in their bird watching, tree naming, plant identifying, butterfly knowing, beetle picking, stone recognizing. And thus I escaped the clutches of the fair sex through those perilous years, thirteen to nineteen. Freckles do it. I became bewitched by the lovely elusive world of nature. And it has remained my love for more than sixty years.

But now I come to the point where I must tell the truth, the whole truth, and nothing but the truth, so help me!

I had fallen in love at the age of thirteen.

She was eleven.

To this day, I can show you the fire hydrant beside the Royal Conservatory of Music in Toronto where I dropped my four public library books and pretended to tie my shoe lace.

I watched them go by.

She was being dragged along by an older big blonde sister named Beth (as I later found out) but she was small and dark, with the most beautiful great eyes I ever saw or have ever seen. As she swept past, she looked at me. But she did not see me. (As I later found out.)

As a matter of fact, she did not see me for seven long years.

But, oh, I saw her.

They turned into Orde street, which was the first street down University avenue behind the Conservatory. Quick as a weasel, I snatched up my books and followed. Orde street is gone now, a blind street off University; tall skyscrapers loom. The old houses are all gone. But when I nipped around the corner, I saw the two of them scamper up the front steps of one house. And I could tell they were home.

I walked past the house. No. 6 Orde street. When I was safely out of its sight, I flew. Like a swallow, I flew up and along College street, up St. George, along Bloor street to the drug store of Mr. Norris at the corner of Howland. He was my friend. He also had a fat yellow book called a City Directory. Breathlessly, I told Mr. Norris of my need to know who lived at 6 Orde street. He was a perceptive man.

"Reverend James Murray," he said, looking in the Directory.

After a moment's reflection, and having no doubt been thirteen years old himself once, he then took the skimpy telephone book of that time and looked up Reverend James Murray.

"College 608," he said to central when she answered. (Though this was sixty years ago, I still remember that number.)

"Pardon me, ma'am," said Mr. Norris when someone answered. "But at what church does the Reverend Mr. Murray officiate? Erskine Presbyterian? Thank you."

And hung up.

"Erskine Presbyterian," Mr. Norris informed me with a smile I like to think I remember too.

Ah, well, from there on it is just the usual story. I had to go to Bloor street Presbyterian Church with my family at the morning service. But each Sunday evening, I was in the balcony of Erskine Church. This in time gave rise, by the time I was sixteen, to the general belief in my family and their friends that I was intending to enter the Presbyterian ministry. And they were all very pleased.

Year after year, every Sunday evening, I sat and watched. Oh, sometimes I would lose heart. Especially when, the moment the service ended, I would hastily skip down and mingle with the crowd that always gathered outside for a little while. And I would see her. She never saw me, I think now that if she had looked at me, I would have collapsed into a blob of jelly on the pavement. But what tormented me was that she grew more beautiful every year, far beyond my wildest reach of hope.

When I was seventeen or eighteen and started to Varsity, I was old enough to realize my folly, and for weeks I would not go to Erskine Church. But then, like a dog, I would creep back. Never had I heard her voice. So in my dreams I gave her a soft, contralto voice. Never had I seen her teeth, for she was a Presbyterian Murray who did not go about smiling in all directions. So I gave her beautiful white teeth. I gave her a character gentle, serene, compassionate. She was so perfect, by the time I was finished with her, that at the age of twenty, having had one last fearful look at her in the outpouring crowd of Erskine Church, I abandoned all hope, all dreams.

On the 17th of January, 1913, age twenty, I was a cub reporter on a newspaper. The University had thrown me out when I failed the first year twice, due to my devotion to the University newspaper, *The Varsity*. Each Friday, at 3 P.M., the staff of my new employers could draw their salaries. Mine was $12 a week. With this, around 4:30 in the afternoon, I would proceed to the Little Blue Tea Room on Yonge street, up a flight of stairs. There I would generously entertain my erstwhile Varsity friends to tea and cinnamon toast, or crumpets, or cocoa in winter. With about $3 I could play host in high style.

At 4:30 of January 17 I walked up the stairs and into the tea room. There were numbers of people sitting at the different tables. I headed for the alcove which was reserved for our Varsity party.

"Greg," said a young man whose name I have forgotten, rising to beckon me.

There was a girl with her back to me at his table.

"I'd like to introduce . . ." he began.

It was like being struck by lightning.

She smiled with the lips and teeth I had given her. At close range, she was more beautiful than I had painted her in my most magical dreams.

I took her home that afternoon. And no man ever took her home again. I was invited to supper. Reverend Mr.

Murray, who was a tall, dark handsome man, looked at me with an expression I had long been familiar with in the passing brief glances of people. He told me long afterwards that on that first occasion he thought I was the dullest young man he had ever encountered.

I wasn't dull! I just wasn't THERE. I was in the Seventh Heaven, where no one speaks. The big blonde sister Beth whom first I had seen seven years before dragging my love along by the hand tried to monopolize the conversation at the supper table. But Mr. Murray and my love talked about fishing in Nova Scotia, and how the reverend gentleman had taught his little dark daughter to cast trout flies.

That was ONE thing I did not design for her. But when I heard about the trout fishing, I knew she was mine.

We were engaged six months later. We were married on the eve of the day before I sailed overseas to be absent from her two and a half years of war. For all but three years of half a century, we lived a joyous life, with only the one great tragedy when our first-born son was killed in battle in the second war. She died in my arms.

But you see I was possessed. That is why the fair sex have not bothered with me. They must sense when they see a man possessed.

Now why, you may ask, on this wintry night, do I tell so secret and idle a tale as this?

Well, on a wintry night such as this, the young, the ones on the threshold of life, are likely to be at home on a Saturday night. And on a Saturday, *Weekend Magazine* comes in. Maybe more often than at other times, the young, on the threshold of thirteen, fourteen, are more likely to come upon this story.

I tell you what you do, boy. Or girl.

Go and look at the western sky where the new moon, the silver shaving of the moon, hangs.

Look at it over your LEFT shoulder, and wish.

Wish that your first love shall be your last love.

And if your wish is granted, you will have put on the whole armour of life.

James Reaney   **THE
BOX-SOCIAL**

"Do you know where I put my gold paint, Auntie?"

She painted some. Swans under bridges with water lilies.
Old ladies at windows reading lugubrious Bibles. Tonight she
was decorating a shoe-box for the box-social they were having
at the school the next night. No one expected her to come.
She had been quite ill for the last three weeks and hadn't
appeared at the last Institute meeting; now, however, she felt
well enough. She was a bit pale and looked much thinner, but
she simply had to go. All that evening she sat in the kitchen
cutting up old scraps of wallpaper and pasting them on the
shoe-box, in various patterns with flour paste. Her box of
lunch would be the prettiest there and the men would bid so
high for it. . . . All she needed now was some gold paint, but
of course Aunt had gone to bed hours ago. If Sylvia had any
profession at all, it was doing pretty little things like this.
Little useless things, for her real vocation had apparently been
to stay home and help her aunt with the housework. What
she needed now was something to line the box with. It would
look so much more beautiful with the sandwiches and the
little bottle of olives set against some deep rich colour. Shoe-
boxes were so wonderfully white.

The rain was falling in soft applause outside.

Her fingers were white from the paste she had been using. The candle in her hand sprouted a yellow willow leaf. She was in the outhouse searching in the tiny attic for a roll of gorgeous parlour wallpaper she remembered her aunt having left there. Her father always forgot to put down the lids; the two holes stared at her like a man with a large eye and a small one. Finding what she wanted, she stepped out and stood still for a moment. The rain slopped the candle out. There was the wind in the elderberry bushes; the little things were breathing as hard as if they were swimming across the North Sea, and another sound—that of Saint James' bells all the way from town. Some notes were lost but she gathered it must be twelve. No clock should have any less to say than twelve, unless it were one at such an hour, so silent and so black. Twelve black strokes: twelve black hair-ribbons.

She walked along the fence beneath the fir trees a bit. The nightshade berries grew here with their wicked fruit. The very next field was lined with furrows as if it had been a large frown or a copy-book. It was not her father's field. Someone else had plowed it. Furrow after furrow after furrow his house lay away where he now lay sleeping and she hated him. Then, her own house—a faint pale light from the two kitchen windows. There the decorated shoe-box lay almost ready for the box-social. Every room of the house, both in their ancient, and modern styles met in parliament on its flat thin sides. Already the event, the box-social gleamed in the distance like a lantern at the end of a dark stable.

There were half a dozen cars parked at the school. Cars have such beautiful behinds with ruby-red roses that wink at you. Sylvia walked across the fields; neither her aunt nor her father wished to go. She held the precious box in her arms. It was wrapped in brown paper to protect it from the rain.

Why you're better.

Yes, I am.

There were thirty people there; no one was as pale as she was. She looked like the queen on a playing card—in her rich red dress holding the gay box in her lap. All the children's desks were cowering in one corner, for there was to be dancing. Already, somebody was sprinkling boracic acid on the floor. Not that it really makes the floor slippery, but everyone is so sure that it does and it feels that much more exciting. The fiddler played six tunes (he only knew five). Mrs. Twite wasn't dancing at all, not even with her husband, because they used the school as a Sunday school on Sundays and it would be like dancing in a church. Then, out stole a little green table, and then another green table and another and another; everyone was playing euchre until they should dance again.

I pass, paleface; joker.

They wouldn't be dancing now until after the lunch. Mr. Deloney (one of the three farmers in the neighbourhood who owned a silo) was arranging the boxes on the teacher's desk. Sylvia was very careful with her hands lest she eat them. And the teacher had pinned up the Winter ornamental border above the west blackboard with all the gay coaches galloping from the north of the room to the south. . . .

This lovely box wrapped in green. What young gentleman wants to eat with a pretty young lady who has wrapt her box in green?

All the men crowded up.

Hers was almost the last and he was bidding for it. Five dollars; it had looked so nice. He came straight to her.

"I knew it was yours—recognized the wallpaper. Very pretty. You aren't mad at me anymore?"

He sat down quite comfortably and began untying the black ribbon. The school clock that they had both looked at together to see if it were recess time ticked loudly above them. He lifted the lid and sat staring at what lay inside. His great hands unusually white on the top of the green baize card table.

And between them, the little shoe-box glistening with scarlet wallpaper and gilt like a fairy coffin. Inside it, there was the crabbed corpse of a still-born child wreathed in bloody newspaper.

"I hated you so much," she said softly.

Alice Boissonneau **THE McCRIMMONS**

Mr. and Mrs. McCrimmon sit beside each other in the office room speaking turn about, with slowness. They are ordinary like the many people who enter and walk upon the oiled worn boards of official hallways, who sit waiting on the straight chairs beside brass memorial plaques. Their voices can be heard behind some closed door, telling their story in sentences which are vivid and ungrammatical. If you were to write the words down something would be lost, a directness which cannot be captured except by the ear.

Mrs. McCrimmon wears a plain coat with a collar of some indeterminate fur, a felt hat pressed on. Her straight hair shows at each side in the manner of the twenties. Her face is without makeup and her eyes twinkle a little as she talks, like raisins in a bun. Mr. McCrimmon is also wearing a plain black coat, his face is heavy and plain with the two grooved lines, thick white eyebrows pasted on above deep-set blue eyes.

They are applying to board a foster child. They have always loved children, and their only daughter died earlier this year in an accident. They would like to give to a child the love in themselves which is searching for an outlet. They will draw from that inward source in themselves to heal the hurt places of a deprived child. They picture in a gratifying way to themselves the little joys rising like fountains which they will lavish around the child's life.

They start talking about children whom they know, and then about two coloured children living on the same street. The family occupies a large attic room above stores. The mother will have to go into Sanitarium and they do not know what will become of the children. They themselves would like to take the children but cannot because of the restrictions of the apartment building. The children are quiet and shy, they say. They never speak. It is because they do not play with other children but spend so much time together in the attic room away from the traffic of the street. They have not mixed with other children and are very close and dependent on each other. When the two come to visit at the McCrimmons they will play during the entire time in complete silence, never opening their mouths. Only at the last as they are leaving they will shout out "Bye-Bye," laughing and jumping as they run out the door. But their mother says that after the children get home it is a different story. Here their favourite game is playing with a toy telephone. They have long conversations on it with "Crimmon." "You be Crimmon," one will say to the other, and the things they will tell!

Then I can see all that back of them as they talk: the world of Bathurst near Dundas, the world of floors without rugs, sleet, eviction notices. I see a landlord with a cold putty-coloured face as he stands in a doorway out of the February wind. He is cursing at a coloured woman who carries in bar by bar, piece by piece, the iron frame of a baby's second-hand crib. I see the thick musty darkness of the hall, the warped linoleum underfoot, the narrow stairway leading up to the row of waiting doors. In the back room is a table covered with oilcloth beside the peeling wallpaper. The window faces an alleyway and another wall. Here they eat bowls of mashed potatoes to keep from starvation.

And like a map I can see the whole miserable territory down there, the sleety canal corridor of Bathurst reaching down to Tip Top Tailors and the lake, past the high walled warehouses where Florence worked. I see Florence in the too-short gray dress, her face dark, walnut-coloured, impassive, her hair springing like stiff grass away from her head.

She walks teetering with the ungainliness of pregnancy, her lips curl back to frame the polite replies.

I can see quite clearly the house wedged in down there, in the porched, wine-coloured row; within, the repetition of doors padlocked against the tunnelling hall; can hear the drunk woman's jeering laugh. Below, like an evil uncle, the landlord watches by the porch for Florence to go out. It is in the days of official papers, relief vouchers.

And I remember how in the month before they were evicted, she took to walking all over the city. In the afternoon the two of them could be seen setting out (Paul a small dark shape dangling from her hand), Florence with that determined unseeing gaze she got. And the maze of streets would seem a world strange and glittering through which they walked in cold shadow, searching in determined, frantic perplexity. I see again the deteriorated section of brick dwellings worn now to a dark prune, the fringed gratings black and lace-like, gardening off roofs. They have now a twilight Spengler-like air around five o'clock. The window-glass is dark, blank, there are FOR SALE signs above the doors.

And I remember how it all ended in one of those war years, how the end was precipitated (could have been foreseen), after the baby was born. "Like a match to a straw-tick," the psychiatrist said, meaning child-birth; "post-partum psychosis, a very interesting case."

And the thought of it again grows sharp in the mind, expands gothically, trying to shape comprehension of the horror. The mind hungers for small things—crumbs and sparrows in the snow beside the tall ashcans. And Florence is seen a small speck, dwindling in the distance of the eye, wandering in those strange afternoons of the city before she foundered. Groping forward still, you see her stumble and fall heavily, a dark heap of clothing against the white. And she begins to cry then, the tears making two channels along the brown skin of her face, like runnels of water against dry earth. A time to weep. And Paul stands looking down with his hands dangling in their blue mitts helplessly.

The McCrimmons would begin to evoke all that. As they talk about these coloured children it would begin to come back, thinking, will it ever be over, ever atoned—what is the cure? And at the end, as Mrs. McCrimmon speaks again of their daughter, she stands in the hallway waiting braced before the finality of their own loss, held like a block within her breast. I see again how her smile breaks through, the light of her eyes bright as knives in the glittering tears, and I think—who is to say how it shall come, out of what tentacles one draws oneself up.

Alice Munro

WALKER BROTHERS COWBOY

After supper my father says, "Want to go down and see if the Lake's still there?" We leave my mother sewing under the dining-room light, making clothes for me against the opening of school. She has ripped up for this purpose an old suit and an old plaid wool dress of hers, and she has to cut and match very cleverly and also make me stand and turn for endless fittings, sweaty, itching from the hot wool, ungrateful. We leave my brother in bed in the little screened porch at the end of the front verandah, and sometimes he kneels on his bed and presses his face against the screen and calls mournfully, "Bring me an ice cream cone!" but I call back, "You will be asleep," and do not even turn my head.

Then my father and I walk gradually down a long, shabby sort of street, with Silverwoods Ice Cream signs standing on the sidewalk, outside tiny, lighted stores. This is in Tuppertown, an old town on Lake Huron, an old grain port. The street is shaded, in some places, by maple trees whose roots have cracked and heaved the sidewalk and spread out like crocodiles into the bare yards. People are sitting out, men in shirt-sleeves and undershirts and women in aprons—not people we know but if anybody looks ready to nod and say, "Warm night," my father will nod too and say something the same. Children are still playing. I don't know them either because my mother keeps my brother and me in our own yard, saying he is too young to leave it and I have to mind him. I am not so sad to watch their evening games because the games themselves are ragged, dissolving. Children, of their own will, draw apart, separate into islands of two or one under the heavy trees, occupying themselves in such solitary ways as I do all day, planting pebbles in the dirt or writing in it with a stick.

Presently we leave these yards and houses behind, we pass a factory with boarded-up windows, a lumberyard whose high wooden gates are locked for the night. Then the town falls away in a defeated jumble of sheds and small junkyards, the sidewalk gives up and we are walking on a sandy path with burdocks, plantains, humble nameless weeds all around. We enter a vacant lot, a kind of park really, for it is kept clear of junk and there is one bench with a slat missing on the back, a place to sit and look at the water. Which is generally grey in the evening, under a lightly overcast sky, no sunsets, the horizon dim. A very quiet, washing noise on the stones of the beach. Further along, towards the main part of town, there is a stretch of sand, a water slide, floats bobbing around the safe swimming area, a life guard's rickety throne. Also a long dark green building, like a roofed verandah, called the Pavilion, full of farmers and their wives, in stiff good clothes, on Sundays. That is the part of the town we used to know when we lived at Dungannon and came here three or four times a summer, to the Lake. That, and the docks where we would go and look at the grain boats, ancient, rusty, wallowing, making us wonder how they got past the breakwater let alone to Fort William.

Tramps hang around the docks and occasionally on these evenings wander up the dwindling beach and climb the shifting, precarious path boys have made, hanging onto dry bushes, and say something to my father which, being frightened of tramps, I am too alarmed to catch. My father says he is a bit hard up himself. "I'll roll you a cigarette if it's any use to you," he says, and he shakes tobacco out carefully on one of the thin butterfly papers, flicks it with his tongue, seals it and hands it to the tramp who takes it and walks away. My father also rolls and lights and smokes one cigarette of his own.

He tells me how the Great Lakes came to be. All where Lake Huron is now, he says, used to be flat land, a wide flat plain. Then came the ice, creeping down from the north, pushing deep into the low places. Like *that*—and he shows me his hand with his spread fingers pressing the rock-hard ground where we are sitting. His fingers make hardly any impression at all and he says, "Well, the old ice cap had a lot more power behind it than this hand has." And then the ice went back, shrank back towards the North Pole where it came from, and left its fingers of ice in the deep places it had gouged, and ice turned to lakes and there they were today. They were *new*, as time went. I try to see that plain before me, dinosaurs walking on it, but I am not able even to imagine the shore of the Lake when the Indians were there, before Tuppertown. The tiny share we have of time appalls me, though my father seems to regard it with tranquillity. Even my father, who sometimes seems to me to have been at home in the world as long as it has lasted, has really lived on this earth only a little longer than I have, in terms of all the time there has been to live in. He has not known a time, any more than I, when automobiles and electric lights did not at least exist. He was not alive when this century started. I will be barely alive—old, old —when it ends. I do not like to think of it. I wish the Lake to be always just a lake, with the safe-swimming floats marking it, and the breakwater and the lights of Tuppertown.

My father has a job, selling for Walker Brothers. This is a firm that sells almost entirely in the country, the back country. Sunshine, Boylesbridge, Turnaround—that is all his territory. Not Dungannon where we used to live, Dungannon is too near town and my mother is grateful for that. He sells cough medicine, iron tonic, corn plasters, laxatives, pills for female disorders, mouth wash, shampoo, liniment, salves, lemon and orange and raspberry concentrate for making refreshing drinks, vanilla, food colouring, black and green tea, ginger, cloves and other spices, rat poison. He has a song about it, with these two lines:

> And have all liniments and oils,
> For everything from corns to boils. . . .

Not a very funny song, in my mother's opinion. A pedlar's song, and that is what he is, a pedlar knocking at backwoods kitchens. Up until last winter we had our own business, a fox farm. My father raised silver foxes and sold their pelts to the people who make them into capes and coats and muffs. Prices fell, my father hung on hoping they would get better next year, and they fell again, and he hung on one more year and one more and finally it was not possible to hang on any more, we owed everything to the feed company. I have heard my mother explain this, several times, to Mrs. Oliphant who is the only neighbour she talks to. (Mrs. Oliphant also has come down in the world, being a schoolteacher who married the janitor.) We poured all we had into it, my mother says, and we came out with nothing. Many people could say the same thing, these days, but my mother has no time for the national calamity, only ours. Fate has flung us onto a street of poor people (it does not matter that we were poor before, that was a different sort of poverty), and the only way to take this, as she sees it, is with dignity, with bitterness, with no reconciliation. No bathroom with a claw-footed tub and a flush toilet is going to comfort her, nor water on tap and sidewalks past the house and milk in bottles, not even the two movie theatres and the Venus Restaurant and Woolworths so marvellous it has live birds singing in its fan-cooled corners and fish as tiny as fingernails, as bright as moons, swimming in its green tanks. My mother does not care.

In the afternoons she often walks to Simon's Grocery and takes me with her to help carry things. She wears a good dress, navy blue with little flowers, sheer, worn over a navy-blue slip. Also a summer hat of white straw, pushed down on the side of the head, and white shoes I have just whitened on a newspaper on the back steps. I have my hair freshly done in long damp curls which the dry air will fortunately soon loosen, a stiff large hair-ribbon on top of my head. This is entirely different from going out after supper with my father. We have not walked past two houses before I feel we have become objects of universal ridicule. Even the dirty words chalked on the side-walk are laughing at us. My mother does not seem to notice. She walks serenely like a lady shopping, like a *lady* shopping, past the housewives in loose beltless dresses torn under the arms. With me her creation, wretched curls and flaunting hair bow, scrubbed knees and white socks—all I do not want to be. I loathe even my name when she says it in public, in a voice so high, proud and ringing, deliberately different from the voice of any other mother on the street.

My mother will sometimes carry home, for a treat, a brick of ice cream—pale Neapolitan; and because we have no refrigerator in our house we wake my brother and eat it at once in the dining room, always darkened by the wall of the house next door. I spoon it up tenderly, leaving the chocolate till last, hoping to have some still to eat when my brother's dish is empty. My mother tries then to imitate the conversations we used to have at Dungannon, going back to our earliest, most leisurely days before my brother was born, when she would give me a little tea and a lot of milk in a cup like hers and we would sit out on the step facing the pump, the lilac tree, the fox pens beyond. She is not able to keep from mentioning those days. "Do you remember when we put you in your sled and Major pulled you?" (Major our dog, that we had to leave with neighbours when we moved.) "Do you remember your sandbox outside the kitchen window?" I pretend to remember far less than I do, wary of being trapped into sympathy or any unwanted emotion.

My mother has headaches. She often has to lie down. She lies on my brother's narrow bed in the little screened porch, shaded by heavy branches. "I look up at that tree and I think I am at home," she says.

"What you need," my father tells her, "is some fresh air and a drive in the country." He means for her to go with him, on his Walker Brothers route.

That is not my mother's idea of a drive in the country.

"Can I come?"

"Your mother might want you for trying on clothes."

"I'm beyond sewing this afternoon," my mother says.

"I'll take her then. Take both of them, give you a rest."

What is there about us that people need to be given a rest from? Never mind. I am glad enough to find my brother and make him go to the toilet and get us both into the car, our knees unscrubbed, my hair unringleted. My father brings from the house his two heavy brown suitcases, full of bottles, and sets them on the back seat. He wears a white shirt, brilliant in the sunlight, a tie, light trousers belonging to his summer suit (his other suit is black, for funerals, and belonged to my uncle before he died) and a creamy straw hat. His salesman's outfit, with pencils clipped in the shirt pocket. He goes back once again, probably to say goodbye to my mother, to ask her if she is sure she doesn't want to come, and hear her say, "No. No thanks, I'm better just to lie here with my eyes closed." Then we are backing out of the driveway with the rising hope of adventure, just the little hope that takes you over the bump into the street, the hot air starting to move, turning into a breeze, the houses growing less and less familiar as we follow the short cut my father knows, the quick way out of town. Yet what is there waiting for us all afternoon but hot hours in stricken farmyards, perhaps a stop at a country store and three ice cream cones or bottles of pop, and my father singing? The one he made up about himself has a title—"The Walker Brothers Cowboy"—and it starts out like this:

> Old Ned Fields, he now is dead,
> So I am ridin' the route instead. . . .

Who is Ned Fields? The man he has replaced, surely, and if so he really is dead; yet my father's voice is mournful-jolly, making his death some kind of nonsense, a comic calamity. "Wisht I was back on the Rio Grande, plungin' through the dusky sand." My father sings most of the time while driving the car. Even now, heading out of town, crossing the bridge and taking the sharp turn onto the highway, he is humming something, mumbling a bit of a song to himself, just tuning up, really, getting ready to improvise, for out along the highway we pass the Baptist Camp, the Vacation Bible Camp, and he lets loose:

> Where are the Baptists, where are the Baptists,
> where are all the Baptists today?
> They're down in the water, in Lake Huron water,
> with their sins all a-gittin' washed away.

My brother takes this for straight truth and gets up on his knees trying to see down to the Lake. "I don't see any Baptists," he says accusingly. "Neither do I, son," says my father. "I told you, they're down in the Lake."

No roads paved when we left the highway. We have to roll

up the windows because of dust. The land is flat, scorched, empty. Bush lots at the back of the farms hold shade, black pine-shade like pools nobody can ever get to. We bump up a long lane and at the end of it what could look more unwelcoming, more deserted than the tall unpainted farmhouse with grass growing uncut right up to the front door, green blinds down and a door upstairs opening on nothing but air? Many houses have this door, and I have never yet been able to find out why. I ask my father and he says they are for walking in your sleep. *What?* Well if you happen to be walking in your sleep and you want to step outside. I am offended, seeing too late that he is joking, as usual, but my brother says sturdily, "If they did that they would break their necks."

The nineteen-thirties. How much this kind of farmhouse, this kind of afternoon, seem to me to belong to that one decade in time, just as my father's hat does, his bright flared tie, our car with its wide running board (an Essex, and long past its prime). Cars somewhat like it, many older, none dustier, sit in the farmyards. Some are past running and have their doors pulled off, their seats removed for use on porches. No living things to be seen, chickens or cattle. Except dogs. There are dogs, lying in any kind of shade they can find, dreaming, their lean sides rising and sinking rapidly. They get up when my father opens the car door, he has to speak to them. "Nice boy, there's a boy, nice old boy." They quiet down, go back to their shade. He should know how to quiet animals, he has held desperate foxes with tongs around their necks. One gentling voice for the dogs and another, rousing, cheerful, for calling at doors. "Hello there, Missus, it's the Walker Brothers man and what are you out of today?" A door opens, he disappears. Forbidden to follow, forbidden even to leave the car, we can just wait and wonder what he says. Sometimes trying to make my mother laugh he pretends to be himself in a farm kitchen, spreading out his sample case. "Now then, Missus, are you troubled with parasitic life? Your children's scalps, I mean. All those crawly little things we're too polite to mention that show up on the heads of the best of families? Soap alone is useless, kerosene is not too nice a perfume, but I have here—" Or else, "Believe me, sitting and driving all day the way I do I *know* the value of these fine pills. Natural relief.

A problem common to old folks, too, once their days of activity are over—How about you, Grandma?" He would wave the imaginary box of pills under my mother's nose and she would laugh finally, unwillingly. "He doesn't say that really, does he?" I said, and she said no of course not, he was too much of a gentleman.

One yard after another, then, the old cars, the pumps, dogs, views of grey barns and falling-down sheds and unturning windmills. The men, if they are working in the fields, are not in any fields that we can see. The children are far away, following dry creek beds or looking for blackberries, or else they are hidden in the house, spying at us through cracks in the blinds. The car seat has grown slick with our sweat. I dare my brother to sound the horn, wanting to do it myself but not wanting to get the blame. He knows better. We play *I Spy*, but it is hard to find many colours. Grey for the barns and sheds and toilets and houses, brown for the yard and fields, black or brown for the dogs. The rusting cars show rainbow patches, in which I strain to pick out purple or green; likewise I peer at doors for shreds of old peeling paint, maroon or yellow. We can't play with letters, which would be better, because my brother is too young to spell. The game disintegrates anyway. He claims my colours are not fair, and wants extra turns.

In one house no door opens, though the car is in the yard. My father knocks and whistles, calls, "Hullo there! Walker Brothers man!" but there is not a stir of reply anywhere. This house has no porch, just a bare, slanting slab of cement on which my father stands. He turns around, searching the barnyard, the barn whose mow must be empty because you can see the sky through it, and finally he bends to pick up his suitcases. Just then a window is opened upstairs, a white pot appears on the sill, is tilted over and its contents splash down the outside wall. The window is not directly above my father's head, so only a stray splash would catch him. He picks up his suitcases with no particular hurry and walks, no longer whistling, to the car. "Do you know what that was?" I say to my brother. "*Pee*." He laughs and laughs.

My father rolls and lights a cigarette before he starts the car. The window has been slammed down, the blind drawn, we never did see a hand or face. "Pee, pee," sings my brother ecstatically. "Somebody dumped down pee!" "Just don't tell your mother that," my father says. "She isn't liable to see the joke." "Is it in your song?" my brother wants to know. My father says no but he will see what he can do to work it in.

I notice in a little while that we are not turning in any more lanes, though it does not seem to me that we are headed home. "Is this the way to Sunshine?" I ask my father, and he answers, "No ma'am it's not." "Are we still in your territory?" He shakes his head. "We're going *fast*," my brother says approvingly, and in fact we are bouncing along through dry puddle-holes so that all the bottles in the suitcases clink together and gurgle promisingly.

Another lane, a house, also unpainted, dried to silver in the sun.

"I thought we were out of your territory."

"We are."

"Then what are we going in here for?"

"You'll see."

In front of the house a short, sturdy woman is picking up washing, which had been spread on the grass to bleach and dry. When the car stops she stares at it hard for a moment, bends to pick up a couple more towels to add to the bundle under her arm, comes across to us and says in a flat voice, neither welcoming nor unfriendly, "Have you lost your way?"

My father takes his time getting out of the car. "I don't think so," he says. "I'm the Walker Brothers man."

"George Golley is our Walker Brothers man," the woman says, "and he was out here no more than a week ago. Oh, my Lord God," she says harshly, "it's you."

"It was, the last time I looked in the mirror," my father says. The woman gathers all the towels in front of her and holds on to them tightly, pushing them against her stomach as if it hurt. "Of all the people I never thought to see. And telling me you were the Walker Brothers man."

"I'm sorry if you were looking forward to George Golley," my father says humbly.

"And look at me, I was prepared to clean the hen-house. You'll think that's just an excuse but it's true. I don't go round looking like this every day." She is wearing a farmer's straw hat, through which pricks of sunlight penetrate and float on her face, a loose, dirty print smock and running shoes. "Who are those in the car, Ben? They're not yours?"

"Well I hope and believe they are," my father says, and tells our names and ages. "Come on, you can get out. This is Nora, Miss Cronin. Nora, you better tell me, is it still Miss, or have you got a husband hiding in the woodshed?"

"If I had a husband that's not where I'd keep him, Ben," she says, and they both laugh, her laugh abrupt and somewhat angry. "You'll think I got no manners, as well as being dressed like a tramp," she says. "Come on in out of the sun. It's cool in the house."

We go across the yard ("Excuse me taking you in this way but I don't think the front door has been opened since Papa's funeral, I'm afraid the hinges might drop off"), up the porch steps, into the kitchen, which really is cool, high-ceilinged, the blinds of course down, a simple, clean, threadbare room with waxed worn linoleum, potted geraniums, drinking-pail and dipper, a round table with scrubbed oilcloth. In spite of the cleanness, the wiped and swept surfaces, there is a faint sour smell—maybe of the dishrag or the tin dipper or the oilcloth, or the old lady, because there is one, sitting in an easy chair under the clock shelf. She turns her head slightly in our direction and says, "Nora? Is that company?"

"Blind," says Nora in a quick explaining voice to my father. Then, "You won't guess who it is, Momma. Hear his voice."

My father goes to the front of her chair and bends and says hopefully, "Afternoon, Mrs. Cronin."

"Ben Jordan," says the old lady with no surprise. "You haven't been to see us in the longest time. Have you been out of the country?"

My father and Nora look at each other.

"He's married, Momma," says Nora cheerfully and aggressively. "Married and got two children and here they are." She pulls us forward, makes each of us touch the old lady's dry, cool hand while she says our names in turn. Blind! This is the first blind person I have ever seen close up. Her eyes are closed, the eyelids sunk away down, showing no shape of the eyeball, just hollows. From one hollow comes a drop of silver liquid, a medicine, or a miraculous tear.

"Let me get into a decent dress," Nora says. "Talk to Momma. It's a treat for her. We hardly ever see company, do we Momma?"

"Not many makes it out this road," says the old lady placidly. "And the ones that used to be around here, our old neighbours, some of them have pulled out."

"True everywhere," my father says.

"Where's your wife then?"

"Home. She's not too fond of the hot weather, makes her feel poorly."

"Well." This is a habit of country people, old people, to say "well", meaning, "is that so?" with a little extra politeness and concern.

Nora's dress, when she appears again—stepping heavily on Cuban heels down the stairs in the hall—is flowered more lavishly than anything my mother owns, green and yellow on brown, some sort of floating sheer crepe, leaving her arms bare. Her arms are heavy, and every bit of her skin you can see is covered with little dark freckles like measles. Her hair is short, black, coarse and curly, her teeth very white and strong. "It's the first time I knew there was such a thing as green poppies," my father says, looking at her dress.

"You would be surprised all the things you never knew," says Nora, sending a smell of cologne far and wide when she moves and displaying a change of voice to go with the dress, something more sociable and youthful. "They're not poppies anyway, they're just flowers. You go and pump me some good cold water and I'll make these children a drink." She gets down from the cupboard a bottle of Walker Brothers Orange syrup.

"You telling me you were the Walker Brothers man!"

"It's the truth, Nora. You go and look at my sample cases in the car if you don't believe me. I got the territory directly south of here."

"Walker Brothers? Is that a fact? You selling for Walker Brothers?"

"Yes ma'am."

"We always heard you were raising foxes over Dungannon way."

"That's what I was doing, but I kind of run out of luck in that business."

"So where're you living? How long've you been out selling?"

"We moved into Tuppertown. I been at it, oh, two, three months. It keeps the wolf from the door. Keeps him as far away as the back fence."

Nora laughs. "Well I guess you count yourself lucky to have the work. Isabel's husband in Brantford, he was out of work the longest time. I thought if he didn't find something soon I was going to have them all land in here to feed, and I tell you I was hardly looking forward to it. It's all I can manage with me and Momma."

"Isabel married," my father says. "Muriel married too?"

"No, she's teaching school out west. She hasn't been home for five years. I guess she finds something better to do with her holidays. I would if I was her." She gets some snapshots out of the table drawer and starts showing him. "That's Isabel's oldest boy, starting school. That's the baby sitting in her carriage. Isabel and her husband. Muriel. That's her room-mate with her. That's a fellow she used to go around with, and his car. He was working in a bank out there. That's her school, it has eight rooms. She teaches Grade Five." My father shakes his head. "I can't think of her any way but when she was going to school, so shy I used to pick her up on the road—I'd be on my way to see you—and she would not say one word, not even to agree it was a nice day."

"She's got over that."

"Who are you talking about?" says the old lady.

"Muriel. I said she's got over being shy."

"She was here last summer."

"No Momma that was Isabel. Isabel and her family were here last summer. Muriel's out west."

"I meant Isabel."

Shortly after this the old lady falls asleep, her head on the side, her mouth open. "Excuse her manners," Nora says. "It's old age." She fixes an afghan over her mother and says we can all go into the front room where our talking won't disturb her.

"You two," my father says. "Do you want to go outside and amuse yourselves?"

Amuse ourselves how? Anyway I want to stay. The front room is more interesting than the kitchen, though barer. There is a gramophone and a pump organ and a picture on the wall of Mary, Jesus' mother—I know that much—in shades of bright blue and pink with a spiked band of light around her head. I know that such pictures are found only in the homes of Roman Catholics and so Nora must be one. We have never known any Roman Catholics at all well, never well enough to visit in their houses. I think of what my grandmother and my Aunt Tena, over in Dungannon, used to always say to indicate that somebody was a Catholic. *So-and-so digs with the wrong foot*, they would say. *She digs with the wrong foot.* That was what they would say about Nora.

Nora takes a bottle, half full, out of the top of the organ and pours some of what is in it into the two glasses that she and my father have emptied of the orange drink.

"Keep it in case of sickness?" my father says.

"Not on your life," says Nora. "I'm never sick. I just keep it because I keep it. One bottle does me a fair time, though, because I don't care for drinking alone. Here's luck!" She and my father drink and I know what it is. Whisky. One of the things my mother has told me in our talks together is that my father never drinks whisky. But I see he does. He drinks whisky and he talks of people whose names I have never heard before. But after a while he turns to a familiar incident. He tells about the chamberpot that was emptied out the window. "Picture me there," he says, "hollering my heartiest. *Oh, lady, it's your Walker Brothers man, anybody home?*" He does himself hollering, grinning absurdly, waiting, looking up in pleased expectation and then—oh, ducking, covering his head with his arms, looking as if he begged for mercy (when he never did anything like that, I was watching), and Nora laughs, almost as hard as my brother did at the time.

"That isn't true! That's not a word true!"

"Oh, indeed it is ma'am. We have our heroes in the ranks of Walker Brothers. I'm glad you think it's funny," he says sombrely.

I ask him shyly, "Sing the song."

"What song? Have you turned into a singer on top of everything else?"

Embarrassed, my father says, "Oh, just this song I made up while I was driving around, it gives me something to do, making up rhymes."

But after some urging he does sing it, looking at Nora with a droll, apologetic expression, and she laughs so much that in places he has to stop and wait for her to get over laughing so he can go on, because she makes him laugh too. Then he does various parts of his salesman's spiel. Nora when she laughs squeezes her large bosom under her folded arms. "You're crazy," she says. "That's all you are." She sees my brother peering into the gramophone and she jumps up and goes over to him. "Here's us sitting enjoying ourselves and not giving you a thought, isn't it terrible?" she says. "You want me to put a record on, don't you? You want to hear a nice record? Can you dance? I bet your sister can, can't she?"

I say no. "A big girl like you and so good-looking and can't dance!" says Nora. "It's high time you learned. I bet you'd make a lovely dancer. Here, I'm going to put on a piece I used to dance to and even your daddy did, in his dancing days. You didn't know your daddy was a dancer, did you? Well, he is a talented man, your daddy!"

She puts down the lid and takes hold of me unexpectedly around the waist, picks up my other hand and starts making me go backwards. "This is the way, now, this is how they dance. Follow me. This foot, see. One and one-two. One and one-two. That's fine, that's lovely, don't look at your feet! Follow me, that's right, see how easy? You're going to be a lovely dancer! One and one-two. One and one-two. Ben, see your daughter dancing!" *Whispering while you cuddle near me Whispering where no one can hear me. . . .*

Round and round the linoleum, me proud, intent, Nora laughing and moving with great buoyancy, wrapping me in her strange gaiety, her smell of whisky, cologne, and sweat. Under the arms her dress is damp, and little drops form along her upper lip, hang in the soft black hairs at the corners of her mouth. She whirls me around in front of my father—causing me to stumble, for I am by no means so swift a pupil as she pretends—and lets me go, breathless.

"Dance with me, Ben."

"I'm the world's worst dancer, Nora, and you know it."

"I certainly never thought so."

"You would now."

She stands in front of him, arms hanging loose and hopeful, her breasts, which a moment ago embarrassed me with their warmth and bulk, rising and falling under her loose flowered dress, her face shining with the exercise, and delight.

"Ben."

My father drops his head and says quietly, "Not me, Nora."

So she can only go and take the record off. "I can drink alone but I can't dance alone," she says. "Unless I am a whole lot crazier than I think I am."

"Nora," says my father smiling. "You're not crazy."

"Stay for supper."

"Oh, no. We couldn't put you to the trouble."

"It's no trouble. I'd be glad of it."

"And their mother would worry. She'd think I'd turned us over in a ditch."

"Oh, well. Yes."

"We've taken a lot of your time now."

"Time," says Nora bitterly. "Will you come by ever again?"

"I will if I can," says my father.

"Bring the children. Bring your wife."

"Yes I will," says my father. "I will if I can."

When she follows us to the car he says, "You come to see us too, Nora. We're right on Grove Street, left-hand side going in, that's north, and two doors this side—east—of Baker Street."

Nora does not repeat these directions. She stands close to the car in her soft, brilliant dress. She touches the fender, making an unintelligible mark in the dust there.

On the way home my father does not buy any ice cream or pop, but he does go into a country store and get a package of licorice, which he shares with us. *She digs with the wrong foot,* I think, and the words seem sad to me as never before, dark, perverse. My father does not say anything to me about not mentioning things at home, but I know, just from the thought-fulness, the pause when he passes the licorice, that there are things not to be mentioned. The whisky, maybe the dancing. No worry about my brother, he does not notice enough. At most he might remember the blind lady, the picture of Mary.

"Sing," my brother commands my father, but my father says gravely, "I don't know, I seem to be fresh out of songs. You watch the road and let me know if you see any rabbits."

So my father drives and my brother watches the road for rabbits and I feel my father's life flowing back from our car in the last of the afternoon, darkening and turning strange, like a landscape that has an enchantment on it, making it kindly, ordinary and familiar while you are looking at it, but changing it, once your back is turned, into something you will never know, with all kinds of weathers, and distances you cannot imagine.

When we get closer to Tuppertown the sky becomes gently overcast, as always, nearly always, on summer evenings by the Lake.

Shirley Faessler **A BASKET OF APPLES**

This morning Pa had his operation. He said I was not to come for at least two or three days, but I slipped in anyway and took a look at him. He was asleep, and I was there only a minute before I was hustled out by a nurse.

"He looks terrible, nurse. Is he all right?"

She said he was fine. The operation was successful, there were no secondaries. instead of a bowel he would have a colostomy, and with care should last another—

Colostomy The word has set up such a drumming in my ears that I can't be sure now whether she said another few years or another five years. Let's say she said five years. If I go home and report this to Ma she'll fall down in a dead faint. She doesn't even know he's had an operation. She thinks he's in the hospital for a rest, a checkup. Nor did we know—my brother, my sister, and I—that he'd been having a series of X-rays.

"It looks like an obstruction in the lower bowel," he told us privately, "and I'll have to go in the hospital for a few days to find out what it's all about. Don't say anything to Ma."

"I have to go in the hospital," he announced to Ma the morning he was going in.

She screamed.

"Just for a little rest, a checkup," he went on, patient with her for once.

He's always hollering at her. He scolds her for a meal that isn't to his taste, finds fault with her housekeeping, gives her hell because her hair isn't combed in the morning and sends her back to the bedroom to tidy herself.

But Ma loves the old man. "Sooner a harsh word from Pa than a kind one from anyone else," she says.

"You're not to come and see me, you hear?" he cautioned her the morning he left for the hospital. "I'll phone you when I'm coming out."

I don't want to make out that my pa's a beast. He's not. True, he never speaks an endearing word to her, never praises her. He loses patience with her, flies off the handle and shouts. But Ma's content. Poor man works like a horse, she says, and what pleasures does he have. "So he hollers at me once in a while, I don't mind. God give him the strength to keep hollering at me, I won't repine."

Night after night he joins his buddies in the back room of an ice-cream parlour on Augusta Avenue for a glass of wine, a game of klaberjass, pinochle, dominoes: she's happy he's enjoying himself. She blesses him on his way out. "God keep you in good health and return you in good health."

But when he is home of an evening reading the newspaper and comes across an item that engages his interest, he lets her in on it too. He shows her a picture of the Dionne quintuplets and explains exactly what happened out there in Callander, Ontario. This is a golden moment for her—she and Pa sitting over a newspaper discussing world events. Another time he shows her a picture of the Irish Sweepstakes winner. He won a hundred and fifty thousand, he tells her. She's entranced. *Mmm-mm-mm!* What she couldn't do with that money. They'd fix up the bathroom, paint the kitchen, clean out the backyard. *Mmm-mm-mm!* Pa says if we had that kind of money we could afford to put a match to a hundred-dollar bill, set fire to the house and buy a new one. She laughs at his wit. He's so clever, Pa. Christmas morning King George VI is speaking on the radio. She's rattling around in the kitchen, Pa calls her to come and hear the King of England. She doesn't understand a word of English, but pulls up a chair and sits listening. "He stutters," says Pa. This she won't believe. A king? Stutters? But if Pa says so it must be true. She bends an ear to the radio. Next day she has something to report to Mrs. Oxenberg, our next-door neighbour.

I speak of Pa's impatience with her; I get impatient with her too. I'm always at her about one thing and another, chiefly about the weight she's putting on. Why doesn't she cut down on the bread, does she have to drink twenty glasses of tea a day? No wonder her feet are sore, carrying all that weight. (My ma's a short woman a little over five feet and weighs almost two hundred pounds.) "Go ahead, keep getting fatter," I tell her. "The way you're going you'll never be able to get into a decent dress again."

But it's Pa who finds a dress to fit her, a Martha Washington Cotton size 52, which but for the length is perfect for her. He finds a shoe she can wear, Romeo slippers with elasticized sides. And it's Pa who gets her to soak her feet, then sits with them in his lap scraping away with a razor blade at the calluses and corns.

Ma is my father's second wife, and our step-mother. My father, now sixty-three, was widowed thirty years ago. My sister was six at the time, I was five, and my brother was four when our mother died giving birth to a fourth child who lived only a few days. We were shunted around from one family to another who took us in out of compassion, till finally my father went to a marriage broker and put his case before him. He wanted a woman to make a home for his three orphans. An honest woman with a good heart, these were the two and only requirements. The marriage broker consulted his lists and said he thought he had two or three people who might fill the bill. Specifically, he had in mind a young woman from Russia, thirty years old, who was working without pay for relatives who had brought her over. She wasn't exactly an educated woman; in fact, she couldn't even read or write. As for honesty and heart, this he could vouch for. She was an orphan herself and as a child had been brought up in servitude.

Of the three women the marriage broker trotted out for him, my father chose Ma, and shortly afterward they were married.

A colostomy. So it is cancer . . .

As of the second day Pa was in hospital I had taken to dropping in on him on my way home from work. "Nothing yet," he kept saying, "maybe tomorrow they'll find out."

After each of these visits, four in all, I reported to Ma that I had seen Pa. "He looks fine. Best thing in the world for him, a rest in the hospital."

"Pa's not lonesome for me?" she asked me once, and laughing, turned her head aside to hide her foolishness from me.

Yesterday Pa said to me, "It looks a little more serious than I thought. I have to have an operation tomorrow. Don't say anything to Ma. And don't come here for at least two or three days."

I take my time getting home. I'm not too anxious to face Ma—grinning like a monkey and lying to her the way I have been doing the last four days. I step into a hospital telephone booth to call my married sister. She moans. "What are you going to say to Ma?" she asks.

I get home about half past six, and Ma's in the kitchen making a special treat for supper. A recipe given her by a neighbour and which she's recently put in her culinary inventory—pieces of cauliflower dipped in batter and fried in butter.

"I'm not hungry, Ma. I had something in the hospital cafeteria." (We speak in Yiddish; as I mentioned before, Ma can't speak English.)

She continues scraping away at the cauliflower stuck in the bottom of the pan. (Anything she puts in a pan sticks.) "You saw Pa?" she asks without looking up. Suddenly she thrusts the pan aside. "The devil take it, I put in too much flour." She makes a pot of tea, and we sit at the kitchen table drinking it. To keep from facing her I drink mine leafing through a magazine. I can hear her sipping hers through a cube of sugar in her mouth. I can feel her eyes on me. Why doesn't she ask me, How's Pa? Why doesn't she speak? She never stops questioning me when I come from hospital, drives me crazy with the same questions again and again. I keep turning pages, she's still sucking away at that cube of sugar—a maddening habit of hers. I looked up. Of course her eyes are fixed on me, probing, searching.

I lash out at her. "Why are you looking at me like that!"

Without answer she takes her tea and dashes it in the sink. She spits the cube of sugar from her mouth. (Thank God for that; she generally puts it back in the sugar bowl.) She resumes her place, puts her hands in her lap, and starts twirling her thumbs. No one in the world can twirl his thumbs as fast as Ma. When she gets them going they look like miniature windmills whirring around.

"She asks me why I'm looking at her like that," she says addressing herself to the twirling thumbs in her lap. "I'm looking at her like that because I'm trying to read the expression in her face. She tells me Pa's fine, but my heart tells me different."

Suddenly she looks up, and thrusting her head forward, splays her hands out flat on the table. She has a dark-complexioned strong face, masculine almost, and eyes so black the pupil is indistinguishable from the iris.

"Do you know who Pa is!" she says. "Do you know who's lying in the hospital? I'll tell you who. The captain of our ship is lying in the hospital. The emperor of our domain. If the captain goes down, the ship goes with him. If the emperor leaves his throne, we can say goodbye to our domain. That's who's lying in the hospital. Now ask me why do I look at you like that."

She breaks my heart. I want to put my arms around her, but I can't do it. We're not a demonstrative family, we never kiss, we seldom show affection. We're always hollering at each other. Less than a month ago I hollered at Pa. He had taken to dosing himself. He was forever mixing something in a glass, and I became irritated at the powders, pills and potions lying around in every corner of the house like mouse droppings.

"You're getting to be a hypochondriac!" I hollered at him, not knowing what trouble he was in.

I reach out and put my hand over hers. "I wouldn't lie to you, Ma. Pa's fine, honest to God."

She holds her hand still a few seconds, then eases it from under and puts it over mine. I can feel the weight of her hand pinioning mine to the table, and we sit a moment in an unaccustomed gesture of tenderness, with locked hands.

"You know I had a dream about Pa last night?" she says. "I dreamt he came home with a basket of apples. I think that's a good dream?"

Ma's immigration to Canada had been sponsored by her Uncle Yankev. Yankev at the time he sent for his niece was in his mid-forties and had been settled a number of years in Toronto with his wife, Danyeh, and their six children. They made an odd pair, Yankev and Danyeh. He was a tall two-hundred-and-fifty-pound handsome man, and Danyeh, whom he detested, was a lackluster little woman with a pockmarked face, maybe weighing ninety pounds. Yankev was constantly abusing her. Old Devil, he called her to her face and in the presence of company.

Ma stayed three years with Yankev and his family, working like a skivvy for them and without pay. Why would Yankev pay his niece like a common servant? She was one of the family, she sat at table with them and ate as much as she wanted. She had a bed and even a room to herself, which she'd never had before. When Yankev took his family for a ride in the car to Sunnyside, she was included. When he bought ice-cream cones, he bought for all.

She came to Pa without a dime in her pocket.

Ma has a slew of relatives, most of them émigrés from a remote little village somewhere in the depths of Russia. They're a crude lot, loud-mouthed and coarse and my father had no use for any of them. The Russian Hordes, he called them. He was never rude; anytime they came around to visit he simply made himself scarce.

One night I remember in particular; I must have been about seven. Ma was washing up after supper and Pa was reading a newspaper when Yankev arrived, with Danyeh trailing him. Pa folded his paper, excused himself, and was gone. The minute Pa was gone Yankev went to the stove and lifted the lids from the two pots. Just as he thought—*mamaliga* in one pot, in the other one beans, and in the frying pan a piece of meat their cat would turn its nose up at. He sat himself in the rocking chair he had given Ma as a wedding present, and rocking, proceeded to lecture her. He had warned her against the marriage, but if she was satisfied, he was content. One question and that's all. How had she bettered her lot? True, she was no longer an old maid. True, she was now mistress of her own home. He looked around and snorted. A hovel. "*And* three snot-nose kids," he said, pointing to us.

Danyeh, hunched over in a kitchen chair, her feet barely reaching the floor, said something to him in Russian, cautioning him, I think. He told her to shut up, and in Yiddish continued his tirade against Ma. He had one word to say to her. To *watch* herself. Against his advice she had married this no-good Rumanian twister, this murderer. The story of how he had kept his first wife pregnant all the time was now well known. Also well known was the story of how she had died in her ninth month with a fourth child. Over an ironing board. Ironing his shirts while he was out playing cards with his Rumanian cronies and drinking wine. He had buried one wife, and now was after burying a second. So Ma had better *watch* herself, that's all.

Ma left her dishwashing and with dripping wet hands took hold of a chair and seated herself facing Yankev. She begged him not to say another word. "Not another word, Uncle Yankev, I beg you. Till the day I die I'll be grateful to you for bringing me over. I don't know how much money you laid out for my passage, but I tried my best to make up for it in the three years I stayed with you, by helping you in the house. But maybe I'm still in your debt? Is this what gives you the right to talk against my husband?"

Yankev, rocking, turned up his eyes and groaned. "*You* speak to her," he said to Danyeh. "It's impossible for a *human being* to get through to her."

Danyeh knew better than to open her mouth.

"Uncle Yankev," Ma continued, "every word you speak against my husband is like a knife stab in my heart." She leaned forward, thumbs whirring away. "*Mamaliga?* Beans? A piece of meat your cat wouldn't eat? A crust of *bread* at his board, and I will thank God every day of my life that he chose me from the other two the *shadchan* showed him."

In the beginning my father gave her a hard time. I remember his bursts of temper at her rough ways in the kitchen. She never opened a kitchen drawer without wrestling it—wrenching it open, slamming it shut. She never put a kettle on the stove without its running over at the boil. A pot never came to stove without its lid being inverted, and this for some reason maddened him. He'd right the lid, sometimes scalding his fingers—and all hell would break loose. We never sat down to a set or laid table. As she had been used to doing, so she continued; slamming a pot down on the table, scattering a handful of cutlery, dealing out assorted-size plates. More than once, with one swipe of his hand my father would send the plates crashing to the floor, and stalk out. She'd sit a minute looking at our faces, one by one, then start twirling her thumbs and talking to herself. What had she done now?

"Eat!" she'd admonish us, and leaving table would go to the mirror over the kitchen sink and ask herself face to face, "What did I do now?" She would examine her face profile and front and then sit down to eat. After, she'd gather up the dishes, dump them in the sink, and running water over them, would study herself in the mirror. "He'll be better," she'd tell herself, smiling. "He'll be soft as butter when he comes home. You'll see," she'd promise her image in the mirror.

Later in life, mellowed by the years perhaps (or just plain defeated—there was no changing her), he became more tolerant of her ways and was kinder to her. When it became difficult for her to get around because of her poor feet, he did her marketing. He attended to her feet, bought her the Martha Washingtons, the Romeo slippers, and on a summer's evening on his way home from work, a brick of ice cream. She was very fond of it.

Three years ago he began promoting a plan, a plan to give Ma some pleasure. (This was during Exhibition time.) "You know," he said to me, "it would be very nice if Ma could see the fireworks at the Exhibition. She's never seen anything like that in her life. Why don't you take her?"

The idea of Ma going to the Ex for the fireworks was so preposterous, it made me laugh. She never went anywhere.

"Don't laugh," he said. "It wouldn't hurt you to give her a little pleasure once in a while."

He was quite keen that she should go, and the following year he canvassed the idea again. He put money on the table for taxi and grandstand seats. "Take her," he said.

"Why don't you take her?" I said. "She'll enjoy it more going with you."

"Me? What will I do at the Exhibition?"

As children, we were terrified of Pa's temper. Once in a while he'd belt us around, and we were scared that he might take the strap to Ma too. But before long we came to know that she was the only one of us not scared of Pa when he got mad. Not even from the beginning when he used to let fly at her was she intimidated by him, not in the least, and in later years was even capable of getting her own back by taking a little dig at him now and then about the "aristocracy"—as she called my father's Rumanian connections.

Aside from his buddies in the back room of the ice-cream parlour on Augusta Avenue, my father also kept in touch with his Rumanian compatriots (all of whom had prospered), and would once in a while go to them for an evening. We were never invited, nor did they come to us. This may have been my father's doing, I do not know. I expect he was ashamed of his circumstances, possibly of Ma, and certainly of how we lived.

Once in a blue moon during Rosh Hashanah or Yom Kippur after shul, they would unexpectedly drop in on us. One time a group of four came to the house, and I remember Pa darting around like a gadfly, collecting glasses, wiping them, and pouring a glass of wine he'd made himself. Ma shook hands all around, then went to the kitchen to cut some slices of her honey cake, scraping off the burnt part. I was summoned to take the plate in to "Pa's gentle folk." Pretending to be busy, she rattled around the kitchen a few seconds, then seated herself in the partially open door, inspecting them. Not till they were leaving did she come out again, to wish them a good year.

The minute they were gone, my father turned on her. "Russian peasant! Tartar savage, you! Sitting there with your eyes popping out. Do you think they couldn't see you?"

"What's the matter? Even a cat may look at a king?" she said blandly.

"Why didn't you come out instead of sitting there like a caged animal?"

"Because I didn't want to shame you," she said, twirling

her thumbs and swaying back and forth in the chair Yankev had given her as a wedding present.

My father busied himself clearing table, and after a while he softened. But she wasn't through with him yet. "Which one was Falik's wife?" she asked in seeming innocence. "The one with the beard?"

This drew his fire again. "No!" he shouted.

"Oh, the other one. The pale one with the hump on her back," she said wickedly.

So . . . notwithstanding the good dream Ma had of Pa coming home with a basket of apples, she never saw him again. He died six days after the operation.

It was a harrowing six days, dreadful. As Pa got weaker, the more disputatious we became—my brother, my sister, and —arguing and snapping at each other outside his door, the point of contention being should Ma be told or not.

Nurse Brown, the special we'd put on duty, came out once to hush us. "You're not helping him by arguing like this. He can hear you."

"Is he conscious, nurse?"

"Of course he's conscious."

"Is there any hope?"

"There's always hope," she said. "I've been on cases like this before, and I've seen them rally."

We went our separate ways, clinging to the thread of hope she'd given us. The fifth day after the operation I had a call from Nurse Brown: "Your father wants to see you."

Nurse Brown left the room when I arrived, and my father motioned me to undo the zipper of his oxygen tent. "Ma's a good woman," he said, his voice so weak I had to lean close to hear him. "You'll look after her? Don't put her aside. Don't forget about her—"

"What are you talking about!" I said shrilly, then lowered my voice to a whisper. "The doctor told me you're getting better. Honest to God, Pa, I wouldn't lie to you," I whispered.

He went on as if I hadn't spoken. "Even a servant if you had her for thirty years, you wouldn't put aside because you don't need her anymore—"

"Wait a minute," I said, and went to the corridor to fetch Nurse Brown. "Nurse Brown, will you tell my father what you told me yesterday. You remember? About being on cases like this before, and you've seen them rally. Will you tell that to my father, please. He talks as if he's—"

I ran from the room and stood outside the door, bawling. Nurse Brown opened the door a crack. "*Ssh!* You'd better go now; I'll call you if there's any change."

At five the next morning, my brother telephoned from hospital. "You'd better get down here," he said. "I think the old man's checking out. I've already phoned Gertie."

My sister and I arrived at the hospital within seconds of each other. My brother was just emerging from Pa's room. In the gesture of a baseball umpire he jerked a thumb over his shoulder, signifying OUT.

"Is he dead?" we asked our brother.

"Just this minute," he replied.

Like three dummies we paced the dimly-lit corridor, no speaking to each other. In the end we were obliged to speak we had to come to a decision about how to proceed next.

We taxied to the synagogue of which Pa was a member and roused the shamus. "As soon as it's light I'll get th rabbi," he said. "He'll attend to everything. Meantime g home."

In silence we walked slowly home. Dawn was just breaking and Ma, a habitually early riser, was bound to be up now an in the kitchen. Quietly we let ourselves in and passed throug the hall leading to the kitchen. We were granted an unex pected respite; Ma was not yet up. We waited ten minutes fo her, fifteen—an agonizing wait. We decided one of us ha better go and wake her; what was the sense in prolonging it The next minute we changed our minds. To awaken her wit such tidings would be inhuman, a brutal thing to do.

"Let's stop whispering," my sister whispered. "Let's tal in normal tones, do something, make a noise, she'll hear u and come out."

In an access of activity we busied ourselves. My sister pu the kettle on with a clatter; I took teaspoons from the drawe clacking them like castanets. She was bound to hear, thei bedroom was on the same floor at the front of the house— but five minutes elapsed and not a sound from the room.

"Go and see," my sister said, and I went and opened the door to that untidy bedroom Pa used to rail against.

Ma, her black eyes circled and her hair in disarray, was sitting up in bed. At the sight of me she flopped back and pulled the feather tick over her head. I approached the bed and took the covers from her face. "Ma—"

She sat up. "You are guests in my house now?"

For the moment I didn't understand. I didn't know the meaning of her words. But the next minute the meaning of them was clear—with Pa dead, the link was broken. The bond, the tie that held us together. We were no longer her children. We were now guests in her house.

"When did Pa die?" she asked.

"How did you know?"

"My heart told me."

Barefooted, she followed me to the kitchen. My sister gave her a glass of tea, and we stood like mutes, watching her sipping it through a cube of sugar.

"You were all there when Pa died?"

"Just me, Ma," my brother said.

She nodded. "His kaddish. Good."

I took a chair beside her, and for once without constraint or self-consciousness, put my arm around her and kissed her on the cheek.

"Ma, the last words Pa spoke were about you. He said you were a good woman. 'Ma's a good woman,' that's what he said to me."

She put her tea down and looked me in the face. "Pa said that? He said I was a good woman?" She clasped her hands. "May the light shine on him in paradise," she said, and wept silently, putting her head down to hide her tears.

Eight o'clock the rabbi telephoned. Pa was now at the funeral parlour on College near Augusta, and the funeral was to be at eleven o'clock. Ma went to ready herself, and in a few minutes called me to come and zip up her black crepe, the dress Pa had bought her six years ago for the Applebaum wedding.

The Applebaums, neighbours, had invited Ma and Pa to the wedding of their daughter, Lily. Right away Pa declared he wouldn't go. Ma kept coaxing. How would it look? It would be construed as unfriendly, unneighbourly. A few days before the wedding he gave in, and Ma began scratching through her wardrobe for something suitable to wear. Nothing she exhibited pleased him. He went downtown and came back with the black crepe and an outsize corset.

I dressed her for the wedding, combed her hair, and put some powder on her face. Pa became impatient; he had already called a cab. What was I doing? Getting her ready for a beauty contest? The taxi came, and as Pa held her coat he said to me in English, "You know, Ma's not a bad-looking woman?"

For weeks she talked about the good time she'd had at the Applebaum wedding, but chiefly about how Pa had attended her. Not for a minute had he left her side. Two hundred people at the wedding and not one woman among them had the attention from her husband that she had had from Pa. "Pa's a gentleman," she said to me, proud as proud.

Word of Pa's death got around quickly, and by nine in the morning people began trickling in. First arrivals were Yankev and Danyeh. Yankev, now in his seventies and white-haired, was still straight and handsome. The same Yankev except for the white hair and an asthmatic condition causing him to wheeze and gasp for breath. Danyeh was wizened and bent over, her hands hanging almost to her knees. They approached Ma, Danyeh trailing Yankev. Yankev held out a hand and with the other one thumped his chest, signifying he was too congested to speak. Danyeh gave her bony hand to Ma and muttered a condolence.

From then on there was a steady influx of people. Here was Chaim the schnorrer! We hadn't seen him in years. Chaim the schnorrer, stinking of fish and in leg wrappings as always, instead of socks. Rich as Croesus he was said to be, a fish-peddling miser who lived on soda crackers and milk and kept his money in his leg wrappings. Yankev, a minute ago too congested for speech, found words for Chaim. "How much money have you got in those *gutkess*? The truth, Chaim!"

Ma shook hands with all, acknowledged their sympathy, and to some she spoke a few words. I observed the Widow Spector, a gossip and trouble-maker, sidling through the crowd and easing her way toward Ma. "The Post" she was called by people on the street. No one had the time of day for her; even Ma used to hide from her.

I groaned at the sight of her. As if Ma didn't have enough to contend with. But No! here was Ma welcoming the Widow Spector, holding hand out to her. "Give me your hand, Mrs. Spector. Shake hands, we're partners now. Now I know the taste, I'm a widow too." Ma patted the chair beside her. "Sit down partner. Sit down."

At a quarter to eleven the house was clear of people. "Is it time?" Ma asked, and we answered, Yes, it was time to go. We were afraid this would be the breaking point for her, but she went calmly to the bedroom and took her coat from the peg on the door and came to the kitchen with it, requesting that it be brushed off.

The small funeral parlour was jammed to the doors, every seat taken but for four up front left vacant for us. On a trestle table directly in front of our seating was the coffin. A pine box draped in a black cloth, and in its centre a white Star of David.

Ma left her place, approached the coffin, and as she stood before it with clasped hands I noticed the uneven hemline of her coat, hiked up in back by that mound of flesh on her shoulders. I observed that her lisle stockings were twisted at the ankles, and was embarrassed for her.

She stood silently a moment, then began to speak. She called him her dove, her comrade, her friend.

"Life is a dream," she said. "You were my treasure. You were the light of my eyes. I thought to live my days out with you—and look what it has come to." (She swayed slightly, the black shawl slipping from her head—and I observed that could have done with a brushing too.) "If ever I offended you or caused you even a twinge of discomfort, forgive me for it. As your wife I lived like a queen. Look at me now. I'm nothing. You were my jewel, my crown. With you at its head my house was a palace. I return now to a hovel. Forgive me for everything, my dove. Forgive me."

("Russian peasant," Pa used to say to her in anger, "Tartar savage." If he could see her now as she stood before his bier mourning him. Mourning him like Hecuba mourning Priam and the fall of Troy. And I a minute ago was ashamed of her hiked-up coat, her twisted stockings and dusty shawl.)

People were weeping; Ma resumed her place dry-eyed, and the rabbi began the service.

It is now a year since Pa died, and as he had enjoined me to, I am looking after Ma. I have not put her aside. I get cross and holler at her as I always have done, but she allows for my testiness and does not hold it against me. I'm a spinster, an old maid now approaching my thirty-seventh year, and she pities me for it. I get bored telling her again and again that Pa's last words were Ma's a good woman, and sometimes wish I'd never mentioned it. She cries a lot, and I get impatient with her tears. But I'm good to her.

This afternoon I called Moodey's, booked two seats for the grandstand, and tonight I'm taking her to the Ex and she'll see the fireworks.

Where the myth touches us

E. W. Thomson

GREAT GODFREY'S LAMENT

"Hark to Angus! Man, his heart will be sore the night! In five years I have not heard him playing 'Great Godfrey's Lament,'" said old Alexander McTavish, as with him I was sitting of a June evening, at sundown, under a wide apple-tree of his orchard-lawn.

When the sweet song-sparrows of the Ottawa valley had ceased their plaintive strains, Angus McNeil began on his violin. This night, instead of "Tullochgorum" or "Roy's Wife" or "The March of the McNeils," or any merry strath-spey, he crept into an unusual movement, and from a distance came the notes of an exceeding strange strain blent with the meditative murmur of the Rataplan Rapids.

I am not well enough acquainted with musical terms to tell the method of that composition in which the wail of a High-land coronach seemed mingled with such mournful crooning as I had heard often from Indian voyageurs north of Lake Superior. Perhaps that fancy sprang from my knowledge that Angus McNeil's father had been a younger son of the chief of the McNeil clan, and his mother a daughter of the greatest man of the Cree nation.

"Ay, but Angus is wae," sighed old McTavish. "What will he be seeing the noo? It was the night before his wife died that he played yon last. Come, we will go up the road. He does be liking to see the people gather to listen."

We walked, maybe three hundred yards, and stood leaning against the ruined picket-fence that surrounds the great stone house built by Hector McNeil, the father of Angus, when he retired from his position as one of the "Big Bourgeois" of the famous Northwest Fur Trading Company.

The huge square structure of the four stories and a basement is divided, above the ground floor, into eight suites, some of four, and some of five rooms. In these suites the fur-trader, whose ideas were all patriarchal, had designed that he and his Indian wife, with his seven sons and their future families, should live to the end of his days and theirs. That was a dream at the time when his boys were all under nine years old, and Godfrey little more than a baby in arms.

The ground-floor is divided by a hall twenty-five feet wide into two long chambers, one intended to serve as a dining-hall for the multitude of descendants that Hector expected to see round his old age, the other as a withdrawing-room for himself and his wife, or for festive occasions. In this mansion Angus McNeil now dwelt alone.

He sat out that evening on a balcony at the rear of the hall, whence he could overlook the McTavish place and the hamlet that extends a quarter of a mile further down the Ottawa's north shore. His right side was toward the large group of French-Canadian people who had gathered to hear him play. Though he was sitting, I could make out that his was a gigantic figure.

"Ay—it will be just exactly 'Great Godfrey's Lament,'" McTavish whispered. "Weel do I mind him playing yon many's the night after Godfrey was laid in the mools. Then he played it no more till before his ain wife died. What is he seeing now? Man, it's weel kenned he has the second sight at times. Maybe he sees the pit digging for himself. He's the last of them."

"Who was Great Godfrey?" I asked, rather loudly.

Angus McNeil instantly cut short the "Lament," rose from his chair, and faced us.

"Aleck McTavish, who have you with you?" he called imperiously.

"My young cousin from the city, Mr. McNeil," said McTavish, with deference.

"Bring him in. I wish to spoke with you, Aleck McTavish. The young man that is not acquaint with the name of Great Godfrey McNeil can come with you. I will be at the great door."

"It's strange-like," said McTavish, as we went to the upper gate. "He has not asked me inside for near five years. I'm feared his wits is disordered, by his way of speaking. Mind what you say. Great Godfrey was most like a god to Angus."

When Angus McNeil met us at the front door I saw he was verily a giant. Indeed, he was a wee bit more than six and a half feet tall when he stood up straight. Now he was stooped a little, not with age, but with consumption,—the disease most fatal to men of mixed white and Indian blood. His face was dark brown, his features of the Indian cast, but his black hair had not the Indian lankness. It curled tightly round his grand head.

Without a word he beckoned us on into the vast withdrawing-room. Without a word he seated himself beside a large oaken centre-table, and motioned us to sit opposite.

Before he broke silence, I saw that the windows of that great chamber were hung with faded red damask; that the heads of many a bull moose, buck, bear, and wolf grinned among guns and swords and claymores from its walls; that charred logs, fully fifteen feet long, remained in the fireplace from the last winter's burning; that there were three dim portraits in oil over the mantel; that the room contained much frayed furniture, once sumptuous of red velvet; and that many skins of wild beasts lay strewn over a hard-wood floor whose edges still retained their polish and faintly gleamed in rays from the red west.

That light was enough to show that two of the oil paintings must be those of Hector McNeil and his Indian wife. Between these hung one of a singularly handsome youth with yellow hair.

"Here my father lay dead," cried Angus McNeil, suddenly striking the table. He stared at us silently for many seconds, then again struck the table with the side of his clenched fist. "He lay here dead on this table—yes! It was Godfrey that straked him out all alone on this table. You mind Great Godfrey, Aleck McTavish."

"Well I do, Mr. McNeil; and your mother yonder,—a grand lady she was." McTavish spoke with curious humility, seeming wishful, I thought, to comfort McNeil's sorrow by exciting his pride.

"Ay—they'll tell hereafter that she was just exactly a squaw," cried the big man, angrily. "But grand she was, and a great lady, and a proud. Oh, man, man! but they were proud, my father and my Indian mother. And Godfrey was the pride of the hearts of them both. No wonder; but it was sore on the rest of us after they took him apart from our ways."

Aleck McTavish spoke not a word, and big Angus, after a long pause, went on as if almost unconscious of our presence:—

"White was Godfrey, and rosy of the cheek like my father; and the blue eyes of him would match the sky when you'll be seeing it up through a blazing maple on a clear day of October. Tall, and straight, and grand was Godfrey, my brother. What was the thing Godfrey could not do? The songs of him hushed the singing-birds on the tree, and the fiddle he would play to take the soul out of your body. There was not white one among us till he was born.

"The rest of us all were just Indians—ay, Indians, Aleck McTavish. Brown we were, and the desire of us was all for the woods and the river. Godfrey had white sense like my father, and often we saw the same look in his eyes. My God, but we feared our father!"

Angus paused to cough. After the fit he sat silent for some minutes. The voice of the great rapid seemed to fill the room. When he spoke again, he stared past our seat with fixed, dilated eyes, as if tranced by a vision.

"Godfrey, Godfrey—you hear! Godfrey, the six of us would go over the falls and not think twice of it, if it would please you, when you were little. Oich, the joy we had in the white skin of you, and the fine ways, till my father and mother saw we were just making an Indian of you, like ourselves! So they took you away; ay, and many's the day the six of us went to the woods and the river, missing you sore.

It's then you began to look on us with that look that we could not see was different from the look we feared in the blue eyes of our father. Oh, but we feared him, Godfrey! And the time went by, and we feared and we hated you that seemed lifted up above your Indian brothers!

"Oich, the masters they got to teach him!" said Angus, addressing himself again to my cousin. "In the Latin and the Greek they trained him. History books he read, and stories in song. Ay, and the manners of Godfrey! Well might the whole pride of my father and mother be on their one white son. A grand young gentleman was Godfrey,—Great Godfrey we called him, when he was eighteen.

"The fine, rich people that would come up in bateaux from Montreal to visit my father had the smile and the kind word for Godfrey; but they looked upon us with the eyes of the white man for the Indian. And that look we were more and more sure was growing harder in Godfrey's eyes. So we looked back at him with the eyes of the wolf that stares at the bull moose, and is fierce to pull him down, but dares not try, for the moose is too great and lordly.

"Mind you, Aleck McTavish, for all we hated Godfrey when we thought he would be looking at us like strange Indians—for all that, yet we were proud of him that he was our own brother. Well we minded how he was all like one with us when he was little; and in the calm looks of him, and the white skin, and the yellow hair, and the grandeur of him, we had pride, do you understand? Ay, and in the strength of him we were glad. Would we not sit still and pleased when it was the talk how he could run quicker than the best, and jump higher than his head—ay, would we! Man, there was none could compare in strength with Great Godfrey, the youngest of us all!

"He and my father and mother more and more lived by themselves in this room. Yonder room across the hall was left to us six Indians. No manners, no learning had we; we were no fit company for Godfrey. My mother was like she was wilder with love of Godfrey the more he grew and the grander, and never a word for days and weeks together did she give to us. It was Godfrey this, and Godfrey that, and all her thought was Godfrey!

"Most of all we hated him when she was lying dead here on this table. We six in the other room could hear Godfrey and my father groan and sigh. We would step softly to the door and listen to them kissing her that was dead,—them white, and she Indian like ourselves,—and us not daring to go in for the fear of the eyes of our father. So the soreness was in our hearts so cruel hard that we would not go in till the last, for all their asking. My God, my God, Aleck McTavish, if you saw her! she seemed smiling like at Godfrey, and she looked like him then, for all she was brown as November oak-leaves, and he white that day as the froth on the rapid.

"That put us farther from Godfrey than before. And farther yet we were from him after, when he and my father would be walking up and down, up and down, arm in arm, up and down the lawn in the evenings. They would be talking about books, and the great McNeils in Scotland. The six of us knew we were McNeils, for all we were Indians, and we would listen to the talk of the great pride and the great deeds of the McNeils that was our own kin. We would be drinking the whiskey if we had it, and saying: 'Godfrey to be the only McNeil! Godfrey to take all the pride of the name of us!' Oh, man, man! but we hated Godfrey sore."

Big Angus paused long, and I seemed to see clearly the two fair-haired, tall men walking arm in arm on the lawn in the twilight, as if unconscious or careless of being watched and overheard by six sore-hearted kinsmen.

"You'll mind when my father was thrown from his horse and carried into this room, Aleck McTavish? Ay, well you do. But you nor no other living man but me knows what came about the night that he died.

"Godfrey was alone with him. The six of us were in yon room. Drink we had, but cautious we were with it, for there was a deed to be done that would need all our senses. We sat in a row on the floor—we were Indians—it was our wigwam— we sat on the floor to be against the ways of them two. Godfrey was in here across the hall from us; alone he was with our white father. He would be chief over us by the will, no doubt,—and if Godfrey lived through that night it would be strange.

"We were cautious with the whiskey, I told you before. Not a sound could we hear of Godfrey or of my father. Only the rapid, calling and calling,—I mind it well that night. Ay, and well I mind the striking of the great clock,—tick, tick, tick, tick, tick,—I listened and I dreamed on it till I doubted but it was the beating of my father's heart.

"Ten o'clock was gone by, and eleven was near. How many of us sat sleeping I know not; but I woke up with a start, and there was Great Godfrey, with a candle in his hand, looking down strange at us, and us looking up strange at him.

" 'He is dead,' Godfrey said.

"We said nothing.

" 'Father died two hours ago,' Godfrey said.

"We said nothing.

" 'Our father is white,—he is very white,' Godfrey said, and he trembled. 'Our mother was brown when she was dead.'

"Godfrey's voice was wild.

" 'Come, brothers, and see how white is our father,' Godfrey said.

"No one of us moved.

" 'Won't you come? In God's name, come,' said Godfrey. 'Oich—but it is very strange! I have looked in his face so long that now I do not know him for my father. He is like no kin to me, lying there. I am alone, alone.'

"Godfrey wailed in a manner. It made me ashamed to hear his voice like that—him that looked like my father that was always silent as a sword—him that was the true McNeil.

" 'You look at me, and your eyes are the eyes of my mother,' says Godfrey, staring wilder. 'What are you doing here, all so still? Drinking the whiskey? I am the same as you. I am your brother. I will sit with you, and if you drink the whiskey, I will drink the whiskey, too.'

"Aleck McTavish! with that he sat down on the floor in the dirt and litter beside Donald, that was oldest of us all.

" 'Give me the bottle,' he said. 'I am as much Indian as you, brothers. What you do I will do, as I did when I was little, long ago.'

"To see him sit down in his best,—all his learning and his grand manners as if forgotten,—man, it was like as if our father himself was turned Indian, and was low in the dirt!

"What was in the heart of Donald I don't know, but he lifted the bottle and smashed it down on the floor.

" 'God in heaven! what's to become of the McNeils! You that was the credit of the family, Godfrey!' says Donald with a groan.

"At that Great Godfrey jumped to his feet like he was come awake.

" 'You're fitter to be the head of the McNeils than I am, Donald,' says he; and with that the tears broke out of his eyes, and he cast himself into Donald's arms. Well, with that we all began to cry as if our hearts would break. I threw myself down on the floor at Godfrey's feet, and put my arms round his knees the same as I'd lift him up when he was little. There I cried, and we all cried around him, and after a bit I said:

" 'Brothers, this was what was in the mind of Godfrey. He was all alone in yonder. We are his brothers, and his heart warmed to us, and he said to himself, it was better to be like us than to be alone, and he thought if he came and sat down and drank the whiskey with us, he would be our brother again, and not be any more alone.'

" 'Ay, Angus, Angus, but how did you know that?' says Godfrey, crying; and he put his arms round my neck, and lifted me up till we were breast to breast. With that we all put our arms some way round one another and Godfrey, and there we stood sighing and swaying and sobbing a long time, and no man saying a word.

" 'Oh, man, Godfrey dear, but our father is gone, and who can talk with you now about the Latin, and the history books, and the great McNeils—and our mother that's gone?' says Donald; and the thought of it was such pity that our hearts seemed like to break.

"But Godfrey said: 'We will talk together like brothers. If it shames you for me to be like you, then I will teach you all they taught me, and we will all be like our white father.'

"So we all agreed to have it so, if he would tell us what to do. After that we came in here with Godfrey, and we stood looking at my father's white face. Godfrey all alone had straked him out on this table, with the silverpieces on the eyes that we had feared. But the silver we did not fear. Maybe you will not understand it, Aleck McTavish, but our father never seemed such close kin to us as when we would look at him dead, and at Godfrey, that was the picture of him, living and kind.

"After that you know what happened yourself."

"Well I do, Mr. McNeil. It was Great Godfrey that was the father to you all," said my cousin.

"Just that, Aleck McTavish. All that he had was ours to use as we would,—his land, money, horses, this room, his learning. Some of us could learn one thing and some of us could learn another, and some could learn nothing, not even how to behave. What I could learn was the playing of the fiddle. Many's the hour Godfrey would play with me while the rest were all happy around.

"In great content we lived like brothers, and proud to see Godfrey as white and fine and grand as the best gentleman that ever came up to visit him out of Montreal. Ay, in great content we lived all together till the consumption came on Donald, and he was gone. Then it came and came back, and came back again, till Hector was gone, and Ranald was gone, and in ten years' time only Godfrey and I were left. Then both of us married, as you know. But our children died as fast as they were born, almost, for the curse seemed on us. Then his wife died, and Godfrey sighed and sighed ever after that.

"One night I was sleeping with the door of my room open, so I could hear if Godfrey needed my help. The cough was on him then. Out of a dream of him looking at my father's white face I woke and went to his bed. He was not there at all.

"My heart went cold with fear, for I heard the rapid very clear, like the nights they all died. Then I heard the music begin down stairs, here in this chamber where they were all laid out dead,—right here on this table where I will soon lie like the rest. I leave it to you to see it done, Aleck McTavish, for you are a Highlandman by blood. It was that I wanted to say to you when I called you in. I have seen himself in my coffin three nights. Nay, say nothing; you will see.

"Hearing the music that night, down I came softly. Here sat Godfrey, and the kindest look was on his face that ever I saw. He had his fiddle in his hand, and he played about all our lives.

"He played about how we all came down from the North in the big canoe with my father and mother, when we were little children and him a baby. He played of the rapids we passed over, and of the rustling of the poplar-trees and the purr of the pines. He played till the river you hear now was in the fiddle, with the sound of our paddles, and the fish jumping for flies. He played about the long winters when we were young, so that the snow of those winters seemed falling again. The ringing of our skates on the ice I could hear in the fiddle. He played through all our lives when we were young and going in the woods yonder together—and then it was the sore lament began!

"It was like as if he played how they kept him away from his brothers, and him at his books thinking of them in the woods, and him hearing the partridges' drumming, and the squirrels' chatter, and all the little birds singing and singing. Oich, man, but there's no words for the sadness of it!"

Old Angus ceased to speak as he took his violin from the table and struck into the middle of "Great Godfrey's Lament." As he played, his wide eyes looked past us, and the tears streamed down his brown cheeks. When the woeful strain ended, he said, staring past us: "Ay Godfrey, you were always our brother."

Then he put his face down in his big brown hands, and we left him without another word.

Morley Callaghan **ANCIENT LINEAGE**

The young man from the Historical Club with a green magazine under his arm got off the train at Clintonville. It was getting dark but the station lights were not lit. He hurried along the platform and jumped down on the sloping cinder path to the sidewalk.

Trees were on the lawns alongside the walk, branches drooping low, leaves scraping occasionally against the young man's straw hat. He saw a cluster of lights, bluish-white in the dusk across a river, many lights for a small town. He crossed the lift-lock bridge and turned on to the main street. A hotel was at the corner.

At the desk a bald-headed man in a blue shirt, the sleeves rolled up, looked critically at the young man while he registered. "All right, Mr. Flaherty," he said, inspecting the signature carefully.

"Do you know many people around here?" Mr. Flaherty asked.

"Just about everybody."

"The Rowers?"

"The old lady?"

"Yeah, an old lady."

"Sure, Mrs. Anna Rower. Around the corner to the left, then turn to the right on the first street, the house opposite the Presbyterian church on the hill."

"An old family," suggested the young man.

"An old-timer all right." The hotel man made it clear by a twitching of his lips that he was a part of the new town, canal, water power, and factories.

Mr. Flaherty sauntered out and turned to the left. It was dark and the street had the silence of small towns in the evening. Turning a corner he heard girls giggling in a doorway. He looked at the church on the hill, the steeple dark against the sky. He had forgotten whether the man had said beside the church or across the road, but could not make up his mind to ask the fellow who was watering the wide church lawn. No lights in the shuttered windows of the rough-cast house beside the church. He came down the hill and had to yell three times at the man because the water swished strongly against the grass.

"All right, thanks. Right across the road," Mr. Flaherty repeated.

Tall trees screened the square brick house. Looking along the hall to a lighted room, Mr. Flaherty saw an old lady standing at a sideboard. "She's in all right," he thought, rapping on the screen door. A large woman of about forty, dressed in blue skirt and blue waist, came down the stairs. She did not open the screen door.

"Could I speak to Mrs. Anna Rower?"

"I'm Miss Hilda Rower."

"I'm from the University Historical Club."

"What did you want to see Mother for?"

Mr. Flaherty did not like talking through the screen door. "I wanted to talk to her," he said firmly.

"Well, maybe you'd better come in."

He stood in the hall while the large woman lit the gas in the front room. The gas flared up, popped, showing fat hips and heavy lines on her face. Mr. Flaherty, disappointed, watched her swaying down the hall to get her mother. He carefully inspected the front room, the framed photographs of dead Conservative politicians, the group of military men hanging over the old-fashioned piano, the faded greenish wallpaper and the settee in the corner.

An old woman with a knot of white hair and good eyes came into the room, walking erectly. "This is the young man who wanted to see you, Mother," Miss Hilda Rower said. They all sat down. Mr. Flaherty explained he wanted to get some information concerning the Rower genealogical tree for the next meeting of his society. The Rowers, he knew, were a pioneer family in the district, and descended from William the Conqueror, he had heard.

The old lady laughed thinly, swaying from side to side. "It's true enough, but I don't know who told you. My father was Daniel Rower, who came to Ontario from Cornwall in 1830."

Miss Hilda Rower interrupted. "Wait, Mother, you may not want to tell about it." Brusque and businesslike, she turned to the young man. "You want to see the family tree, I suppose."

"Oh, yes."

"My father was a military settler here," the old lady said.

"I don't know but what we might be able to give you some notes," Miss Hilda spoke generously.

"Thanks awfully, if you will."

"Of course you're prepared to pay something if you're going to print it," she added, smugly adjusting her big body in the chair.

Mr. Flaherty got red in the face; of course he understood, but to tell the truth he had merely wanted to chat with Mrs. Rower. Now he knew definitely he did not like the heavy nose and unsentimental assertiveness of the lower lip of this big woman with the wide shoulders. He couldn't stop looking at her thick ankles. Rocking back and forth in the chair she was primly conscious of lineal superiority; a proud unmarried woman, surely she could handle a young man, half-closing her eyes, a young man from the University indeed. "I don't want to talk to her about the University," he thought.

Old Mrs. Rower went into the next room and returned with a framed genealogical tree of the house of Rower. She handed it graciously to Mr. Flaherty, who read, "The descent of the family of Rower, from William the Conqueror, from Malcolm

1st, and from the Capets, Kings of France." It bore the *imprimatur* of the College of Arms, 1838.

"It's wonderful to think you have this," Mr. Flaherty said, smiling at Miss Hilda, who watched him suspiciously.

"A brother of mine had it all looked up," old Mrs. Rower said.

"You don't want to write about that," Miss Hilda said, crossing her ankles. The ankles looked much thicker crossed. "You just want to have a talk with Mother."

"That's it," Mr. Flaherty smiled agreeably.

"We may write it up ourselves some day." Her heavy chin dipped down and rose again.

"Sure, why not?"

"But there's no harm in you talking to Mother if you want to, I guess."

"You could write a good story about that tree," Mr. Flaherty said, feeling his way.

"We may do it some day but it'll take time," she smiled complacently at her mother, who mildly agreed.

Mr. Flaherty talked pleasantly to this woman, who was so determined he would not learn anything about the family tree without paying for it. He tried talking about the city, then tactfully asked old Mrs. Rower what she remembered of the Clintonville of seventy years ago. The old lady talked willingly, excited a little. She went into the next room to get a book of clippings. "My father, Captain Rower, got a grant of land from the Crown and cleared it," she said, talking over her shoulder. "A little way up the Trent River. Clintonville was a small military settlement then . . ."

"Oh, Mother, he doesn't want to know all about that," Miss Hilda said impatiently.

"It's very interesting indeed."

The old woman said nervously, "My dear, what difference does it make? You wrote it all up for the evening at the church."

"So I did too," she hesitated, thinking the young man ought to see how well it was written. "I have an extra copy." She looked at him thoughtfully. He smiled. She got up and went upstairs.

The young man talked very rapidly to the old lady and took many notes.

Miss Rower returned. "Would you like to see it?" She handed Mr. Flaherty a small gray booklet. Looking quickly through it, he saw it contained valuable information about the district.

"The writing is simply splendid. You must have done a lot of work on it."

"I worked hard on it," she said, pleased and more willing to talk.

"Is this an extra copy?"

"Yes, it's an extra copy."

"I suppose I might keep it," he said diffidently.

She looked at him steadily. "Well ... I'll have to charge you twenty-five cents."

"Sure, sure, of course, that's fine," he blushed.

"Just what it costs to get them out," the old lady explained apologetically.

"Can you change a dollar?" He fumbled in his pocket, pulling the dollar out slowly.

They could not change it but Miss Rower would be pleased to go down to the corner grocery store. Mr. Flaherty protested. No trouble, he would go. She insisted on asking the next-door neighbour to change it. She went across the room, the dollar in hand.

Mr. Flaherty chatted with the nice old lady and carefully examined the family tree, and wrote quickly in a small book till the screen door banged, the curtains parted, and Miss Hilda Rower came into the room. He wanted to smirk, watching her walking heavily, so conscious of her ancient lineage, a virginal mincing sway to her large hips, seventy-five cents' change held loosely in drooping fingers.

"Thank you," he said, pocketing the change, pretending his work was over. Sitting back in the chair he praised the way Miss Rower had written the history of the neighbourhood and suggested she might write a splendid story of the family tree, if she had the material, of course.

"I've got the material, all right," she said, trying to get comfortable again. How would Mr. Flaherty arrange it and where should she try to sell it? The old lady was dozing in the rocking-chair. Miss Rower began to talk rather nervously about her material. She talked of the last title in the family and the Sir Richard who had been at the court of Queen Elizabeth.

Mr. Flaherty chimed in gaily, "I suppose you know the O'Flahertys were kings in Ireland, eh?"

She said vaguely, "I daresay, I daresay," conscious only of an interruption to the flow of her thoughts. She went on talking with hurried eagerness, all the fine talk about her ancestors bringing her peculiar satisfaction. A soft light came into her eyes and her lips were moist.

Mr. Flaherty started to rub his cheek, and looked at her big legs, and felt restive, and then embarrassed, watching her closely, her firm lower lip hanging loosely. She was talking slowly, lazily, relaxing in her chair, a warm fluid oozing through her veins, exhausting but satisfying her.

He was uncomfortable. She was liking it too much. He did not know what to do. There was something immodest about it. She was close to forty, her big body relaxed in the chair. He looked at his watch and suggested he would be going. She stretched her legs graciously, pouting, inviting him to stay a while longer, but he was standing up, tucking his magazine under his arm. The old lady was still dozing. "I'm so comfortable," Miss Rower said, "I hate to move."

The mother woke up and shook hands with Mr. Flaherty. Miss Rower got up to say good-bye charmingly.

Half-way down the path Mr. Flaherty turned. She was standing in the doorway, partly shadowed by the tall trees, bright moonlight filtering through leaves touching soft lines on her face and dark hair.

He went down the hill to the hotel unconsciously walking with a careless easy stride, wondering at the change that had come over the heavy, strong woman. He thought of taking a walk along the river in the moonlight, the river on which old Captain Rower had drilled troops on the ice in the winter of 1837 to fight the rebels. Then he thought of having a western sandwich in the café across the road from the hotel. That big woman in her own way had been hot stuff.

In the hotel he asked to be called early so he could get the first train to the city. For a long time he lay awake in the fresh, cool bed, the figure of the woman whose ancient lineage had taken the place of a lover in her life, drifting into his thoughts and becoming important while he watched on the wall the pale moonlight that had softened the lines of her face, and wondered if it was still shining on her bed, and on her throat, and on her contented, lazily relaxed body.

George Elliott

THE WAY BACK

She lay big and comfortable with Dan inside her, the familiar patchwork quilt over her knees. When the pains started once more it would be time for her husband to go for the doctor.

Thin and sharp-faced, he sat on the cedar chest at the foot of the bed. He pushed out a little with his lower lip: a new habit he had gotten into to try and get a knowing and confident look that he wanted. She didn't like it when he did this, but never spoke about it. She connected the pouting lip with his endless gossip about the people in the axe-handle factory.

When she was a girl at home—she thought of it just that moment—there was no such talking about business at the supper table. So she didn't permit it in her house after she got married.

But it was an effort for him to keep up the innocent flow of talk and planning. It was easier for him to come home nights and talk about the people he worked with: sort of flow them on into his life at home.

The pains started coming. He looked at her, his eyebrows raised.

"Yes. Go now, go now," she whispered.

He got up and she made a motion with her hand. He turned. He knew what she wanted.

"You'll get the grinder man too?" she pleaded. He frowned as he shook his head.

"Please? This last time?"

He left. He left the door open. She heard his steps on the porch, along the cement walk, on the sidewalk of the street, under the oaks leading to the main street.

She didn't know whether the grinder man would be standing outside the house for this birth. He had been there for the other two children. Both times before, her husband had gone for the grinder man when he went for the doctor.

She knew that all you had to do to get the grinder man was stand on Doc Fletcher's back stoop and call for him. He'd show up in a minute.

There'd be no grinder man this time. Just Doc Fletcher.

People in town never considered the possibility of a birth-giving without the familiar old figure standing on the walk outside the house. Without ever thinking twice about it, people knew a woman's time had come as soon as they saw the old man outside her house. There he'd be: a gnarled, brown old man, his back curved, standing still, his sharpening machine down on the walk in front of him. It was his living.

So this day, the people saw Doc Fletcher's horse and buggy tied up outside, but no grinder man. Somebody must be sick, they thought at first. But it dawned on them with terror for the unborn and with shame for the father: this birth was to happen without the grinder man.

So Dan was born. A healthy gurgling child he was. But the people were ashamed for his father and were full of pity for his mother. She could say nothing, she couldn't defend or ignore. She was ashamed too.

Looking at his third and last child for the first time, Dan's father was sharply aware of the shame and sympathy, and pressed his back molars down hard and shoved out his lower lip that way he had.

He paid. There was the time Dan turned four years old. His shaking old aunt in New York sent him a blown ostrich egg for a birthday present. In another family it would have become a private treasure to be looked at and held and wondered at. Dan did his best to keep his father from enjoying it. He kept it carefully wrapped in cotton batting in an old jewellery box and hid the box under the bed.

Then there was the dead June bug hanging by a thread on the bedroom wall. Dan kept it alive in a match-box for a few days. When the bug died, he hung it by a piece of silk thread so it was a few inches from his head when he lay in bed. First his father asked in a friendly way what it meant and Dan screamed. Then his father wanted it taken down and Dan screamed louder and almost got sick.

A boy grows up that way, it's no wonder his father starts worrying over the grinder man.

It was a May day when things were quiet and Dan was home from school for lunch. He played a secret game of buck-buck, how many fingers up, bouncing gently on his chair at the table and making whispered grunting noises. His father sat thin and isolated, chips of hickory in his hair. His mother, placid and hopeful, served the meal efficiently.

The sound of the grinder man's bell was heard far off, coming from maybe three streets over, through the trees, over the houses, into this window. His mother sat up and smiled. He noticed she turned her head a little as though to hear every sound of the bell. His father frowned. He noticed that too. Dan didn't know what to do. He knew that the kids would be running out of their houses now, down this street, across that side street, looking up and down for the grinder man. He did it once himself, but he would never do it again. Not after what happened.

He got up from the table slowly, pushed his chair back in carefully, and went out the back door. The sound of the grinder man's bell was loud. He wanted to go to it.

"That's the grinder man's bell," his mother said.

"I know, I know," his father said.

"Why doesn't, Dan run to it, the way we used to, I wonder?"

"You know why. What do you ask for? It's ridiculous."

"All the other kids are running over. Dan's still out in the back yard."

"Listen. I'll take that kid out of school and put him to work if you don't shut up. Grinder man. Shut up."

"Work?"

"Yes, work. Work's what matters nowadays. Nothing else. Stuff like that grinder man gives me the pip. He's nothing better than a bogeyman women are scared of."

"But he's not for the women," she cried softly. "Women aren't frightened of him. They like him. He's for the men, for the fathers. It's the fathers that benefit. You know that."

He knew she was right by what their parents had told them, but it was a story, mystery, something concealed, a feeling. That was bad. He got up and banged his chair into place and went out the front door quickly. She was left crying in shame and sympathy.

Dan watched his father go down the street and heard the sound of the bell grow louder and louder from the other direction. The old man was coming on this street.

Crouched in the bushes waiting, Dan knew that it was the grinder man that had somehow caused the anger between his mother and father, but he didn't think about it for long. He wished he could go to the old man with the other kids. He saw them walking and skipping along behind and around him.

Dan couldn't go with them because of his father. He knew.

My name's Dan. Yes, I'm marrying the last of the Salkald girls. Twenty-third of next month. Oh, it'll be quite a wedding. The Salkalds should be good at putting on a wedding by now. Vicky's the youngest of five daughters, the other four all married. It'll be in their rose garden, with a trellis of roses behind the preacher and two nieces of mine carrying wicker baskets of roses and two of Vicky's nephews in sailor suits. Everybody'll be there, sitting on chairs borrowed from the Orange Lodge and everything'll go smoothly, even the photograph after it's over.

I met her at the factory of course. Where else could I meet her? Don't you know who I am? I'm the only man in this town born without the grinder man standing outside the day I was born. It was no oversight. My old man could have afforded it, all right. He just decided it didn't mean anything and he was bound he'd try it once. It broke my mother's heart. Didn't do me any good either. Thing like that, if you don't have a feeling for it, it'll separate you from the kids in school. It doesn't matter if your family's one of the oldest in town. You just don't live it down.

For a long time I thought my old man had the right idea. The grinder man was an old-fashioned idea. Times were changing. There had to be a break some time. He did it. When I was a kid I was kind of proud of him. Proud. Now I'm old enough and I'm ashamed of him, the way my mother is, the way my brothers are. I feel sorry for them and him the way everybody in town does. It wasn't a question of fashion or times changing.

Honey Salkald will be my brother-in-law. That makes me proud. Honey's a good man. He won't have anything to do with me, though. Last Saturday night we were in Mac's office, sitting around kidding Mac about his map with all the pins in it and about the money he makes peddling insurance, the way we always do Saturday nights, and Honey and me, we had it out finally. Honey sneered at me. I said it wasn't my fault, but that didn't matter. Honey's right to sneer. I should get out of town as soon as we're married, but I can't leave. It's all I know. If only there was a place for me. A connection.

I remember when I was just a kid playing with the others, nice as you please, when there was the sound of the grinder man's bell, the only sound on a lazy summer day, coming from away off. We all jumped and ran for it as fast as we could go. But as soon as we caught up with him, the others laughed at me and told me to go on home, the grinder man'd have nothing to do with me.

You know, I was sixteen years old before I found out. I heard what everybody else knew at a garden party down at the river church. There were two girls from town there. I sat beside one in particular during dinner and her skin was clear and she smiled at me when I looked at her and we talked and got along first rate. We kind of kept together after dinner. We watched the softball game together, sometimes standing a little apart pretending not to be together when any of our relatives walked near. Her girl friend sort of hung around.

When it got dark, the gas lamps were lit on the stage back of the church. The stage was really John Reid's wagon rack. They used it for a stage because it was tongue-and-groove hardwood and smooth from all the loads of hay and grain that had rubbed it for ten years. This girl and her girl friend and I went with the crowd from the ball park across the road to the church. Most all of the good seats were taken, but there was a sleigh tipped up on its side against the drive shed and a bunch of us sat on it and had a good view of the stage.

She decided to sit with her girl friend, so I was kind of left out, but I hung around and managed to sit right behind her only a little up. The programme got started and everybody was watching the stage except me. I was thinking about her the way a boy would and wondering what I could get away with. I moved closer to her, willing her to do what I wanted her to do. I spread my knees apart and put my hands down between my knees. Then, slowly, as the programme went on, I moved my hands closer to her until I touched her back. Nothing happened. I made my hands move more around on her sides and felt the softness there. And she didn't move at all. I knew she was a quiet one and I knew she would come with me if I dared ask. Then the programme was over and the violinist and some baritone from up country led in "God Save the Queen" and there was a lot of talking and laughing. The girl friend turned around and caught me with my hands where they shouldn't have been. She whispered all about me to the girl I wanted. I heard then what everybody else knew and I knew and I walked all the way home and I was late and my father was mad at me and I didn't care.

Shortly after that I met Victoria Salkald. Don't you see? I had to marry a girl from the country. It couldn't be one from town. They all knew. I told Vicky all about it, but it didn't bother her somehow.

On the Sunday she said she would marry me, I asked her what her family thought about it. She said it didn't matter what her family thought as long as her grandfather was around. I never knew the old blister had it over the family the way he did. I asked Vicky what she meant.

"You mean about the way you were born?"

"Of course."

"Oh, it came up at Sunday dinner once when I told them that I thought you would be asking me to marry you."

"What happened?"

"Grandma got mad and left the table. Granfer made her

come back and behave. Granfer kept eating away, looked at me now and then. Finally he said there is always hope of return. That was the end of it."

Things are working out too smoothly. I guess that's not a thing to say less than a month before your wedding day, but it's a fact. Vicky's happy. I'm happy. My mother's happy. And my old man has it in his head that this all proves something. The other night when I showed him the wedding ring he said to me flatly, "You worked out all right after all, eh?"

"What do you mean?"

"Oh, just that you're getting married to a nice girl and all."

"No thanks to you."

"I mean some people figure you got off to a bad start," he said lightly. "It looks now as though maybe you didn't."

Then I saw the confidence in him was a November hoar frost that disappears in the heat of the day. I left him and thought of going to my mother, but knew that would be warm and useless and this terrible undertone of regret. I couldn't face it.

As I went down the street it dawned on me where my father's confidence came from. His father would have seen to it that the grinder man was outside the day my father was born. So my father had been given the right to a serene life, and to things I can't speak of.

I wanted to know how it had happened. Surely my grandfather had planned it differently. But we had experienced the contempt and shame of the others. I didn't know how it had happened. My father was the end and I was the beginning.

"I guess I'll wait until after the week-end to wean the baby," Victoria said, and the word was there in front of Dan so he could think of nothing else and he got out of the house and down the street to be alone with the word and the act and to wonder what to do.

He avoided the old man who sat under the willow tree by the pond because the old man knew and his pity would be too real. He avoided the high school and he avoided the Seaton place and walked out the township road to where it was unfamiliar.

He thought of it all and tried to see Victoria the way she was, but couldn't. He tried to feel the way of his life from the time he first learned about the grinder man, but couldn't. He wondered when he last saw the grinder man, but it didn't matter because the figure of him was there and Dan considered a new reason for the old man: to let the mother and the father acknowledge the child as an adult at the right time. So it wasn't exactly for the fathers, the way his mother always said. It was for mothers and fathers, and Dan needed a way back. Victoria's father said there was hope of return. He had hope but Dan hadn't, so Dan was tired and isolated and wanting to believe in Victoria's father.

If something would only come to him, he hoped on his way back home, a little ashamed for having run from the house at the sound of the word. Why should it bother him now? He had heard it before, had seen the act twice before. This was the third weaning. There was nothing unusual about it. Yes. This was the last. That was it. The last weaning. Where is the hope of return now, Mister Salkald?

He came home at last and saw there was a light in the parlour and knew Victoria was there, and he loved her, but he went in by the back door, quietly, knowing she heard, but not wanting her to see him the way he was. He sat down at the bare table and his head felt tired and he said over to himself the few ideas he wanted to hold. The grinder man is there, outside the door to a birth-giving so that the father and the child can love. He is there so that the father and the mother will assert the child's adulthood at the right times. He wasn't there when I was born, Dan thought, so I see the difference between the life of my father and the life of the heart. I want the life of the heart and Mister Salkald says there is hope, there is a way back. This is the connection.

He sat up straight in the red kitchen chair and his knee bumped the table leg, and the knives, forks and spoons in the drawer rattled against each other. Victoria came in the kitchen then and he wondered if it was wrong to think about hating her. She led him to the bedroom. They undressed and went to bed.

Early in the morning, he went into the basement and got his hatchet, his draw-knife, his axe and the rusty old scythe that belonged to Mr. Salkald, Victoria's father. The familiarity and the reality of them all soothed him and he planned confidently what he was going to do. He placed them carefully in the grass by the side door. Then, while Victoria went, with the baby, down the street to shop, he cleared the kitchen table drawer of the paring knives, the long butcher knife, the kitchen scissors, and he remembered to get the scissors from her sewing basket.

Standing on the sidewalk, with some of them in his hands and the others in the grass, he waited for the grinder man.

When Victoria came home, Dan was not around. The hatchet, the axe, the blade of the scythe, the two pairs of scissors, the draw-knife, all her kitchen knives, all sharpened, were on the kitchen table.

She knew. If she had not known, she would have left Dan that day and gone to the farm to live with her brother, for good. But she knew. She had always known. She had remembered what her grandfather had said. She hoped this was the way.

She picked up the draw-knife and noticed the way the light flashed on the newly-sharpened surface. So he had been around.

This was Granfer's knife, she thought. He had made shingles with it and rough-shaped wheel spokes and axe handles with it. It had been his knife. Maybe this was the way. And that was Granfer's scythe, too. She saw his tall figure in memory, moving slowly along the fence by the roadside, the scythe swinging in rhythm, and she remembered the sound of the seeuhree-seeuhruh of the stone on the blade of the scythe as Granfer sharpened it. Maybe this was the way.

She heated the gruel on the back of the stove and was impatient to get on with it. She put a little of the gruel in a bowl on a tray and moved with it out of the kitchen door towards the bedroom where the baby was. As she left the kitchen, Dan came in from the yard and saw that the scythe blade was missing from the kitchen table and regretted his wonder about hating Victoria, then he was impatient too.

The baby cried a lot and the gruel was on his face, and Victoria was kind with him. She waited for him to want it. She wished that she could be near a window so she could see out on the street. She wondered where Dan was. The baby cried and the tears mixed with the gruel and Victoria looked under the bed over and over again to make sure she had really put the shining blade there.

Then the baby took a few spoonfuls of the gruel and managed it very easily. She set the bowl aside and hurried out to the kitchen where Dan was. They smiled to each other. They went out the front door and onto the porch and looked down the street. Then they heard the bell and the grinder man walked up their street and stopped on their path and put his grinding machine down. He fiddled with the leather carrying-strap, put his hands in his pockets, looked up at them at last and smiled back.

Hugh Hood

**WHERE
THE MYTH
TOUCHES
US**

People still listen to their radios, evading the corpse-like glare
of the man who breaks down the fat globules. Joe Jacobson
has a radio shaped like the fat point of a late Gothic arch,
with a fretwork face in front of a faded red curtain, which
shields the speaker cone, and below three knobs of which the
third—the one on the right—does nothing, although a tiny
decalcomania under it says TONE. The other knobs are for
volume and tuning but the condenser is shot in the volume
control. Sometimes the old set won't speak above a chaste
murmur for days and then, all at once, it booms out with an
enormous tinny rattle of the speaker and a great crackling
noise. Joe swats it with an open palm, hardly looking up from
his typewriter or book, and it subsides.

He doesn't want a new radio; this one was in the family for
thirty years. When he was still a baby his father burst excitedly
into his bedroom late one night, past nine-thirty, with a pair
of earphones in his hand and a long black cord trailing behind.

"Babele," said his father, "it's a miracle, listen!" And he
clamped the headset on Joe's ears, startling the child. There
was music in the earphones.

"CKOC Hamilton," crooned his father, "like it was in
the next room! Amazing!" Hamilton was forty-six miles away.

The next day the "Atwater Kent" appeared in the living room and Joe's mother brought him up next to it, sewing her way through eight daytime serials every afternoon. After his parents were dead, he asked his brothers for the radio as his share of the inheritance, wanting nothing else—somebody has to die before you inherit—placing it on his bureau, over the drawer where he keeps his family pictures.

The plywood veneer is peeling at the back of the set and parts of it have flaked off, exposing the cheap pine frame. Every week or so he takes a butter knife and spreads wood glue into the crack, pressing the veneer down, and for a while it holds. Then in the evening, while he writes, he'll hear a pinging sound and know that it's sprung up again. He means to go along, gluing it together as long as he can.

Toby Frankel came to his room that time and made fun of the radio; she couldn't be blamed, knowing nothing about it.

"Joey, on what you make! An associate professor!"

He looked at her blankly and gave the peeling wood a squeeze with the palm of his hand. He will marry Toby anyway, he thinks, when the book comes out. A first-novelist ought to be a bachelor, but on a second-novelist it looks queer unless he writes about North Africa. Once, visiting her in the Group Dynamics Lab, he offered comically to "take you away from all this" but she didn't get the joke, pushing him away when he patted her. She looked up fearfully at the one-way window, unsure, unsure.

So for the moment he lives alone in his room with his radio and his screened sun-porch, not too eager to round off this course of life. Tonight he turns off his desk-lamp while the radio babbles quietly, sits for a moment in the warm summer darkness rubbing his eyes, then he gazes off at the lake two blocks away down Frontenac Street, gets up from his desk and manipulates the volume control on the radio with some care, hoping that it won't scream. He manages to get the Wednesday Night Talk and, lighting a cigarette, lies down on his couch to listen and think of nothing, perfectly aware that his veins will tingle like this until the morning of August twenty-fifth when he can go down to the University Bookstore and admire the display. He understands that one novel isn't a career, that publication day is the day he'll have to start all over again, but hard covers are hard covers, and the bees will buzz in assorted hives; Evanston, Berkeley, Toronto, Madison, Cambridge.

As the slow dark relaxes him and his eyes lose the image of his lamp, the smell of his cigarette sharp and pleasant in his nostrils, he moves his legs tiredly on the couch and listens to the voice on CBC Wednesday Night, peppery, combative, lucid, engaging, and it is, who else, David Wallace. "Summer in the City," Jesus, he's been doing that in the papers, in magazines, in novels, he ought to hire a plane, skywrite the piece in permanent smoke, and get maximum coverage all at once, "Summer in the City." And at that it is a good talk, and nobody will read informal essays any more. He tunes the set more carefully, to get the shriek out of the speaker, stretches out again, and listens.

"Doing what I do for a living," says the familiar, old friend's voice, "I don't get out onto the streets until the middle of the afternoon. You know, we should have the custom of the siesta, as they do in the Latin countries, and most of all in August in the city. My siesta lasts until two-thirty and by then the sun is beginning to get down the other side of the sky, that summer sky, always light grey, nearly white, not the blue of spring or fall. So . . . anyway . . . I take my time getting into my clothes. Maybe some day I'll tell you my secret, how to keep from getting sticky in August. But I don't get sticky and I don't move very fast at all. I walk slowly across the bridge, looking down at the poplars and elms in the ravine, and the children from the Hunt Club on their ponies on the bridle path. Sometimes on the other side I have an ice-cream soda. Then I walk to the Subway, taking my time and admiring the girls' blouses, and the lovely way their hair moves in the light air and the heat. It's cool in the Subway going downtown and I don't have to rush because I'm just coming into the studio to record this talk. The studio is air-conditioned and very cool, and about four o'clock I begin to wake up, just as the office workers downtown are going home. That way I have the downtown to myself after dinner."

Lying on the couch in the summer dark, Joe smiles very soberly to himself, remembering the places, the studios, the quiet discussions, the beer, a cold-beef plate in the Morrissey Dining Room, with a mint parfait to follow, and David asking his producer to please do something about echo noises on the tape. He can't yet wish himself back there but all the same he remembers—and wonders what Toby would think.

"I might take the ferry to the island if I'm alone at night," says David to the nation and to Joe remembering, "or go to the ball game and sit in the pavilion, the best seventy-five cents' worth in town, watching the gamblers pass large bills from hand to hand, the light planes at the airport, ships in the Western Gap. But usually I'm in a group that talks for a few hours, a drama critic, a young writer from Kingston, in town for a day to see his publisher," and Joe thinks to himself, I wish he'd stop doing that, but David is a paragraph further on now, "and about twelve, when they close the lounges, I say goodnight to my friends, and by now the city is growing quiet. I wander along Bloor Street as people come out of the lounges, getting into their cars, or deciding to go somewhere else for something to eat and another drink, or just walking up Avenue Road hand in hand, under the trees in the dark. I might buy a morning paper at the corner of Avenue Road and talk for a minute to Sammy, who has the newsstand there. Now there aren't many cars, and you can hear the streetcars blocks away. I stroll along, taking my time, going home to work. Because this, you see, is when my working day begins, hours after midnight. I hop a streetcar and go along to the bridge over the ravine, dark now, and the bridle path a grey strip between the deep black masses of the trees.

"When I get home I turn on the sprinkler and the fountain in the garden and sit for a few minutes in the best part of the night, about one o'clock to one-thirty. Far away across the ravine I can hear the night traffic. But there isn't a sound on my street except the splash of water around the cupid in the fountain. Then I go into my screened porch—just to keep off the mosquitoes, don't you see—turn my desk light on, and go to work." He makes it sound wonderful; there was always a wide streak of romance in him.

"I'm halfway into the manuscript of a new book, to follow the one that comes out later this summer. I'm excited about it, and as it grows quieter around me my ideas seem to get brighter and brighter, because I work best at night, best or an after-midnight summer night. And that's my summer in the city. Goodnight, everybody, and stay cool, won't you."

The announcer, another old acquaintance—the Wednesday Night series is like old home week for Joe—comes on to give David his plug, and is particular about urging his listeners to buy and read the new novel which is to appear late in August. Then he does the station break and is followed by strings playing an allegro from one of the Handel Opus Six Concertos.

"Jesus," says Joe violently, aloud, trying to wrench his thoughts away and remembering in spite of himself, "Jesus!"

Seven undergraduates are arguing in the kitchen, making a hideous racket, while Rabbit Wallace pokes angrily around in a pile of cartons and old newspapers beside the radiator.

"Jesus!" says Rabbit with terrible scorn, "will you look at that?" His face is wrathy and terrible and the seven boys, Joe among them, break off their wrangle to stare at him.

"What is it?" asks one, and they silently follow his finger. Behind the pile of rubbish are lined up six pints of beer, a little cache concealed by some unsportsmanlike drinker so that when everyone else has drunk his last there will be some left for him.

"That's MY BEER," says Rabbit. "Which of you has done this?"

Nobody in the kitchen will confess to it and there are fifteen other possible culprits in the house.

"That's the trick of an alcoholic," says Rabbit angrily, "and it's damned selfish besides. I'll tell you, one of those stinking brandy-drinkers did this. We'll watch and see who comes for it later on, when everything else is gone. He picks up the six beers with tender loving care and puts them in the refrigerator, already a solid phalanx of green glass.

"These aren't cold," he says considerately, the perfect host, "I'll fish out some cold ones." He begins to yank out the bottles next the freezing unit, handing them back over his shoulder.

"Got enough?"

"I'm drinking gin," says one of the boys.

"And I'm not drinking," says another, who is in residence at Emmanuel.

"We'll hang on to the extra ones," says Rabbit to Joe, throwing his arm over his shoulders affectionately, "come on, I'll show you around."

It is all new to Joe, who has never lived in this part of town, this big old house across the ravine with the cupid in the fountain. The Wallaces have just bought it and are doing it over room by room, painting it and choosing the colours themselves. Rabbit leads him upstairs by winding back passages and downstairs by the graceful main staircase, showing him what they mean to do.

"Dad bought it after he came back from New York for good."

"For good?" Joe finds this incomprehensible. He has always believed that anyone who has the option will live in New York forever.

"Dad doesn't like New York. He thinks it hurts his writing. Paris didn't. He liked Paris and wrote well there. But there are too many writers in New York, all sitting around trying to impress each other. You know, Joey, a writer's career is very fragile; it has to be guarded carefully. Joe knows Rabbit can only be quoting his father, that he doesn't know anything about a writer's career at first hand, but what he says has an air of second-hand authenticity and shouldn't be ignored. Rabbit has already chosen his profession, the law, and can't be suspected of harbouring secret writing inclinations, so he can likely be trusted to report his father accurately."

"It's precious," says Joe.

"What is?"

"A writer's career. It has a certain shape of its own. The early works, the middle period, the periods of stagnation and doubt, the triumphant later years, and the final apotheosis."

They are standing at the foot of the staircase and as he rounds off this summary with proper sonority there comes a muffled shout of laughter from the coat closet and lavatory under the stairs. Joe starts nervously and takes a long drink of beer.

"That's Dad," says Rabbit, "I didn't know he was home. Hey, Dad, come on out. I know you're in there." He rattles the closet door. "What are you doing?"

"Shut up, Rabbit," says a voice, "I'm hiding the whiskey. I just got in." Then the closet door opens and Mr. Wallace emerges wearing a sheepish grin, looking first at Joe and then at his son. "It's like the marriage feast of Cana," he says, "except that I won't serve the good wine at the end; they wouldn't appreciate it. Who's this?"

"Joe Jacobson. Goes to U.C. My year."

Mr. Wallace looks at Joe. "You went to Malvern Collegiate," he says quickly but politely, "you got a scholarship," he takes another look, "and I would guess that your father's dead."

Joe stares at him, aware how easy the trick is, but half-impressed anyway.

"Sure it's a trick," says David Wallace, "a trick of observation. I didn't mean to speak lightly about your father." He is a small, lightly built man of fifty or so, with a suspiciously mild manner that conceals a terrifying alertness; he misses nothing. "I read that story of yours in *The Varsity*," he says now, to Joe's enormous gratification. "Rabbit brought it home and told me to look at it. That's one of those lucky subjects, isn't it," he gives it professional consideration, "that you just daydream your way through. You didn't have to build that story, did you? It told itself."

"That's right," says Joe peaceably, although it isn't strictly true, "I didn't have to invent anything. It just came along and I put it down."

"I wish they were all like that," says Mr. Wallace, whose best-known book is a collection of stories, a marvellous collection, almost every story an anthology piece. "People read my stories," he says with humorous regret, "and they say: 'How easy. All he had to do was set it down as it came.'" He laughs. "I'll tell you something, Mr. Jacobson, there'll be a dozen or so, maybe twenty, stories that you can daydream your way through, that you don't have to build like you were building a house. Don't sit down and write up all those easy stories right off the bat, do you see? Save them, and build your early stories while you're learning how to write. When you've formed your style, then you can do those stories that come along line for line. Don't shoot them off all at once."

Since he hasn't yet read everything Mr. Wallace has written, Joe is on infirm ground. "The story of yours I like best," he says tentatively, "is 'The Girls in Their Summer Dresses.' That's a terrific story."

Rabbit gives Joe a peculiar look, smothering a grunt of laughter. "Joey," he says, "Joey, finish your beer!"

"'The Girls in Their Summer Dresses,'" says Mr. Wallace slowly and kindly, "I remember it. The young married couple on Fifth Avenue and he's looking over the other girls. You know," he smiles, "that's a story of Irwin Shaw's. When it came out I told him how much I liked it. It's in the first *New Yorker* collection, isn't it?" Seeing that Joe is about to die of mortification, he goes into the library to look for the book.

"I'd have sworn your father wrote it," says Joe to Rabbit helplessly.

But Rabbit has disappeared into the host of beer drinkers leaving him to face the music as Mr. Wallace comes back with a book in his hands.

"You're right, you know," he says comfortingly, "it's a subject I might have done myself, and it's about my length for that kind of piece, but it's Irwin's story. I'd never have done it that way. I remember telling him that and he wasn't very pleased with me." Then he leads Joe by degrees into the living room where there are only one or two slowly settling drinkers and begins to reminisce, as though he were talking to himself, in a way that opens Joe's eyes to an hitherto only half-suspected life.

"When I dropped Scribners and they dropped me—it was mutual but I made the first move—Max said to me: 'I'm sorry David that you've been so much under Ernest's shadow. Like Ruth and Gehrig. We know you're not a second-string Ernest but what can we do?' I suppose he had a point although I'd been selling pretty well, especially the collection, which was a famous book for years. Maybe it will be again, one day, though of course you can't tell about these things. A lot of people have compared me to Anderson because I write about simple people in small towns quite a lot. But I'm not a primitive. I've had some intellectual training of a kind that Sherwood never had, and it hurt him. He had no judgment."

At this moment Joe could listen forever. Sherwood, Ernest, Max, and it is all real because David Wallace is the authentic thing with the fully formed career, with all the contacts. He really has known all these men and what's more they've known him and still do, except that Max and Sherwood are dead and so are Tom and Scott and Ernest.

"I was trained as a lawyer and was actually called to the bar after I left college," says Mr. Wallace, "and whatever you might think about some lawyers, the law is one of the great humane disciplines which can form the mind and give it a toughness that Sherwood never had. I still practise law now and then, just to keep the forms in my mind." He stares alertly at Joe. "Are you going to have a purely literary education?"

Nobody ever put such a question to him before; nobody from his neighbourhood could have thought of it; so he hasn't thought of it himself. "I don't know," says Joe.

"There's no telling, writers grow up like weeds, everywhere, in the most surprising circumstances, and there aren't any laws. I think it helps to have a kind of . . ." he casts around for the word.

"Urbanity?" says Joe, off the end of his tongue.

"The very word. North American writers are rarely urbane—they're afraid to death of it. That's why we don't have those dozens of pretty good second-rate writers like the English have, writers whose good manners and schooling make up for their defects in imagination and talent."

"Is that so?" says Joe, who can think of nothing else to say.

"I don't know. I just thought of it. It might be true."

They are interrupted by the arrival in the living room of Rabbit, four undergraduates with beer bottles who have just heard that Mr. Wallace is in the house and who want to talk impressively with the celebrity, and a fifth miserable creature whom Rabbit accuses of hiding his beer.

"What a trick," he shouts with disgust, "so the rest of us wouldn't have any."

"Honest, Rabbit," moans his victim, "I brought them with me and there was no room in the icebox."

"Balls you did! Where's the empty carton?"

"I had them in my coat pockets. I'd have shared them with you."

"Oh you would, would you?" Rabbit is too good-natured to embarrass the culprit any further. "I believe you," he says, though he obviously does not.

The eager undergraduates surround Mr. Wallace and ply him with technical questions of a breathtaking naivety.

"Do you feel that you can divorce art from morality?" asks the lad from Emmanuel, and with a polite smile Mr. Wallace turns to answer him. It astonishes Joe that nothing the thronging admirers can say, no matter how terrible, causes Mr. Wallace to lose his courtesy. He files this in his memory as the real professionalism.

"What do you do about myths?" asks another lad, maybe the most dreadful of all.

"I don't quite understand that," begins Mr. Wallace, just the least bit haltingly, and at this Joe quits the living room in search of his raincoat, finds it, and quietly leaves the house.

Afterwards he went there for years, all the way through that literary education which he decided to undergo in the face of Mr. Wallace's hints. Joe reckoned himself to be in a special situation not covered by the older man's mandate. He and all the other Jacobsons were strangers to every literature but the Rabbinical. There could be nothing discomforting, pedantic, unhealthy academic, in a formal literary training for a man who started from scratch as it were, who had to pack into himself the generations of evolution that the mannerly second-rate talents from Oxford would possess from instinct. Years later, when the going was good, when Joe thought that he had some control over his powers of expression and the English sentence generally, he still sometimes recognized that he was fundamentally an untrained writer, and that you couldn't acquire all the instincts of the mannerly Oxford second-rater in a single lifetime. Never mind, he would say to himself, your grandsons will have it in their marrow.

When he came to have something like a personal signature—for he wouldn't of course call it a "style"—he could still feel in his muscles the ache of holding the rules of expression together, and he understood what David had said about Anderson. The lacks, the gaps, not in one's formal education which grew in time to be mighty formidable, but in the larger lovelier urbanity of the achieved European, were what hurt the first-generation writer.

When he found out that Proust was thought by the French uniquely the master of the imperfect and the past definite, he marvelled and marvels still at the notion of a society which honours a man for his command of a tense. Suppose there were a North American writer who possessed a great and unique mastery of, let's say, the present progressive. What decorations would he receive from a grateful civil authority, what honours reap from literate society?

Imagine a literary hostess: "I want you to meet Mr. Jones, the master of the present progressive." Imagine the response!

Sometimes Joe's friends would ask him, "Why do you go to see Wallace? There's nothing for you there, the guy's written out and has been since the Spanish Civil War." Cozy Walker said it to him first, and the nasty imputation made Joe stiffen his spine against the padding in the booth.

"That doesn't happen to the good ones."

"Sure it does," said Cozy, who had just magisterially completed a doctoral dissertation on the public life of Matthew Prior, "it happens to everybody on this continent. They all start off very brave and big, and in fifteen years they're done, because they've worked through themselves and they never, but never my hopeful little friend, get on to anything else."

"Not true!" said Joe, muddling his Manhattan vortically.

"David Wallace is no good for you, Joe. You can't learn a thing from him, he's a primitive. He never had the least idea how to write, he's a transcriber."

Joe looked fiercely at Cozy. "I read your thesis, Buster, and if that doesn't shut you up, nothing will."

"I don't profess to be a writer."

"I should hope not."

"But you do."

"Yes," said Joe, "and that's my affair. Why don't you drop it, since you don't know what you're talking about?"

"I've never in my life found that a deterrent," said Cozy cheerfully, signalling for another drink.

"Just remember, nobody's ever written out. That's a term used by the ignorant, like you."

"So O.K. We're all ignorant about something."

"But we don't all talk about it."

He never used to go to David's house for his "local" literary education, not wanting to talk to him about tenses, or the management of relative clauses, but mostly to learn how the literary life was lived, where the stories came from and how they grew, why it was that peoples' careers took this or that shape, why some guys couldn't do anything after forty and some could do nothing before, though these were rare. And on this last point there was always a certain constraint because David had written nothing so good as his first half-dozen books for ten years and was just then trying to work around the difficulty with every atom of craft, technique, ingenuity, he could command.

When Joe asked him about it, he couldn't tell. "They just came," he said, "and neither Helen nor I knew how lucky we were. I just wrote them up and sent them out and they sold, like that."

"I remember," said Helen from the depths of her armchair, "one time David and I were in Chicago, I don't recall what for. But that day *Scribner's Magazine* published two stories by David. There was a little belt of paper around each copy with his name on it. 'Two new stories by David Wallace.' And we just took it for granted."

"They came so easy," said David, smiling affectionately at Helen, "but they don't anymore. There was one story that I simply transcribed from a magistrate's court record. The whole story was in the re-arrangement of course; the trick was to see the story there."

"Edward O'Brien loved that story," said Helen reminiscently.

"Sure. He sent me a four-page letter about it. How do you see the story in the facts? Where does it come from? I used to see them all the time, clear as crystal, and now I have to jockey around, weigh this fact against that, and try to guess which are the right ones."

"It's a question of maturity," said Helen, with her queerly passive certainty, "because to write the story you have to think it important. When we're young, we think every little perception we have is fundamental. But in middle age we're more critical. You simply don't write so hastily nowadays, because you've seen more of the world, and you know that a lot of the moving little occurrences that you witness are not important. Twenty years ago you'd write them up immediately and therefore some of those early stories are naive. But this new novel—it won't come easily and it won't be naive."

"Well, Joe's a young man. How about it, Joe, do you have second thoughts about your story ideas?"

"No. The editors have to do that for me, and they do. When I've had ten rejections on a story I figure that maybe it wasn't such a good idea at that. I don't know. I still can't tell the authentic ones from the fake or the dull. I wish to God I could."

"But they get winnowed out when you send them around?"

"And how."

"I don't understand that," said David regretfully, "because it's an experience I never had. I sold almost everything I wrote for fifteen years, without any effort. Maybe you're lucky."

"But I've written forty stories," said Joe, a little desperately, "which is pretty good for a man my age, and some of them are not too bad. You've read them and you know. And I've sold exactly two of them. Now how am I different from you?"

"You might be less talented," said David candidly, "but not enough to make that much difference."

"He's lucky, he's lucky. Do you know what I read the other day?" said Helen. "I read an article about some screenwriter. He might not be a real writer at all; few of them are. But he said one very interesting thing. When he was asked how he became a writer he said, 'Five hundred thousand people started out to be writers the same day I did. All the others stopped. I'm the only one left.' I think he's got a point."

"If he said that," said David, "he's probably pretty good."

"The trick is simply not to stop?"

"That's it, that's it."

Joe sighed. "I wish there were a surer way."

All at once David crossed the room and turned off the television which had been glowing, pictureless, for two hours. "Could we have some buns and coffee?" he asked Helen.

"Yes," she said, "should we expect Rabbit?"

"If he isn't home now, I don't expect he will be."

"He's at a party," said Joe. "I was supposed to go."

"But you came here instead," said Helen at the door, "that's charming."

Joe laughed. "I wasn't trying to make an impression."

"I know, sweetie," she said, "Buns. . . ." she muttered abstractedly, trailing it out the door. David came and stood beside Joe's chair and lowered his voice.

"It's this damned novel that's upset her," he said, "she's really pulling for me to bring it off. The trouble is, she knows me too well."

"I wish there were something I could do," said Joe, "but. . . ."

"But there isn't, is there? I haven't written a novel since just before the war. I did a full-length juvenile, and a collection of memoirs that ran to novel-length, and a lot of travelling and broadcasting, and maybe twenty stories. But I haven't kept up. Boy," he said fervently, "this one better go."

"It'll go," said Joe loyally, "because it's going to be a great book."

"My agent thinks so but then he's prejudiced and besides he's anxious to make some money out of me. I haven't put a dime on his books in ten years."

"He isn't getting tough about it?"

"Lord, no, he's a personal friend! I was his second client.

But he wants a picture sale or maybe a play out of it and I'm not certain they're there. It's a difficult subject."

"It'll go," said Joe again. There wasn't anything else to say. And then Helen came back with cinnamon buns and coffee and they talked for a few minutes about Rabbit, who was beginning to have second thoughts about the legal profession.

"He has that uneasy look," said David, "that presages a sudden flight to Paris. I know it well. And I wish I weren't middle-aged." He grinned. "My middle period, my transitional phase." Then all at once he decided to round off the evening with a benediction. "Maybe I can tell you once and for all how it is, Joe, for me, and perhaps for you too. Some idiot once asked me about the myths, and how I used them. Now I don't know about that. I'm not a man for the technical terms of criticism and I wouldn't recognize a myth, I guess, if I tripped over one. But I *can* tell you this: there's a point where the myth, if you want to call it that, the great story of which you've stumbled into a small part, assumes a kind of possession of you. You don't use it; it uses you. I don't mean that you're inspired. But the myth touches you, gets into you and begins to tell the story for you, through you, making the decisions for you. When that happens, and control of the tale passes out of your hands, you almost begin to be in the story yourself. I don't mean to sound poetic but it's like a laying-on of hands. You're touched, you're possessed, you're all committed, engaged, and if the story doesn't please or beguile of itself, you're lost, because you have to set down what is dictated. You have to live your way into the story. And that's how it is." He set down his coffee cup and stretched, and looked embarrassed.

"Living under the myth," said Joe thoughtfully. It sounded like magic to him.

"In and under it—that's the trouble with this new book."

He heard no more of this curious doctrine from David himself but he saw how it worked when the "middle-period, transitional" novel appeared, was revised with utter incomprehension on every side, was dumped and written-off by its publishers, and early allowed to disappear into the limbo of excellent books that haven't sold. Wrong myth, he thought to himself, as he saw David become more and more a journalist, getting his living in television and radio and from magazine and newspaper articles. Wrong myth!

Just as David had prophetically guessed, the design of the "middle period, transitional" book had baffled everyone who read it. With every inner consistency, with marvellous truth to itself, the myth had made him its scapegoat. For not content with dictating a narrative that wouldn't beguile, the myth, or whatever had composed the book, positively offended people and made them dislike the novel and its writer for affronting them with a narrative that didn't fit their sense of where a story ought to come from and go. Wrong myth, wrong audience! And David left in the middle, still trying in the middle of all his journalism to work through those late nights into the middle of another book, trying to get from "the period of stagnation and doubt" to "the triumphant later years."

When Joe left town, the highest diploma clutched tightly in his hand, David was still trying, still reassuring Helen that he would make it, working on a new book, this one about innocence, crystal clear, no puzzlements, with none of the characters on two sides at the same time, with none of the illogicalities which Joe thought nearly Shakespearian but which the public found idiotic.

The two men had their struggles, and to some extent shared them, although Joe never wrote directly to David, so much his senior, so much still compelling a filial piety. He wrote instead to Rabbit who had by now given up the law, or been given up by it, and who was operating a feature syndicate, the first in the country, for a Toronto daily that had visions of national influence. Rabbit, Joe knew, was nurturing secret writing inclinations and might at any moment commit a novel. So they corresponded and he heard incidentally, in Evanston or Cambridge, how the new book was going, how slowly and silently it was evolving. And this secret submarine evolution of a new book which cost David five years' work, and upon which he was risking everything, began to coincide more and more closely with the gestation of Joe's own novel, not his first, but the first that looked anywhere near publishable.

He had gone on turning out stories year by year and by now one-tenth of them sold, an improvement over his earlier ratio of two in forty. Of his newer stories, one in ten was picked up by a quarterly and he banked the rest in a trunk against the day when everybody would know what he was talking about, instead of an occasional perceptive editor, and in the spring of this year he printed his sixth story and began to call himself a writer. He had always told himself that six stories would justify the name and there were times when the slender figure looked unattainable.

Statistics have nothing to do with composition but it is curious how regular a curve describes the early publications of a new writer. There will be at first the hundred and twenty printed slips which give way in time to printed slips with a word in ink at the bottom. This goes on for a while and Joe studies those inked monosyllables and wonders who wrote them, what the initials stand for, what the reader thought.

And then there are the letters which say "We are holding the story for further consideration." These come very late in the day, labourers of the eleventh hour, and now Joe feels the force of the screenwriter's aphorism. "Five hundred thousand began the same year. All the others stopped. I'm the only one left." But the stories "held for further consideration" march back one by one and he tells himself comfortingly that someday somebody will buy them. It'll be slow coming but it'll come, it'll come. "All the others stopped. I'm the only one left."

But no myth has ever possessed Joe and done the story for him; he builds them up with carpentry, nailing the clumsy pieces together and hoping the nail-holes don't show, apologizing by the things he can do for the things he can't, as every writer must.

"Why don't you write a best-seller under an alias?" asks Toby Frankel, the fourth time he takes her out; they are sitting in the LaSalle Beverage Room in the heart of downtown Kingston, having an economical date, three dollars worth of draught beer which is a fair amount of beer at that. He looks at her upper arms which are lovely, round but not fat, one might call them plump, perhaps. Anyway they will cover a multitude of sins.

"You mean a pseudonym," he says hungrily.

"I mean an alias," she says, "I know perfectly well you'd consider it immoral." She is a practising clinical psychologist, or will be very soon, and her ideas of motivation are not his.

"I couldn't do it anyway," he says, "it requires a special skill that I don't have. I couldn't write for a newspaper either without taking the time to learn the technique. And it's taken me ten years to learn the technique of the short story and I'm not finished yet." He thinks this over for a minute and is rueful. "I haven't even started."

"I wonder if anything that takes that long can be worth it?" she says with womanly pragmatism. "You can become a heart specialist or a psychoanalyst in twelve years, and a Jesuit, I'm told, in thirteen."

She is being subtle, for her. "And a short story writer knows more of the secrets of the heart than all three," says Joe, "isn't that what I'm supposed to say?"

She is engaging. "I set it up for you."

"Well, he probably doesn't—but he knows as much. Thirteen years of study ought to yield something in the way of practised application of one's knowledge."

"If the talent is there."

Joe shudders. "My theory," he says hopefully, "is that the talent is in the application to study. The talent *is* the diligence."

"Then anyone can become an artist of the short story?"

"No. Not everyone can do the thirteen years' work."

"I see. The empiricist view of talent. The talented are those who last thirteen years."

"There's no other way to measure it," he sighs, "and I wish you were not studying psychology. I sold a story this morning."

"Joey, you didn't!"

"I did and that makes five; one more to go."

"To go for what?"

"Never mind," he says, "and I'll get an agent out of this one, because I made some money out of it for a change." He watches with amusement as her eyes widen.

"How much?"

"Seven hundred and fifty."

"How long did you take to write it?"

"Thirteen years."

"I mean the actual writing-time."

"Counting revisions, about a month."

"But on your spare time?"

"Uh-huh."

"If you could do that once a month, over and above your salary, you'd be doing very well, wouldn't you?"

He starts to laugh. "I would, but I don't expect they'll all bring that good a price."

"Oh, but it's something to think about, and why are we going on this cheap date anyway? We ought to celebrate." She is already taking that proprietorial tone.

"And spend the whole seven hundred and fifty?"

"Just the odd fifty."

"It's these odd fifties that kill you." He stirs thoughtfully in his chair. "I'll buy your dinner and we can go someplace after. The important thing is, I may be able to get an agent."

"Does it really help?"

"Not unless you're selling a lot. Stories are bought on their own merits, by and large, but an agent helps you to get a careful reading and he looks after the paper work, mailing and such. They're most useful if you're really in business with both feet."

"You will be," she says, with a very friendly gleam.

"Yeah. An agent might help me place a novel, which is very hard. Come on, I'll buy you something to eat. Maybe even steak."

So small a world is the circle of editors, publishers, writers and agents, that even before his big sale appears in print Joe begins to receive cautious non-committal notes from people who would like, without making any positive declarations, to see what else he can do that may be of use to them. In no other market does word-of-mouth play so important a part. Long long before a new writer's name is known to the general public, sometimes several years before, the little group centred on New York, with trading posts in Boston, Philadelphia, Cleveland, Toronto, knows all about him, what he can do, what his prospects are, whether he is ever likely to be any good. The writers themselves, though not so concentrated geographically, are even more inbred. A youngster who lives in Phoenix, Arizona, who is twenty-six, who has printed three stories, can be certain that fifty of his near contemporaries (who are personally utterly unknown to him) nevertheless know through the channels all that they need to know about him, and how much they need to fear him, perhaps because they have met somebody who was in the same graduate school, or because an editor-acquaintance has read him extensively, or maybe because he once worked for six months in New York and went to the parties. It makes altogether for a good deal of taking in each others' washing and it is sometimes doubtful whether anybody reads new fiction except the two thousand men who write, edit and try to market it.

Joe begins to get these feelers and they give him the worst six months of his life as each of seven publishing houses reads his three novel-length manuscripts, every editor earnestly searching for something he can "save"—this curious technical term "save" which means "make marketable"—and out of the twenty-one chances, twenty are blanks. But, oh, that glorious twenty-first!

He clicks when the last of the friendly salvationists takes a chance on the latest of the three manuscripts, writing a letter to Kingston and taking the manuscript to the higher echelons—the editorial conference—where the gist of his defense is "we won't make a nickel on this book but with moderate promotion we shouldn't lose anything, which is nice, and anyway we've got a strong fall list and we can afford the risk, and who knows, who knows?"

"Does he have an agent?"

"Yeah, but he won't make trouble, we're doing him a favour. I tell you, George, in all honesty, this is a real borderline case."

"Give them the standard contract and specify the promotional appropriation. Now, where were we?"

"You wanted to discuss the merger, George."

"Sure. Sure. This is a quality house, gentlemen, and I want you to know that the merger won't affect our trade policy one bit. Not one bit. You may think otherwise and you're going to be surprised."

"Textbooks!" says a disgusted voice in a corner but George ignores the interruption and goes calmly on. Of such is the kingdom of Heaven or so it seems to Joe when he gets word of the acceptance from his agent almost concurrently with the sale of his sixth story, that achieved half-dozen, the magic figure. On his next credit-application he describes himself as "Writer, Teacher."

In late May the city sky is topless, clear and blue, you can see through it, and the still oppressive heat of later summer hasn't yet come on to immobilize everyone in the middle of the day. His examination papers graded, the scholastic year behind him, Joe feels free to take a week to go and see the Canadian publishers who will handle his book as agents for New York, to examine if he can the dust-jacket design and the layout of any point-of-sale promotional material that they may have in mind. It really isn't any of his business and he ought to keep his nose out of it; he wouldn't dare go near the New York office for a similar purpose. But he has friends in Toronto and things are conducted more informally, so he is willing to take the chance. Also, he thinks with enormous pleasure, he can see David and Helen and tell them all about it, and maybe he can even tell them about Toby, what there is to tell, which is nothing specific except that it is time he got married and she is a girl he knows. After lunch, his first day in, he makes his phone call, forgetful of David's schedule.

"He isn't up yet," says Helen, "but we both want to see you."

"I'd forgotten. And it's nearly one-thirty."

"You know David! He was working very late last night. I guess he finished up around six, six-thirty."

"I can't do that. I have to get it done by midnight or the day is wasted. What's he working on?"

"Another novel, to follow the one that's coming out in August. But he'll want to tell you about it himself. When are we going to see you?"

"Tonight, if it's all right."

"Of course it's all right. Come any time."

He tarries downtown, repressing his eagerness for the meeting, until seven o'clock, when he goes to the Morrissey Dining Room for the sake of his recollections, hoping that he will see somebody he knows; it is handy to the studios and the publisher's Toronto offices and there, sure enough, is Cozy Walker with a nameless girl, a beauty, whom Cozy hastens to exhibit with an air of proprietorship, though without revealing her name or origins.

"What are you doing in here?" asks Joe. It is a kind of desecration to find Cozy in the place, which is really not for academics.

"I'm in television, didn't you know?" says Cozy defensively. "I'm a producer."

"No!" says Joe flatly. "No, you're not!" He doesn't see how it can be true.

"Oh, but I am and this is my script assistant. We do 'Studio,' the half-hour drama series. And that reminds me, Joe, why don't you submit to us?"

"I'll submit to your script assistant any time, if that's what she wants."

"I mean manuscripts," says Cozy crossly, "don't you write plays?"

"I write fiction. That's all I know about."

"Then you'd better learn something else or you'll never get anywhere. Haven't you heard about the anti-novelists? Fiction is dead. What's wanted now is stuff for the mass media. John Osborne writes for TV."

"Sure, and Kingsley Amis writes for the magazines, and have you read his last book?"

"No."

"Read it! All you guys think that writing is dead but it isn't. I'm doing all right."

"You've got a novel coming out in August, haven't you?" says the beautiful script assistant, with respect and envy in her voice. She looks from one man to the other, patently preferring the man in the outmoded medium. "August 25th?"

"I didn't think anybody knew. I thought the publishers were keeping it our little secret."

"August 25th," says Cozy with malicious pleasure, "an interesting coincidence. I wonder what David Wallace will make of it."

"Why should David make anything out of it?"

"Because his book comes out on the twenty-sixth."

"Oh."

"Yes, oh! And I think I can predict that he won't like it very much, dear boy. He's counting on this book to bring him back."

"He's never been away."

"Oh ho ho ho. Go and ask him! Just you go and ask him, my uptown friend."

"I think I will. Good-bye Cozy, good-bye Miss Script Assistant, I wish I knew your name, but poor old Cozy. . . ." He stalks out of the place, feeling his face grow red. He hasn't for several years wanted to punch anybody quite that much. He can quite see the academician as a producer on the parochial little TV network with its ten half-baked writers competing with each other, but not as the doyen and arbiter of the forms of new art. And the remark about David and himself keeps him a little short of breath all the way across town on the streetcar. He doesn't recover his equanimity until the slow walk across the ravine cools him out. But by the time he knocks on the familiar door he is restored and as eager for the meeting as when he'd planned it.

Behind the door is David, unchanged, a year or two short of sixty now but the same slight mild-mannered friend of almost a decade, his face creased in a welcoming grin.

"Come in, come in, Helen's here and I've decided not to work tonight, so we've got the whole of it to ourselves. Are you in town for long?"

"Three or four more days. I wanted to see Fred Callan."

"About your book, wonderful, sure. Are they treating you decently?"

"You know how it is; they aren't spending a cent over the budget."

"It won't be that way next time," says David, which is exactly what he ought to say, so why does Joe feel uneasy? "They'll spend thousands next time. We haven't heard much about the book, all the same."

"That doesn't matter," says Joe, heading him off, "tell me about the new novel." The three of them seat themselves squarely in the same old trio of easy chairs, settling down for what looks like a long night.

"I've seen the jacket," says David eagerly, "I've got one here." He goes to a writing cabinet in the corner, takes out the brightly-coloured piece of paper and flips it to Joe. "They've featured my name on purpose," he says with naive pride, "and they're playing up my European reputation in the promotion. You know, I went to the Plaza for a drink with Jack MacCartney the afternoon we signed the contracts. He did all the work on the book himself. And after we'd had about three drinks he said to me, 'David, you were a GREAT reputation. What happened?' The drinks had loosened his tongue, don't you see? And then he said, 'I'm going to bring it all back.' I believe he wants to play God and that's all right with me because they're spending a lot of money on the book; they're giving me a cocktail party on publication day—that's August twenty-sixth—and they've sent everybody advance copies. They've got a quote from Bill Faulkner which they're going to use. He always liked my things. I tell you, Joe, I'm very high on this book. I think perhaps this is the one."

"It's really good, Joey," says Helen surely, and maybe her testimony is the best of all, and Joe feels more and more uneasy, "it's *his* book. You'll see that the minute you read it. It's about innocence and it makes Leslie Fiedler look gauche."

"You've put a lot of yourself into it?" asks Joe lamely.

"Boy, as Helen says, it's *my* book, Joe. This one is for me."

"A writer's career has a perilous shape," says Joe with a careful smile.

"That's right. 'The triumphant later years, the final apotheosis.' I had a tough middle period but I think that's all over now. You're going to find out, after you've finished 'the early works,'" and at last he puts the awkward question. "When is your book coming out?"

"Oh, that." There is nothing for it but to tell him. "As a matter of fact it's coming out the day before yours."

"The day before mine?"

Helen sits up abruptly in her deep chair, looking from one man to the other wordlessly.

"August twenty-fifth," whispers Joe.

David stands looking at him in amazement. "What do you think you're up to?"

"David, you know how it is with a first novel. You don't tell them; they tell you. It won't hurt your book."

"What a trick!"

"David, there'll be twenty novels coming out that week. Mine won't make any difference to you. You're famous. Your book will be a publishing event. Nobody's going to notice mine."

"He's right, David," says Helen sharply. "It won't make an atom of difference. You aren't competing with each other."

Without taking his eyes from Joe, he puts her view aside. "We're all competing. What's he trying to do to me? There's only so much review space. Of course we're competing. The same week, the day before. Why it's all been planned, hasn't it? Everybody knows you're supposed to be my friend. Some friend! I need all the help I can get." He is terribly upset.

"When they assigned me that date, I hadn't any idea when your book was coming out, not the least idea."

"And you think they didn't? I've had dealings with George before this. They're simply trying to kill my book, blanket it with yours. What happens if yours is very good, tell me that?"

Joe is now a little stung. "It's pretty good," he says.

"It ought to be, for Christ's sake, you've been at it long

enough. And then you have the nerve to walk into my house to tell me about it."

"David, be fair," says Helen.

"Be fair, be fair," he says, "was anybody fair to my last book? Fairness has nothing to do with it," and he stands looking at Joe in bewilderment, "and taking the silver," he quotes, "the chief priests bought with it a potter's field which is called Haceldama, that is, the field of blood, even to this day."

Joe picks it up and the implication that because he's a Jew he won't catch the reference freezes him, absolutely freezes him, rooting him motionless in his chair for a second as Helen stares regretfully from one to the other. Talking about myths, he thinks in a flash, talking about being possessed, the guy's possessed, he's disappeared into the myth; it's swallowed him. What am I sitting here for?

Without a word, waiting until later for reflection and self-doubt to assail him, he walks out of the house, the city spoiled for him, the pleasant life he'd looked forward to rejoining spoiled for him, the name of Judas whispering in his ear as he goes.

The strings are still playing Handel as he stands before his old "Atwater Kent" with his hand on the useless knob which says TONE. All at once, miraculously, the shriek and rattle in the speaker fade out and the orchestra becomes smooth and lovely, displaying the movement of the master's mind. He looks blankly at the curtain of faded velvet behind the fretted scrolls and remembers the childlike enthusiasm his father had for all such wonderful contrivances. "It's a miracle, Babele, listen!" He puts his hand gently on the volume control and turns the sound down, way down, until the strings are only a murmur, and he thinks of the dedication to his book, TO MY FATHER, and thinks to himself, I'm glad it's for him, for my father, for my real father, and he moves his wrist slightly and the music stops.

Alice Munro

THE PEACE
OF UTRECHT

I

I have been at home now for three weeks and it has not been a success. Maddy and I, though we speak cheerfully of our enjoyment of so long and intimate a visit, will be relieved when it is over. Silences disturb us. We laugh immoderately. I am afraid—very likely we are both afraid—that when the moment comes to say goodbye, unless we are very quick to kiss, and fervently mockingly squeeze each other's shoulders, we will have to look straight into the desert that is between us and acknowledge that we are not merely indifferent; at heart we reject each other, and as for that past we make so much of sharing we do not really share it at all, each of us keeping it jealously to herself, thinking privately that the other has turned alien, and forfeited her claim.

At night we often sit out on the steps of the verandah, and drink gin and smoke diligently to defeat the mosquitoes and postpone until very late the moment of going to bed. It is hot; the evening takes a long time to burn out. The high brick house, which stays fairly cool until midafternoon, holds the heat of the day trapped until long after dark. It was always like this, and Maddy and I recall how we used to drag our mattress downstairs onto the verandah, where we lay counting falling stars and trying to stay awake till dawn. We never did, falling asleep each night about the time a chill drift of air came up off the river, carrying a smell of reeds and the black ooze of the riverbed. At half-past ten a bus goes through the town, not slowing much; we see it go by at the end of our street. It is the same bus I used to take when I came home from college, and I remember coming into Jubilee on some warm night, seeing the earth bare around the massive roots of the trees, the drinking fountain surrounded by little puddles of water on the main street, the soft scrawls of blue and red and orange light that said BILLIARDS and CAFE; feeling as I recognized these signs a queer kind of oppression and release, as I exchanged the whole holiday world of school, of friends and, later on, of love, for the dim world of continuing disaster, of home. Maddy making the same journey four years earlier must have felt the same thing. I want to ask her: is it possible that children growing up as we did lose the ability to believe in—to be at home in—any ordinary and peaceful reality? But I don't ask her; we never talk about any of that. No exorcising here, says Maddy in her thin, bright voice with the slangy quality I had forgotten, we're not going to depress each other. So we haven't.

One night Maddy took me to a party at the Lake, which is about thirty miles west of here. The party was held in a cottage a couple of women from Jubilee had rented for the week. Most of the women there seemed to be widowed, single, separated or divorced; the men were mostly young and unmarried —those from Jubilee so young that I remember them only as little boys in the lower grades. There were two or three older men, not with their wives. But the women—they reminded me surprisingly of certain women familiar to me in my childhood, though of course I never saw their party-going personalities, only their activities in the stores and offices, and not infrequently in the Sunday schools, of Jubilee. They differed from the married women in being more aware of themselves in the world, a little brisker, sharper and coarser (though I can think of only one or two whose respectability was ever in question). They wore resolutely stylish though matronly clothes, which tended to swish and rustle over their hard rubber corsets, and they put perfume, quite a lot of it, on their artificial flowers. Maddy's friends were considerably modernized; they had copper rinses on their hair, and blue eyelids, and a robust capacity for drink.

Maddy I thought did not look one of them, with her slight figure and her still carelessly worn dark hair; her face has grown thin and strained without losing entirely its girlish look of impertinence and pride. But she speaks with the harsh twang of the local accent, which we used to make fun of, and her expression as she romped and drank was determinedly undismayed. It seemed to me that she was making every effort to belong with these people and that shortly she would succeed. It seemed to me too that she wanted me to see her succeeding, to see her repudiating that secret, exhilarating, really monstrous snobbery which we cultivated when we were children together, and promised ourselves, of course, much bigger things than Jubilee.

During the game in which all the women put an article of clothing—it begins decorously with a shoe—in a basket, and then all the men come in and have a race trying to fit things on to their proper owners, I went out and sat in the car, where I felt lonely for my husband and my friends and listened to the hilarity of the party and the waves falling on the beach and presently went to sleep. Maddy came much later and said, "For heaven's sake!" Then she laughed and said airily like a lady in an English movie, "You find these goings-on distasteful?" We both laughed; I felt apologetic, and rather sick from drinking and not getting drunk. "They may not be much on intellectual conversation but their hearts are in the right place, as the saying goes." I did not dispute this and we drove at eighty miles an hour from Inverhuron to Jubilee. Since then we have not been to any more parties.

But we are not always alone when we sit out on the steps. Often we are joined by a man named Fred Powell. He was at the party, peaceably in the background remembering whose liquor was whose and amiably holding someone's head over the rickety porch railing. He grew up in Jubilee as we did but I do not remember him, I suppose because he went through school some years ahead of us and then went away to the war. Maddy surprised me by bringing him home to supper the first night I was here and then we spent the evening, as we have spent many since, making this strange man a present of our childhood, or of that version of our childhood which is safely preserved in anecdote, as in a kind of mental cellophane. And what fantasies we build around the frail figures of our child-selves, so that they emerge beyond recognition incorrigible and gay. We tell stories together well. "You girls have got good memories," Fred Powell says, and sits watching us with an air of admiration and something else—reserve, embarrass-ment, deprecation—which appears on the faces of these mild deliberate people as they watch the keyed-up antics of their entertainers.

Now thinking of Fred Powell I admit that my reaction to this—this *situation* as I call it—is far more conventional than I would have expected; it is even absurd. And I do not know what situation it really is. I know that he is married. Maddy told me so, on the first evening, in a merely informative voice. His wife is an invalid. He has her at the Lake for the summer, Maddy says, he's very good to her. I do not know if he is Maddy's lover and she will never tell me. Why should it mat-ter to me? Maddy is well over thirty. But I keep thinking of the way he sits on our steps with his hands set flat on his spread knees, his mild full face turned almost indulgently toward Maddy as she talks; he has an affable masculine look of being diverted but unimpressed. And Maddy teases him, tells him he is too fat, will not smoke his cigarettes, involves him in private, nervous, tender arguments which have no meaning and no end. He allows it. (And this is what frightens me, I know it now: he allows it; *she needs it*.) When she is a little drunk she says in tones of half-pleading mockery that he is her only real friend. He speaks the same language, she says. Nobody else does. I have no answer to that.

Then again I begin to wonder: *is* he only her friend? I had forgotten certain restrictions of life in Jubilee—and this holds good whatever the pocket novels are saying about small towns —and also what strong, respectable, never overtly sexual friendships can flourish within these restrictions and be fed by them, so that in the end such relationships may consume half a life. This thought depresses me (unconsummated relation-ships depress outsiders perhaps more than anybody else) so much that I find myself wishing for them to be honest lovers.

The rhythm of life in Jubilee is primitively seasonal. Deaths occur in the winter; marriages are celebrated in the summer. There is good reason for this; the winters are long and full of hardship and the old and weak cannot always get through them. Last winter was a catastrophe, such as may be expected every ten or twelve years; you can see how the pavement in the streets is broken up, as if the town had survived a minor bombardment. A death is dealt with then in the middle of great difficulties; there comes time now in the summer to think about it, and talk. I find that people stop me in the street to talk about my mother. I have heard from them about her funeral, what flowers she had and what the weather was like on that day. And now that she is dead I no longer feel that when they say the words "your mother" they deal a knowing, cunning blow at my pride. I used to feel that; at those words I felt my whole identity, that pretentious adolescent construction, come crumbling down.

Now I listen to them speak of her, so gently and ceremoniously, and I realize that she became one of the town's possessions and oddities, its brief legends. This she achieved in spite of us, for we tried, both crudely and artfully, to keep her at home, away from that sad notoriety; not for her sake, but for ours, who suffered such unnecessary humiliation at the sight of her eyes rolling back in her head in a temporary paralysis of the eye muscles, at the sound of her thickened voice, whose embarrassing pronouncements it was our job to interpret to outsiders. So bizarre was the disease she had in its effects that it made us feel like crying out in apology (though we stayed stiff and white) as if we were accompanying a particularly tasteless sideshow. All wasted, our pride; our purging its rage in wild caricatures we did for each other (no, not caricatures, for she was one herself; imitations). We should have let the town have her; it would have treated her better.

About Maddy and her ten-years' vigil they say very little; perhaps they want to spare my feelings, remembering that I was the one who went away and here are my two children to show for it, while Maddy is alone and has nothing but that discouraging house. But I don't think so; in Jubilee the feelings are not spared this way. And they ask me point-blank why I did not come home for the funeral; I am glad I have the excuse of the blizzard that halted air travel that week, for I do not know if I would have come anyway, after Maddy had written so vehemently urging me to stay away. I felt strongly that she had a right to be left alone with it, if she wanted to be, after all this time.

After all this time. Maddy was the one who stayed. First, she went away to college, then I went. You give me four years, I'll give you four years, she said. But I got married. She was not surprised; she was exasperated at me for my wretched useless feelings of guilt. She said that she had always meant to stay. She said that Mother no longer "bothered" her. "Our Gothic Mother," she said, "I play it out now, I let her be. I don't keep trying to make her *human* any more. You know." It would simplify things so much to say that Maddy was religious, that she felt the joys of self-sacrifice, the strong, mystical appeal of total rejection. But about Maddy who could say that? When we were in our teens, and our old aunts, Aunt Annie and Auntie Lou, spoke to us of some dutiful son or daughter who had given up everything for an ailing parent, Maddy would quote impiously the opinions of modern psychiatry. Yet she stayed. All I can think about that, all I have ever been able to think, to comfort me, is that she may have been able and may even have chosen to live without time and in perfect imaginary freedom as children do, the future untampered with, all choices always possible.

To change the subject, people ask me what it is like to be back in Jubilee. But I don't know, I am still waiting for something to tell me, to make me understand that I am back. The day I drove up from Toronto with my children in the back seat of the car I was very tired, on the last lap of a twenty-five-hundred-mile trip. I had to follow a complicated system of highways and sideroads, for there is no easy way to get to Jubilee from anywhere on earth. Then about two o'clock in the afternoon I saw ahead of me, so familiar and unexpected, the gaudy, peeling cupola of the town hall, which is no relation to any of the rest of the town's squarely-built, dingy grey-and-red-brick architecture. (Underneath it hangs a great bell, to be rung in the event of some mythical disaster.) I drove up the main street—a new service station, new stucco front on the Queen's Hotel—and turned into the quiet, decaying side streets where old maids live, and have birdbaths and blue delphiniums in their gardens. The big brick houses that I knew, with their wooden verandahs and gaping, dark-screened windows, seemed to me plausible but unreal. (Anyone to whom I have mentioned the dreaming, sunken feeling of these streets wants to take me out to the north side of town where there is a new soft-drink bottling plant, some new ranch-style houses and a Tastee-Freez.) Then I parked my car in a little splash of shade in front of the house where I used to live. My little girl, whose name is Margaret, said neutrally yet with some disbelief, "Mother, is that your house?"

And I felt that my daughter's voice expressed a complex disappointment—to which, characteristically, she seemed resigned, or even resigned *in advance*; it contained the whole flatness and strangeness of the moment in which is revealed the source of legends, the unsatisfactory, apologetic and persistent reality. The red brick of which the house is built looked harsh and hot in the sun and was marked in two or three places by long grimacing cracks; the verandah, which always had the air of an insubstantial decoration, was visibly falling away. There was—there *is*—a little blind window of coloured glass beside the front door. I sat staring at it with a puzzled lack of emotional recognition. I sat and looked at the house and the window shades did not move, the door did not fly open, no one came out on the verandah; there was no one at home. This was as I had expected, since Maddy works now in the office of the town clerk, yet I was surprised to see the house take on such a closed, bare, impoverished look, merely by being left empty. And it was brought home to me, as I walked across the front yard to the steps, that after all these summers on the Coast I had forgotten the immense inland heat, which makes you feel as if you have to carry the whole burning sky on your head.

A sign pinned to the front door announced, in Maddy's rather sloppy and flamboyant hand: VISITORS WELCOME, CHILDREN FREE, RATES TO BE ARRANGED LATER (YOU'LL BE SORRY) WALK IN. On the hall table was a bouquet of pink phlox whose velvety scent filled the hot air of a closed house on a summer afternoon. "Upstairs!" I said to the children, and I took the hand of the little girl and her smaller brother, who had slept in the car and who rubbed against me, whimpering, as he walked. Then I paused, one foot on the bottom step, and turned to greet, matter-of-factly, the reflection of a thin, tanned, habitually watchful woman, recognizably a Young Mother, whose hair, pulled into a knot on top of her head, exposed a jawline no longer softly fleshed, a brown neck rising with a look of tension from the little sharp knobs of the collarbone—this in the hall mirror that had shown me, last time I looked, a commonplace pretty girl, with a face as smooth and insensitive as an apple, no matter what panic and disorder lay behind it.

But this was not what I had turned for; I realized that I must have been waiting for my mother to call, from her couch in the dining-room, where she lay with the blinds down in the summer heat, drinking cups of tea which she never finished, eating—she had dispensed altogether with mealtimes, like a sickly child—little bowls of preserved fruit and crumblings of cake. It seemed to me that I could not close the door behind me without hearing my mother's ruined voice call out to me, and feeling myself go heavy all over as I prepared to answer it. Calling, *Who's there?*

I led my children to the big bedroom at the back of the house, where Maddy and I used to sleep. It has thin, almost worn-out white curtains at the windows and a square of linoleum on the floor; there is a double bed, a washstand which Maddy and I used as a desk when we were in high school, and a cardboard wardrobe with little mirrors on the inside of the doors. As I talked to my children I was thinking—but carefully, not in a rush—of my mother's state of mind when she called out *Who's there?* I was allowing myself to hear—as if I had not dared before—the cry for help—undisguised, oh, shamefully undisguised and raw and supplicating—that sounded in her voice. A cry repeated so often, and, things being as they were, so uselessly, that Maddy and I recognized it only as one of those household sounds which must be dealt with, so that worse may not follow. *You go and deal with Mother,* we would say to each other, or *I'll be out in a minute, I have to deal with Mother.*

It might be that we had to perform some of the trivial and unpleasant services endlessly required, or that we had to supply five minutes' expediently cheerful conversation, so remorselessly casual that never for a moment was there a recognition of the real state of affairs, never a glint of pity to open the way for one of her long debilitating sieges of tears. But the pity denied, the tears might come anyway; so that we were defeated, we were forced—to stop that noise—into parodies of love. But we grew cunning, unfailing in cold solicitude; we took away from her our anger and impatience and disgust, took all emotion away from our dealings with her, as you might take away meat from a prisoner to weaken him, till he died.

We would tell her to read, to listen to music and enjoy the changes of season and be grateful that she did not have cancer. We added that she did not suffer any pain, and that is true—if imprisonment is not pain. While she demanded our love in every way she knew, without shame or sense, as a child will. And how could we have loved her, I say desperately to myself, the resources of love we had were not enough, the demand on us was too great. Nor would it have changed anything.

"Everything has been taken away from me," she would say. To strangers, to friends of ours whom we tried always unsuccessfully to keep separate from her, to old friends of hers who came guiltily infrequently to see her, she would speak like this, in the very slow and mournful voice that was not intelligible or quite human; we would have to interpret. Such theatricality humiliated us almost to death; yet now I think that without that egotism feeding stubbornly even on disaster she might have sunk rapidly into some dim vegetable life. She kept herself as much in the world as she could, not troubling about her welcome; restlessly she wandered through the house and into the streets of Jubilee. Oh, she was not resigned; she must have wept and struggled in that house of stone (as I can, but will not, imagine) until the very end.

But I find the picture is still not complete. Our Gothic Mother, with the cold appalling mask of the Shaking Palsy laid across her features, shuffling, weeping, devouring attention wherever she can get it, eyes dead and burning, fixed inward on herself; this is not all. For the disease is erratic and leisurely in its progress; some mornings (gradually growing fewer and fewer and farther apart) she wakes up better; she goes out to the yard and straightens up a plant in such a simple housewifely way; she says something calm and lucid to us; she listens attentively to the news. She has wakened out of a bad dream; she tries to make up for lost time, tidying the house, forcing her stiff trembling hands to work a little while at the sewing machine. She makes us one of her specialties, a banana cake or a lemon meringue pie. Occasionally since she died I have dreams of her (I never dreamt of her when she was alive) in which she is doing something like this, and I think, why did I exaggerate so to myself, see, she is all right, only that her hands are trembling—

At the end of these periods of calm a kind of ravaging energy would come over her; she would make conversation insistently and with less and less coherence; she would demand that we rouge her cheeks and fix her hair; sometimes she might even hire a dressmaker to come in and make clothes for her, working in the dining room where she could watch— spending her time again more and more on the couch. This was extravagant, unnecessary from any practical point of view (for why did she need these clothes, where did she wear them?) and nerve-racking, because the dressmaker did not understand what she wanted and sometimes neither did we. I remember after I went away receiving from Maddy several amusing, distracted, quietly overwrought letters describing these sessions with the dressmaker. I read them with sympathy but without being able to enter into the once-familiar atmosphere of frenzy and frustration which my mother's demands could produce. In the ordinary world it was not possible to re-create her. The picture of her face which I carried in my mind seemed too terrible, unreal. Similarly the complex strain of living with her, the feelings of hysteria which Maddy and I once dissipated in a great deal of brutal laughter, now began to seem partly imaginary; I felt the beginnings of a secret, guilty estrangement.

I stayed in the room with my children for a little while because it was a strange place, for them it was only another strange place to go to sleep. Looking at them in this room I felt that they were particularly fortunate and that their life was safe and easy, which may be what most parents think at one time or another. I looked in the wardrobe but there was nothing there, only a hat trimmed with flowers from the five-and-ten, which one of us must have made for some flossy Easter. When I opened the drawer of the washstand I saw that it was crammed full of pages from a loose-leaf notebook. I read: "The Peace of Utrecht, 1713, brought an end to the War of the Spanish Succession." It struck me that the handwriting was my own. Strange to think of it lying here for ten years—more; it looked as if I might have written it that day.

For some reason reading these words had a strong effect on me; I felt as if my old life was lying around me, waiting to be picked up again. Only then for a few moments in our old room did I have this feeling. The brown halls of the old High School (a building since torn down) were re-opened for me, and I remembered the Saturday nights in spring, after the snow had melted and all the country people crowded into town. I thought of us walking up and down the main street, arm in arm with two or three other girls, until it got dark, then going in to Al's to dance, under a string of little coloured lights. The windows in the dance hall were open; they let in the raw spring air with its smell of earth and the river; the hands of farm boys crumpled and stained our white blouses when we danced. And now an experience which seemed not at all memorable at the time (in fact Al's was a dismal place and the ritual of walking up and down the street to show ourselves off we thought crude and ridiculous, though we could not resist it) had been transformed into something curiously meaningful for me, and complete; it took in more than the girls dancing and the single street, it spread over the whole town, its rudimentary pattern of streets and its bare trees and muddy yards just free of the snow, over the dirt roads where the lights of cars appeared, jolting towards the town, under an immense pale wash of sky.

Also: we wore ballerina shoes, and full black taffeta skirts, and short coats of such colours as robin's egg blue, cerise red, lime green. Maddy wore a great funereal bow at the neck of her blouse and a wreath of artificial daisies in her hair. These were the fashions, or so we believed, of one of the years after the war. Maddy; her bright skeptical look; my sister.

I ask Maddy, "Do you ever remember what she was like before?"

"No," says Maddy. "No, I can't."

"I sometimes think I can," I say hesitantly. "Not very often." Cowardly tender nostalgia, trying to get back to a gentler truth.

"I think you would have to have been away," Maddy says, *"You would have to have been away these last—quite a few— years to get those kind of memories."*

It was then she said: No exorcising.

And the only other thing she said was, "She spent a lot of time sorting things. All kinds of things. Greeting cards. Buttons and yarn. Sorting and putting them into little piles. It would keep her quiet by the hour."

II

I have been to visit Aunt Annie and Auntie Lou. This is the third time I have been there since I came home and each time they have been spending the afternoon making rugs out of dyed rags. They are very old now. They sit in a hot little porch that is shaded by bamboo blinds; the rags and the half-finished rugs make an encouraging, domestic sort of disorder around them. They do not go out any more, but they get up early in the mornings, wash and powder themselves and put on their shapeless print dresses trimmed with rickrack and white braid. They make coffee and porridge and then they clean the house, Aunt Annie working upstairs and Auntie Lou down. Their house is very clean, dark and varnished, and it smells of vinegar and apples. In the afternoon they lie down for an hour and then put on their afternoon dresses, with brooches at the neck, and sit down to do hand work.

They are the sort of women whose flesh melts or mysteriously falls away as they get older. Auntie Lou's hair is still black, but it looks stiff and dry in its net as the dead end of hair on a ripe ear of corn. She sits straight and moves her bone-thin arms in very fine, slow movements; she looks like an Egyptian, with her long neck and small sharp face and greatly wrinkled, greatly darkened skin. Aunt Annie, perhaps because of her gentler, even coquettish manner, seems more humanly fragile and worn. Her hair is nearly all gone, and she keeps on her head one of those pretty caps designed for young wives who wear curlers to bed. She calls my attention to this and asks if I do not think it is becoming. They are both adept at these little ironies, and take a mild delight in pointing out whatever is grotesque about themselves. Their company manners are exceedingly lighthearted and their conversation with each other falls into an accomplished pattern of teasing and protest. I have a fascinated glimpse of Maddy and myself, grown old, caught back in the web of sisterhood after everything else has disappeared, making tea for some young, loved, and essentially unimportant relative—and exhibiting just such a polished relationship; what will anyone ever know of us? As I watch my entertaining old aunts I wonder if old people play such stylized and simplified roles with us because they are afraid that anything more honest might try our patience; or if they do it out of delicacy—to fill the social time—when in reality they feel so far away from us that there is no possibility of communicating with us at all.

At any rate I felt held at a distance by them, at least until this third afternoon when they showed in front of me some signs of disagreement with each other. I believe this is the first time that has happened. Certainly I never saw them argue in all the years when Maddy and I used to visit them, and we used to visit them often—not only out of duty but because we found the atmosphere of sense and bustle reassuring after the comparative anarchy, the threatened melodrama, of our house at home.

Aunt Annie wanted to take me upstairs to show me something. Auntie Lou objected, looking remote and offended, as if the whole subject embarrassed her. And such is the feeling for discretion, the tradition of circumlocution in that house, that it was unthinkable for me to ask them what they were talking about.

"Oh, let her have her tea," Auntie Lou said, and Aunt Annie said, "Well. When she's *had* her tea."

"Do as you like then. That upstairs is hot."

"Will you come up, Lou?"

"Then who's going to watch the children?"

"Oh, the children. I forgot."

So Aunt Annie and I withdrew into the darker parts of the house. It occurred to me, absurdly, that she was going to give me a five-dollar bill. I remembered that sometimes she used to draw me into the front hall in this mysterious way and open her purse. I do not think that Auntie Lou was included in that secret either. But we went on upstairs, and into Aunt Annie's own bedroom, which looked so neat and virginal, papered with timid flowery wallpaper, the dressers spread with white scarves. It was really very hot, as Auntie Lou had said.

"Now," Aunt Annie said, a little breathless. "Get me down that box on the top shelf of the closet."

I did, and she opened it and said with her wistful conspirator's gaiety, "Now I guess you wondered what became of all your mother's clothes?"

I had not thought of it. I sat down on the bed, forgetting that in this house the beds were not to be sat on; the bedrooms had one straight chair apiece, for that. Aunt Annie did not check me. She began to lift things out, saying, "Maddy never mentioned them, did she?"

"I never asked her," I said.

"No. Nor I wouldn't. I wouldn't say a word about it to Maddy. But I thought I might as well show you. Why not? Look," she said. "We washed and ironed what we could and what we couldn't we sent to the cleaners. I paid the cleaning myself. Then we mended anything needed mending. It's all in good condition, see?"

I watched helplessly while she held up for my inspection the underwear which was on top. She showed me where things had been expertly darned and mended and where the elastic had been renewed. She showed me a slip which had been worn, she said, only once. She took out nightgowns, a dressing gown, knitted bed-jackets. "This was what she had on the last time I saw her," she said. "I think it was. Yes." I recognized with alarm the peach-coloured bed-jacket I had sent for Christmas.

"You can see it's hardly used. Why, it's hardly used at all."

"No," I said.

"Underneath is her dresses." Her hands rummaged down

through those brocades and flowered silks, growing yearly more exotic, in which my mother had wished to costume herself. Thinking of her in these peacock colours, even Aunt Annie seemed to hesitate. She drew up a blouse. "I washed this by hand, it looks like new. There's a coat hanging up in the closet. Perfectly good. She never wore a coat. She wore it when she went into the hospital, that was all. Wouldn't it fit you?"

"No," I said. "*No.*" For Aunt Annie was already moving towards the closet. "I just got a new coat. I have several coats. Aunt Annie!"

"But why should you go and buy," Aunt Annie went on in her mild stubborn way, "when there are things here as good as new."

"I would rather buy," I said, and was immediately sorry for the coldness in my voice. Nevertheless I continued, "When I need something, I do go and buy it." This suggestion that I was not poor any more brought a look of reproach and aloofness into my aunt's face. She said nothing. I went and looked at a picture of Aunt Annie and Auntie Lou and their older brothers and their mother and father which hung over the bureau. They stared back at me with grave accusing Protestant faces, for I had run up against the simple unprepossessing materialism which was the rock of their lives. Things must be used; everything must be used up, saved and mended and made into something else and used again; clothes were to be worn. I felt that I had hurt Aunt Annie's feelings and that furthermore I had probably borne out a prediction of Auntie Lou's, for she was sensitive to certain attitudes in the world that were too sophisticated for Aunt Annie to bother about, and she had very likely said that I would not want my mother's clothes.

"She was gone sooner than anybody would have expected," Aunt Annie said. I turned around surprised and she said, "Your mother." Then I wondered if the clothes had been the main thing after all; perhaps they were only to serve as the introduction to a conversation about my mother's death, which Aunt Annie might feel to be a necessary part of our visit. Auntie Lou would feel differently; she had an almost superstitious dislike of certain rituals of emotionalism; such a conversation could never take place with her about.

"Two months after she went into the hospital," Aunt Annie said. "She was gone in two months." I saw that she was crying distractedly, as old people do, with miserable scanty tears. She pulled a handkerchief out of her dress and rubbed at her face.

"Maddy told her it was nothing but a check-up," she said. "Maddy told her it would be about three weeks. Your mother went in there and she thought she was coming out in three weeks." She was whispering as if she was afraid of us being overheard. "Do you think she wanted to stay in there where nobody could make out what she was saying and they wouldn't let her out of her bed? She wanted to come home!"

"But she was too sick," I said.

"No, she wasn't, she was just the way she'd always been, just getting a little worse and a little worse as time went on. But after she went in there she felt she would die, everything kind of closed in around her, and she went down so fast."

"Maybe it would have happened anyway," I said. "Maybe it was just the time."

Aunt Annie paid no attention to me. "I went up to see her," she said. "She was so glad to see me because I could tell what she was saying. She said Aunt Annie, they won't keep me in here for good, will they? And I said to her, No. I said, No.

"And she said, Aunt Annie ask Maddy to take me home again or I'm going to die. She didn't want to die. Don't you ever think a person wants to die, just because it seems to everybody else they have got no reason to go on living. So I told Maddy. But she didn't say anything. She went to the hospital every day and saw your mother and she wouldn't take her home. Your mother told me Maddy said to her, I won't take you home."

"Mother didn't always tell the truth," I said. "Aunt Annie, you know that."

"*Did you know your mother got out of the hospital?*"

"No," I said. But strangely I felt no surprise, only a vague physical sense of terror, a longing not to be told—and beyond this a feeling that what I would be told I already knew, I had always known.

"Maddy, didn't she tell you?"

"No."

"Well she got *out*. She got out the side door where the ambulance comes in, it's the only door that isn't locked. It was at night when they haven't so many nurses to watch them. She got her dressing gown and her slippers on, the first time she ever got anything on herself in years, and she went out and there it was January, snowing, but she didn't go back in. She was away down the street when they caught her. After that they put the board across her bed."

The snow, the dressing gown and slippers, the board across the bed. It was a picture I was much inclined to resist. Yet I had no doubt that this was true, all this was true and exactly as it happened. It was what she would do; all her life as long as I had known her led up to that flight.

"Where was she going?" I said, but I knew there was no answer.

"I don't know. Maybe I shouldn't have told you. Oh, Helen, when they came after her she tried to run. She tried to *run*."

The flight that concerns everybody. Even behind my aunt's soft familiar face there is another, more primitive old woman, capable of panic in some place her faith has never touched.

She began folding the clothes up and putting them back in the box. "They nailed a board across her bed. I saw it. You can't blame the nurses. They can't watch everybody. They haven't the time.

"I said to Maddy after the funeral, Maddy, may it never happen like that to you. I couldn't help it, that's what I said." She sat down on the bed herself now, folding things and putting them back in the box, making an effort to bring her voice back to normal—and pretty soon succeeding, for having lived this long who would not be an old hand at grief and self-control?

"We thought it was hard," she said finally. "Lou and I thought it was hard."

Is this the last function of old women, beyond making rag rugs and giving us five-dollar bills—making sure the haunts we have contracted for are with us, not one gone without?

She was afraid of Maddy—through fear, had cast her out

for good. I thought of what Maddy had said: nobody speaks the same language.

When I got home Maddy was out in the back kitchen making a salad. Rectangles of sunlight lay on the rough linoleum. She had taken off her high-heeled shoes and was standing there in her bare feet. The back kitchen is a large untidy pleasant room with a view, behind the stove and the drying dishtowels, of the sloping back yard, the CPR station and the golden, marshy river that almost encircles the town of Jubilee. My children who had felt a little repressed in the other house immediately began to play under the table.

"Where have you been?" Maddy said.

"Nowhere. Just to see the Aunts."

"Oh, how are they?"

"They're fine. They're indestructible."

"Are they? Yes I guess they are. I haven't been to see them for a while. I don't actually see that much of them any more."

"Don't you?" I said, and she knew then what they had told me.

"They were beginning to get on my nerves a bit, after the funeral. And Fred got me this job and everything and I've been so busy—" She looked at me, waiting for what I would say, smiling a little derisively, patiently.

"Don't be guilty, Maddy," I said softly. All this time the children were running in and out and shrieking at each other between our legs.

"I'm not guilty," she said. "Where did you get that? I'm not guilty." She went to turn on the radio, talking to me over her shoulder. "Fred's going to eat with us again since he's alone. I got some raspberries for dessert. Raspberries are almost over for this year. Do they look all right to you?"

"They look all right," I said. "Do you want me to finish this?"

"Fine," she said. "I'll go and get a bowl."

She went into the dining room and came back carrying a pink cut-glass bowl, for the raspberries.

"I couldn't go on," she said. "I wanted my life."

She was standing on the little step between the kitchen and the dining room and suddenly she lost her grip on the bowl, either because her hands had begun to shake or because she had not picked it up properly in the first place; it was quite a heavy and elaborate old bowl. It slipped out of her hands and she tried to catch it and it smashed on the floor.

Maddy began to laugh. "Oh, hell," she said. "Oh, hell, oh *Hel*-en," she said, using one of our old foolish ritual phrases of despair. "Look what I've done now. In my bare feet yet. Get me a broom."

"Take your life, Maddy. Take it."

"Yes I will," Maddy said. "Yes I will."

"Go away, don't stay here."

"Yes I will."

Then she bent down and began picking up the pieces of broken pink glass. My children stood back looking at her with awe and she was laughing and saying, "It's no loss to me. I've got a whole shelf full of glass bowls. I've got enough glass bowls to do me the rest of my life. Oh, don't stand there looking at me, go and get me a broom!" I went around the kitchen looking for a broom because I seemed to have forgotten where it was kept and she said, "But why can't I, Helen? *Why can't I?*"

Epilogue

Dave Godfrey   **OUT
                                     IN
                                     CHINGUACOUSY**

He left Shad lumbering around outside in the top field while he went into the kitchen to greet his cousin Albert.

The hearth was bricked-in and the room smelled of oil heat.

"Not much going or I'd go out with you," Albert said. "Might try back near the tracks though."

Albert had the *Star* spread out on the kitchen table and was exploring the latest adventures of Colonel Canyon.

He felt there was something he should say to Albert this day, but it was winter and there were no crops to comment upon, and his cousin just sat there reading, with his hair rank over his forehead and the blue metal breakfast plate pushed to one side and the blue metal coffee mug glued to the centre of the plate by drying, hardening egg.

"That used to be some house," he said when he came out and had walked with Shad past the silo and into the far fields.

"It is pretty big." Shad had a careful and polite manner of expressing himself, which some people mistook for deference but which was really his way of reaching out. I've worked myself out of something pretty hard, it said, something which you don't have to know about but for which you are perhaps partly responsible. Although I won't mention that responsibility. It's your word. I've paid my dues. I won't go back. I'm no Bobby Washington; I won't do anything careless. But I'll always be careful talking to you. It said all that.

The front part of the house out in Chinguacousy was unpainted: hasn't seen a paintbrush since the Boer war, as his father used to say. There were no curtains on the side windows, the shades were torn, and you could look straight inside, to mustiness, the falling plaster, trash, rain-stained mattresses. The boards were the colour of long unpolished silver. Albert lived in the back section, which was low and made of brick. He had burned the ivy off one fall afternoon and the brick was pocked and crumbling, as though it were made of sandstone and not the good clay of the region. There was a C cracked almost into an O on the kitchen window.

"It's a pretty big house, if you consider both parts," Shad chose to say. "Has he lived there a long time?"

"Born there. Bred there. Schooled there. He and his father. My great-uncle and his grandfather. And their father before them."

"You're lucky to know all that," Shad said. "About your family. It must be a lot of work to keep a place like that up."

"Depends on what you're interested in," he said. *Tritavis.* An honourable man knows the great-grandfather of his grandfather.

They went through a grain field that had been partly ploughed under for winter wheat and partly just left to rot. There was a thick aisle of weeds ten feet out along the right fence.

"He's going to have a field full of tares next year," Shad said.

"Vetches we call them," he said. "In case you're ever out with farmers. Watch that one now."

The rabbit came out almost at their feet and slipped over to the seeded furrows. He lifted and let it run until it was beyond damage range; hit it; caused its running to cease.

Shad still had the twenty-two cradled in his arm.

"Better make sure you're on my side when the riots start," he said to Shad. He felt embarrassed with the small, brown body of fur when they reached it and he quickly stuffed it into the bird-fold at the back of his jacket. He put in a new shell. The lightest of bird shot.

"We'll clean it at the car," he said.

They went over one of Albert's fences: old cedar rails, straightened from their former snaking flow, with a single strand of barbed wire running along the top rail.

"I guess you have to shoot them in the back," Shad said.

"Back? Ass is the word. Sometimes they run towards you. Not often. Or circle. Or cut in one direction. Mostly it's just straight away from your danger."

"You want to do it at this fence?"

"Coming back; if you're still certain. People are usually careful going out."

"It seems funny, but I don't think there's another way. But I'd rather do it myself."

"It'll look a lot less suspicious if I do it."

They hunted.

At the same fence, coming back, with four rabbits weighing down his jacket, he prepared himself to break the rules, the hard, the long-learned, the defensive and inbred rules. But it was still awkward and not easy. He sent Shad over first and passed him one gun. Then he pushed the safety off on the Beretta and flung one leg up on a rail and then the other leg, balancing, and tipped the barrel over the single strand of barbed wire, while Shad stood there passively, almost ready to laugh; and then awkwardly, when the barrel swung downwards, holding the gun as far from the earth as he could, calculating the pattern, he jerked the trigger, putting on all the grip he could with his right hand and using his left as a restraining block to keep the barrel aimed true, although the recoil was strong with no shoulder to absorb it and the gun fought to break out of his hands. Then he looked at Shad, who was laughing now.

"That'll teach you to stay out of my watermelons, boy," Shad said.

"My line," he said. "My line." And laughed out some of his own uneasiness. "Are you okay?"

Shad kicked his foot at any imaginary football. "Sure. Should have taken a few extra bennies; but it's not as bad as cleats. I was thinking of that night Bobby Washington shot the marine. I was expecting something worse."

"I was too." But he could not laugh.

He pushed the button on the shotgun and smoke wisped out as it snapped open. He tossed the spent shell on the earth. And he thought of Bobby Washington coming back into that midwest bar after the marine had laughed at him and called him a nigger-girl who didn't know enough to wear a skirt, and had offered to fight him right there or out in the alley or on the sidewalk. And Bobby walked out and the marine laughed and joked about what a real woman could do for Martin Luther, and strutted a little, until Bobby walked back in with a pistol in his hand and didn't even call out to the marine but just shot him six times and the marine never even got a chance to turn around and see what was killing him but all six shots entered his body within a small arc circumscribed from the point where a line joining his kidneys would intersect his spinal cord.

The ground was not totally firm beneath him and he thought of those immense dislocations of his youth, when a voyage of five or six miles would make him vomit as the world beyond the bus seemed to fade away into nothingness on all sides. He thought of McNamara sitting on a swivel chair in the Pentagon and answering the questions of the American clergy. "You know, there are two ways to kill a man. You can kill his body, or you can kill his soul. I'd rather kill a few thousand bodies than kill fourteen million souls in Vietnam." He took aim at McNamara, but he kept swiveling away from him and presenting his back and all of a sudden he himself was the marine and Bobby had come through the door and he knew he would never get to finish his beer and then he was just a monkey in the hand of Buddha, a wild monkey with an Italian shotgun in his hands and a feeling of bitterness that the shotgun wasn't engraved in gold.

He laid the gun on the cold-hardened earth and slapped reality back into his face.

"Got six, eh?" Albert said when they came back to the house.

"Five. And one Shad. I did the real city boy thing at the fence. Shot him in the foot passing over the guns."

Shad held out the boot as though he were some sort of

travelling salesman or they were all actors in an early comedy film.

"A little birdshot's good for the soul," Albert said.

He took them inside and Shad unlaced his boot. The foot was bruised and sweaty, but the boot had absorbed most of the damage. Some of the shot had gone well through the tough leather, some taking blue wool from Shad's sock with it so that odd threads curled up like hairs, and pellets were visible as darker bodies within the flesh.

They phoned the doctor and left Shad alone in the kitchen.

"Hear you're thinking of moving into the country," Albert said.

"Charlie tell you? I'm always thinking of it. I hear you've put a price on this place."

"Considering it. Want to see around?" They moved out of the brick portion of the house into the old, frame, two-storied section and walked through the musty rooms. Old mattresses lay on the floor; a cracked wash-stand; cardboard boxes and pile of newspapers. The walls were stained. The wallpaper's floral pattern had been bleached out by time; the torn shades kept out little sunlight. The fireplace was full of settled ashes.

"Used to be a hotel didn't it? A stopping place?"

"Oh, maybe. A hundred years ago. Who knows? I wish I had that whole hundred acres instead of just this here fifty. Got offered two an acre for it. Two thousand. Enough to pay off the mortgage, I guess."

He knew there had never been a dollar borrowed on the land in all the time since the original grant. He looked at his cousin.

"Your American friend didn't like the army, eh?" Albert scraped at his cheekbone with his right thumbnail.

"He never joined."

"A lot of them like that in Toronto now, I guess."

"Some."

"A little cowardly to my way of thinking."

"There's lots of ways to be cowardly." He looked out through the dust on the window. "There's never been a mortgage on this place, has there?" he said. "In more than your lifetime and mine put together."

"Just a way of speaking," Albert said.

"You're quite a way from things here."

"Seven miles from the Rambler plant. Eight miles from the 401."

Modern loci. From the dusty front windows were still visible the masonry walls of the river's mill, the ancient stone heart of the locality. Tritavus.

"Lots of industry coming up," he said. "You might get General Dynamics or Dow to build here."

"Can't tell. If you can't beat them hold out for top dollar on what you got to sell them, I say."

"That's one way of looking at it, I guess."

"I guess."

When the doctor came up from town he gave Shad a local anesthetic, and right there in the kitchen removed all the birdshot.

"Better keep your weight off it for two or three weeks," he said when he was done. "Then you'll be as good as ever."

"It's not going to work," Shad said on the drive back towards the city. "I could laugh last time, when they read off the Attorney-General's list and I said no, I never belonged to any of them, they're all dead, nobody belongs to any of them. And they said sure we know that and that's why we don't change them because when we did they just changed their names anyhow; now we keep the list the same and they don't change their names and we all know where we're at. They said all that and I laughed with them. But this time I'll throttle anybody who jokes about it or if they keep me waiting for five hours at a time. And if I go in, I'll kill somebody within three weeks. As soon as they start running me through their stamping machine. I'm not raw metal now; I'm a grown man. I've fought my wars. And if I stay out and hide out, some day my father'll die and I'll go back and they'll jail me for five years and I'll go mad and kill somebody. I dream of Bobby Washington some nights now, shooting that marine right off the stool, without giving him any warning at all, and I wake up in a worse sweat than after a game. I should have used the rifle myself."

He drove quickly and let Shad talk and fought the sense of

failure that came as he considered that he had been unable to succeed even at the simple task of maiming a friend who desired physical maiming.

When they got on the high part of 401 the city was a sea of light right down to the harbour. Then darkness. Then the islands. Then the greater darkness beyond the islands.

Biographical Notes

Alice (Eedy) Boissonneau was born in Walkerton, Ontario, and educated at the University of Toronto. For a number of years she was a social worker in Toronto and Vancouver; more recently she spent the warm months of the year in Northern Ontario where her husband was doing research in land use. She has lived in Cannington, Ontario, for the past four years. Her stories and sketches have been published in the *Canadian Forum* and *Alphabet*, and heard on the C.B.C. programme "Anthology." "The McCrimmons" was included in Martha Foley's list of "Distinctive Short Stories" for 1952. She has completed a novel and is working on a collection of short stories.

Morley Callaghan (1903-   ) is one of Canada's major novelists. Born in Toronto, he was educated at St. Michael's College and Osgoode Hall Law School. For a short time in 1929 he was a member of the fabled group of expatriate North Americans who haunted the Boulevard Montparnasse in Paris, and he has written an important memoir of the period, *That Summer in Paris* (1963). Since 1929 he has made his home in Toronto, which he once wrote has a quiet, orderly way of life that is good for his writing because it keeps his soul in a state of longing. He has published twelve novels, and his short stories are among the finest ever written in Canada. Both "Last Spring They Came Over" and "Ancient Lineage" first appeared in book form in his early anthology *A Native Argosy* (1929). Callaghan is at present at work on a new novel, *In the Dark and the Light of Lisa*.

Gregory Clark (1892-   ), one of Canada's most delightful journalists, was born in Toronto, the son of an editor of the *Star*. He went to Harbord Collegiate, and married Helen Murray in 1916. Clark was on the staff of the *Star* from 1911 until his retirement in 1945, and since 1936 has been writing his gentle satiric sketches for the *Star Weekly* and *Weekend Magazine*. "May Your First Love Be Your Last" first appeared in *Weekend* in 1958.

Austin Clarke (1932-   ) was born in Barbados, and came to Canada in 1956. He attended the University of Toronto, and has been a newspaperman and free-lance writer, as well as lecturer at several American universities. His tales of West Indians in Toronto catch the social textures of both Barbadian and Torontonian life, and the sharp experience of existence on the frontier between two races. Since 1964 Clarke has published three novels and, in 1971, the collection of short stories *When He Was Free And Young And He Used To Wear Silks*, from which "They Heard a Ringing of Bells" is taken.

Sara Jeanette Duncan (1862-1922) was a lively literary figure in late nineteenth-century Canada. Born in Brantford, she was trained as a teacher, but until her marriage in 1891 was a newspaperwoman; eventually her wit and intelligence earned her the position of parliamentary correspondent for the *Montreal Star*. She spent the latter part of her life in India, and most of her novels appeared under her married name, "Mrs. Everard Cotes." She wrote no short stories as such, but "The Jordanville Meeting," from her novel *The Imperialist* (1904), represents very well her dry wit and the penetration of her social vision.

George Elliott (1923-   ) was born in Ontario. After a career in journalism he became an advertising executive in Toronto, where he still works. His only book is *The Kissing Man* (1962) from which "The Way Back" is taken; it is a cycle of gentle, mystifying tales of life in a small Ontario town. Recently Elliott has been working on some plays and a film script.

Shirley Faessler. "I come of poor people," Shirley Faessler has written; "I grew up in a poor neighbourhood on a poor street." Immigrant Jewish life in the area where she was born in downtown Toronto forms the milieu of her half-dozen published stories. Faessler is a painstaking craftsman, and her first collection has been eagerly awaited for some time. Recently she has been completing a novel, *Everything in the Window*, which will soon be published.

Hugh Garner (1913-   ). Though he was born in England, Garner spent his youth in the Anglo-Saxon slum area of Toronto which he later helped to make famous in his fine realistic novel *Cabbagetown* (1950, complete edition 1968). Besides being a novelist, he is an expert and prolific short-story writer, and won the Governor-General's Award for one of his collections in 1963. "One-Two-Three Little Indians" was written between 1946 and 1948; there is an acid account of its unsuccessful submission to a national short-story contest in Garner's autobiography, *One Damn Thing After Another* (1973).

Dave Godfrey (1938-   ) was born in Winnipeg and attended university in Toronto and the United States. He has been unreliably reported to teach Welsh literature at the University of Toronto, but can sometimes be found in the English Department at Trinity College. He was one of the founders of House of Anansi, new press, and the Independent Publishers Association. "Out in Chinguacousy" is from his collection of "hunting stories," *Death Goes Better With Coca-Cola* (1968). Godfrey is the most challenging young novelist to appear in Canada in this decade; his first novel, *The New Ancestors*, drawn from his experience teaching in Africa, won the Governor-General's Award in 1970.

David Helwig (1938-   ) teaches at Queen's University in Kingston, not too far from the places where he spent his youth, Toronto and Niagara-on-the-Lake. He is a poet and novelist as well as a writer of stories. He has worked extensively with prison inmates who are interested in writing and in 1972 published *A Book About Billie* in collaboration with one of them. "In Exile" is from his collection *The Streets of Summer* (1969).

Hugh Hood (1928-   ). Born in Toronto, Hood now teaches English at the Université de Montréal. He is a productive short-story writer and thoughtful essayist, and has also published four novels, of which the most recent is *You Can't Get There From Here* (1972). Several of the sketches in *The Governor's Bridge Is Closed* (1973) recall the Toronto of the forties and fifties and, like all Hood's work, are imbued with a sardonic power of reminiscence. "Where the Myth Touches Us," which shares the same feeling, is from *Flying a Red Kite* (1962).

Raymond Knister (1899-1932) was born in Blenheim, Ontario, and the landscape of the south-western counties of the province can be seen in his short stories and the novel *White Narcissus* (1929). One of the first Canadians to publish in the modernist periodicals of the twenties, *The Midland, This Quarter,* and *Transition,* he was also deeply interested in the problem of a national Canadian literature and provided a brilliant and prophetic introduction for his pioneer collection *Canadian Short Stories* (1928). "The Loading" appeared in *The Midland* in 1924.

Susanna Moodie (1803-1885) was one of the literary Strickland family, several of whom emigrated from Suffolk to Upper Canada in 1832. *Roughing It in the Bush* (1852) is composed of lively but disillusioned essays about her life here; it has become a classic of nineteenth-century English-Canadian writing. After her departure from the bush, Mrs. Moodie played an active part in Canadian literary life for a number of years as a novelist and editor. "A Trip to the Woods" (not reprinted in the most widely-available text of *Roughing It in the Bush*) describes her family's move from the relative comfort of the Cobourg area to the backwoods of Douro township which was eventually to defeat them.

Alice Munro (1931-   ) was born in Wingham, Ontario, and though she has lived in British Columbia for a number of years, she has continued to write about Western Ontario, both in *Dance of the Happy Shades* (Governor-General's Award winner in 1968, where both "Walker Brothers Cowboy" and "The Peace of Utrecht" were collected) and in her story-cycle *Lives of Girls and Women* (1971). Munro's prose style is one of the most expressive in English-Canadian writing; it is the perfect vehicle for her perceptive evocations of the complex lives of small-town families.

Harvey O'Higgins (1876-1929) was born in London, Ontario. Not long after his education at the University of Toronto (where he gained fame for some verses in imitation of Chaucer) he went to live in the United States, and pursued an active career as a writer. At least two of his twenty books, *Don-a-dreams* (1906) and *Clara Barron* (1926), are partly set in "Coulton," scene also of "Sir Watson Tyler," which appeared in *From The Life* (1919), and was collected in Raymond Knister's *Canadian Short Stories* (1928).

James Reaney (1926-   ) was born near Stratford, Ontario, and much of his poetic activity is centred on the complex imaginative landscape he finds in that area. "The Box-Social" was first published in the University College magazine *Undergrad* when Reaney was a student in 1947. Reprinted in the national magazine *Liberty* a few months later, it provoked a shocked torrent of abuse, and marked Reaney out as the *enfant terrible* of post-war Canadian writing. A three-time winner of the Governor-General's Award, Reaney has become one of Canada's most distinguished dramatists. He has published two collections of plays, *The Killdeer and Other Plays* (1962) and *Masks of Childhood* (1972). His *Poems* were collected in 1972.

Duncan Campbell Scott (1862-1947). One of the half-dozen major Canadian poets of the pre-modern era, Scott was born in Ottawa and lived there most of his life. His talent was at once more reserved and wide-ranging than any of the so-called "Confederation Poets," and his interest in the problems of human relationships sets him apart from many of his contemporaries in Canadian literature. "Expiation," one of his many fine short stories, appeared in *The Witching of Elspie* (1923).

"Patrick Slater" was the nom-de-plume of a Toronto lawyer, John Mitchell (1880-1951). *The Yellow Briar* (1933) is a poignant yet realistic look at nineteenth-century rural life in Ontario, seen from the point of view of a Catholic living in a rigidly Orange province. A cycle of connected stories, it is organized around the reminiscences of the narrator, "old

Paddy Slater," whose life as an immigrant boy in Toronto around 1847 is remembered in "Adrift."

Edward William Thomson (1849-1924) was a pioneer of the modern short story in Canada. Born in Peel County, he fought as a teen-ager on the northern side in the American Civil War. He was eventually educated as an engineer, a profession he practised in the Ottawa Valley, scene of many of his stories. From 1878 on he spent much of his time as a journalist, and lived for a while in the United States. Like Sara Jeanette Duncan and Duncan Campbell Scott, he was intensely interested in new movements in the literary world outside Canada, and struggled with the conflict between outdated sentimental form and modern realistic observation in his own writing, a problem which is overcome with almost mythic force in "Great Godfrey's Lament," which was probably written in the early 1890s.

Nicaragua – History – Revolution, 1979 – – Pictorial works